SERPENTS IN THE COLD

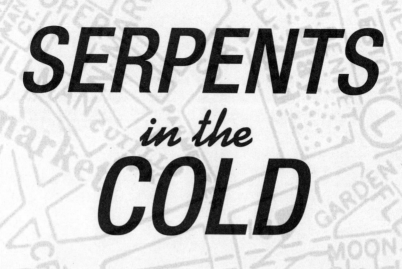

SERPENTS
in the
COLD

THOMAS O'MALLEY
and
DOUGLAS GRAHAM PURDY

MULHOLLAND BOOKS
Little, Brown and Company
New York Boston London

Mulholland Books/Little, Brown and Company
Hachette Book Group
1290 Avenue of the Americas, New York, NY 10104
mulhollandbooks.com

First Edition: January 2015

Mulholland Books is an imprint of Little, Brown and Company, a division of Hachette Book Group, Inc. The Mulholland Books name and logo are trademarks of Hachette Book Group, Inc.

The publisher is not responsible for websites (or their content) that are not owned by the publisher.

The Hachette Speakers Bureau provides a wide range of authors for speaking events. To find out more, go to hachettespeakersbureau.com or call (866) 376-6591.

Photographs by Nishan Bichajian, copyright Massachusetts Institute of Technology, courtesy of MIT Libraries, Rotch Visual Collections

Library of Congress Cataloging-in-Publication Data
O'Malley, Thomas, 1967– author.
  Serpents in the Cold / Thomas O'Malley and Douglas Graham Purdy.—First edition.
     pages cm
  ISBN 978-0-316-32350-5 (hardback)
  1. Serial murderers—Fiction. 2. Boston (Mass.)—History—20th century—Fiction. 3. Mystery fiction. 4. Suspense fiction. I. Purdy, Douglas Graham, author. II. Title.
  PR6115.M347S47 2015
  823'.92—dc23   2014018353

10 9 8 7 6 5 4 3 2 1

RRD-C

Printed in the United States of America

Book design by Marie Mundaca

For Dorothy Purdy,
Dot from the Dot
&
Bartley O'Malley,
"The Mayor of Boston"
Local 223

Sicut Patribus, sit Deus Nobis.
May God be with us, as he was with our fathers.

—Motto on seal of Boston

In Boston serpents whistle at the cold.

—Robert Lowell

SERPENTS IN THE COLD

❧

PORT NORFOLK, DORCHESTER. FEBRUARY 1951

SNOW HAD FALLEN during the night, and in the gray-blue before dawn it shrouded the street with a glittering mica that caught the glow of street lamps and reflected the light like shards of glass. Holding tight to the dog's leash, the children—two girls and their young brother between them—closed the screen door to the house softly behind them so as not to awaken their father, who worked the second shift at the Edison plant across the bay in South Boston. They whispered to the straining dog, telling him to be quiet, to stop making such a racket, that there would be hell to pay and the back of Daddy's belt if he didn't quiet down.

The children shuffled down the steps from the porch, fine flakes of snow swirling from their boots, and made their way down the street toward Neponset and Tenean Beach, where the dog liked to run, chasing gulls across the frost-packed sand. As they came down Pope's Hill, they could see a few cars and tractor-trailers moving like dark shadows on the highway, motors rumbling, headlights pushing against the darkness. The dog, familiar with their route, lifted his snout and, nostrils piqued

3

by the scent of brine and bird, scrabbled at the snowfall beneath his paws.

"Dammit! Be still!" the elder girl shouted and yanked on the leash. With her other hand she held tight to her young brother, who trudged so slowly that both sisters had to drag him along the pathway to the beach. Saw grass and spindly gorse shuddered at the path's edges as they passed the dark façades of sleeping triple-deckers from which, here and there, a single kitchen or bedroom light blazed against the dark, and then the silent, abandoned marina, the crumbling wooden pylons and spars of the deserted marine salvage and boatyard.

The children paused for a moment, their breath smoking the air. A great sheet of ice stretched a hundred yards out into the bay, and there lay a second shore, a ragged border against which the sea hissed and boiled in dark waves, pressing the ice back in large, sharp-looking spears. Points of light pulsated in the sky, and then a plane emerged from the dark bound for Logan. As the plane passed overhead, the children craned their necks to look at its markings, the eldest calling them out and the others nodding and then watching the blinking wing lights receding over the Calf Pasture and into darkness.

A mist swirled in off the ice pack and drifted here and there, a pale silver sheen fogging the beach. Distantly, buoys clanged; boats sounded their horns in the passage and narrows beyond the beach. The dog lunged forward, breaking the girl's hold upon his leash, and raced toward the pylons before the salvage yards where the saw grass bunched and curled in frozen spikes and the ice lay smashed against the spars and throbbed with the current. There was something there and the dog was at it.

"Sam!" she called after him, "leave that alone!" and pulled on her brother's arm as she ran ahead. And then they paused. A few yards before them, half-submerged in the muck yet frozen erect, was the naked body of a woman. They stared at her blue-hued, rigid limbs, her silvering skin, the jut of her hips, and the prominence of her rib cage, her bare, mottled breasts.

They stared at her open mouth, parted as if in surprise, and at her wide-eyed gaze, clouded pupils looking beyond them at some invisible and inevitable horror. And then there was the other mouth: the gaping, torn folds of her neck from which blood hung in thin frozen ropes down to her chest. The children stood there, holding one another's hands, as the morning mist swirled about them. Strakes of snow whirled, snakelike, across the frozen shoreline, and the dog continued to bound about them, sniffing the body and then barking again, the sharp sound of it roiling out across the empty bay to the giant Boston Gas tanks, toward Savin Hill, and the lights of the city blinking in the distance beyond.

1

In winter, in daylight, Scollay Square was a cold and desolate place. The neon lights that brightened the avenues and alleyways at night remained unlit and encased in ice. Here and there along its concrete walkways, in the doorways of betting shops and poolrooms, stood men draped in over-sized coats, hats hiding their eyes, hands buried deep in their pockets. On street corners, small groups of them huddled and lit one another's cigarettes, spoke of things having little consequence. They were killing time, waiting for the night.

Kelly's Rose was a basement dive with one long window and a steel slab for a door. Those walking by wouldn't even register it as a bar. The neon sign hawking Pickwick ale hung crookedly in the lone window and was never turned on, and farther inside, the lights above the bar and booths were kept so low not even a moth would be drawn to them.

In the two-stall, two-urinal bathroom in the back of Kelly's Rose, Dante Cooper had many thoughts going at once, but he didn't have any place to put them. They spun and caught onto memories, dragging them and the rest of the junk into something vast and confusing. And there were voices, too, all conversing in his head, colliding into one cracked and unharmonious symphony. He sat in the stall closest to the wall, a tie tightly wound around his left bicep, his pants down at his ankles, a syringe resting flat on the hard muscle of his thigh. The radiator beside him tapped and echoed. He grasped a spoon in one hand and his lighter in the other, its flame bending bowl-shaped beneath the metal. The noise in his head softened by degrees, and from this quiet he could hear her call out to him, at first muted and distant, and then with clarity: a siren's voice pulled through a fog.

And then she was there with him, his dead wife, like a starlet leaning over their bed and pulling the cigarette out of his mouth and putting it in between her lips. She was in good spirits from their score the night before, and she was singing her favorite song, "These Foolish Things." She lay back on the bed for him, her reddish-brown hair spilled over the white sheets, her pale, naked body so thin and boyish, writhing as she sang, and then her laughter roughened by too many whiskey sours and Pall Malls.

In the stall, he tried to sing back to her, but his mouth felt leaden and his tongue numb.

Oh, how the ghost of you clings—

The tablet started to sizzle and turn the right shade of horse. He bit into his bottom lip and tried to steady his damaged left hand, unable to straighten his thumb and index finger fully. It had happened before, an upturned spoon, or a syringe in pieces on the floor.

He rolled up a tiny piece of cotton and dropped it into the spoon. He picked up the needle off his lap and carefully dipped it into the liquid, sucking it up and filling the glass syringe with dirty gold. He held his breath, steadied his arm, and made a fist so tight his raw knuckles paled. He maneuvered the tip of the needle over a vein, found the right spot, and leaned forward as he pushed down on the plunger. A slight eruption of blood escaped into the syringe and then, after a charged pause, all disappeared under his skin and inside. Dante yanked the tie from around his bicep and reclined backward. It never took long.

The lone light in the bathroom turned pink and soft, flickered, and then went black.

These foolish things remind me of you—

The great emptiness swallowed up the chorus playing in his head, leaving nothing but a cathedral-like hum, until there were voices at the stall door, and the world about him shuddered.

"Blowing up another vein, Dante? I'm surprised you have any left. Advice to a lowlife addict, okay? Just make it easy so Ski here don't need to break the fucking door."

Dante opened one eye. The door to the stall was vibrating under somebody's fist. He opened the other eye. Two reptilian shadows crept along the floor by his feet.

"C'mon, it's not worth it, li'l man. You know why we're here, so let's just make it easy. I like easy."

He struggled to return to the memory of Margo on their bed. He closed his eyes and tried, but she was gone.

"Don't leave me yet, Margo," he called into the darkness.

The stall door split. With one more blow from the shoulder the lock would soon tear free.

"I'm sorry, my love," he said. "I'm so sorry."

I'm sorry for that bad score, sorry for not telling the truth, sorry I left you alone that morning, so fucking sorry I can't bring you back to me.

The stall door burst open and the two shadows rushed in at Dante Cooper.

2

SAVIN HILL, DORCHESTER

HE HAD BEEN in the Hürtgen Forest again, for days now it seemed, advancing in the dark beneath the dense, snow-shrouded canopies of trees through which the violent light of bomb-burst and gunfire flickered. Tracer flares ignited the cordite smoke, and with artillery explosions detonating above the treetops, clouds of phosphorescent light drifted among the tree line, through which other soldiers moved as jerky, misshapen shadows. Cal moved blindly into the clearing, falling in the muddied and bloodstained snow and realizing as he pulled himself up that he was clambering over frozen dead bodies and the parts of dead bodies: arms and legs and faces. Before him a vast fence of barbed wire stretched across the forest and upon it the bodies of soldiers dangled. One soldier, perhaps a year or two younger than himself, still struggled and twitched. Through the bullet holes on his torso pink flesh showed; white bone protruded from his shattered kneecap.

Flares lit up the sky above them and spiraled down, illuminating the clearing, and the enemy fire began again. The young man's face shone, his gaunt cheekbones pulled taut in pain. His eyes rolled back in his head and then rolled forward and stared at Cal. His breath steamed the air. Through the fog of smoke the shadows of the enemy approached, a horizon of figures shuddering in light and shadow, the silhouettes of their rifles spearing the darkness. They moved forward stabbing and then grinding their bayonets into the mounds of bodies upon the ground. Cal watched the raised, pleading arms of the victims, their pleas like the mewling of animals as they were gutted.

Hearing the sounds of the dying, the young soldier jerked his head to the left and right, twisted toward the advancing army, then back to Cal. His mouth opened and closed but no sound came. "Kill me," he whispered. "Please kill me. Don't let me die like that."

Cal moved closer, unholstered his automatic, and aimed it at the soldier's head. The screams were less frequent. The world was becoming empty of sound as fragments of bullets whipped around him, tearing divots in the earth and in the surrounding trees. The enemy was almost upon them.

"It's okay," Cal said, "it's okay," not sure if he was speaking to himself or to the young soldier. And then he believed he'd said, "I can't, I'm sorry, I can't kill you," but he pulled the trigger anyway and shot the young soldier through the forehead. The soldier's head rocked upon his neck and then his body slumped against the wire.

Cal woke and clutched instinctively at his upper thigh, where the muscle tapered to the pelvis. The sheets were in disarray and the mattress damp at his back. At his side Lynne lay on her stomach, breathing deeply in sleep. Gray light filtered through the stained window shades and with it came the sounds from the street outside, of the city waking, cars honking on the Avenue. He could feel the winter cold sifting through the window frame, listened for a moment as a gust of wind set the panes rattling. The subtle tremors of the subway station three streets over reverberated through the timbers of the three-decker. He sat up, pulled his legs over the side of the bed. He rubbed his temples, raked a hand through his black hair. He stretched his aching leg out before him and then back again until he could feel the blood flowing warmly through it—the pain spiking for a moment and then ebbing—and knew he could walk.

In the living room, he poured himself a whiskey, watching his hand as he did so. Then he turned on the radio, and after a moment sound crackled through the speakers. He tuned it to the *Darcy and McGuire Show* and turned it down so that it wouldn't wake Lynne, who'd worked the late shift at the Carney. He sighed, pressed the heel of his hand to a spot just above his eyelid, under the ridge of his brow, where the pain—always after a nightmare—was the most intense. The phone rang, startling him, and after a moment of consideration, he reached to pick it up, grunted into the receiver.

It was his cousin Owen, the cop, asking him if he knew where Dante was. His head spun for a moment. He'd never been able to keep track of family even though they gathered for wakes and reunions in bars around the city at least a few times every year. Owen Mackey was his first cousin—his father's sister's kid—three years younger than himself and a homicide detective for Boston PD, working out of the Dorchester precinct.

"Owen," he said. "What is it?" and then, realizing Owen couldn't hear him, he cleared his throat and spoke louder. "What is it?"

"It's Margo's sister, Cal. We found her body this morning, on the beach. It's a mess. I'm trying to find Dante."

Cal placed the tumbler on the table.

"Cal? You still there? Cal?"

"Yeah," he grunted, turned his head away from the mouthpiece so that he could hack and clear his throat again. "I'm here." He glanced toward the kitchen and the clock above the sink, squinted so that its numbers emerged from blurriness into distinction: six forty. From Owen's end he could hear the early-morning bustle of the station house. He'd known that once, too: the crossover from the graveyard shift to the day, the boisterous, almost jubilant voices of the morning beat cops, cradling their coffees, some still drunk from the night before, shitbirds talking about their wives, the piece of ass they'd been with, the hopped-up kids they'd given the beat-down. He heard the clatter of typewriter keys, the distant ringing of phones, the desk sergeant hollering out duties.

"Just come down with Dante."

"Give me an hour or so to find him," he said. Owen said something that Cal couldn't make out, and then Cal was listening to the hum of the open line. He looked toward the bedroom.

The last three nights he'd lain awake, unable to sleep or experiencing nightmares when he did. Awake, he'd watched Lynne as she slept, and in the early a.m. as she rose and crossed the kitchen to the bathroom in the dark. Six years since the war, three since he'd been kicked off the force, and the only thing that kept him rising in the morning was Lynne and the shitty security business he'd created from war bonds and their meager savings. And lately, all of it going to shit.

He ground his teeth, swallowed the phlegm that had come to his mouth, searched the trash-strewn coffee table for a smoke, but there was none. The operator was squawking at him from the receiver, and he resisted the urge to tell her to go fuck herself. He placed the phone back in its cradle, watching his hand all the while and surprised to find it wasn't shaking.

3

SCOLLAY SQUARE, DOWNTOWN

DANTE KNEW HOW to play the rag doll. It was as though he'd turned bone-less and shut off his nerves so every punch from Grabowski merely echoed in his flesh. He could feel what the damage would be, and the hurt would come later: the rupture of skin on his jaw, a swollen eye, the bruising of a rib, two teeth loosening from his blood-soaked gums. A debt a month old wasn't a ticket to the morgue, even with Sully and his Irish and Pol-ish goons, the Catholic Pride of Dorchester Avenue, but lingering in the back of his head, there was the chance that they'd get carried away, make a mistake, and kill him.

"Dante, you're such a fuckin' waste. You know, back in the old days we all thought you'd make something of yourself. But now look at you with your pants down and your face all pretty. Jesus, a no-good waste, a true piece of shit."

Grabowski held Dante's limp body up with his two scarred hands. He released his right hand, cocking his arm to the side, and sent another blow across Dante's chin. He pulled back again and lowered with a hard rip into the stomach. The thug had been a boxer once, but never much good. Without any discipline or strategy, he'd always been more at home fighting bare-knuckled in the back alleys and outside the social halls up and down the Avenue.

He grabbed a fistful of Dante's unkempt hair and pulled him back toward the stall. Dante made a choking sound and tried to raise an arm. Grabowski hauled his head back and then slammed it into the stall's oak door. Dante bounced, his head snapping back before he crumpled to the floor. Shaw stepped forward, leaned down over Dante, and flicked his half-smoked cigarette. The embers smoldered in the folds of Dante's shirt, singed through to his skin.

"Okay, Ski, hold up a bit. Go check his jacket there by the toilet and see if he has any cash."

Shaw had grown up in Fields Corner with both Cal and Dante. He came from the Shaughnessy family, a ripe brood where the seven sons all wanted to be just like their father, a low-rent criminal who made a substantial mark in gin and whiskey running during Prohibition. Shaw was the youngest, and he was the runt of the litter. As a kid, he was all mouth. He'd always had someone do his dirty work for him. And he hadn't changed one bit since then, always talking like a tough guy, but with the trim, well-manicured hands of an accountant.

He had a habit of sucking his crooked teeth before he spoke. "Sully always liked you and Cal. Good boys, he says, could have really made it good with us if they just knew where their fuckin' bread was buttered. He feels for you, he really does. But it's been over, like, six months since your wife passed on. Sympathy has its limits, it wears thin after a while; even if it's small change, he goes on principle. A man has to work off of principle, right? Otherwise the whole world goes to shit."

Dante looked up at the freckled, flabby, pale face, the curly orange hair escaping like a clown's wig from the sides of the tight hat, and the gray, heavy-lidded eyes. He tried to say something, but blood overflowed his mouth and spilled down his chin. The sharp metallic taste of it filled his nostrils, knotted with the growing pain in his gut as his adrenaline and his high dissolved into sickness.

He tried again. "I'll get it to you soon...just don't have it."

Guttural laughter suddenly came from inside the stall. "The fucker got no money. But he's got these."

Ski came and shoved a handful of morphine syrettes at Shaw, four of them capped except the one that Dante had used earlier.

Shaw wrapped them up in one of his leather gloves and then pocketed them inside his long wool coat. He shook his head, sucked his teeth again. "I guess those niggers at those jazz joints really give you a good deal, no? Five caps and they'll throw in some tubes of morphine just to take the edge off come morning."

Ski caught his breath, rolled his shoulders, stood above Dante, and shook his head in an exasperated manner. He turned and looked over at Shaw, eyes crossed.

"Jesus Christ, how can somebody get this bad off? I feel kinda bad hurtin' somebody who can't even fight back."

Shaw smirked. "If he wasn't such a fuckup, I'd feel kinda bad for him too. Sick bastard finds his wife dead of a junk overdose and then crawls into bed next to her. Three days later, the police get a complaint of something smelling foul, so they come and break down the doors and find him still in bed with her."

"You kiddin' me?"

"Nope."

"No, sleeping with your dead wife, that ain't right."

"Nothing right about it at all."

Ski looked down at Dante on the floor. A look of sympathy briefly flickered in his gray face, hard with thickly knit scars, but then a scowl of disgust pulled at his mouth and he grunted loudly, drew back his leg, and brought another heavy boot to Dante's chest.

4

CAL PULLED HIS battered Chevy Fleetline into a plowed space opposite Epstein's Drug and sat for a moment watching the bundled shapes of pedestrians passing along the sidewalk. The radio was tuned to the news and the news reporter was asking Richard Nixon, congressman and investigator for the House Un-American Activities Committee, about his thoughts on the upcoming trial of Julius and Ethel Rosenberg for conspiracy to commit espionage and on charges that they passed information about the atomic bomb to the Soviet Union.

Cal turned off the engine and glanced at himself in the rearview. His face, still youthful and quick to flush, was lined around startling blue eyes. Black hair shining as if oiled, close back and sides, high and flat on top. He looked better than he felt, and smiled without humor. A wind was howling down the avenue and it whistled in the wheel wells, shook the car, so that Cal had to put his shoulder into the door to open it as he climbed out. His joints ached and the tendons in his legs seemed to be talking to one another, sending sharp pains through him with each step, and he wished he'd taken another slug of whiskey.

He looked down the crooked alleyways stretching toward the cobblestone and crowded tenements of the West End, where tavern signs glowed in bright red and green neon, and farther, where vagrants shifted beneath makeshift shelters—cardboard boxes, wooden crates, and ragged, hole-worn army blankets they'd thawed over subway grates from which tendrils of steam twined. The sun was somewhere above the rooftops, but he'd be damned if he knew where.

He hadn't been to the office in over a week. Their last customer looking for bonded security watchmen had been G. J. Fergusson on Washington Street. Cal had done the walk-through of the six-floor garment factory himself: sixty thousand square feet of overheated, poorly vented space that looked out on the elevated tracks where trolley cars rumbled, groaned, and squealed from dawn to night and where, at rows upon rows of ancient sewing machines, hundreds of Chinese women labored away.

The building was a footsore if ever he'd seen one, but an easy job for a night watchman. Three key stations on each floor; you could pass the night doing whatever the hell you liked as long as you kept an ear out for the property owners making an impromptu drop-by. All property owners did it now and again to check in on their investments, to make sure the guards were where they were supposed to be, that the number of guards they'd requested and paid for were actually on the premises. He liked to hire retired cops, ex-soldiers, and, now and again, cons who he knew had been sent down for misdemeanors, judge bias, or crooked police work and who he knew could, at times, provide him with valuable information the others could not. But the Fergusson Company was out of business now, and others like the Anvil Building had been gutted after the city designated it for the wrecking ball and urban renewal. Pilgrim Security had had contracts with Sears in the Fenway, Woolworth's, Gillette, Necco, the Custom House Tower, the Copley Hotel, and the Eliot, but those days were gone, and now he could count their clients on the fingers of one hand: a tool and die factory on Old Colony Ave in Southie, three package stores in Mattapan, and a bank in Uphams Corner by the Strand Theatre, a couple of warehouses down on Atlantic Ave along the waterfront, some office space downtown and in Post Office Square. Every so often something would come up—a week or two worth of work with the potential for something long-term—and he'd call in the numbers of those who he knew needed the work the most.

Of course, the business was more than just a security company, despite his attempts to make it only that. But when Boston's economy went south, he'd had to take whatever he could, and there were always people looking for someone like him to get things done. And the people in the neighborhood, who needed things done, who didn't trust the police or couldn't call them, reached out to him for help. There were wives whose absentee husbands refused to pay child support; families with loved ones in Suffolk or Charlestown jail and no way to post bond or hire a lawyer; employers who suspected their workers of pilfering goods or stealing from the till; debt collectors and loan sharks who needed to be squeezed back just a little bit; the husband or wife who believed their spouse was cheating on them; the sister who didn't believe the story of how her brother died.

He liked to think that he'd found a way to make a living and pay the bills from what he knew how to do and what he was good at, and that once the economy got better and everyone was back on their feet, he'd get back to running his security company and to hell with everything else, but he also found it hard to leave behind what he'd done as a cop, doing what he thought mattered, which in the end, he'd discovered, had little to do with the law. Perhaps more than that, he often wondered if he was trying to make right all his wrongs from the war.

The windows to the second-floor offices of Pilgrim Security were dark and shuttered, and when he climbed the stairs, snow melting from his shoes onto the worn green carpeting, he found the door locked. The rippled glass painted with the company name was in need of cleaning. Cal stared at the door. One of the children whose parents worked on the floor had been peering into the dark room; a small greasy handprint was smeared on the glass. The white cardboard sign announcing PASSPORT PHOTOS TAKEN HERE and NOTARY PUBLIC hung crookedly at the center of the window. The hallway smelled of boiling cabbage—a wet and ripe, sweaty smell—and of something burnt—eggs perhaps. Voices came muted through other doors: a radio, a telex, and farther down the hall from Franklin Professional Services came the clickety-clack of secretaries at work, of typewriters and the thump and hum of Dictaphones and mimeographs, the sudden short bark of a woman's laugh.

Later, Cal stood just inside the building's entranceway, smoking a cigarette and trying to avoid the wind. Dante might be at Mike Piloti's garage on Summer Street or even out at Uphams Corner Auto doing a bit of spot-welding, as he sometimes did to put cash in his pocket, but then he remembered Dante had put in some hours at his cousin's garage last week right before the latest storm, and as long as Dante could make enough to get by, he wouldn't be looking to make more. And if he had cash in his pockets, he'd give himself over to something else. Cal just hoped he was on the bottle rather than the junk.

THE DOOR TO Dante's apartment was unlocked. Cal knocked, and when there came no reply, he entered. Dante's younger sister, Claudia, sat at the small Formica-topped table in the kitchen. She wore a blue housecoat, bare feet in oversized worn slippers. Pale varicose flesh nestled in thick tufts of fake fur around the ankle. She was sitting sideways in the chair and staring out the window. Her hands lay in her lap, unmoving. Her hair looked damp and hung in lank strings on either side of her ashen face. Her eyes were rimmed with red, and her lips appeared white, bloodless. A cigarette smoldered in a World's Fair ashtray on the vinyl tablecloth.

"Claudia," Cal said and resisted the impulse to touch her before he sensed she was aware of him standing there. Still she gave no response. Melting snow from the rooftop thumped the glass and slid down the window, making everything blurred and indistinct. Claudia stirred and blinked, turned her head at last and looked at him. "Oh," she said, but showed no surprise or curiosity.

Cal came and stood beside her, squeezed her shoulder before pulling out a chair from the table and settling into it. Looking at her, he knew he wouldn't tell her about Sheila; she was in no condition to hear about murder.

"I tried calling," he said and nodded toward the black phone resting in its cradle on the wall, "but they've shut your phone off."

Claudia took a last drag from the cigarette and pressed it down into the tin ashtray. A breeze from somewhere turned the smoke and pushed ash across the table. Claudia looked at the phone on the wall.

"I'm waiting for Dante to call. He said he'd call."

Cal nodded. "He'll probably call soon, Claudia. Any time now. If I see him, is there anything you want me to tell him?"

"We need coffee. Bread, too. And toilet paper. Milk and eggs would be nice."

"I'll take care of it, Claudia. Don't worry about it." He touched her shoulder, so cold it made him shiver, and went to the foldout couch in the living room and returned with a throw blanket, placing it around her shoulders. He considered putting on water to make her some tea, but as he watched her turn back toward the window, he decided against it. At the door he turned up the thermostat to sixty-five, waited until he heard the furnace kick in and water flowing through the radiators. At least they hadn't turned that off yet.

On the street, Charlie, the newspaper hawker, was counting change in his newsstand beside the Rialto. Above them, on the second floor of the theater, the neon cross of the Calvary Rescue Mission glowed, a blue nimbus in the frozen air. Outside the newsstand, pinned to plywood, the covers of *Sports Daily, Bettor's Weekly, Men's Club,* and various local and national papers fluttered and flapped against their pins. The *Globe* was revisiting the Brink's robbery of a year before, what the *New York Times* had called the Crime of the Century, and showed the Superman masks the robbers had used and that now every kid from Charlestown to Quincy wore on Halloween.

Cal held up the paper, looked at the headline: POLICE ASK PUBLIC'S HELP IN BOSTON BUTCHER CASE. NO LEADS IN MURDER OF FOUR WOMEN. At the bottom of the page he read STILL NO SIGN OF $2.5

MILLION SEIZED IN BRINK'S ROBBERY and then turned to the back of the paper and the sports section.

Charlie watched him and chewed on his frayed cigar. There was always cigar pulp around the old man's mouth, and with his deep-set eyes he looked like some manner of mole poking its head out into the sun.

"They think that guy they're calling the Butcher might be a foreigner off the boats coming in," he said. "Maybe a sailor docked over in Charlestown. That's what I'm thinking too. Only a foreigner could do something like that. You know, a Russian or one of those Slavic types. Are Polacks Slavic? You don't think it was a Polack, do you? My mother was Polish."

Cal shook his head. "No, not a Polack off a boat anyway."

"Four girls cut up like that. It's a crying fucking shame. I don't know what the world's coming to."

He glanced over the top of the sports page in Cal's hands.

"Bruins lost again," he said.

And before Cal could ask, Charlie said, "The Canadiens won."

Cal scanned the results himself, sighed. "Still, we face Montreal tomorrow night. We can make up some ground."

"Like hell. I'm just waiting for pitchers and catchers to report to spring training."

"Baseball?" Cal shook his head. "Too early for baseball. I still have faith in the Bruins."

"This year? Are you shitting me? We've got no offense and our defense stinks. Better chance of Mulrooney winning the Senate seat."

"So, all bets are on Foley?"

"Well," Charlie paused as a fit of coughing took him, "I wouldn't bet against him. He's way too connected in this town. And who else would want the mess Cosgrove left behind." He took out a soiled handkerchief, and blew into it. "You know, they say he died on the shitter."

Cal grinned, pulled a crumpled dollar from his pocket, placed it on the counter, made as if he were tipping back a drink, and pointed to the betting slips stacked against the back of the booth. His hands were shaking. "Any chance you saw Dante this morning?"

"Nah, haven't seen that mess in days." Charlie reached behind the betting slips and, after a moment, pushed a fifth of whiskey into Cal's hands. "Is he in trouble again?"

Cal screwed off the top and knocked back a quarter of the bottle, coughed and wiped his mouth with the back of his hand. He breathed deeply and felt the shaking in his hands subside.

"Not with me he's not."

By the time he'd made it to the end of the street, the fifth of whiskey was almost empty. Cal's mind felt sharp, and the aching in his limbs was gone. He felt his heart beating strong in his chest, and when the biting cold pressed through to his skin, his gun was a pocket of warmth just below his ribs.

THERE WERE ONLY two people at the bar, bowed over their half-empty glasses in a dull, drunken silence. When the door opened, one of them looked up. Before an empty stool at the other end of the U-shaped bar, a lone drink sat untouched. It was a whiskey sour and it had a depressed air to it, as if some poor sap had bought it for the girl he admired, thinking she would walk in at any minute.

Next to the drink, an ashtray held a cigarette that had burned through. Cal knew that Dante was here. A whiskey sour wasn't his drink of choice, it was Margo's.

Cal lurched forward, called out to the bartender, a tall balding man with a mustache that hung over his lip. "Have you seen him?"

"I see lots of people, all kinds of people."

"Just do me a favor and at least let me know if he has company in there."

"Aaaah, O'Brien, I just cleaned the toilets. Not a soul in there."

Cal turned and glanced toward the hallway leading to the bathroom.

"You know we don't welcome that kind of stuff here."

"I'll check myself."

Cal reached in under his coat, felt the reassuring weight of his M1911 in the holster. He passed several empty booths along the wall, soiled red-

and-white-checked oilcloth on the tables, glasses of unfinished beer from the night before, past a nickel jukebox with its stained yellow panels, and farther into the hallway toward the bathrooms. The acrid smell of piss gathered in his nostrils. At the door, he heard a heavy grunt followed by a cough thick with phlegm, the squeaking of rubber soles moving on the tiled floor, and then a rip of laughter.

He pulled out his gun, raised it shoulder level, and kicked the door open. Ski dropped Dante to the floor and raised a hand in a silly gesture, as though it wasn't his fault Dante's face was turned inside out. Shaw smiled and sucked his teeth, but before he could speak, Cal made his move. He was a few inches under six feet, had the stocky build of a lightweight, slight bones compressed with muscle, but it was his trip-wire rage that gave him an edge. He charged the big Polish thug, who, stunned by the oncoming blur, tried to raise his hands to protect his face. The grip of Cal's gun opened up his temple; another quick crack on the nose and the big man stumbled, his knees going to jelly and his hip crashing against the radiator as he fell. His nose sprayed a bloody stream.

Cal ran a straight left arm into Shaw's chest, pushed him until his back slammed the wall. He pressed the barrel of the gun against his forehead. The redhead turned to alleviate the pressure, but Cal pushed harder. Shaw's heavy-lidded eyes momentarily shut and his lips pulled over his crooked teeth in pain.

"We're just collecting for Sully, Cal. You need to simmer down."

"Fuck you I will."

Shaw gave Cal's eyes a good reading.

"Just settle down, old friend," he said, "we're all good." The redhead sucked his teeth one final time, raised his accountant hands in the air as a sign of surrender. "He said he'd get us by the end of the week, and we trust him. We're like that. We take care of those from the Corner."

"How much is he in for this time?"

"Not as much as the last time, but enough."

Cal lowered his gun and turned. The big Polish boxer was back on his feet, his right hand clutching his broken nose. A darkening welt grew from the side of his head.

Dante rolled over, spit out a thick glob of blood and saliva.

Shoulders hunched, head lowered, Ski ambled by Cal and mumbled several curse words in Polish, flung open the bathroom door, and disappeared into the darkness of the hallway. But Shaw hung at the door for a moment.

"This is real stupid of you. Sully's in a real shit mood lately, and the last thing he's going to do is give that dirtbag another break."

"Just get the fuck out of here, Shaughnessy."

The door closed, and Cal reached down, grabbed Dante's hand, and pulled him to his feet. "Jesus Christ," he said, "pull up your fucking pants." He turned on the faucet and helped him rinse his face. The white porcelain swam pink. After a while he turned the cold water off.

Cal's anger didn't dissipate. When they entered the bar, he called out to the bartender, who suddenly appeared busy, wiping the bar down.

"Next time I'll do you before I do them, you prick."

The bartender stared after them, waited until Cal and Dante were halfway out the door before shouting after them, "Fuck you, O'Brien!"

Outside, Cal grabbed at Dante's coat front, buttoned up the neck, yanked up the collar, and helped him up the five concrete steps to the sidewalk.

"Do you have your feet?" he asked.

Dante nodded, and Cal let go of him.

5

Inside Joe and Nemo's it was warm and bright. Sudden blasts of wind pushed against the plate glass windows of the diner, startling customers at their meals. Nemo's brother was working the counter. He was a thin older man with wiry gray hair at his temples and a large swell of a belly, but his white pants and shirt looked immaculate. He might have been a banker if not for the location. No one liked him but he didn't much care. It never affected business. He glanced up as Dante and Cal sat at a booth and then went back to the sports page.

"Well, that was smart," Dante said, wincing as he rubbed a hand across his lips. "Fucking up one of Sully's men like that."

"You worry about yourself. I'm not the one owing money."

Dante avoided Cal's eyes.

"So what was it this time? Horses? Numbers?"

"It doesn't matter. I'll pay them back."

"With what?"

Dante shook his head, moved his hands to his pack of cigarettes, and pulled one out.

Cal glanced over the menu. The room smelled of boiling hot dogs, coffee, bacon, and stale grease. He realized he was hungry after not having eaten a thing since late yesterday afternoon.

"What are you having?"

Dante lifted the water glass and drank. When he put it back on the table, blood sank darkly in the glass.

"You need to eat something."

Dante pointed to his face and he grinned. "Does it look like I'm hungry?"

"No, but you still need to eat."

"Eggs, then. And Tabasco sauce, lots and lots of Tabasco sauce."

Cal stared over at the brother, stared at him till he lifted his eyes and made eye contact. "Can we get some coffee over here?" he called. The brother turned a page and went back to his reading.

A waitress scurried by them and Cal reached out an arm and grasped her by the elbow. She looked at his hand and then down at him. "Sorry to bother you, miss, but could we get some coffee here?"

The waitress glanced at Dante and went to move away, but Cal held her elbow. "Some coffee for me and my friend here."

She hesitated for a moment, and then responded dully, "I'll see what I can do."

In a moment, the waitress was back. "Only coffee. The boss says I can't serve you breakfast." She gestured with her head toward Dante. "Not with him looking like that."

"We'd die for some of that apple pie. Don't have to cook nothing, just wrap it all up and we'll be on our way."

"I'll do it, honey, but then you have to go. Take your friend down to Burke's or Joey Glynn's. That's the place for you."

Cal nodded, watched the waitress walk away. "They closed down Joey Glynn's a month ago. The wrecking ball will have it in a week or so. Half the Square is going."

"Going to hell," Dante said. He dabbed at his bloodied mouth with napkins he'd pulled from the dispenser.

Nemo's brother was looking up from his paper and staring at them.

The waitress took the long way about the restaurant, checking in on her other tables before she went behind the counter, filled up two paper cups with coffee, and wrapped the pie. When she returned, Cal took the paper bag from her hand and left two quarters on the table.

THEY STEPPED INTO the Peabody Street alley. Before them the recently excavated lot of Cassidy's Bar jutted out into the barren expanse toward Tremont Street, and a wind whipped down through the avenue with nothing to cut it.

"I need more than coffee," Cal said, and Dante followed him across the street to Court Street Liquors. The lights were off inside, and the narrow aisles were dark in shadow and illuminated by meager slants of daylight poking through the ice-covered windows at the front of the store.

Cal's breath hung in the air. "Why's it so damn cold in here?" he asked. The old cashier wore a multitude of multicolored sweaters, one over the other. His emaciated wrists poked from their ragged cuffs as he reached up to a shelf and grabbed four nips of whiskey, and his hands shook when he handed Cal his change. A red wool cap was pulled tightly down over his ears. He chewed on his thick lips and sputtered when he spoke. "They turned the damn electric and heat off on me, the fuckers."

Back outside, Cal and Dante poured the whiskey into their coffee as they rested against a brick wall and stared at the broken stone and mortar where Cassidy's had been. A crane with wide tracks and a wrecking ball sat immobile, covered with a dusting of snow from the previous night.

They hugged their coats about them as they drank, watched the low clouds churning over the city; traffic rumbled on distant streets, and navy frigates leaving the Charlestown locks blew their long, plaintive horns as they made their way out into the harbor.

"My cousin Owen called me this morning," he said. "The Dorchester detective. You know the guy."

Dante looked up from his stupor and stared at him. A hard wind blew icy crystals against their faces so that they squinted at each other. The bottoms of their overcoats whipped against their legs.

28

Cal finished the last of his coffee dregs, sucked the whiskey from them with his teeth. He turned against the wind and, with his head bowed, managed to light a cigarette. He exhaled, tried to smile, and then gave it up. "Sheila was found murdered this morning, Dante. I'm sorry."

Dante cocked his head like a dog and smiled, his grotesque, deformed grin searching for the joke, and perhaps trying to make sense of what he'd just heard. Cal reached for his shoulder, put his hand there, and held it. "I'm sorry."

Dante's mouth parted as if to say something. After a moment he looked out across the barren lot, gazed blankly at the traffic and the pedestrians passing hunched into themselves against the cold. Cal watched him, studied the damage to his face. He took him by the shoulder and moved him tenderly back onto the street toward the car he'd left parked opposite Epstein's Drug. "C'mon," he said. "We need to go see the body."

6

THE ROOM, TWO levels beneath Boston City Hospital's main floor, was as cold as an icebox. The windowless walls were scrubbed white tile, and beyond the tile Cal knew there lay old stone, many feet thick, that would be damp to the touch. He could sense the bay beneath them and around them, a subtle scent of moist decay, brine, loam, and shale, a smell that three hundred years and hundreds of thousands of tons of landfill couldn't affect or change. It was a place that somnambulists and creeps might haunt while the rest of the city slept, for even now, at three in the afternoon, it was night down here.

Large sheets of sheer plastic hung like soiled shower curtains on hooks separating gurneys upon which bodies lay, visible through the plastic. The coroner, Fierro, stood at the head of a stainless steel autopsy table smoking a cigarette. On the table, covered with a sheet, lay the body of Dante's sister-in-law, Sheila Anderson. The outline of her face pressed against the sheet; Cal stared at the dark contours of eyes and nose and mouth.

Fierro waited with a silent decorum that surprised Cal. When Cal nodded, he rolled down the sheet to just above her neck. Pale, blue-hued, and sleeping, as if she had not suffered at all. Fierro stared at them, squinting through his cigarette smoke, ready to show them the reason why she could never wake and rise ever again.

Cal placed his hat on the stainless steel worktable. "This isn't a formal identification. Owen already ID'd the body, right?"

"He did earlier, but I knew you'd come."

Cal nodded. "Thanks."

Fierro replaced the sheet, pressed at the edges about the stainless steel table as if he were making a bed. The lights above the steel tables flickered and buzzed, and a dull pressure throbbed behind Cal's eyes.

Dante stared at the sheet and looked as if he were somewhere else altogether, perhaps remembering how Margo had been examined, gutted, and stitched back up in this very same room. He'd aged since then. Cal suspected they both had. Only Fierro seemed untouched; his complexion gleamed, absent of wrinkles or age. Years before Cal had mistaken that look for serenity, a man who liked his job, who came home at the end of the day without any worries on his mind, but it was only later that Cal realized Fierro was simply indifferent. To Fierro these people were merely cadavers, and their waxy, soft, once volatile and industrious flesh something to be considered and inspected, then ordered and classified, and then filed away. Living bodies interested Fierro even less.

Dante cleared his throat. "I'd like to see the body."

Cal looked at him.

Fierro put his hand to his mouth and coughed. "A lot of hate went into this. Whoever named him the Butcher wasn't too far off the mark."

"The Butcher killed her?" Cal asked, surprised.

"Didn't Owen tell you that?"

"No," Cal said.

Fierro stepped forward, took hold of the sheet that draped her body, and folded it precisely and efficiently down below her feet. She was naked, just as she'd been found, but the rigor that the police report had spoken of was gone. Now, nine hours later, after Fierro's autopsy, what blood was left in her body had pooled in her back and legs.

Cal stared down the length of Sheila's body. The gash across her neck had been sewn shut once the body had thawed—a violent cross-stitching like the lacing on a football. Cal realized he was no longer looking at Sheila but at something that had once been Sheila. He didn't want to think this way, to think like Fierro did, or to believe that such a thing as one's soul—the essence that made up a person even in death—could be so completely gone.

"Why'd you tag her as a Jane Doe?" Dante asked.

"Couldn't be sure anyone would claim her. I guess if it wasn't for Owen, she'd be lying in the potter's field at Fairview."

"Then change the tag."

Fierro, wearing a black rubber apron and yellow lab boots, kept touching and patting at Sheila's body to break up the pooling effect. "We'll get to it."

Dante stared at Sheila's face, then down her purple bruised breasts and stomach to the thin fan of fair hair over her pubic mound. When he looked up, Cal's eyes were on him and he had to look at the ground. "Jesus, Cal," he said. "She was twenty-three. Twenty-three."

"What's the cause of death?" Cal asked.

Fierro looked up from his heavy massage of Sheila's thigh muscle, the ash of his cigarette powdering her leg. The skin across her lower stomach and hips trembled and shuddered. "Well," he said, and eyed Cal as if he was teasing him, "that seems pretty obvious, doesn't it?"

Dante shuffled in his coat and stepped closer to the table. "She's family, not a fucking ashtray." Fierro looked down at her leg, shook his head apologetically, and quickly rubbed at the ash.

Cal laid a hand on Dante's shoulder to keep him calm. Beneath the coat, he felt the tremors of anger. "She ain't a nobody," Dante continued, muttering to himself. "She's family." He turned and walked toward the back of the room, and Cal watched him trying to light a cigarette. Suddenly he was hacking into his fist, and Cal could tell that he was going to be sick. Dante scrambled to the heavy steel door, flung it open, and left. They listened to his footfalls clattering up the basement corridor, waited a moment in silence.

"What about sex?" Cal said. "Was there sexual assault?"

Fierro shrugged, smiled vacantly. "I can't tell. She was found naked and that usually suggests a sexual attack of some kind. All of his other victims have been violated, sodomized. We've found semen in some, but not all."

"Why can't you tell if she'd been sexually assaulted?"

"There's no trauma and no semen. But that doesn't mean she wasn't sexually assaulted. With a body in this state, out in the elements for hours, and damage to the tissue from the cold—that destroys a lot of evidence, Cal. It's hard to know what happened."

"Or she might have been stripped naked for other reasons, maybe to shame her or make a point, a statement."

Cal walked around to the head of the dissecting table. "What about these," he said, "the marks on her wrists?"

"They're ligature marks. Most likely from a rope."

Fierro held his hands together above his head. "She would have been hanging from something as he tortured her." He put down his hands and sighed. "It's the same as the other girls."

"Did she die where they found her, or was she moved postmortem?"

"Well," Fierro began, and with a gloved hand rubbed at the back of his thick neck, "I'm only the coroner, Cal, not the detective at the crime scene, but there's no sand on the body. Now, that may not be all that significant as the beach is under ice and snow, and the cold would have prevented anything clinging to her—once the epidermis had become frozen—but that there would be no sand at all, especially on her lower sections, is surprising."

"I still don't get it. Why would the son of a bitch plant her in such a ritualistic way—what the hell does that mean?"

"You said it yourself. To shame her, to make an example of her." Fierro shrugged and lit another cigarette from the butt of the one he'd just finished. "I think this guy, the Butcher, he gets off on it—making an example of the particular woman he kills."

"The killer," Cal said, "he's been murdering prostitutes, right?"

"So far, yes."

"Sheila wasn't a prostitute."

"Okay, but how long has it been since you saw her last?"

"What are you saying?"

"Maybe the guy has changed his MO or maybe you don't know this girl as well as you thought."

Cal imagined how the killer held her from behind and drew the knife across her neck, how she struggled and bucked against him as the blade tore into the flesh, and how her blood gushed forth as he tore through the muscle and tendon and opened her fully from ear to ear. He saw Sheila's head lolling forward into the gluey pool of her own gore spilling down her breasts as the Butcher planted her in the ground and the temperatures in the bay froze and held her in final rigor, and her clouding pupils staring at the blinking lights of her old neighborhood and the Calf Pasture and the Edison plant beyond, with its dun smokestacks.

"Why Tenean Beach? Why'd he leave her at Tenean Beach?"

Fierro pulled the sheet up over the body, adjusted Sheila's head, fixing her hair before he covered her face. "Maybe it was easy."

Cal scratched at his cheek. "Sheila lived in Dorchester. Isn't that a bit strange, the only victim to be left where she lives?"

"Might just be coincidence."

"Yeah, or maybe not. Maybe she knew him."

Fierro stamped out his cigarette and, coughing, began to light another. Cal stared at Sheila's toe, the last part of her that lay uncovered, and at the tag strung there declaring: JANE DOE. Fierro watched as Cal lifted the bottom of the sheet and covered her completely. When he was done, he cleared his throat, reached over, and picked up his hat off the worktable. "Thanks again," he said, and turned away.

Fierro stamped out his cigarette, hurried between the examining tables. "Ahh, Cal?" he began, as he reached forward and touched Cal on the shoulder.

"Yeah?"

"Well, it's a terrible time and all and I hate to ask but—"

"What is it, Fierro?"

"Do you still have those Bruins tickets?"

CAL FOUND DANTE in the hallway, back against the wall, his hat crumpled in one hand, and in the other a cigarette, which he tugged at in short, painful breaths. His face was pale and he looked as if at any moment he would rush back into the bathroom to get sick all over again. When he saw Cal he straightened, wiped at his mouth with the back of his hand.

"I keep seeing her," Dante said. "I keep seeing what he did to her."

"I know."

"Will you help me?"

"Anything you need, Dante."

"Good. Help me find the fuck who killed her."

"Dante, slow down. The police are already on it. We should wait it out."

"You know they won't do shit. You saw the tag on her. To them she's just a Jane Doe, a whore." His bloodshot eyes blazed. "I can't do this by myself."

"I run a security company. I'm a fucking bondsman. This is police work. You have to let them handle it."

"I need your help. You knew her too."

Cal gripped Dante's shoulder and squeezed. Desperation pulled at Dante's mouth. "She was family, Cal. I wouldn't ask you if I had a choice."

A worker pushing a gurney banged past them, whistling, and Cal dropped his hand. The whistling continued down the dimly lit hallway with the rattle of wheels reverberating off the stone walls.

"Okay, then," he said. "Okay. But first, let's get you home."

7

DANTE'S APARTMENT WAS on the third floor above the Scollay Grill and the offices of a dentist. He entered the narrow hallway. The odor of burnt hamburgers and steak and onions permeated the stairwell. Once he reached the second floor, he could smell bleach mixed with the faint metallic odor of a drill grinding into enamel. Passing by the door with a smoked-glass window—DR. FLINK—DENTISTRY—he could feel the two teeth loosened by Sully's muscleman, a sharp pain that ran along his jaw and tapped against his eardrum.

The door to his apartment wasn't locked. His sister Claudia never left the apartment. He paused, the doorknob in his hand, and tried to take a deep breath, but his bruised ribs made him wheeze, and the acidic taste of vomit scratched at his throat. He entered the apartment and forced a smile as he took off his hat and dropped it on a hook of the coat rack. A bare yellow bulb hung from a cord in the entranceway, and under its fifty-watt glare he imagined his face must appear misshapen, hideously comic.

Claudia sat in the rocking chair with a book on her lap. She didn't

36

look up when she spoke. "Did you see Cal? He was looking for you this morning."

She was three years younger than him, just turned thirty, and already had OLD MAID stamped on her forehead. She'd had a boyfriend once, but he'd never popped the question. Eventually he left her for another woman he'd met in Worcester, and since then she'd been a mess. She couldn't even listen to or carry on a conversation without nervously coughing or wringing her hands. She took calming pills like they were mints, and sat, smoking cigarettes and half listening to the radio, in her rocking chair most of the day. When she did leave the apartment, she wandered the streets, a perpetual clockwork journey through familiar neighborhoods, staring blankly in storefronts or watching other people as they passed.

"How was your day?"

She kept her eyes on the book. "They shut off the phone again."

Dante unbuttoned his coat as he entered the living room.

The light from the reading lamp exposed the swollen, bruise-colored flesh under her eyes. And not only that, but the lines above her lip, and thin streaks of a premature gray staining the black hair pulled and tied in the back. Such a pretty face still, Dante thought. She might yet turn it around.

Claudia finally looked up at him and saw his face, closed the book, and placed it on the folding aluminum table beside her.

"It's no big deal. Got into it with a drunk at Kelly's."

"For heaven's sake, you look like death. You owe somebody money again."

"Please. Not now. I just need to rest."

"Can you eat? There's some leftovers in the fridge."

He bent over and gently kissed her forehead. "I just need some rest. You should do the same. Those bags under your eyes could carry a week's worth of groceries."

She gave him a weak smile and her voice softened some. "Really, Dante, what happened to you?"

"Nothing. I'm okay."

Dante saw the midday *Herald* folded up on the couch.

"You just get this?" he asked. He reached down and picked it up, glanced at the headlines. BOSTON BUTCHER STRIKES AGAIN. UNIDENTIFIED WOMAN FOUND ON TENEAN BEACH. How quick the news got out; even before he could make sense of it all.

"Isn't it awful?" Claudia asked. "Been thinking about it all day, you know? Could be anybody killing these girls."

"You read too many of those damn crime novels, Claudia."

"Who do you think it was?" she asked.

"Who?"

"The woman they found on Tenean."

"No idea." He moved to the coffee table, grabbed the day's mail—what looked to be a telephone bill from Bell, another from Bigelow Oil, and a letter from the landlord. What good would it do if he told Claudia that it was Sheila found on Tenean? He'd have to console her, and feed her bullshit about Sheila now being in a better place. He decided to wait until she read the papers tomorrow, once Sheila's name was released to the public.

Dante dropped the bills back on the table and went to his bedroom. "Good night," he said, before closing the door.

He took off his shirt and placed it on the wooden chair next to his record player. Several record covers were on the floor. He picked them up and put them back on the shelf with the rest of his collection. He powered up the player and dropped the needle.

Sitting on the edge of his bed, Dante lit a cigarette and watched the tendrils of smoke pass up over his eyes in the dim light. The image of Sheila on the autopsy table returned in a close-up: the blue-and-purple-hued face, her black-stitched throat. Who would kill her like that? Where did that hate come from?

He hadn't seen her since the end of spring, or was it early summer? She ran through the clubs he had frequented, the Hi-Hat, Devereaux's, Savoy Café, and sometimes the Roseland, but in all that time, not a sign of her, not even at the Rose when her favorite, Dizzy, played a string of sets last October.

Sheila had had everything Margo hadn't. The fiery hair and blue eyes, a voluptuous body. That outgoing, sugar-coated exterior and that laugh that carried through the room, warming even the most hardened of men. And she'd had conviction, too, something Margo could never hold on to. Upon Fierro's dissecting table she'd been dead—beyond dead, even, for the brutality of her murder prevented him from seeing her in any other way—but now he imagined her unmarked and every part of her flushed with life.

He tried to let the song from the player ease into his mind, but it wouldn't take hold. He shut off the player without taking the needle off the record, and it slowly ground to a stop. There was a glass of water on the nightstand, and below it on the floor a half-empty bottle of whiskey. He lay on the bed. As his eyes fluttered, he glanced over at the bare wall to the right of the door. The three jagged holes from his fist stood out against the pale blue paint, a reminder of Margo's dying the spring before. When he finally fell asleep, it was of Sheila that he dreamed, talking, whispering hotly in his ear something he could not quite make out, and then she was laughing, head thrown back and neck bared, so pale and vulnerable, and he had the sense that she was laughing at him.

8

SAVIN HILL, DORCHESTER

CAL LAY WITH his head back upon his pillow and stared at the ceiling. The wind whipped unevenly along the street and sent hard scatterings of snow against the house and the windowpanes. Lynne was next to him, turned toward the wall, her bare back above the sheets bowed in a pale curve, and he could feel her warmth. He watched as the darkness outside lightened and leaked down through the curtains, and the ceiling with its fine web of fractured plaster became more visible. He sighed and pushed the sheets off him and, knowing that he wouldn't be able to fall back asleep again, was about to move to the living room and have a cigarette when Lynne stirred beside him.

"What's wrong?" she murmured. It was still an hour or so before dawn, but she was on the day shift at the Carney for the next two weeks and was half-awake, listening to him, he guessed, with her eyes closed.

"Nothing's wrong. Go back to sleep. It's still early yet."

"How long have you been awake?"

"Not long."

"Are you thinking about Dante?"

He reached for his cigarettes on the nightstand and worked at prying one from the packet.

"Yeah. I'm gonna head over there this morning."

Lynne was silent and he waited for her to speak. She inhaled deeply and then sighed, pulled at the sheets and blankets, and covered her shoulders. When she spoke, her voice was muffled. "That sounds like trouble," she said.

He nodded in the dark, exhaled cigarette smoke at the ceiling. "If you'd seen Sheila, what this guy did to her..."

"I see enough at the hospital."

He waited, jaw clenched in the dark. "The cops have written this one off. He's got nowhere else to go."

"Is he paying you?"

"Is he paying me? For Christ's sake."

"Don't get mad, I'm only asking."

"Dante hasn't got a pot to piss in, you know that."

"He's in trouble again."

"Not so much. Nothing we can't handle."

He sensed her about to say something and then she paused and said, "I'm sorry, I'm just tired is all. This must be terrible for him."

"Shhhhh," he said after a moment and stroked her hip through the blanket. "You go back to sleep."

He waited until her breathing deepened and then got up from the bed, trod the cold linoleum to the kitchen, where the clock said it was a little after five thirty. He put on the coffee, and showered and shaved. He drank his coffee and watched through the window as the street brightened. When the sun was barely above the bay and the ice-packed cars along the street seemed to glow blue and silver and the lights in other houses across the street came on, he took the car's battery off the kitchen table and carried it outside.

9

SCOLLAY SQUARE, DOWNTOWN

AT THE SOUND of the door buzzer Dante came up out of sleep hard and fast, still in the panic of a terrible dream. His fingers covered in blood, poised above the piano keys. His knuckles were shattered: bone showed through ripped skin. In the dark, voices urged him to play on! Give us another song! and he continued, blood spattering across the keys. It took him a moment to realize where he was, and then the buzzer sounded again and he knew it was Cal and that he was waiting for him. He got up from the bed, and wormlike spots flashed and floated in his vision. He stood and had to wait for the dizziness to pass. He tongued his teeth and grimaced; the inside of his mouth seemed to be lined with sticky cotton. He stood shakily in the bathroom and urinated.

When he was done, he put on his shirt and sweater and coat, rummaged in his bureau for a photograph of Sheila. There were several in the top drawer, ones of him with Margo and Sheila at their side, another of them all in the park, and he paused momentarily as he looked at the photo. Sheila in sunglasses and a light summer dress decorated in pastels.

That had been taken on the Common. The sun was at her back, and it shimmered through the thin material and showed the outline of her body. If he hadn't already torn the pictures so that only Sheila remained, his wife would have been standing to her right—she'd worn a blue dress that day—and holding the wicker basket with the remains of their picnic. He took that one and the one from his wedding and went out to the car.

Cal's gray Fleetline idled at the curb, white smoke steaming from its exhaust. Cal looked up and rolled down his window. Hatless, his black hair appeared unruly and disheveled, but Dante noticed the V of his coat, the press of his white shirt, the immaculate tight knot of his tie, his face gleaming from a fresh shave. Still, he looked tired and pale, and Dante imagined that he had barely slept.

"We'll go to where she died first," Cal said.

Dante sighed and his shoulders drooped unconsciously. He absently fingered the brim of his hat.

"I thought you said the cops already have it under wraps."

"Most cops can't even find their own dicks to piss."

Inside the car the air was warm and moist, like a wool coat warming on a radiator after the rain. On the dashboard Cal had coffee and dough-nuts waiting. The steam from the coffee fogged the windows. Cal handed Dante a cup. "Here. You look like shit."

Dante took the coffee and pulled the photographs from his coat pocket. "So that we can show them around," he said, and Cal glanced at them as he sipped his coffee.

"That's good."

He pressed on the accelerator and the car moved into the Square. He wrangled with the clutch, and they eased into a lane of traffic, moved through an intersection, and made their way onto the ramp bound for the South Shore. Occasional glimpses of the sea, iron blue and flat, white-caps rippling across the surface, appeared through buildings to their left. Traffic was light, and within minutes Savin Hill rose up on their left and then the bay opened up before them and the gas tanks before Tenean Beach loomed stark and gray. Dante glanced over his shoulder. Cal's hat sat neatly in the center of the backseat, next to a stack of maps and city ordinances and a police slicker. When he looked back, Cal was smiling grimly, squinting through the beads of rain streaking the windshield, the sheen of black road before them. After a moment he put on the indicator, downshifted, and turned the car toward the Neponset off-ramp. Dante patted down his coat for his pack of smokes and Cal pushed in the cigarette lighter.

The outsized blank screen of the Neponset Drive-In rose up on their left and then fell away behind them as the ramp corkscrewed back to earth. They were passing beneath the Neponset overpass, and as Dante held the red coils of the lighter to his cigarette, the triple-deckers of Port Norfolk rose up before them. "This is where they found her?" he asked.

Cal nodded grimly, rolled down the windows to clear the glass. The smell of the sea came in to them, and they could see the small spit of sand with its frothy gray shore and the city beyond: the beach of their childhood.

10

CAL AND DANTE stood out as black silhouettes upon the frozen beach, looking as if they'd been cut from hard angles of metal, and stared at the white, untouched expanse of snow. Even the track of the coroner's wagon and the familiar tread of cops' boots had been covered by the previous night's storm.

Dante flicked his cigarette toward a clump of frozen seaweed but the wind returned it at his feet. "Hard to believe this is the same place we used to come as kids," he said, turning to his left, where the small shuttered shower stalls and snack shack stood in stark relief against the ashen sky.

"I'm going to check the bathrooms," Dante said as he began his walk toward the building, his coat whipping off his legs. Cal watched him and tried to suppress his suspicion. He shook his head. "Don't you go fucking up before we even get started."

THE FIRST DOOR that Dante checked was padlocked. The other, facing the ocean, appeared to be locked from the inside, but he stepped back and kicked it open. Cautiously, he stood before the darkness. It felt like looking into a mausoleum.

His mother had taken him and Claudia here all the time, June to September. His family—and Cal's, too—didn't have the money to vacation on the Cape, on one of the islands, or up north on some quaint little lake. This was all they'd had.

He turned and looked at the ocean and saw himself as a young boy swimming in the brownish harbor waves, all the way out to the piers where older boys dove in headfirst from twenty feet above. He saw his sister, all skin and bones, wearing a pink bathing cap. She was at the scummed shoreline with a stick, prodding a jellyfish that lay cooking in the sun. He saw his mother sitting cross-legged on a blanket, wearing that black bathing suit that was far too tight on her thick frame, accenting the rolls on her back and stomach, and him sitting next to her eating sandwiches hot from the sun. And then when the light of day began to soften, and the traffic of cars behind them became louder with the commute home, he remembered that sharp sense of melancholia as he watched families roll up their blankets and pack up their books and baskets and gather their children together, fearing that soon his mother would do the same. Thankfully, she always liked those moments at the end of the day when the beach was deserted and she could have a clear view of the harbor without anybody getting in the way. He and his sister would play by themselves, chasing gulls or playing in the dirty sand until the sun dipped toward the horizon and their mother called out to them, telling them it was time to pack up and head home to Fields Corner, where later in the evening he had a piano lesson with Mrs. Gilchrist, an old widow with severe rheumatoid arthritis whose hands stank of camphor and eucalyptus, and who, when he made a mistake, pinched him hard in the soft part of his upper arm until he got it right. He could see his mother standing in the sunset, hands cupped around her mouth as she called out in Italian and then even louder in English. And him sprinting the length of the beach toward the small peninsula covered in tall grass as if it were an enchanted place instead of a dumping ground for the factories just off the bay.

Dante blew into his hands and turned back around to face the darkness of the stalls. Now in winter, the place smelled of human feces mingled with cheap cigar. There had been people here, bums or kids perhaps—teenagers drinking and smoking, doing what teenagers did. He turned down the narrow hallway between the bathrooms and the locker rooms. Two windows were partially boarded up, the light forcing its way through the uneven plywood slats. He turned to the last window in the hallway and tore off a slat of wood that was nailed weakly to the window frame. It allowed in more light, enough for him to feel secure before opening the door to the men's locker room.

He called out to the darkness as the door creaked open, and stepped inside. There were two high windows, and he went to one and pried off its shutters also. This one was nailed more securely. He put his hat back on and used both hands until the daylight glimmered through. Several blankets were crumpled in among sheets of newspaper and soot-stained towels. He pulled at one of the blankets, and the fetid stench of human shit that wafted up made him wince. He pulled out his lighter, moved its flame around with a shaking hand until he saw something in a tin coffee can. Around it were a few empty beer cans, a wine bottle, a woman's sweater, soiled underthings. He picked up the sweater—it was nothing Sheila would have worn. He grabbed the can, walked back into a square of daylight, and, trembling, emptied the contents of the can onto a wooden bench beneath the window.

The shakes were coming stronger now and he licked at his lips. Wouldn't it be nice to have it all laid out for him, a clean fix and some clean works, a quick taste in the darkness before he made it back out to Cal. Just a taste, something to help him carry on the rest of the day. He bit his lip and erased the thought. If there was any good time to fold, it wasn't now.

Just a bunch of coins, a pouch of dry tobacco and rolling papers, a pencil, what looked to be a tooth, and a silver lighter. He raised it to the open window, and the morning light reflected off the silver. He flicked it open and the spark caught and flamed. He pocketed it, stood back in the

47

doorway, and looked out over the beach, the distant view of Moon Island beneath a darkening sky, and then the open Atlantic with its waves ragged and threatening. He lowered his hat and headed back to the beach.

CAL PAUSED AND looked back the way he'd come, his footsteps small, dark divots in the blanket of white. He tracked them to the parking lot, where, even after the recent snowfall, he could make out the deep frozen rills left by the big trucks and tractor-trailers. He turned back and watched the waves crash and foam under the wooden pylons and against the sheet of rippling ice that last night would have been thicker, blacker, reaching farther out into the bay. He trudged across the frozen grass to the marine salvage and boatyard and stood looking at the beach.

Dante was standing there, staring at him. He called out to Cal, his voice fighting against the wind. "I found nothing."

Two planes passed overhead in quick succession. Dante lowered his head and lit another cigarette.

"It's like nothing ever happened here," Cal said. "Beginning to think Fierro was right. She wasn't killed here."

Cal gestured for Dante's cigarette, took a drag, and handed it back. "It's too cold to stand around and bullshit. Let's get going."

In the car they sat in silence, the engine of the Chevy running. Cal watched Dante roll the lighter about in his hands and he resisted the impulse to tell him to stop. "We'll hit some of these streets next."

"I need to go Somerville," Dante said, but wouldn't look at him. The lighter seemed to move more frenetically from hand to hand.

"What the fuck's in Somerville?"

"It's more of a hunch than anything. It's where Sheila used to live."

"I thought she was living in Dorchester."

"I have no idea where she was last living. I'm talking about where she used to live with Margo, a boardinghouse."

Cal cupped his hands and blew into them, spread them open before the heating vents. "And you have to go now, right this fucking minute?"

"Yeah."

"How long has it been since she was there?"

"I don't know, a year and a half maybe. It used to be a safe place for Margo. I'm thinking maybe it was a safe place for Sheila, too." Dante stared out the window. "Jesus, I just said it was a hunch."

He was becoming morose, and Cal didn't want him to steep in it, to start thinking of the past again, the mistakes that he'd made and that Cal knew he always reminded himself of.

"Okay," he said, and shrugged. "I'll hump around here, pop in on some of the neighbors. You take the car. I know how you are behind the wheel, so just take it slow, okay?"

They opened the doors and the wind tore at them. At the driver's side, Cal paused. Dante slid in behind the wheel, clutched it tightly. "I hate to make you walk home," he said.

"The walk will do me good. Just be careful. Look both ways, and go slow. You look like a fucking accident waiting to happen."

Cal watched as Dante pulled the Fleetline out of the lot and rumbled off down the secondary road. He rubbed at his temple and cursed. It wasn't Dante's driving that worried him.

11

WITH DANTE GONE, Cal spent the next two hours canvassing the neighborhood above Tenean, knocking on doors that never opened. Inner doors slammed and rattled in distant hallways and above shadowy staircases. Curtains parted slightly and then fell back against the window. He heard the volume of a radio being raised, a mother scolding her child. He'd managed to speak to only a dozen or so people, and everyone he'd showed Sheila's picture to had shaken their heads, including an old woman who'd let him in and served him bitter tea, and he'd sat with her and her cats in a room that stank of urine as she proudly showed him her sons' class pictures from Saint Mark's of twenty years before, and he'd recognized them, too—Mark, Pat, and Conor Fitzgerald, all doing time at either Charlestown or Plymouth.

At the end of the street he turned and, looking back over Dorchester Bay with its long sliver of shore stretching toward the city, he thought of Sheila. The last time he'd seen her she'd been nothing more than a girl, a teenager who had taken his hand and asked him to dance at Dante and Margo's wedding at the Polish American Social Club in the Polish Triangle.

Sheila was wearing a pink silk dress that seemed to float around her waist, with a black bodice sheath and matching black shoes with three-inch heels. She was trying to act grown-up, but the dress only made her look younger. Lynne had looked on with amusement, her eyes like a cat's below her slightly arched eyebrows, her teeth bared in a smile and lightly pinching her bottom lip. When she strode to the bar, hips trembling beneath the dress, and ordered a glass of wine, he'd watched her greedily. She'd looked over then with that look of hers and he'd smiled fiercely, alcohol flushing his face and coursing through his body, so that the young girl in his arms had perhaps taken it for something meant for her.

The air had been heavy and sultry and smelled of sweating bodies and spilled beer and electric lights blazing above them, dust burning on the bare bulbs. There were skylights, and a rain had begun to fall sometime during the night and the glass was stippled with it. It hammered and drummed on the tin and pelted the asphalt roof as the band played faster and the crowd hollered and cheered in Polish.

Afterward Sheila had whispered something in his ear and then eyed him as she blew cigarette smoke with practiced precision, pouting her lips and exhaling slowly toward the ceiling elaborate hazy blue rings, trying to affect an elegance and sexual maturity she must have taken from the movies.

At the end of the night she had lifted her glass to him as he placed a stole about Lynne's shoulders. Her lipstick was smeared and her mascara had begun to run with sweat. He could hear, even now, the jangle of the bracelets on her thin wrist as she raised her glass. He'd realized only much later how she'd been drinking steadily all night, and finishing her drinks in the same manner, mock-toasting Margo and Dante. Strange how that sound should come to him now in her death, and the sudden, forgotten knowledge that Sheila had been drunk and so very young and alone at her only sister's wedding.

He stood atop the hill above Port Norfolk and watched the cars and trucks moving north and south over the highway. Below, at Tenean Beach, various trucks, long trailers and short-beds, idled on the street as drivers read papers, smoked, ate their lunch, or waited for their scheduled deliveries. One truck pulled in, killed its engine, and another started up and moved slowly down the street, and disappeared beneath the highway overpass toward Gallivan Boulevard. They moved with the consistency of the planes breaking the clouds over the peninsula and thrumming overhead on their way to Logan.

Steeling his leg for the journey, he strode down the hill. As tripledeckers gave way to beachfront, the wind howled through the crumbling spars and pylons and ripped against him, frozen particles of sand stinging his face. His feet and hands were numb. Needle-sharp pinpricks stabbed his eyes. He stared at the ice-covered snow beyond the crime scene and searched for fading telltale signs—small collapses in the snow that might show him where and how a man carrying a body had moved in the late hours of the night—and then in toward the parking lot, for engine oil frozen in a black pool just beneath the recent snow, or a car's tire track captured in a perfect sparkling mold. But he could only see the gray, thick-ridged icy grooves that had been cut and shaped over the long winter by the big rigs. He poked at them with his foot, those created weeks before and hardened like permafrost, and the more recent, crumbling against his shoe.

A white Peterbilt with BOSTON MEATS written across its side panels was one of the last trucks left on the street. In the distance Saint Mark's tolled two o'clock. Cal blew into his hands and knocked on the door, and the driver rolled down his fogged window. A brown-and-green-tweed scally cap was pushed aslant his head; a cigarette dangled from his mouth. He had pale blue eyes that reminded Cal of a child's.

"Jesus, Mac, it's fuckin' cold. What you doing out there?"

"A buddy of mine has a route out of Boston, supposed to pick me up here on his lunch break today. Here I am freezing my ass off and he's a no-show. Maybe you know him?"

"Maybe, if he's out of the wholesale terminal. I make my first pickups there and then my last at the end of the day. What's his name?"

"Murphy, Paul Murphy."

"Nah, don't know him. But there's a lot of trucks coming out of there."

"Might that be the only place he drives for? He's got a big reefer unit just like this one."

"He might be outta someplace else, but if he's driving the city and he's got a reefer, maybe Chelsea, but he'll probably end up at the terminal one way or the other.

"Look, I'll be done with my lunch in a few minutes and I'm heading back in that way if you want a ride."

"I'd appreciate that." Cal reached up his hand to the cab's window. "Cal O'Brien."

The driver took his hand and grimaced with the cold shock of it. "Jesus, the name's Jimmy Gleason, but will you get in here for Christ's sake so I can shut the fuckin' window."

The cab smelled of grease and cigarette smoke, of old sweat and coffee. But Jimmy Gleason was an immaculate man: Cal noticed his fingernails, spotless and neatly trimmed, and the manner in which, after he ate, he grabbed a rag from a bench box between their seats and wiped down the instrument panel and then the dash and steering wheel. And yet there was a pervasive smell of rot in the cab, as if mildewed and soiled clothing had been piled there and with that, old food. Cal wondered if the odor was coming from the refrigeration unit behind the cab or from within the cab itself. Jimmy seemed oblivious to the smell. He caught Cal looking at him and offered him a cigarette, which he'd been in the process of removing from a pack and placing in his own mouth.

As Jimmy smoked, he pointed to his open lunch pail on the bench box between them. "The wife packs me way too much. It's baloney and cheese and it'll fill a hole if you're hungry."

"Thanks, but I'm good," he said.

Wind howled in the hollows of the wheel wells and around the cab's doorframes as the rig climbed the ramp to the highway and they headed north, back into the city. The fan's engine cut in from behind them, on the nose of the trailer, loud and thundering so that the cab shuddered with the vibrations. After a moment Cal became used to the sound, and

Jimmy, seeming to sense this, spoke. "At least I don't have to put as much ice in the bunker with days like this."

"Surprised you need any ice at all."

"You can't have it too cold, else you'll ruin the meat. All depends what you're haulin'. The temperature has to be regulated just so. Fresh-cut meat: high thirties; apples, peaches, grapes, lettuce: mid-thirties; potatoes: forty-five to fifty; dairy: just above freezing."

"So, if my friend drives a reefer like this one, you think he'd be out of South Street?"

Jimmy nodded. "Yeah, most of 'em come out of South Street. Flowers, fruit, hanging meats, fish."

"Hanging meats?"

"Yeah, y'know, cuts of cow put up on hooks, suspended from the ceiling of the trailer—'hanging.' Sends the rig all over the place. I wouldn't do it long haul if you paid me."

"Where do you go, then?"

"North and South Shore. Sometimes down to New Bedford and Fall River into Rhode Island." He grinned. "I also get up to Portsmouth, New Hampshire, Maine, Canada sometimes too."

Jimmy wiped at the gear knob with his cloth and gazed at it appreciatively when he was done, as if he were admiring the luster of freshly polished silver. "She's powered by a Cummins two-hundred-and-sixty-two-horsepower engine with a five-speed main and three-speed auxiliary transmissions. They don't make them like this anymore."

They passed the Dorchester gas tanks and Jimmy pointed out toward the point, where black smoke from the tire factory and the city dumps twined in the air. "Out there, on the Calf Pasture, that's the graveyard where all the dead trucks go. Like elephants, they all end up there." He touched the console tenderly. "She'll end up there too."

"As salvage?"

Jimmy nodded. "She's got go in her yet, though." He picked at his teeth with a free hand and seemed to be lost in thought for a moment. "When I was a young man I used to haul produce from Nogales, Arizona, into Los Angeles during the summer months. Now that's when we needed ice. Load up the front of the trailer with as much ice as the bunker would hold, twenty one-hundred-pound blocks I'd swing in with my own hands. Had to stop and cool down the load with ice every two hundred miles. I was in some shape then."

He nodded and smiled, a pleasant memory shifting the wintry highway before him into a sweltering West Coast vista, and he suddenly seemed much younger. "This very same rig. Worked hard to buy it, took ten years to pay it off. No more leasing for me—drain your life, those fuckers will. Fifty-one years old and I got a truck and a house. Ain't bad in these times."

"You don't look so old, Jimmy."

"I got a good wife. That helps."

"Yeah. I guess it does."

"How old are you, son?"

"Thirty-two."

"Hate to say it, but you don't look so hot."

Cal laughed. "I've been told that."

"Since the end of the war I've seen lots of guys look like you. You were over there, I'd guess. Could tell the way you limped over to the truck. Where were you?"

Cal was quiet for a moment as he looked out the window, feeling the gray and the cold seep into his bones. He gestured to the city around them, to the tenements, warehouses, triple-deckers, the sea always off to their right. "All over," he said. "I was all over."

"You've got a wife," Jimmy said matter-of-factly, and Cal glanced down to check for his wedding ring; he often forgot whether he was wearing it or not.

"Sure."

"I bet she's a good one."

"What's that?"

"Your wife. I bet she's a good one."

Cal looked at him.

"She's stuck by you, hasn't she?"

"She tries to."

"Sure she does. Through thick and thin. Sickness and sorrow. Till death do us part. All that bullshit."

Jimmy nodded, chuckled to himself. "Don't get company much. I live in my own world so much, I tend to forget some of the more social graces. I ain't making apologies or nothing." He shrugged. "But I shouldn't be butting into no one else's business. You'll have to excuse that. I didn't mean any offense."

The truck's right-front tire hit a pothole, the crashing thud jolting the front end. The sharp reverberation penetrated up through Cal's legs into his scarred hip and thigh, stirring up a sudden pain that made him briefly wince. He gritted his teeth as the truck, downshifting, its engine a roaring backwash, bellowed down through the empty canyons of Dorchester Ave. They turned into Andrew Square, and Cal glimpsed through the fogged window the Polish American Social Club, and then they turned onto Albany and rumbled toward the South Street warehouses, adjoined on the east by the city's central train tracks. In the distance he could make out the square tower and strange medieval turrets of Boston City Hospital. A fucking web, he thought, everything in Boston connected in some way to everything else. Every*one*, too, for that matter. It reminded him that he needed to give Fierro and Owen a call after this next stop, and hope Dante, wherever the hell he was, could get both himself and the car home in one piece.

12

THE TRAFFIC ON Massachusetts Avenue was sluggish. Behind him and in front of him, impatient drivers laid on their horns as if the shrill noise would make everything move. The BPW plows hadn't done a good job clearing the roads; chunks of icy snow lay scattered on the street, and patches of ice grew where the trucks hadn't sanded. A white Buick in front of him slowed and then came to a complete stop.

As he crossed the bridge, the Charles River reflected the high sun that momentarily forced its way through the clouds, stretching its glare across the marbled ice. Below it, he imagined a vast cold current of nothing, and Sheila trapped inside the dark waters, her eyes sealed shut, her throat a frozen gash.

"I'm a fucking mess," he said aloud, wiping his knuckles across his wet cheek, tears he hadn't been aware of. A weight continued to press on his chest. That he hadn't seen Sheila in so long got to him. It had been late July, a month after he'd been released from the hospital, and he'd gone to the Pacific Club to hear Sonny Stitt and his trio. From his usual spot standing with his back to the bar, he'd glimpsed her sitting at a small ring-side table with a guy wearing a broad-shouldered suit that matched the color of his black pompadour. He'd watched her from across the red-lit room, noticing how she leaned into the guy every time he spoke, the gentle touches she placed upon his arm, the smile and the sly nod she gave him when he lit her cigarette. When the band took a short break to refill their glasses, he found her walking to the bathroom, watched the motion of the dress sliding across her hips, the thin material clinging to the cleft of her bottom and the backs of her thighs, and he reached out to her as she passed.

"How about a drink with your brother-in-law?" he said, realizing too late how much it sounded like a pickup line. And even though she smiled, her eyes betrayed her. He gently grabbed her arm and pulled her in closer to a space at the bar and, slurring his words, told her that he'd missed her. He waved to the bartender, Bowie, and asked for another whiskey and a whiskey sour.

When their drinks came, she turned to her table, where her stylish escort sat, gesturing with his hands, beckoning her back. She raised an index finger and mouthed the words "One minute, just one more minute."

"Who's the sharp dresser?" Dante asked, and she laughed and her eyes drifted back to the table.

"Just a friend," she said. Sheila was never a good liar, not to him at least.

"Well, I hope he's treating you well." He looked her over for a moment. She had lost some weight and it showed in her face. Gone was the dreamy curiosity she'd often exhibited. It was now replaced with a self-assured elegance. She wore white gloves that ran all the way up to her elbows and made the pink satin dress even more chic, perhaps too much so for an after-hours club like the Pacific. He stared at her gold necklace and the swell of her cleavage. He was about to ask how she could afford such jewelry, but she was already preparing to leave. "Good to see you, Dante," she said, and he stumbled and pulled her into him and said he loved her. Her body went tight and he loosened his embrace and stepped back.

"It's been hard for us all," he said, trying to sound normal despite the anxiety building in his chest and throat. He wanted to say how much he truly cared for her, that they were family, that he loved her and desired her, yes, but before he could utter the words, she extinguished her cigarette, kissed him on the cheek, and said good-bye. That was it. And then she was gone.

PARKING THE CAR off River Street just outside Central Square, Dante walked two streets over to the corner of Winston. The faint odors of chocolate and burnt fudge carried half a mile from the Necco candy factory. He lit another cigarette, exhaled smoke from his nostrils.

He paused before the green house, a square, flat-roofed two-family without a back or front porch. He pushed the doorbell once and then repeated, hearing the sharp buzzing echo in the hallway inside. All the houses in this neighborhood were built in a rush during the first war, and they were squared up tightly on narrow streets and sidewalks barely wide enough to hold a hydrant. He watched two little boys skip on the sidewalk toward him. Each was wearing a tattered sweater that was a size too big. They looked up, chins raised, and stared at him, a look that an adult might give somebody who wasn't from the neighborhood, and even though they were just children, the look got under his skin.

The door opened, and a voice like a breaking dish made him turn around. "Jesus Christ, look who crossed the bridge! If it ain't Dante Cooper, it must be whatever is left of his ghost."

Dante hadn't seen Karl in over two months. He was wearing a thin robe and a pair of blemished chinos. A beard hid his lopsided chin and thinned over his stick neck, where his Adam's apple protruded like something infected. His heavy eyes were bloodshot. He wasn't a large man, didn't look like he'd be much in a fight, but the diseased look usually kept those who wanted to brawl in check; he had the look of a man who found many uses for razor blades besides shaving.

"I was in the neighborhood. Just thought I'd say hello."

"Is that right? Came all the way here just to see me?"

One never knew what to expect with Karl. Either he was pissed off or ecstatic, and he could switch back and forth with the ease of a well-kept switchblade. Right at this moment, Dante couldn't get a good read on him.

Once up the bare wooden stairs to the second floor, Dante could smell the marijuana. It wasn't a good sign. Things must have been dry, and without any of the heavy stuff, Karl was resorting to the green leaf to help pass the time.

Dante didn't want to waste any more effort on him than he had to. "I just thought I'd pop by."

"You make it sound like we're friends, Dante. You're here for the same reason everybody comes here. You think I'm stupid?"

The second-floor hallway was crammed with nearly a dozen cardboard boxes.

"No, I don't think you're stupid, Karl. I've seen you do some stupid things before, but no."

Karl's thin lips curled up around his gums, an attempt at a grin. "God's on my side, you know. See these boxes here?" He pulled back one of the flaps. Inside were miniature statues of Christ on the cross, resting on beds of shredded newspaper. "With this many Jesuses, I'd say the big guy's got my back. Yesterday I wasn't holy; today I might as well be the fucking pope."

"You got enough of these to fill every windowsill in the North End."

Karl reached out and put his hand on Dante's arm. "C'mon, there's someone I want you to meet." Karl gave him a wink, and pushed open the door. "Dante, this here is my friend Cassie. She'll take care of you while you're waiting."

The small living room stank of cheap incense and marijuana. On the couch sat a thin black girl no more than eighteen. She was wearing an off-white silk shirt halfway unbuttoned. The bottom of a billowing skirt spread up around her skinny thighs. She looked at him, her eyes moving in and out of focus, and Dante could tell that she was flying high from junk.

"Have some fuckin' manners, Cassie," Karl snapped. "Say hello. An old friend like him deserves it."

She managed a raspy "Hello," and her head lolled suddenly as though some cosmic puppeteer had sneezed, tweaking the wrong string. A slight impression of fog escaped from her mouth as she tried to smile, and Dante felt how cold it was in the room.

"Take a seat, Dante. Please, make yourself at home."

"I can't stay long." It all felt wrong to him.

Karl crossed the room and flipped a record on the player. The stirring of a blues ballad came on, barely audible with all the skips and pops on the vinyl and dust clogging the needle. He turned back to Dante. "C'mon, at least stay for a side. To be honest, I'm having a great day and I'd like you to share it with me."

"I don't have much time."

The girl on the couch broke out in raspy laughter. "He doesn't sound like a true friend, does he? He really ain't here to see you."

Dante gave her a look-over and made sure she felt it. "Karl, if you don't want to part with any, I understand. I just need something to take the edge off. I've been clean for a while. It won't take much."

"Don't like our company, do you?"

"It's not that. I'm just busy with something."

"Saving the world, are you?"

"No, just helping somebody out."

"But you'll only end up making it worse like always, no?" Karl laughed.

Dante didn't respond, so Karl continued, slightly apologetic. "Okay, I understand. How much you got on you?"

"Ten."

"I'll fix you up something. You can join all of us, if you want. I think we're ready, aren't we, Cass?"

The girl laughed again. "This pale boy looks like he could use some of that love. A face that bruised-up means he a little lonely." She spread her legs apart and Dante saw the wiry mass of pubic hair.

Karl said, "Don't mind her, she gives too much lip and not enough head is what it comes down to. I'll be right back." He opened a door off the living room and went inside. Dante could hear him talking to somebody.

A man's wool peacoat hung on the back of the chair. He sat down and looked at the Oriental rug. Two Christ figurines were lying there, each snapped in two at the waist. He reached down and picked one up. It was hollow inside. His thumb pressed into the abdomen, and the plaster crumbled in his hand. So this was where Karl stored it. Dante shook his head, let what was left of Christ drop to the floor, and wiped his chalky fingers on his pant leg.

"Hey you, look." The girl had lifted her skirt higher, spread her legs farther apart. She rubbed the inside of her spotty thighs for a bit before parting the hair and exposing the pink folds, which she spread with skinny fingers. She leered and then leaned forward, inspected her sex as if it had been removed from her body and placed on a dinner plate.

"Close your damn legs," he said.

She cackled in response and probed deeper with her thumb and index finger. Dante stood and made his way to the bedroom. Karl was already on his way out. The door was open and Dante could see inside.

A white teenage girl was wiping down her breasts with a tissue. She couldn't have been more than thirteen years old. Her lipstick was smeared over her lips and chin, and her legs were wide open and bent at the knees as if she were giving birth. Before her a man of about fifty was pulling up his boxer shorts. His half-erect penis looked as though it had been bloodied. He wore oval gold-rimmed glasses and looked like a minister, his pale face shaved so clean it shone like polished ivory. Sick bastards like him were the ruin of this world, Dante thought. He looked back at the girl on the bed. Unflinching, she balled up the tissue and threw it on the floor near Dante. "What the fuck you lookin' at?"

Karl put his hand on Dante's arm and pulled him back into the living room, closed the door behind him. "Jesus, Dante. What the fuck is wrong with you?" He handed him six fixes tied in a balloon.

Dante gave him the ten. His jaws clenched and he chewed on the insides of his mouth; he wanted to crack the skull of the sick bastard.

In the hallway Karl said, "I'll see you again, soon."

"No you won't. I'm giving up after this, I'm going clean."

"Sure, Dante, sure. I've heard that one a million times. Sorry, brother."

"No, I mean it. I'm done."

"I'll see you in two days, tops, maybe even sooner. And you know it's only me you can come to. The whole city is dried up and it has been for months. Canto and Boris ain't carrying, and Gordon is up in Concord. Unless some of your nigger friends can feed you some overpriced shit, probably cut with fuckin' pancake mix, I'm the only one."

"Karl, you're nothing but a lowlife."

"But this lowlife always gives people like you what they need."

"Like selling underage girls to get fucked? Karl, they should put you on a pedestal. Then light a fucking match."

Karl bared his teeth. He didn't like sarcasm. "You've been lonely since she's gone, don't say you aren't. I could see it in your eyes when you saw those little tits and that tight li'l cunt staring right up at you. You're no different from the rest of us animals, so don't be a fuckin' hypocrite."

"You don't know me for shit, Karl. I won't be seeing you again."

"That's a good one, Dante. Morning after next you'll be back. You'll always come back to Brother Karl."

On the street, Dante inhaled deeply to cleanse the clinging odors of incense, bitter reefer, cum, and pussy that had permeated the apartment and had made their way into his clothes. He lit a cigarette and found it tough to drag on. He shuddered with a disgust and loathing he hadn't felt in some time.

Hate was the only thing that could make one stronger, and he hated not just himself but every low-down bookie, thug, and peddler of junk and underage girls. Someday the fires of hell would take them all away, and he wished that he'd be able to sit on the precipice, taking in his last fix, and watch them all burn and suffer, knowing that soon enough the flames would come his way and pull him down to join them.

13

THE WAREHOUSE TERMINAL at the fraying edges of Dorchester, Roxbury, and South Boston spread out on the west bank of the Fort Point Channel like a vast industrial wasteland with trucks rumbling in and out of warehouse bays. Cal had often passed it coming from Uphams Corner without giving it a second thought, but as they came in through the Southampton Street entrance, the size of the place momentarily overwhelmed him.

"Jesus, how many warehouses are there here?"

"I dunno, maybe fifty? Sixty?"

"And how many of them are cold storage?"

"Most of 'em."

"Christ."

"Keep the faith. You might get lucky straight off."

A quarter of a mile in Jimmy waited for a truck to pull out and then turned the rig wide before a row of empty bays beneath the sign BOSTON MEATS and slowly backed it to the dock. Inside the warehouse Cal followed Jimmy to the dispatcher's office, where a woodstove burned by the desk and drivers were drinking coffee and waiting for their loads. A blackboard covered the far wall listing the truck numbers and times in and out and their scheduled pickups and drops in glaring white chalk, pressed hard to the board. Jimmy led him over to a desk by the loading dock where a large ledger showed the drivers' assignments, their rigs, and their times, signed in and out with each return to the hub. The door to the office was propped open by a cinder block, and from the warehouse beyond came the sound of blaring forklifts and shouting loading-dock workers.

Cal looked at the log. He didn't know what he was looking for other than a sign that something was off. If someone was using a reefer to pick up, kill, transport, and then dump bodies, it would take time, time that had to show up somewhere. Forty trucks, and every truck accounted for in the last twenty-four hours, including Jimmy Gleason's, his neat script logging his most recent run. And every truck on the page within twenty minutes of its scheduled pickup and drop-off.

Jimmy waited. "Any luck?"

"No. This isn't the place. I'd better get my walking shoes on."

"Jesus, that's a shame. Listen, I've got to drop my load and get to Fall River, but a quick tip. Most of the warehouses here do retail food sales to locals, so they usually don't mind people coming by the docks. But stay out of the way of the loading—that's the fastest way to piss people off. Just tell the dispatcher your story, lie where you need to, and perhaps you'll get what you're looking for."

Cal extended his hand. "Thanks, Jimmy. It was a pleasure meeting you."

Jimmy's grip was like a vise. "Same here," he said. "You remember to look after that wife of yours, okay? She sounds like a peach if she's stuck by you," and he laughed.

"Sure thing, Jimmy."

CAL HAD SPENT the better part of the day searching the terminal, and now, nearing dusk, his thigh was throbbing. The place was the size of an airport field. He'd watched refrigerated semis coming in, loading, and leaving from one warehouse after the other, their rumblings jolting the tarmac beneath his feet and trains on the B&A line—the Boston-to-Albany Twilight Express—churning back and forth out of South Station in the distance. He passed the cold storage fish warehouses with their dumpsters reeking of rotting fish and upon which big harbor seagulls fought and screeched. Whatever reefer carried her body to Tenean, he doubted it was carrying fish. The pallet loading aboard the trucks wouldn't allow it, never mind the smell.

The need for a drink to ebb the pain pressed at the forefront of his thoughts, but he pushed it back down, unwilling to give in to it until he had something that he and Dante could work on. He climbed the ladder to the loading dock of another warehouse—his twenty-third, if he was counting. A sign for Fat Fong Choy—鴻鈞老祖—hung over the dock, looking like the type of business sign that might be replaced in a month by another.

The dock workers were a mix of white and Asian. An Asian kid was smoking a cigarette by the trucking log and signing his initials. When he was done, he looked up. "I was hoping you might be taking that load sitting out there to New Bedford, but you ain't a driver."

His accent was townie all the way. "No, I'm looking for a friend who drives a rig out of here."

"What's his name?"

"I figure if I look at the log it'll jog my memory."

The driver raised his eyebrows, clearly suspicious but waiting him out.

Cal scanned down the log. Twenty trucks and every truck accounted for in the last twenty-four hours but one: number 36, Scarletti.

"What happened to thirty-six, Scarletti?" he asked.

"That your friend?"

"Might be."

"How much is it worth to you?"

Cal considered this. He had limited funds and wasn't about to give anyone a handout, but he still had an additional ticket for the hockey game tonight. It was the Bruins, after all, and it was still Boston.

"A ticket to the Bruins and the Canadiens," he said. The driver looked at him and shrugged.

"Guess it's not worth that much to you. The Bruins fucking stink."

"That's what everyone tells me." He pulled a five from his wallet.

The driver turned and called out to a stump of a man as wide as a rain barrel who had his back to them and was gesturing at one of the forklift drivers. "Hey, Peter! Have you seen Mike Scarletti come in? His friend here is looking for him."

Peter half turned, an unlit stogie mashed in his mouth, and Cal could see the face of the Asian forklift driver, tight-lipped and angry as hell. Peter held up his index finger, telling them one minute, and then went back to screaming at the driver. The kid was looking at him, grinning. "You're full of shit, gwai lo," he said and put out his hand.

THE DISPATCHER PLODDED into the office as if the weight of the world rested upon his shoulders. He was even more barrel-like close up. A heavy red-and-black-plaid flannel shirt rode up from his waistband.

"I swear most of these morons don't know their ass from their elbows," he said, pulling the wet cigar from his mouth and laying it tenderly across a rusted tin ashtray. "What the fuck you want?"

"Scarletti, the driver of number thirty-six." Cal gestured to the log. "Have you seen him?"

"Who are you?"

"I'm looking for a friend who drives one of those rigs, maybe out of here."

"Yeah? Your friend got my truck, red and green Peterbilt?"

"Maybe. Who's this driver?"

"Fucking Scarletti, he's a big stupid punk from Providence." He looked at Cal. "I thought you was friends?"

"From way back when. Long time ago. Didn't know he moonlighted as a working stiff, but then it's been a long time since I've seen him."

"Working stiff? Well, that's not Scarletti, and when I see him he's fucking through. I got a guy down in Buzzards Bay pissing and screaming his customers never got their meat, a half ton of fucking cow that never gets to where it's going because my driver decides to take a fucking powder."

"When did he miss his load?"

"Two days ago. He's been AWOL since."

"This Scarletti, if it's the same guy, how would I know him?"

"You couldn't miss him. Built like a brick shithouse, big as a fucking moose. Just as dumb, too. Curly orange hair." He pointed a stubby finger to his upper lip. "And one of those ugly deformed lips, you know, a harelip."

Cal kept his expression measured. "Yeah, that sounds like him."

In the warehouse someone was shouting for the dispatcher. He cursed, jammed the stogie back in his mouth, and left the office. Cal followed. Forklifts hummed past, forks rattling in their braces. Before the open truck bays, workers hollered at trucks reversing into their spots, signaling the drivers to cut their wheels or waving them off and telling them to start again. Someone swung open a truck's rear doors and cried, "Fuckin' load's crushed! Some asshole double-stacked the pallets!"

"What's that over there?" Cal said, gesturing out beyond an open truck bay toward the Fort Point Channel and the South Station rail yards. In the distance, beside stacks of crushed cars were rows of identical-looking trailers.

"What's what?"

"Over there at the end of the lot, those trailers. Are they waiting to be loaded?"

"Nah." The dispatcher waved them away. "They're useless. The refrigeration units are done on some; on others the floors are rotted away, or the brake lines are shot, or a hundred other frigging things. They're waiting to be towed away."

"Out to the city dump?"

"That's right."

The dispatcher chewed on his cigar so that bits of it flew about the room as he turned his head, frowning. "Listen, guy, not to be a rude son of a bitch, but I really don't give a shit about your friend. I don't know where the fuck he is. If you want to waste your time, go check out those trailers, go the fuck over to the city dump. Be my fucking guest, but I got a warehouse to run."

He followed as Cal limped to the loading dock, wrapped a beefy hand around the chains that raised and lowered the dock doors, and lowered the door to just above Cal's head so that Cal had to duck beneath. Cal jumped down off the dock, and the shock of the impact shot through his legs. His hat fell to the ground, and he stumbled awkwardly as he went to pick it up. With his hands in his pockets, he walked gingerly toward the rail yard, pulling his coat tight about him. He heard the rollers against the chains as the dispatcher hollered, "And if you find Scarletti, you tell him I want my fucking truck!" and then the dock door slammed down behind him.

A short distance across the abandoned lot, toward the trains at South Station and the subway home, the wind came at him, pushing him back, and his feet and hands felt frozen. His thigh had stiffened with all the walking, and the rail yard was farther away than it seemed, so that when he looked back, he was surprised to see how little distance he'd come, the lights of the terminal and its trucks glowing feebly no more than two hundred yards away.

14

BALL SQUARE, SOMERVILLE

DANTE SAT IN the car as it grew cold, watching the boardinghouse where Margo and Sheila had once lived together. One seventy-four Russell Street looked like it could have been a small nursing home, or a place where addicts like himself, or broken war heroes like Cal, came to forget the messes they'd left behind. The large boardinghouse was built in the Greek Revival style, and it sat upon a small hill, peeling white paint against the white of the snow. The bare arthritic maple trees gave the house a haunting perspective from the sidewalk. None of the steps had been cleared, and the smooth, untouched snow gave the place an aura of seclusion despite being in a relatively crowded neighborhood.

He kept the car's engine running. The driver's-side window fogged over, and he wiped at the moisture and watched the building for any signs of life. A gust of wind pulled pieces of newspaper across the front lawn. Two squirrels jumped from the long porch, one chasing the other, and then climbed the dark silhouette of a tree, scurrying one moment and, the next, seeming to disappear. The house was over a hundred years old, and it looked the worse for wear. The three columns on the front porch appeared slanted, perhaps one rough winter away from collapse. And the shutterless windows on the three floors had no curtains, giving the feeling that the place was vacant. He turned off the engine, leaned back in the seat. How awful Margo and Sheila had had it as foster children during the depression, a time when parents struggled to put food on the table for their own children, let alone ones they felt charitable enough to take in and give shelter to.

More bad things had happened to Sheila and Margo than good, and during his and Margo's marriage, he regretted that she had kept all those things to herself. But sometimes in a rare moment of sharing, she had given him enough of a story to put the pieces together and form a sort of crude map of their lives. Their mother had left them at Saint Mark's when Margo was seven and Sheila was three. And they'd gone from foster home to shelter to a new city to another town—from Quincy Center to Roslindale, Mattapan, Weymouth, a stint in Fields Corner and then Jamaica Plain. They'd once had their heads shaved for fear of their bringing lice into a new home; a man at an orphanage had broken Margo's arm and it never set properly and got infected; when Sheila was six, she fell ill with pneumonia and missed a year of school. And the house before him was the first place Margo, and then Sheila, could call home—thanks to an old Brahmin couple, the Baxters, who, in return for their helping with cleaning and cooking, offered them the small room in the attic.

The windshield was now glazed with ice. The quiet in the car ate at him and filled him with anxiety. He felt like he was falling off the world again. A fix was waiting in his pocket, whispering a remedy. Just return the car to Cal, admit that your hunch went nowhere, and then go away for a while, see you tomorrow. But there was the thought that needed absolution, and it helped carry Dante out of the car and up onto the sidewalk that hadn't been shoveled in weeks. For a moment he stood looking up at the lone window on the uppermost attic floor, a small black square that, against the white paint of the house, seemed impenetrable from the outside.

Dante pulled up his collar and moved through the snow along the sloping front lawn. Most of it was frozen solid, and every few steps the crust of ice caved in, leaving him in up to his knees. Eventually he made it up the hill and to the stairs slanted with snowdrift, up onto the long, wide front porch. He rang the doorbell and heard the chimes ring out a brief and stately melody, part of a Protestant hymn long forgotten. He waited and then opened the screen and knocked on the wooden door.

He peered in through one of the windows. A slight tapping on the pane startled him. It was a fly seeking escape. He left the columned porch and passed around the side of the house. Empty trash barrels without their lids tilted crookedly, half submerged and frozen in the snow. Using the wooden railing, he climbed the short porch that led to the kitchen. He knocked on the door, waited a moment, and then turned the door-knob. It opened. In the kitchen, the rotting stink of garbage, only slightly disturbed by the gust of cold air that poured in behind him.

A plate of untouched food sat on the kitchen table, what might have been mashed potatoes and carrots turned gray and black with mold. A lump of shriveled meat seemed to convulse as maggots squirmed upon it. Another fly crept over the fetid mass, and then paused and remained motionless, as if it were looking at him. Dante scanned the room. Pots and pans hung on their hooks beside the stove. The sink and countertops, though now covered in a fine layer of dust, had recently been clean. He turned back toward the plate of food, watched the fly exit the kitchen into the hallway.

He closed the door behind him. Beneath the silence, he could hear the house shifting, moaning as the wind pressed against it. There was a back staircase that led from the kitchen up the three floors to the attic. He remembered this, somehow, and entered the narrow, musty staircase, and in the darkness felt for a light switch. He found one and flipped it. The bulb was out.

His lighter provided enough light, a flickering glare that traveled a foot in front of him. The wood of the stairs groaned under his weight. He paused, feeling as if something or somebody was in the house listening to him, and he thought of the crippled woman who had once been a tenant here. She'd had a stroke at a young age, no more than thirty, and it had paralyzed half her body and left her with a shuffling limp. The woman's hair had fallen out, and she had refused to eat, and had slowly wasted away, her body becoming emaciated and sexless. She hid in her locked bedroom all day, but at night she would roam the house barefoot, wearing nothing but her robe. Margo and the other women had complained of her frightening them: sitting in the bathroom with the lights off, just staring into the tiles on the floor, hiding in the basement where the washing tubs were, or in this very same dark staircase, waiting hours and hours until somebody came and found her.

He made it up to the third floor, paused for a moment at the door he knew led out to a long hallway past five of the bedrooms, and then continued up the narrow staircase to the fourth and uppermost floor, the attic. In the hallway he found a lightbulb and pulled on the cord with fingers still numb from the cold. The light chased away the darkness, as well as the memory of the woman. He opened the door and took one step into the room where Margo and Sheila had lived. A single window allowed in the weakening light of late afternoon. Except for a small bed where a sheet and a blanket lay strewn at one end, the room appeared stripped of everything else, as if it had always been this bare and empty, as if nobody had ever lived here.

Dante walked farther into the room. To his left, a small dresser stood against the wall. The drawers had been pulled out, forced from their runners. Whatever had been inside them was scattered about the floor: a pair of white panties, a small purse with floral design stitching, a silk slip, a roll of lace, several tins of rouge and powder, and crimson stockings. Someone had been through the room, and they'd done a thorough job, but had they found what they were looking for? He crouched to his knees, reached down, and grabbed the purse. Its lining had been torn out and nothing was left inside. He tossed it back into the mess of scattered clothes. A gust of wind pressed against the old wooden window frame, set the loose screen on the other side of the glass clacking loudly. Dante stood back up and, in fear of dirtying the clothes with his wet shoes, stepped carefully over them, only realizing after a moment that Sheila would never be wearing them again.

On the other side of the dresser, a small mirror had been smashed on the floor. In the pieces he saw fragments of himself, a shadow in reflection. Seven years' bad luck for you, he thought, and reached over to the closet, the same closet that Margo used to store her meager belongings in. It was empty except for a few wire hangers. Deeper inside he saw a human shape, a pale torso. Startled for a moment, he realized it was just a dressmaker's dummy, a headless, armless body on a pole. A sudden weight came down on him and he had to sit on the mattress.

This was the room where he and Margo had spent their first night together. And this had been their bed. The thin mattress bowed beneath him. For a moment it seemed he could smell her here, the cool touch of her arms on the back of his neck.

He looked down and spotted the board that didn't quite match the rest of the floor, a slightly different grain against the dark-stained maple—the place where Margo used to keep her fixings. He tapped on the board with the heel of his shoe, and the echo of it ran hollow. He got on his knees, cigarette resting at the edge of his lip, and pushed at the floorboard. It was loose and without any nails holding it in. There was a groove beside it, not big enough for a finger to fit into. From the closet he grabbed a metal coat hanger and straightened the hook out. Forcing the metal into the hole, he raised the slat high enough to pull it free with his fingers. The space was empty. He sat back on his haunches, took a long pull on the cigarette. He didn't know why he thought there would be something still here after all this time. He leaned facedown to the floor and peered first left and then right along the line of the joist.

A small box sat deeper in the hole in the shadow beneath the joists. He reached in, fingers scrabbling for a hold, and pulled it out, returned to the bed with the box on his lap. He wiped the dust and the cobwebs from the top and then slowly opened it. A nude photograph of Sheila propped up on an elbow and reclining amid the cushions on an ornate couch glared up at him. Through slitted eyes, thick with eyeliner and mascara, she stared at him, smeared lips puckered, blowing a kiss to whoever held the camera.

Another one of her standing naked in what looked to be a hotel room, posing like Betty Grable, with a leg bent upward behind her and her head thrust back as if in the midst of laughter. One was taken from the foot of a bed and centered on her spread legs, her glistening vagina thrust toward the camera lens. Her head was propped awkwardly upon the pillow, and the smile plastered to her face seemed unsure and anxious. There were others of her also, but in these the face was purposely blurred or the photos were cropped from the neck up. From the body alone he knew they were Sheila.

Repulsion turned in Dante's stomach. He stared at the pictures even though he felt dirty, guilty, a Peeping Tom. This was all his fault. He inhaled, exhaled slowly, trying to stave off the sudden shame and guilt pressing in on him.

Beneath the stack of smut there were more photos, unlike the others. They were of Sheila at the dog track, smoking in the dim light of a club, on the Swan Boats in the Public Garden. And then there were older ones, blistered and cracked, taken from when she was a child. One showed a young Sheila holding the hand of Margo, probably nine years old at the time, each of them wearing dresses far too big and both staring blankly at the camera with coal-dark eyes. Another showed them standing out in front of Saint Mark's church, the same church where their mother had abandoned them, the same church he and Cal had attended as children. Both of them stood beside a sturdy older woman who may have been the senile woman they called Auntie, the one they briefly lived with in South Boston. Also in the stack was a picture from Dante and Margo's wedding, the bride and groom beaming in the bright flash, Cal standing next to him, squinting, and Sheila next to her sister, her eyes looking not at the camera but somewhere off in the distance.

He placed the photographs on the floor and began to search the rest of the box. To his side, the picture of Sheila's spread legs and shockingly

75

bared vagina stared up at him, and he found it hard not to glance at it. In the box there was a charm ring, a rabbit's foot, a first report card, jewelry, trinkets, a dance card from a cocktail banquet at the Emporium Hotel, junk. It was like looking through the secret belongings of a young girl. But at the very bottom of the box was an envelope. Inside were ten one-hundred-dollar bills, perfectly pressed, without line or crease, all sticking to one another as if they had never been counted. He put the bills to his nose. Fresh off the press, steeped in that sharp tang of new money. He looked at his hands as if he expected to see green ink there, as if it might bleed from the notes and stain his skin.

He stood and folded the bills before sliding them into his pants pocket. He reached back down and picked up the photos, looking at the girl in them again. He flipped them over, searched for a photo shop imprint, a date, a name, but every one of them was blank except for the one pose that mimicked Grable, and on it was written *My Only Pin-Up, Love, Your Man, Mario.* He collected the trinkets and photos, placed them into his coat pocket, returned the box to its space in the floor, and left the room.

HE WALKED THE hallway floors, bare, water-damaged, and warped ply-wood, passing before open doors of empty bedrooms. All of them were gone; the middle-aged widows, or the wife waiting and praying for her husband to return home from Europe unharmed, the single girls who ached for a romance that wouldn't materialize until the war was over, and the spinster who had told the younger girls that hearts could be broken only once. The sad, horrifying, deformed stroke victim in her early thirties, forever limping alone through the dark.

Downstairs he suddenly had the feeling of somebody's presence in the next room and, feeling foolish, he called out, "Hello. Anybody there?"

There was only the distant buzzing of flies. He had seen two flies earlier, and now as he walked closer to the front room, he could hear, and smell, where the rest of them gathered. He pulled out a handkerchief from his pocket, covering his nose and mouth before entering the dining room.

The body lay on the floor. Its head was like a large decomposing vegetable that had fallen from its vine. The face was stretched and splitting. A blackened gouge ran along the side of the forehead and led down to a puddle of dried blood covering the edge of the carpet. The hair on the scalp was a sandy pale white, the hands liver spotted and bloated, one upturned on the floor, the other resting on his chest.

Mr. Baxter, the owner and patriarch of the house. Someone had used a tool to bash in the poor bastard's skull. Probably the same someone who'd ransacked Sheila's bedroom searching for something. At the body's feet, the rug was ruffled and bunched up. With the handkerchief held tightly to his mouth, Dante offered up a muffled prayer. He glanced about the room. A small table and a wooden chair tucked under it. A phonograph, an unmade hospital bed in the corner, and a reading chair next to an aluminum table covered in books. With his free hand, Dante took an old afghan from the arm of the reading chair and tried to lay it over the upper body and head, but it bunched together and fell to the side. With the motion, a black cloud of buzzing flies flew up from their feasting, causing the head to shudder slightly, and then the head canted to the right and the skin came away from the skull. Fighting the urge to vomit, Dante backpedaled from the room.

15

FIERRO AND OWEN were already seated in the nosebleed section high in the rafters of the Boston Garden when Cal arrived, out of breath and clutching three beers. Far below them on the undersized rink, the hockey players were throwing themselves against one another, fighting for the puck against the boards where heckling fans crowded. As Cal watched, the Bruins' captain, Milt Schmidt, crushed one of the Habs just past the visitor's bench so violently the wood shook and the crowd went wild banging the boards.

"You boys look like you've got a head start on me." Cal squeezed by them to his seat, handing out the beers as he passed.

Owen, still in his police blues, stood and leaned back. "All in your honor, Cal," he said, and squeezed Cal's shoulder. "All in your honor."

"You made it," Fierro said. "Jesus, your balls must be frozen blue."

Cal grinned, but it was a tired gesture without humor. "What balls? Can't feel anything below my waist."

He sat hard in the wooden chair, took off his hat. He left his coat on, drew his shoulders in; the cold had seeped deep into his bones and his mood had soured.

Owen lit a cigarette and handed it over.

"Thanks," he said.

"Terrible thing about Sheila," Owen said. "How's Dante taking it?"

"Seems like he's holding up, but you never can tell. I didn't think he had anything left after Margo's death." Cal shrugged. "I guess we'll see."

"Yeah, we'll see."

"What does that mean?"

Owen sucked on his cigarette till his cheeks hollowed. When he was done he was still frowning. "It means to watch your back. I don't trust him."

"Jesus, that's a hell of a thing to say after what's just happened."

"He's a junkie."

"You don't even know him." They were both looking down at the game as they spoke.

"I know junkies. I know he'd sell his own mother out to get what he needs when he needs it."

"Dante's always done the right thing by me."

"Look, I'm not arguing with you, I'm just saying. The guy can't help himself. I mean, look at him. He could have saved his wife, and he didn't. He knew she was sick and he left her rotting away in their apartment, never once went for help. He let his own fucking wife die. And how many days did he lie in that bed with her for?"

"I don't know."

"I don't know," Owen mockingly echoed. "Well, I know. Four fucking days, that's how long. They should have kept him in Mattapan State for the rest of his life."

There was a pileup in front of the Canadiens' net and a Bruin came free with the puck on his stick. A great roar went up from the crowd and everyone stood in their seats and then swore and moaned. Fierro stumbled back into his seat, spilling his beer. When the crowd sat, Cal could see that the Canadiens were driving past the blue line, three on one.

Owen turned to him. "You gonna let the cops do their job?"

Cal squinted through the cigarette smoke. "Sure," he said.

"Sure?"

"Yeah, I'm fucking sure. What gives?"

Owen raised his hands in mock surrender and laughed. "Okay, okay. I had to ask even though I already knew the answer. Giordano, you remember him, don't you?"

"Giordano, Jesus, I went through the academy with that piece of shit."

"Well, he rose through the ranks while you were away, and he's in line to be promoted to commander this year, so I'm betting he doesn't want anything messy on his plate. Just stay out of his way."

WHEN HE HAD finally settled into the game, he found he had to lean around one of the iron beams to see the action on the left side of the rink, and he cursed Owen and Fierro aloud for taking the good seats, but they were already drunk and took no notice of him. He scanned across the other seats, the rafters from which the 1929, 1939, and 1941 Stanley Cup championship banners hung. He fumed for a few minutes, knocked back his third beer in silence, and tried to follow what he could see of the game. Suddenly, Owen and Fierro were loudly discussing the ponies.

He waited a moment and then said, "We're watching a hockey game," and they turned to look at him bleary-eyed. "Never mind," he said, gesturing for them to continue. "Carry on. It's just a fucking hockey game against the Canadiens and we only need to win the damn thing if we have a shot of getting into the play-offs. And it's the middle of fucking February for Christ's sake, but if talking the odds at Suffolk Downs is more important to you, then be my guest, go ahead."

An usher in a red sport coat and a hat with gold trim on the brim eyed them warily from the upper concourse. Cal slapped the back of his hand against Owen's shoulder and gestured that it was time for another beer. "I have to hit the head," he said, took up his hat, and made his way back down the line of chairs. Fierro rose awkwardly and followed him. They climbed the steep stairs to the top concourse. At other times the long lines outside the few toilets snaked through the Garden's musty concrete corridors, but tonight they were in luck and the urinals were mostly empty. "The drunks are all staying in their seats," Cal said. "They're too cold to move."

"I agree, Captain," Fierro said, and Cal glanced back at him, watched him lurch up to the olive-green cast iron basin that ran the length of the bathroom.

A grime lay upon the glass sconces above the toilets, and the light they gave off cast an oily sheen over everything. The radiators thumped with steaming water, and a long stream of hissing air sounded miserably through the valves. From one of the stalls came a painful-sounding groan, and someone shouted, "For Christ's sake, give us a fucking mercy flush, would you!" Outside, the sound of the game, the growing cheers, and then the sudden, exasperated moans of the Garden crowd. The amplified, barely intelligible voice of Frank Ryan came from the loudspeaker.

Fierro swayed at the urinals and splashed the tin loudly. Cal stepped to his right away from him and when he was done went outside and waited. He stared into the dark stands. It was so cold inside the Garden, most of the fans hadn't bothered to remove their overcoats. He cupped his hands together and blew into them. Fierro was at his shoulder. "C'mon," he said, "follow me to the bar."

At the beer stand Fierro ordered two cold ones. He raised his glass and eyed Cal blearily. "You need something warm in you," he slurred, reached into his overcoat and pulled out a silver flask.

Cal watched Fierro as he drained half his beer. "Anthony, I've never seen you so drunk. Something get under your skin today?"

Fierro nodded slowly, pursed his lips. "You could say that."

"You found something, yeah?"

"She was pregnant, Cal."

"Pregnant? Sheila was pregnant?"

"It sure seems that way. She'd given birth recently."

Cal reached for the flask, unscrewed it, and poured a liberal shot into his mouth.

"How long before her death, you think?"

"I don't know. It's tough to say. She was still healing. A few days perhaps—a week at the outside. She wouldn't have been in good shape before her death. Very weak."

"She had no chance, then, before he tied her up and tortured her."

"She would have had a hard time fighting back."

Cal hit the flask again. He drained what was left of his beer and he turned the empty glass in his hand. Fierro stared at his own.

"Is this in the medical report?" Cal asked.

"Yes, of course, but we don't release that to the press. Owen doesn't think it's a big deal. But I just thought you—and Dante—should know."

"Thanks, Tony."

Cal went to move his feet, but they were stuck to the concrete floor. He lifted his shoe, tried to scrape off what was stuck there: popcorn, peanut shells, bits of hot dogs and buns made sticky by spilled beer. As he turned away from the counter, he looked up and caught the malevolent glare of two rats staring at him from beneath the slatted seats in the top row of the balcony, and he paused, glared back at them, but the rats didn't budge. Rats thrived in the Garden. It had been this way when he was a kid, too, and he wondered if they ever cleaned the Garden's floors. If anything the number of rats had multiplied.

"So," Fierro said, spreading his hands, "what do we do now?"

Two blood-smeared fans were trading blows in the balcony and they'd caught the attention of the crowd, who seemed to be more interested in watching the two men go at it than watching the game. Cal looked toward the scoreboard and lowered his head. The Canadiens were up, 4–1. An uproar of cheers and screams and taunts came from the left side of the balcony as another group of men went at it, a drunk man falling headfirst over into the next row and a big square-jawed man pulling him up by the hair and driving a fist into his face. It seemed hopeless at this point, Cal thought. Fucking savages everywhere.

Below, Cal could see that Owen had left his seat and was making his way up to the beer stand, weaving among and momentarily lost in the crowd. He sighed, turned back to Fierro, and smiled grimly. "What do *we* do now? We get the fuck out of here and get us a drink somewhere more civilized. That's what we do."

16

NEAR DUSK CAL wandered Scollay's back alleys and side streets. He'd made the rounds of the abortion doctors in the West End down to Fort Point and back again, asking about Sheila, but none of them remembered a girl of her description. Only Chang on Milk Street had given him any grief, but he'd put an end to that, too, by threatening to bring the detectives down on him to investigate the death of a Chinatown teenager, named Anita Chan, from the year before. She'd died from a botched abortion—Fierro had told him about that one—and Cal had always known that Chang had to be involved.

In the Square the lights of the Old Howard, ringed in phosphorescence, blazed across the sidewalk. Fresh-shaved young men, Harvard students, gray middle-aged businessmen, hair patted down with pomade, stood around smoking, stamping their feet in the cold, waiting for the burlesque star Sharon Harlow, main attraction of the marquee skin show, to come out. Cal heard the hollers as she exited the side doors. Slick-haired Harvard boys from over the bridge in Cambridge and young ruddy-faced hicks down from New Hampshire and Maine called out her name or waited red-cheeked and silent as she slowed to autograph napkins and photographs.

At the other end of the Square, beyond the cold glitter of the burlesque shows and bars, a flatbed and truck were parked before the two intersections of Tremont Row, blocked by BPD sawhorses. On both sides of the truck large placards announced CONGRESSMAN MICHAEL FOLEY FOR U.S. SENATE and showed the stoic, strong-jawed face of the congressman, his prematurely silver hair held down with oil and combed back from his forehead. At the tailgate, volunteers were handing out voter registration slips and bread rolls and, from the spigot of a dented vat, cups of steaming soup to a growing crowd of down-and-outs. Cal stopped for a moment, sheltering out of the wind, and watched the spectacle. A group of bums with their backs to him stood a little ways away, looking at the same scene.

The line at the flatbed was forty deep, and more were quickly pressing in. Off to the side of the flatbed, six cops stood with billy clubs in gloved hands, leather collars up and hats lowered just above the eyes. There were two other cops farther down the street, standing by a black limousine. Smoke billowed from the tailpipe, reflected the red neon lights of the Crescent Grill.

A gasoline-powered generator chugged dully on the flatbed and from speakers mounted atop poles on the cab of the truck came a distorted and crackling version of Boston College's fight song, "For Boston," the words altered to sing the praises of the congressman. The sound reverberated tinnily throughout the Square so that the barkers for the vaudeville shows halfway down the block might have been calling from miles away. During the chorus one of the volunteers shouted through a bullhorn, "Who you gonna vote for?" And the other volunteers shouted, "Foley!"

With the urging of the volunteers and the promise of hot soup and bread, the crowd slowly began to reply in the same manner to each subsequent rallying call, and gradually a hesitant response rose to a loud if monotone refrain. When a few dozen registration slips had been handed out, a volunteer clambered onto the rear of the truck and slid its door up. From the back he began to heft frozen hams to other volunteers, who handed them to those with slips, crowding the truck in staggered lines.

Cal watched as a group began to gather by the idling limousine. Someone was stepping out of the car; flashes from camera bulbs lit the air. He heard one of the bums say, "There he is."

"Who?"

"Michael Foley."

There seemed to be a photographer from each of the five city papers snapping shots of the congressman talking and shaking hands with several bums handpicked for the purpose. Another pair of policemen wearing long navy trench coats now stood outside the group, and farther off, a cop atop a horse.

Cal lit a cigarette, bent his face low against the flame. Michael Foley looked better fed than he had in their days together on the Avenue as kids and more like his father, a longshoreman who'd turned to politics and graft and had dominated the unions in the late thirties. There had even been a time long before that when both his own father and Foley's had been friends. The congressman stood over six feet, broad-shouldered, wearing a tan wool coat, leather gloves, and a fine fedora with a feather angled under the black silk band. He shook hands with a few vagrants, patted one on the shoulder, and nodded enthusiastically when another said something to him. A reporter called out beside him, and he turned with a natural grace, put his hand on the back of a bearded man wearing a tattered raincoat, and posed as several more flashes went off.

"Christ, what a load of shit," someone said.

Cal tightened his collar and moved to the rear of the crowd. There, the wind cut a little bit less and he could hear Foley speaking.

"I'm not going to stand here and tell you I can give you a home and a job right away. And I'm not going to say that the road ahead will be an easy one. But I can tell you that as your future senator, I can bring more opportunity, more money into this city, eventually get you back on your feet, and put some pride back into your lives."

More bulbs went off as the photographers moved within the circle trying to capture the best angle; Foley in the forefront, tall, almost regal, and all those decrepit faces looking up at him. Foley even took off his fedora to create the brief illusion that he and those before him were more alike than not, and so the crowd and the press could see his face plainly, the harsh wind pressing back his oiled, leonine hair. It was an image taken right out of Mayor Curley's notebook, and Cal could imagine how it would look on tomorrow's front page.

"Foley, you're a fucking lowlife!" someone hollered, and Foley paused as heads turned searching for the culprit. Then it came again, and an old man standing shook his fist. "Who do you think is the bigger crook?! You, or your no-good brother?!"

One of the cops hooked his club through the loop on his belt and went to the man. Foley raised a hand as a peace offering—another flash-bulb went off—shook his head, and went back to conversing with two homeless men.

"You're a crooked blowhard, Foley! Just like your father who fucked up the unions, just like your criminal brother. Full of shit, that's what you are!"

A thin man with a hard, sharp face and wearing a fur-collared great-coat whispered something in Foley's ear and then walked back to the limousine, where a chauffeur stood. The chauffeur opened the rear door and, after the man climbed in the backseat, carefully shut the door behind him.

"You're a no-good, cocksucking crook!" the old man continued, and then gestured wildly to the crowd. "Don't fall for his bullshit, none of you fall for it!"

The cop grabbed the old man by the arm and pulled him away from the crowd. The man spat in the direction of Foley, but with the wind against him, it didn't get very far. Phlegm hung from his lower lip; he struggled and cursed the cop holding him. "Get your filthy hands off me!" he shouted as another cop took hold of him and dragged him out of the crowd.

Cal turned to watch them, and a young woman with bright cheeks and a red, white, and blue stovepipe hat came at him out of the crowd, pressed a large button into his hands.

"What's this?" Cal said, looking at Foley's face on the embossed tin smiling up at him.

"It's in support of Congressman Foley, our next senator."

"What makes you think I'd vote for him?"

The young woman opened her mouth, stared at him wide-eyed and incredulous. The wind whipped the hair into her face, and she pushed it roughly away.

"Why, if you want a better Boston, a better state, of course you'll vote for him, sir. Are you registered to vote? If you come over to the truck we can have you registered in no time. It's every American's duty to vote."

Cal shook his hand free. "Lady, I already did my duty," he said, thrust the button into his coat pocket, and stepped away from the crowd.

On the next street over, Cal stopped at the top of the alley, watched as the two cops worked on getting the old man from the rally into a paddy wagon. One reached for his arm, but the old man shook him off with surprising strength and vehemence. Spittle caked about his lips, his mouth clamped down on the nearest cop's hand and the cop hollered, "He bit me, he fucking bit me," and then the two of them went to work on him with billy clubs. The sound of wood smacking flesh and then the cracking of bone came to him and he fought the impulse to step in. He didn't need any trouble with the cops—not yet, anyway, and not with him and Dante searching for Sheila's killer. The cops' arms came down again and again, fog pouring out of their mouths as their breath ran ragged, and soon the old man stopped flailing and was still.

17

TREMONT STREET, SOUTH END

IN A CORNER of the flophouse a large man wearing a woman's yellow fleece coat lay amid dirty sheets and torn cushions. He hadn't moved since Dante arrived just before midnight: no snoring or stirrings of dreams; only the stink of his bowels, which he'd let go of earlier, now wafted about the derelict room. Candles sputtered on the floor and upon old furniture, white flames flickering in the cold that made their faces look hollow and skeletal and pressed the shadows toward the high water-stained ceilings. Besides the man in the corner, there were four of them. A haggard woman in her late forties, Rosie, was in her own special place on the floor, lying on her back with a childish smirk pulling at her horribly chapped lips. In a wooden chair a doughy man with a perpetually sweating brow occasionally peered at them from thick, owl-eyed glasses. He didn't speak much, and when he did, it sounded like Russian or some other Slavic language.

The only one Dante knew well was Lawrence, an old queer with an overcooked grin and a rusty, well-manicured beard like van Gogh's, whom he and Margo used to buy from at the Tic-Toc Club years back. Tonight he looked bad. He sat cross-legged on the floor, gently rocking to some long-lost ballad that played in his head.

With trembling, nearly deformed hands, he rolled a cigarette, lit a match, and let the sulfur burn off before touching the flame to the to-bacco. He looked across at Dante sitting in his chair, blew smoke from his thin, chapped lips. His eyes appeared white in the candlelight.

"Dante, my man," he whispered. "I'm sorry, I really am. Just trying to place it, you know, how somebody could have so much rage to go and do that to her..."

"Why do that, right?" he added, scratching at the crook of his needle-scarred arm. "She broke some animal's heart, that's what she did."

Dante stared at him for a moment, and then closed his eyes trying to remove the image from his mind. He hoped Lawrence wouldn't bring it up again.

Lawrence relit a candle and placed it on a cracked white saucer. "Not too much space between love and hate in this world," he said, as if to himself. "Maybe a stone's throw or..."

Dante fixed another round over the candle flame even though he knew he needed to be rationing what he'd bought from Karl, spreading it out so he could try and get clean again. When it was ready, he filled the syringe and pushed the needle into the vein. His head lolled slowly back on his neck. After a little bit he found himself speaking. "I wonder if Sheila is with Margo now, looking down on us sitting here in the slums. Maybe they're laughing at us, maybe they're just shaking their heads."

Lawrence ran his fingers through his thinning blond hair and extin-guished his cigarette in the saucer. The candle flame flickered momentar-ily and Dante closed his eyes.

The room fell quiet, and all that moved was the flickering candlelight and the shadows at the tops of the walls. He was stepping backward into the white noise that prefaced dreams, and he swung gently in its tide, his breath coming in even rhythms until he saw blue skies open up above him and felt summer air, breezeless and warm, pressing down on him. It felt as if he were being held up to the heavens, but only for a moment before he had the feeling that he was being let go.

"You couldn't ask for a better day."

Margo reached over the patchwork quilt, damp from the ground, placed her hand on his, and pushed down on it, all to remind him how much he meant to her. Her pale blue summer hat matched the sky above them, and below the wide round brim, a sharp swath of shadow cut through her face, exposing only her chin to the June sun. Her dark lips quivered for a moment, and then turned up in a skeptical grin. He pulled his hand out from under hers and playfully reached around her bare shoulders, held her to him.

"A day almost as gorgeous as you," he told her, and she tried pushing away from him in mock discomfort.

He tightened his grip around her, amazed at how cold she felt despite it being so warm out. "C'mon," he said, "you know I mean it."

"I guess it's the best you can do, my man of so many words. I guess I have no other option but to take it."

Sheila sat across from them with her legs crossed, closing an old copy of *Life* magazine and dropping it beside an issue of *McCall's*.

"It really is so good to see you two taking advantage of this weather. I told you it would do you some good."

Then the quiet settled in again, despite the sparse Sunday traffic on Tremont and the crowds surrounding the Brewer Fountain, where streams of water arched and sparkled like glass.

The grass on the Common had never been greener. And across it, heading all the way up to Beacon Hill, a lustrous field where couples clustered along its expanse, reminding him of a description in a crusty old English novel where courting couples shared precisely cut sandwiches and well-mannered flirtations. Dante held his eyes shut and let the sun envelop him, felt its warm fingers reaching into the cold spots scattered inside him.

"Ham or turkey?" Sheila asked as she reached into the basket and pulled out a sandwich wrapped in wax paper, smearings of yellow mustard all over the fold.

"I'm not that hungry," Margo said.

"Me neither," added Dante.

"You two and your appetites," Sheila said as she dropped the sandwich back inside the basket. She stood up on her bare feet, and Dante watched her as she anxiously stretched off the boredom that, he could tell, was growing under her limbs and in her thoughts. The narrow sunglasses didn't cover the thick lines of her brow, and he could see that she was squinting. She pulled at her auburn hair tied back into a ponytail and slowly searched over the park as if looking for somebody.

"She's getting antsy again," Margo whispered into his ear.

Dante looked at his wife and her sleeveless blue dress that once fit her perfectly just a year ago but now covered her like a hospital robe, hiding all those sharp angles that made him ache when he watched her move.

A bead of sweat crept down his widow's peak followed by several others. On the edge of the blanket by his left hand, three red ants crawled. "Make sure that basket is shut tight. We've got company."

The heat was gathering as humidity filtered into the air, thickening it and making it tough to breathe, and all those people on the Common, figures in a painting, were starting to bend, their shapes muddied like mirages.

And he said it again, only this time to himself: *We've got company.* Between them and the fountain, there were six men watching her, and then suddenly there were eight, nine, ten, all looking at Sheila standing there in the sun. Two of them held bouquets of roses, and in their Sunday wardrobes, hair slicked to the side, their postures steeped in youthful eagerness, as if waiting at a front door for their first date to answer. Two others were bedraggled and unshaven with leering glances. One even massaged himself, rubbing out a growing ache, staring at her in a predatory way, perhaps imagining a knife to her throat and a hand covering her mouth; the others, he figured, were desperate, love-hungry men of all ages, their faces young one moment and then wrinkled and hollow-eyed the next.

"I think we should head back home." He hated to say those words to Margo, who finally seemed to be relaxing, not secluded in the apartment with heavy curtains on the window and ghostly refrains of muted trumpets bleeding from the radio. "Get ready, you two. I think we've had enough for the day."

Sheila was glaring down at him, and her upper lip curled into a coy, somewhat sinister smile. Dante clenched his fists and stood up from the blanket. "It's time to go, Sheila."

"Leave her be," Margo called out. "Remember it's me you're married to."

"It's just that we've had enough sun for the day," Dante said as he watched Sheila reach up her right hand and hook the strap of her dress with one finger, sliding it higher up on her shoulder.

"You can't do anything for her now," Margo said.

"Will you just fucking listen to me? We're leaving now."

"But I don't want to go yet. Not until I find the right hole," Margo said with frustration, her voice terse.

Margo had taken her hat off, and her face was exposed in the sunlight, a lurid and pained anticipation pulling the skin tightly over her sharp cheekbones. Ribbons of open sores ran along her arm, purple and festering barnacles splitting the flesh. And as though she were inspecting fruit to see which was the ripest, she began to press her fingers into each one.

"I can't find a good spot, love. Help me find one, will you?" She pulled out an absurdly fat needle, as thick as a pipe cleaner.

"Jesus Christ, put that fucking thing away."

As Margo sank the needle down below the crease of her arm, Sheila's sudden laughter slapped at the back of his neck, immediately doubling his panic. Sheila had spotted somebody, and raised a hand to wave. Dante squinted against the sun and saw the man appear again, against the green grass and blue skies above, the shape of him bending in the heat as he raised an arm and waved in return. Sheila left the safety of their blanket and began walking toward him with a possessed grace to her movements, a sleepwalker following a treasure or a trap. A hot wind

94

carried through the park and the fabric of her dress clung to her buttocks and her thin shoulder blades. Dante called out to her again. She turned around, and Dante could see the full profile of her sharp jutting breasts. She gave him a painted smile, a "fuck me" smile, pursed her lips, and blew him a mocking kiss before turning back around. He watched her hips swaying through the thin material of her dress as she continued across the green.

"Get back here now, Sheila. He's no good." He took a few steps toward her, but Margo reprimanded him again.

"She'll be fine, honey. That's just her new man, the one she's so hung up on. Besides, she'll get attention from wherever she can get it. Come over here and help me find the magic spot."

Dante watched the man walk up to Sheila, spread out his arms and embrace her. He lifted her momentarily off the ground and managed to keep the bouquet he was holding from falling. He gently placed her back down and, resting his free hand on the crook of her back, pulled her in to him, and they kissed, long and deep. When they were done, he handed her the flowers, and she kissed him again on the cheek. He reached for her hand and she took it and led him back to Dante and Margo.

"Bobby, I'd like you meet my sister and brother-in-law. This is Dante, and that's Margo."

The man smiled, showed teeth that blazed white against his deeply tanned skin. His hair was styled in a pompadour cut, oiled curls glistening in the sun, and his shirt was a lime color with big pearly buttons and a sharp-pointed collar.

He reached out a hand. Dante halfheartedly shook it. The man's grip tightened around his and squeezed even harder as he spoke. "Hey, Dante. Nice to meet you."

Dante lowered his eyes, pulled his hand away. "Yeah."

The man looked toward Margo, nodded with the same self-assured smile. "My pleasure, Margo. I've heard so much about you." He turned back to Sheila, who was sniffing at the bouquet, and kissed her on the cheek again. "Honey, let's go for a walk. Got lots to tell you."

Sheila walked toward the picnic basket to where her sandals rested on the grass. She slid her feet into them, carefully rested the bouquet on the blanket beside Margo, and then stood back up, reached back to her ponytail, and pulled off the elastic band. Dante watched her hair spill about her shoulders, watched the way she licked her lips to moisten them, watched how the thin fabric of her dress pressed tightly against her.

"We'll be back in a bit, then maybe we can all go out for a drink. Wouldn't that be nice?"

"We won't be here when you get back," Dante said, but she turned away and paid him no attention.

He watched the two of them move across the green of the Common, Bobby lowering a hand to one of her buttocks, which he firmly grasped and then squeezed. Sheila began to cackle in high-pitched laughter, and even from a distance, it pierced through him. It was clear to Dante that she was laughing at him.

"Sheila's so private," Margo said. "We never meet any of her suitors. This one must be real special."

Sweat stung his eyes and he stood there and smoked a cigarette, seeing them pass up and over a hill heading toward the other side of the park. Margo called out to him again. "I don't feel so good, love."

Dante knelt back down on the blanket, but now it wasn't on the moist grass of the Boston Common anymore, but on their bed back in the Scollay Square apartment with the curtains thick as velvet blocking out the sun, and the lamp next to them emitting a somber haze. And Margo was dead, already starting to stink, her eyelids peeled back and her eyes pushing wetly from their sockets. He began to weep as he always did, for he'd been through this memory many times, but this time, without a pulse and her skin so cold, she reached over to him and told him to let it out, that it was just a bad dream. And when he turned to her, pulling her closer to him and staring into her face, all he could see was the straightened death-kissed lips and the protruding eyes.

"You're giving up on me, Margo, you can't fucking give up on me," he screamed, pushing her off him and leaving the bed.

"Dante, dear, what can I do? You gave up on me a long time ago."

"That's bullshit. How'd I give up? Tell me, how'd I give up?"

"Don't think I'm stupid. I could smell her on you. All those times you'd come home late, you were too drunk to notice."

"Smell like who? If you know who, then just fucking say it."

He waited for her to answer, wished that she'd just say her name, *Sheila,* and with that finally spoken, he'd finally be able to say *sorry,* admit to his infidelity once and for all. But she turned her face away from him, rested her head on the pillow, and spoke no more. All the tears, the guilt, were burning in him, and he refused to let them consume him. He moved over to the nightstand, grabbed the glass vial they'd kept their junk in, and squeezed it with his hand until his knuckles went white. It wouldn't shatter under his grip, so he moved over to the wall across the bedroom and released a hard right hook, fist breaking and smashing through the plaster, and pulling his hand back out as shards of the wall snagged deep into his skin, and punched it a second time, pulling roughly so that the gash widened as if caught on a nail, the blood pooling up and gushing over his wrist, dripping down to the floor in blackish streams. He stood back and hit the wall a third time.

"It's all my fault, isn't it?" he asked her. His hand was still bleeding and he was amazed he had any blood left at all. He crawled into bed next to her, slowly, carefully, as if not to wake her, lowered her eyelids with his bloodied fingers, tenderly kissed her cheek, which felt cold and waxlike, and caressed her chin, her neck, leaving trails of blood along her skin. The walls and the rest of the room soon dissolved around them. And like a tearful voice skipping on a dusty old record, he told her over and over how much he loved her until there was nothing left in him but the simple desire to get her warm again, holding her close to his body, so close that even with the most gentle whisper she could hear how he had always loved her, that he would always love her.

The silence in the room was disturbed by the sound of broken voices coming from the holes he'd punched into the wall. He pulled his naked, blood-smeared body off the sheets and pressed his ear against the wall, listened to the multitude of pained cries reaching up from down below, below the city, perhaps even below the crust of the earth. Each echoed cavernous and full of sorrow, creating the sleepless, anesthetized melody of an asylum, filled with hunger, guilt, and shame. He reached into a hole and felt the heat of an open furnace curl the hairs on the back of his hand. A sharp tickling carried over his bare arm, which soon became a burning, and he pulled his arm out into the light. Hundreds of termites were crawling over him, feasting on him as though he were made of wood. He stared at their large heads and fat, pale, urine-colored bodies churning like a garment over him. He brushed at them and they fell off, a disintegrating sleeve, but others reappeared as quickly. In the black wiry mass of his pubic hair, they covered him and chewed at him, in between his buttocks, in the soft part of his thighs, moving up and blanketing his chest and covering his neck like a scarf. He couldn't scream, for he felt them in his mouth, filling in the spaces between his teeth and his cheeks, moving down his throat to warmer things.

DANTE WOKE IN a chair, feverish. The candles were all guttered out and a gelid light spilled though the room's windows. He stared at the ceiling sagging from water damage and mold, the broken furniture scattered about, the black spots where a past fire had eaten away at a section of the floor and halfway up the wall. Upon the floor, Lawrence lay with his head resting on the crook of his arm, saliva shining on the side of his face. The emaciated woman, Rosie, had curled herself into a fetal position in an armchair. Her skirt was bunched up around her waist, and through torn nylons Dante could make out a map of yellowed bruises on her pale legs. The Slavic man with the thick glasses was gone. The large man in the yellow fleece stirred in the corner. Something between a moan and a death rattle escaped his mouth, and an overpowering stench of hot shit wafted in the air.

Dante climbed to his feet, stood shakily before the window, and watched the sky brighten as the junk lost its grip on him. As the sun rose, the red brick of the surrounding buildings regained their color and he understood that he was back in the present time, on his own feet, and no longer floating in a nightmare, and the face of the man—Sheila's lover—came to him again; on that day in early summer at the Boston Common, the man she had introduced to them. He looked down at the scars on his knuckles, turned over his hand, and looked at the long scar staggering across his palm. He clenched his fingers and made a fist, felt a throbbing pound away at his wrist.

The guy on the Common was the same guy at the Pacific Club, the sharp dresser who had beckoned Sheila back to the table and away from him, and his name was Bobby, he remembered. Sunlight began to shine through the window and he winced against it. Maybe this Bobby was just a low-rent hood, a good-looking Italian who used his greasy charm to win people over, especially Sheila. Maybe it wasn't even his charm and good looks that interested Sheila but something he had, something she'd wanted for herself. The visions of the nightmare had faded completely, and the need for real sleep called out to him; his muscles ached as if they'd been scraped with a wire. He made his way back to the chair, grabbed his works, what was left of his heroin, and walked out of the room and down the shattered staircase.

18

ON THE PARK bench a bum, a woman wearing a wool hat striped like a candy cane, lay stretched out beneath cardboard and rolled newspapers. The fountain was laced with fresh snow from the night before. Hoarfrost covered her face. A clouded VOTE FOR FOLEY button hung crookedly from the collar of her coat and shone with ice. Cal placed his hand above the woman's mouth, rested his fingers on her throat just below her jawline. After a moment he reached down and pulled the stiff makeshift blanket up over her head. Snow tumbled to the ground about his feet. He made the sign of the cross instinctively and looked about the park. A mounted cop, riding high atop a wide brown quarter horse, was making his way through the Common, heavy leather and wool collar pulled up tight against the wind. Cal waved him down and the cop trotted the horse toward him.

The horse snorted and stamped its hooves, eager to keep moving. Its hindquarters quivered and white smoke steamed from its nostrils. The cop's eyes were on him. A real hard guy but then Cal knew quite a few like him.

Cal gestured toward the park bench, and the cop's eyes followed. "Dead," he said.

"Yeah," the cop said, and sighed. "You know this guy?"

Cal didn't think it would matter to tell him that it was a woman. He shook his head.

"Another fucking John Doe. More John Does in the morgue this winter than citizens."

"It's a bitch of a winter."

"And it ain't ending anytime soon. We try to round them up every night, many as we can, try to get them to the shelters, in out of the cold. But you can't make people do what they don't want to do. This is the sixth body in two days."

"A bitch of a winter," Cal repeated, and shook his head. He sucked on his teeth, and the bitter taste of tobacco filled his mouth.

"A regular *Farmer's Almanac*, you," the cop said but without malice, and Cal nodded. He offered the cop a cigarette, but the cop shook his head.

"Thanks, but I've got to call this in."

The cop turned the horse around and made his way toward the call box on Church Street and Cal watched as the large animal's shanks rippled as it trod away, metal shoes scraping bare cobblestone that showed between patches of snow. He stared at the dead woman again and watched as one of her arms swung free from beneath the newspaper and cardboard and the knuckles of her hand cracked loudly against the iron leg of the bench. A crumpled card fluttered to the snow, and he bent to pick it up. *Bernadette Murphy*, it read. *Registered Voter City of Boston. Address: Room 1114, The Emporium Hotel, Tremont Street.*

He shook his head. With the election for the vacant Senate seat coming up, half the frozen dead in the city probably had rooms at the Emporium, rooms they'd never occupied and never would. He doubted the doorman would even have let them step into the lobby out of the cold. He pushed the card back into Bernadette's rigid hand and walked slowly east, then uphill toward Beacon. The startling laughter of children skating on the frozen Frog Pond not two hundred yards away came to him. Above the skeletal tree line the gold dome of the State House caught the cold sun and for a brief, transitory moment appeared glittering and almost beautiful.

19

SCOLLAY SQUARE, DOWNTOWN

Outside Scollay Station the wind twisted the ragged coat about Dante's legs, pushed at his back, and sent him stumbling. There was no traffic on the street or on the sidewalk, and Charlie hadn't even made his first appearance yet, his booth on the corner with its wood slats still locked down and stacks of this morning's newspapers waiting to be racked and sold. Dante ducked his head and carried himself on weak legs off the island exit onto Tremont toward Epstein's Drug. Once at the corner, he dodged into a doorway and stood for a moment in the windbreak, hands upon the walls, taking pleasure in the ache of blood returning to his fingers. He walked back out, kept his head low, and let the wind guide him. From the corners of his eyes he glimpsed windblown trash scurrying through the snow-packed gutters, the brief glances of people on their way to work, leaving doorways and turning street corners, the cold sucking all shape and color and leaving them muddy silhouettes.

He made it up the stairs, opened the door to his apartment, and paused. Claudia wasn't in her usual chair by the window. The morning light cast its slow, dull illumination over the bare cushion and the end table where one of her crime novels lay open. An electric current of panic vibrated inside his chest and in his empty stomach. Without bothering to take off his jacket or place his hat on the rack, he moved slowly into the room. He held his breath and approached the hallway by their bedrooms, but stepped back into the living room when the toilet suddenly flushed and the lid banged down. He looked nervously about the hallway. Out the door, that's where you want to go. Be a coward in your own home, that's okay. He fought the urge to flee and walked ahead, stomping his feet, wanting to be heard. The odors of burning tobacco and hot coffee came toward him from the kitchen. The dull stirrings of conversation sounded off the walls.

Claudia sat at the kitchen table in her bathrobe, a cup of tea in front of her, a faint dusting of rouge on her cheeks, and a feverish smile on her face. Across from her, with a cup of coffee, a bottle, and a glass, was Shaw. His sheepskin jacket hung over the back of the wooden chair and he sat with his legs outstretched, his small feminine hand running through the wiry curls of red hair. Opposite him sat Blackie Foley, lean and youthful-looking, wearing dark jeans and a leather bomber jacket. He seemed unusually pale, his pupils small pinpricks of black in the bright blue irises. He seemed to be making a great effort to appear calm and still when it was obvious he was bored and impatient, and when he looked up, his face brightened in the same mischievous way that Dante knew was trouble. Suddenly it seemed as if no time at all had passed since their childhood together, and Dante felt as small and insignificant as he had in those days.

"Look who's here, the pride of Saint Mark's. Welcome home, old pal." Shaw cackled.

"Dante," Blackie said, staring at him.

The bathroom door opened and down the hall came the Pole from Kelly's Rose, a thick white bandage crisscrossed over the wide bridge of his nose, a swollen, livid welt like a hot wire burnt across his brow. Smiling, he pushed past Dante, forcing him into the room.

"C'mon, Dante," said Shaw, "don't look like you just stepped in dog shit. We were in Scollay to take in a quick bite and thought we'd pop on by to say hello to you and your sister. We're old neighborhood, remember? Blackie came along for the ride to see how we get things done."

When Blackie spoke, his voice was flat, emotionless. "I came because Sully asked me to come."

Shaw swallowed his whiskey and then, coughing, nodded. "Sure, Blackie, sure. Whatever you say."

Dante stared at Shaw, took the face in, imagined it turned inside out and scattered like glass all over some sidewalk. The words came out of his mouth with more conviction than he would have thought possible. "You're in my house uninvited, drinking my whiskey at my kitchen table in the apartment I pay rent for. You have no right to come here. You've taken advantage of my sister who doesn't know any better. Show us a bit of respect."

"You hear that, Blackie? Most inhospitable. All we were discussing were old memories, lots of old memories. No reason to get red."

Claudia stood. "Dante, there's no need for this. We've been here talking about Dorchester, about the old neighborhood, and they've been filling me in on who's doing what. Why don't you just sit down and have a moment with us."

Dante glared at her, his jaws clenching, and she sat back down. As though she would explode with unease if she didn't move, her hand went for the radio that sat on the kitchen table.

"Shut it off, Claudia." Dante stepped farther into the room, and the Pole straightened up, as if waiting for the bell to ring.

Dante reached for the bottle, poured himself a quick one, and downed it with a strange desperation that bordered on recklessness.

"Can we talk in the living room, just you and me?"

Shaw nodded approvingly, shook off the Pole, and then eyed Blackie briefly before getting up from his chair.

Dante entered the living room with Shaw following leisurely at his back, the pungent smell of his exotic Turkish cigarettes billowing before him. Dante turned his head slightly. "You came in mighty early to shake me up. Guess you thought I'd still be asleep."

"Besides taking a good beating, one thing you do well is hide. I give you that, Cooper."

"I remember he always did find the best hiding spots when we were kids, right, Dante? None of us could ever find him."

Dante looked toward the voice. Blackie stood in the doorway behind Shaw. It was brighter in the room, the many windows letting in the snow-cast light, and his eyes seemed as pale as dimes.

"Sometimes we'd just call the game and go home, and he'd stay hidden for hours and hours, afraid to come out."

Shaw cackled dismissively, sucked air through his teeth.

"You remember that far back, Dante?" Blackie asked.

"I remember." Dante slowly reached into his pants pocket, felt the fold of crisp one-hundred-dollar bills he'd found in Somerville. In some way he had to distract Shaw and Blackie. Once they went through his pockets and found the money, they'd get suspicious, wonder where it came from, and ask him questions he couldn't answer.

"I need another day or two. I promise, that's all I need to get it."

"Jesus Christ, Cooper. Your promises mean shit," Shaw said and stepped in closer.

His fingers were still numb from the cold, and in a sudden, careless move, Dante reached both of his hands into his coat pockets, turned them out as if to show in dramatic fashion that he was flat broke, not one cent on him.

Half a dozen of the photographs came out with his left hand and fell to the floor. He quickly dropped to his knees and clawed at what he could, pulling them together as though he was grabbing at the winnings of an alley craps game before any weapons were pulled. Sheila's bare crotch gaped obscenely up at him, slick fingers splaying her vagina open. He stammered, reaching and grasping for another photo to cover it with.

Shaw put a foot into his shoulder, knocking him to the floor. "Not so fast there."

Claudia and the Pole had entered from the hallway and stood beside Blackie, all of them watching.

Shaw's mouth opened in surprise as he reached down to the floor for one of the photos. "This ain't some joke, old friend?"

Blackie stepped up beside him. "What is it?"

Shaw handed it to Blackie. He raised the photo to his eyes, squinted as if his vision were taking its time focusing on the body inside the glossy frame. The corner of the photo crumpled between his thumb and index finger. He looked at Dante.

Shaw rubbed at his chin and looked over the photo again, grinned as if he had figured it all out. "Like a goddamn wet-brain beggar, Dante. Just look at you. And to make it worse, you're turning to peddling smut. And you're fucking half-rate at that, too. You can't even see the girl's face in these, they're all pussy and asshole. That's real classy, real fucking classy."

Dante tried to get up on his knees, but Shaw kicked him in the shoulder again, softer this time, breaking his balance and sending him onto his rear, where he remained in a sitting position.

"Look, I don't give a shit about this smut. Where's our fucking money?"

Claudia came to him, grabbed him by the arm as he mustered the strength to pull himself to his knees. He pushed her aside with a straight arm, and she inched back to the doorway, hands reaching up to her mouth.

She began to cry, and with her voice cracking, screamed into the room, "I'll give you the money, just leave him alone!" The tendons in her neck were tightly drawn under her flushed skin. She looked down at her brother with eyes full of desperation and then fled to her bedroom, feet thudding heavily on the hardwood.

Dante eyed Shaw with sudden rage, and when he spoke, spittle flew from his mouth. "I know now never to come to that fat Paddy bastard for nothing."

Shaw didn't seem offended that his boss had just been insulted, and instead carried on as if Dante hadn't spoken a word. "You can keep the photos of the whore."

Claudia came out with a handful of bills balled up in her hand. She reached over and handed them to Shaw. "That's all I have," she said, sobbing, her voice sounding stripped and raw. "There's fifty-three dollars. Now leave him alone."

For a brief moment, Shaw appeared almost sympathetic. He looked away from her, glanced over at Blackie, who had seated himself in a chair next to an old rolltop desk and was watching their interaction with his arms crossed and a wry, crooked grin on his face. Shaw handed the money over to the big Pole; with one large hand, the Pole shoved the bills into his pants pocket.

"That's good for now," Shaw said. "I want the rest by the end of the week."

Blackie laughed coldly. "This is top-notch vaudeville. Wake me up when the fucking clowns come out."

"Just shut it, for Christ's sake. Why'd you even come along?"

"Maybe I came along to see how piss-poor of a job you do shaking down junkies. Maybe Sully asked me keep an eye on you." He leaned forward in the chair, arms still crossed against his chest. His eyes didn't budge from Shaw, who suddenly knew better.

"Fetch my hat and coat, Ski," Shaw called out to the Pole, who lumbered toward the kitchen. Standing with her shoulder on the wall, quietly sobbing, Claudia turned and followed him.

Shaw watched the two of them leave the room and turned back to Dante, lowering his voice. "God, your sister looks like she's aged twenty years in a year. Do something nice for her, why don't you? When you finally pay us off the rest, you go out and get a fucking job like a real man. And with that money you take in, bring her to Filene's and get her a dress and a hat, make the dog feel pretty."

"Go fuck yourself."

"Just saying, if she had some Irish in her, maybe she'd have a chance

108

still. But it looks like she got the worst of your no-good Polish father and that Italian heifer of a mother."

Dante watched Shaw's eyes momentarily drift, and he shot off the ground, threw a haphazard left that connected on the side of Shaw's head, and sent the short man stumbling sideways into the end table. He charged at him and put all his weight behind a fist that landed hard against his chest. Dante watched him stagger and fall, and he relished the brief moment of victory. He waited for Shaw to get to his feet so he could give it to him again, but from behind him came the sound of heavy footsteps, and as he turned, large hands locked on his shoulders and flung him to the floor.

Dante rolled onto his stomach, wrapped his arms about his head, and closed his eyes, wincing under the heavy boots kicking at his chest, stomach, hips, spine, buttocks, and balls. Ski and Shaw kicked at him until their breaths were ragged, and if not for Claudia's screams, they would have kept going until there was nothing left of him.

Sounds came to him disembodied and fragmented. Light flickered weakly on the undersides of his eyelids. They'd been talking and then they were gone, their footsteps fading, reverberating in the stairwell along with the Pole's raucous laughter, and then he heard Claudia talking to herself in the kitchen between fits of sobbing.

He heard the sound of a glass shattering, but instead of rising to his feet and going to comfort her, he lay on the floor, listening to the clock ticking slowly upon the mantel, and heaving deeply, waiting for his lungs to work properly again. He curled into himself, went to cradle his tender balls, but the mere touch made bile rise in his throat.

"Dante, what the fuck have you done to yourself?" Blackie was still in the room with him, sitting in the chair by the old desk, watching him with those cold yet startlingly clear blue eyes. "All of us from Fields Corner, we thought you'd be the next Gershwin. Your name up in the big lights, you wearing a fancy suit and playing for a bunch of rich fucks. But you had to piss it all away."

Blackie shifted in the chair, the wooden legs squeaking against the seat. "I got no idea why you dealt with those kike and spic backers. They shouldn't have taken a hammer to your hand over such a small debt. You could have come to me. I would have made that debt go away."

Dante looked at him rising from the chair and then walking toward him. He closed his eyes, expecting a fist across the face. "Get the fuck outta my house, Foley," he managed.

"That's no way to talk to me, Dante."

Blackie was leaning over him now, his licorice breath on his neck, and in a near-whisper: "This was the worst those fucking idiots could do to you. And they think that's something. You don't know what I can do to you."

Dante heard the floorboards creak, as though Blackie was walking to the front door, but suddenly they stopped, and Blackie's voice came to him one final time. "And tell my old buddy Cal that I saw his fine wife walking along Dot Ave a few weeks back. He should be careful, watch out for a looker like that—anything could happen. No problem, though. I followed her to make sure she got home okay."

When the front door closed, Dante knew he was alone again, and once he began to breathe right he climbed to his feet, rose up full of sharp pain. He moved through the hall into the kitchen.

Claudia sat with her head lowered over the table, black hair pooled on the Formica. Her cup of tea and the bottle were in pieces on the worn linoleum: shards of glass and ceramic in a puddle of whiskey.

"Claudia, I am the one who has an excuse to be this way. I lost something. You, you never lost a goddamn thing."

She continued to sob with her face hidden. He wanted to step behind her, pull her hair back to make sure she saw him. "Lose what I have, Claudia, then you can act this way. There's no excuse for you. At least I've tried. And, shit, I've failed. But there's a big difference between the both of us, and you're probably never going to live enough to understand it. A fucking spinster with her head in the clouds, that's all you'll ever fucking be."

He slammed the door to his bedroom, fell onto the unmade bed, and tried to fight back the tears, but they rose thick in his throat until he had to give in. He felt blood leaving his mouth, trickle and pool onto the fabric of the pillow. When there was nothing left he turned over in the bed, pulled his knees up to his chest, and let sleep take him.

20

An icy rain rolled down the office windows of Pilgrim Security. Cal had turned on the heat after a few days with the office left unoccupied, and now the room smelled of dust burning atop the radiators, stale cigarette smoke, and old moldy things. The radiators pinged and rattled, and the lower sections of the windows that looked out on the avenue were filmed with steam. Through the bleared glass they could see the vacant expanse that Scollay Square was becoming. It seemed that whenever he looked out the windows these days, the landscape of Scollay had changed yet again; sunlight glaring through the spaces where buildings had once been.

Dante dragged his hand across the stubble on his face, rubbed at his bruised jaw, put the phone back in its cradle, and with a pen drew a line across the final hospital listing on the pad before him.

"Nothing?" Cal was staring at a map of Boston amid the larger map of Massachusetts on the wall. His eyes had grown blurry and all he could see were the interstices of highways and roadways interspersed and conjoined like the entrails of a body all across the state. He thought of the trucks parked along Tenean Beach, their exhausts steaming the cold air, and just beyond them the heavy traffic moving along the highway. Someone had brought Sheila's body by truck, he knew it, and that someone was still traversing the highways out there.

He sipped from his coffee cup and swiveled his chair back to the desk. He fingered the few personal belongings the Boston police had retrieved: a simple gold-colored watch with a matching chain strap, its hands now forever stuck at eleven o'clock; one clover-shaped topaz-colored earring; and then there was the manila envelope containing the trinkets and the photographs that Dante had discovered at the boardinghouse, some personal belongings, including letters to Margo that she had never sent; and pay stubs from her job at the State House. He looked at the dance card from the Emporium Hotel and thought of the dead bum, Bernadette Murphy, from the Common. When he went to open it, a cocktail napkin, gilt edged and with the hotel's logo in scrolling script at its center, fell out. There was a handwritten number scrawled beneath the logo in pen: 8001.

"Dante, make another call, would you? The Emporium Hotel."

"The Emporium? Sure."

Dante asked the switchboard operator for the hotel and waited as she connected him.

"Ask the receptionist for room eight zero-zero one." He held up the napkin so that Dante could see.

"What then?"

"Just see if anyone answers."

Dante spoke to the person on the end of the line, was asked for his name, thanked the operator, and then put down the phone.

"It's a private listing," he said. "No one's talking to anyone in room eight zero-zero one unless they've already got an in."

"You ever been inside the Emporium?"

"Are you kidding? Have you?"

"No, way too rich for me, but it looks like Sheila had an invite."

He stared at the chain on Sheila's watch. When he moved so that it twinkled beneath the fluorescent office lights, he could make out the hardened blood caught on its entwined strands, blood that had remained even after the rest had been washed clean by, he assumed, Fierro's assistant.

"Did Sheila still go to church?"

"You mean was she religious? Yeah, I think so."

"Where?"

"Depends on where she was living, I guess."

"In Cambridge, Somerville, or back in the old neighborhood?"

Dante looked up, bleary-eyed, harried. "I have no idea."

Cal wondered if that was true or if he'd simply given up. Ever since he'd told Dante about Sheila's pregnancy, he'd gone quiet and retreated into himself, but perhaps there was more to it. They both lit up cigarettes, leaned back in their chairs. Smoke slowly filled the room. The dust had burned off the pipes, and as the day beyond the glass darkened, the room seemed to grow even warmer. Cal sniffled and wiped at his nose, hawked into a tissue, balled it up, tossed it into the wastepaper basket.

"She could have used an alias or else gone out of town," Dante said.

"Why?"

Dante shrugged. "Maybe she was ashamed, didn't want anyone to find out."

"Perhaps she wanted nothing to do with the father." Cal rose and limped over to the kitchenette, poured some more coffee. "The church certainly wouldn't look with favor on a birth outside of wedlock. Where would a young unwed Catholic girl go if she were about to have a child, if she decided an abortion was out?"

"Maybe she put it up for adoption?"

"You knew her much better than me. Do you think she would abandon her child the way her mother did to her and Margo?"

"No."

Cal sipped from his cup, grimaced, and drank some more. At his desk he retrieved his cigarette from the lip of the ashtray. "If she was a regular at Mass, someone would have noticed, people would've talked, so, yeah, maybe she goes away for a bit until the baby's born."

As he exhaled smoke, he wound the chain around his hand, scratched at the hardened blood with his fingernail. Dante stared at him from across the table, watched as Cal worked at the fake-gold chain and small flakes of Sheila's blood crumbled down between his gnarled hands and spotted his white desk blotter.

Cal looked up. Dante's bruised face was impassive, unreadable. "What is it?"

Dante shifted in his seat, groaned as he reached into his coat pocket. "I was going to show you this." He tossed the fold of bills across the table, where Cal picked them up and thumbed through each bill.

"What the fuck, Dante."

"They were in the box too."

Cal took one bill out, held it with both hands, and whistled as he raised it to his eyes. "This stinks to me. These shouldn't even be in circulation. How does she come by newly minted bills?"

Dante winced as he reached toward the table to grab another cigarette. "Of course it stinks. It all stinks. Somebody goes looking for Sheila, tears up her old place, kills an old guy for nothing. It all fucking stinks to me."

Cal grabbed another of the bills, inspected its number. "Jesus Christ, these bills are from the same print run." He reclined back in his chair, took in a deep breath.

"This is Brink's money," he said.

"You can't be sure of that."

"This is Brink's money and you know it. No wonder Blackie was at your place with Shaw."

"Sheila wasn't in on that. Not her."

"But she sure knew someone who was, and if Blackie thought the two of you were connected, we probably wouldn't be talking now. He was looking for someone else."

Cal glanced over at him. "He scare you yesterday?"

"Who?"

"'Who?" he said. "Blackie fucking Foley, that's who."

"Yeah. A little bit. He always did."

"It's how the prick operates."

"And what about you?"

Cal considered this, took a swig of his coffee. "No, I'm not scared of him." And then he laughed wryly. "Did you know that my old man and the Foleys," he said, "they used to be good friends."

Dante looked at him. "For as long as I can remember, your old man and the Foleys had it in for each other. The whole neighborhood knew that. My mother used to say, 'You see Mr. O'Brien and Mr. Foley on the street at the same time, you run the other way.'"

"I know, but back when they both worked the docks together they were friends. They used to come home after work on a Friday together, and have a few beers at the kitchen table even though they were already drunk. I was so small I can barely remember it, but I do.

"And then in the thirties, Foley ran for city council and tried to gang-bust the unions, and it ended their friendship. I was with my father at a longshoremen's rally for Curley at the Sons of Erin, couldn't even see over the seat in front of me, when three different factions went at it. One of the agitators was Foley. He was trying to make a name for himself running as a councilman on Curley's card. My dad called him a lying rat bastard scab and then the shooting began. People were screaming and running. My father threw me beneath the chairs and lay over me, covering my body with his. He got a bullet in the leg—his calf—but I never knew at the time. He never said a word."

"Your old man, he was a real tough guy."

Cal nodded, and echoed hollowly, "Yeah, a real tough guy."

"But that's not why you hate Blackie Foley."

"You don't need much of a reason to hate Blackie Foley. He's a fucking psycho, always has been."

Dante looked at him and waited. There wasn't going to be any good time to say it.

"He was asking for you."

Cal glanced up.

"Blackie, he said he saw Lynne on Dot Ave."

"Yeah?"

"He said you should be careful, that anything could happen to her."

It took a moment for it to register, and then Dante saw clarity develop in Cal's eyes, his face become stony and impenetrable. "What else did he say?"

"Nothing. That was it."

Cal reached for the manila envelope and one by one pulled out the pictures, spread them out upon his desk. His jaws worked relentlessly, and Dante had the sense he wasn't seeing the pictures at all.

"You okay?"

"I'm good."

"If you want we can—"

"I'll take care of it."

"What are you going to do?"

"He's a fucking animal."

"He was just trying to get a rise out of you. Like when we were kids."

"Well, it worked."

"What do you want me to do?"

"Nothing. I said I'll take care of it."

Cal tried to concentrate, but the image of Blackie following Lynne on the streets of Dorchester held him in place. He saw his thugs, the Kinneallys, stepping from a side alley, and Blackie smiling as they pulled her into the shadows. Rage constricted his throat and he coughed to clear it, stood and got water from the tap, tried to drink it slowly even as his heart hammered in his chest. Dante was watching him.

"If he goes near Lynne, I'll kill him," Cal said.

Dante had turned away, leaned back in his chair, the springs squealing, and watched ice sliding down the window. Cal lit a cigarette and took his time smoking it. He held up the fold of bank notes. "The only place this money is going is in the safe, and it's staying there. It's too dangerous to be caught with it." He opened the small floor safe, put the money in a safe-deposit box, then slammed the door shut and spun the combination dial.

"You sure this is it? There were no love letters, mementos, nothing else besides the note on the back of the photo?"

Dante leaned forward in the chair. "Nothing else."

"You're sure about that? I can't have you keeping things from me, Dante."

"I know, I know. Don't fucking worry about it."

Cal pressed him again. "Is there anything I should know about her, some secret life, some problems she had that you're not telling me?"

"What the fuck? Are you even listening to me? There's nothing else, nothing that I know. After Margo died, she wanted nothing to do with me. I haven't seen her since last summer. End of fucking story."

Dante rose from the chair, went to make a new pot of coffee. He made a lot of noise emptying the old grounds and then rinsing the pot in the sink.

Cal looked at the photos on his desk and at the images of Sheila there, smudged by fingertips: Sheila smoking, her lips pursed over the end of a cigarette, and the hazily lit background of a bar or club; outdoors, on a Swan Boat in the Public Garden, with her eyes closed and face raised toward the sun; pictures of her smiling, and then openmouthed, mock-kissing the camera. A picture of Sheila leaning over a balustrade, gazing out at an intentionally unfocused background: a hazy dog track and the blurred shapes of speeding dogs streaming by. Another of her at the same dog track perhaps, sitting in a chair and intently watching the races. And then one of her with the greyhounds, head lowered to them and laughing as they licked her face—always Sheila thrown into sharp foreground focus and everything behind her blurred and amorphous. And then as he delved further into the stack of photos, Sheila nude or in various stages of undress, but with her face blurred and out of focus or else cropped entirely.

He fanned the pictures out as he would a deck of cards, moved the pictures about, trying to create some manner of order or pattern. But the longer he spent examining them, the more confused and light-headed he became. He sighed as he put the pictures back into their envelope. He didn't feel shame necessarily. It was as if he was not looking at Sheila at all. The woman in the pictures was suddenly a stranger to him.

"What do you think?" he asked, although he didn't want to interrupt the silence. It somehow felt sacrilegious, disrespectful to do so. He listened to the clock ticking on the wall—the second hand was broken—and began again. "Well, are these the shots of two lovers playing games and having some fun, or is this smut? Was she caught up in something bad?"

It took Dante a moment to speak. He separated the photographs, pushed the ones showing Sheila's face across the table. "The cropped ones, we know what they're for, but these," and he tapped a picture, stared at her face taunting him with puckered, brightly painted lips, "no one else was supposed to see these but her and one other person, this Mario maybe."

Cal considered this, pursed his lips. "This other person might know something that only Sheila knew too. This might be who Blackie was looking for."

21

A LITTLE PAST two p.m. a Greek family came in to have their passport photographs taken. Cal rose from his chair, helped them fill out their passport applications for a trip back to the motherland, which they'd been saving for since their youngest was born. "At least you'll get the fuck out of this cold," Cal said as he mimeographed their paperwork, but the family didn't understand him, which was just as well. When they left, he opened the mail and found a check from Merchant Tool and Die in Southie. It wasn't much, but he thought he might be able to make it last a while.

It had been shortly before Christmas since the last good money had come in: Walter McGrath, a wealthy World War I pensioner, ex-army quartermaster, who lived in an eighteenth-century colonial on a rambling twenty-acre estate out in rich and exclusive Dover, called him, convinced that his chauffeur was abusing his privileges, using the Lincoln Continental sedan for personal use and depositing his checks into his own account. The chauffeur's name was Roland Baggs, an ex-con from Mattapan who'd spent two years in Concord after being pulled over by state troopers for driving a truck with out-of-date tags, and when they searched the back, they discovered twenty television sets stolen from Sears, Roebuck in the Fens just days before.

Baggs could charm the skin off a cat, and Cal had actually liked the sap. But the quartermaster had been right. Roland was taking him for a ride, and he wasn't smart enough to be inconspicuous about it. Cal had one of his security guards who needed some cash for the holidays, a first-generation American Pole named Wolaski, sit in the parking lot of the Wellesley train station and watch Baggs, on one of his weekends off, pick up the quartermaster's great-niece, coming off the midday train from New Haven. After the train left, they'd parked the Lincoln in a corner of the lot and remained there for half an hour before Baggs took them on a jaunt into the city, first stopping to visit the Indian Head National Bank in Cambridge to deposit McGrath's checks into his own account, and then to the Stuart Hotel in the Theater District, where they stayed for two successive nights.

After sacking Baggs, McGrath had given Pilgrim Security a large Christmas bonus. But that was two months ago, and now Cal hoped he could keep the heat on throughout the rest of the winter so that the pipes wouldn't freeze and burst. If that happened, Pilgrim Security would be done, and with it all of his and Lynne's savings.

With the money from Merchant Tool and Die, Cal wrote out checks to the half-dozen Pilgrim Security watchmen they still managed and, in the lobby, dropped them in the building's mailbox, then crossed the avenue for a pint bottle at Trident Liquors on the corner of Brattle. The rain had let up a bit. He picked up a pint, two cold prepackaged bologna and cheese sandwiches, and cigarettes and the *Globe* and *Bettor's Weekly* for Dante, and was about to cross the street and return to the office when he paused. At the corner lot between Hanover and Broad Street, three gleaming limousines idled with white smoke steaming from their exhausts.

In one of the abandoned lots where Caskell's and Amerilio's Pizza had once stood, a group of men were gathered in fine wool overcoats. Out on the street one of the limo drivers stood outside his car, pale from the cold and clearly trying not to show it. Cal rummaged in his pocket for the pint bottle and limped toward him. As he approached, the driver looked up warily. He was tall and thin, sickly-looking; his overcoat hung loosely on his shoulders. In another time, it had probably fit him. Before a fall off a ladder at a four-alarm in Adams Square, he'd been one of Boston's most decorated firemen.

"Jesus, if it isn't Tim Donovan," Cal said. "Why the hell you standing outside?"

"Boss's orders." He nodded toward the four men gathered on the snowy clearing, where one of them was gesturing emphatically with his hands to the others, perhaps conjuring a vision of what would soon be built upon the empty lot.

"I work across the way," Cal said. "Had to get something to keep myself warm." He lifted the pint. "You want a pull?"

Donovan shook his head, sniffed loudly, and ran his gloved hand across his raw nose.

"C'mon, you're half frozen to death. You think they're looking from way over there?"

Donovan shook his head again.

"Who are they anyway?"

"The one on the right, the tall thin one, that's Francis McAllister."

"The developer?"

"That's right."

"Who's the one next to him?"

"That's Congressman Foley."

Cal squinted toward the lot; from this distance they all looked alike, ordinary men in their finely tailored coats and expensive hats. "Is that so? Heard he's going to be our next senator."

"That's what they say. Him and McAllister have got plans for the city."

"They do, huh? Well, the city needs something all right."

Cal looked at the other cars idling at the curb. "So, one of these cars belongs to the congressman too?"

Donovan nodded. "They've had us driving them down here every day, one location after the other for the last two months. Third time this week I've been here."

A car blew its horn, and when they turned to look at it, double-parked in front of Tully's Tattoo Parlor, they had to squint against the wind that nearly pulled the hats from their heads. Cal shivered; he needed the warmth of the office.

"Here," Cal said, handing him the bottle. "Just one pull."

"I can't."

"Sure you can. Standing out here in the cold like this."

"The boss won't like it."

"Your boss sounds like an asshole, making you stand outside while the car's still running."

"Mr. McAllister, he's not an asshole all the time. He pays me well enough."

"Sure he does, but take the bottle anyway."

Cal left him then and trudged back up the street toward the office. The sandwiches, cigarettes, and newspapers in his pocket felt sodden and cold. He glanced back briefly as he looked both ways crossing the avenue: at Donovan by his limousine, standing with his head bowed against the wind, taking a half-concealed pull from the pint, and at the other men still there—the architects of the new Boston, black figures on the white snow—and at the rainwater sweeping down exposed walls from the dislocated and torn gutters atop the brick façade of the next building waiting for the wrecking ball.

22

OUR LADY OF PERPETUAL HELP, MISSION HILL, ROXBURY

As HE DID most evenings after work, Cal took the trolley to Huntington Avenue and walked the two blocks to Mission Church, the Basilica of Our Lady of Perpetual Help. An early winter dark had descended outside, and the lights inside the shops and diners and bars he passed were murky and diminished. Ice hung in colossal glacier ribs from the dual spires of Mission Hill's basilica, its Roxbury puddingstone hauled from the local quarries a hundred years before, the same stone that formed much of the bedrock underlying the city. The sky was the same color as the church, and it pressed down on Cal as he opened one of the heavy oak doors and stepped inside.

He sat in a back pew of the church and stared at the elaborate work of the artists of the Redemptorists and the depictions of the Passion, in each alcove the martyrs and saints. Footsteps reverberated upon the stone tile. Someone shuffled in a seat, coughed. The soothing sound of muted prayer. Old parishioners, mostly women, shuffled back and forth from the pews to the transept to light votive candles and pray for lost loved ones, asking God's intercession for those in limbo and purgatory, and for their own lost and empty souls, perhaps. Before the altar an altar boy practiced the swinging of the censer, his eyes shut, his mouth moving in prayer. The church smelled of beeswax and the heady, sweet thick scent of incense lingering from the midday Mass.

He listened to the hum of benediction, took in the scent of tallow candles burning low and spitting in the dark, and the light at play upon the frescoes and the stone faces of the saints, on Saint Francis, the Virgin Mother before the altar, Christ, and gleaming atop the bowed heads of those bent in prayer. He rested his head against the hard wood of the pew. The candles burned out one by one. Shuffling in the aisle. Shadows lengthening into darkness.

He prayed for his loved ones, the ones still with him, the ones who had moved on. He thought of the homeless woman, frozen dead, and a great sadness, a sentimentality that usually came only when he was inebriated, gathered in his throat. He looked up and watched the altar boy. The boy closed his eyes, raised his head toward the curved and bowed gilt laths above, and mouthed *Miserere mei, Deus.* The boy's arms and hands opened to the vaulted ceiling and the fiery ring of martyrs, their fixed gaze burning all souls for eternity.

AT THE END of Mass, Cal allowed time for Father Nolan to change out of his vestments, then rose stiffly from the pew. In the transept he knelt and lit a votive candle for his mother and another for Lynne. At the sacristy he knocked and waited for Father Nolan to come to the door, but Father Nolan shouted for him to enter. Inside the small room Father Nolan, in black pants and a white T-shirt, was running an iron over a black shirt draped across an ironing board. A cigarette dangled from his mouth. His chasuble and stole were laid out on top of the sacristy credens waiting to be put away.

"Ahh, Cal," he said, half grunting. "I'll be decent in one moment. What can I do for you?"

"I have a question, if you don't mind."

"Okay."

"Where would a young Catholic girl go if she was pregnant and planning to give up the child?"

"Is this someone in the family?"

"A close friend."

"Well, if she's in trouble, I hope you'd advise her to get help, to talk to someone. I'd be happy to see her."

"She's dead."

"Oh, I see. I'm sorry to hear that. *Ar dheis Dé go raibh a anam.*"

It was a common Irish condolence for the bereaved that he'd heard at wakes and funerals when he was young: May her soul be on God's right side. "Thanks," he said.

"May I ask how she died?"

Cal hesitated. He'd known Father Nolan since he was a boy and Father Nolan a young man just off the boat and strutting about the Avenue; he'd been a boxer and after the seminary had served in the war. They said that before entering the priesthood he'd smuggled guns back to Ireland. There wasn't much he hadn't seen or heard.

"She was murdered."

"The poor child." Concern briefly clouded Father Nolan's face and he looked to Cal but understood that Cal would say no more and so resumed his ironing. Ash from his cigarette fell onto the board, speckled the white canvas top. For a moment he was lost in thought.

"The Convent of Saint Clare in JP, by the arboretum. That's a good place to start. You went to Saint Mark's; you'll recognize some familiar faces. You can tell them I sent you."

Cal nodded and then, suddenly feeling awkward, gestured to Father Nolan's shirt. "I'll let you get back to that."

Father Nolan placed the iron upright, steam breathing from its plate. He pulled on the shirt, rolled up the sleeves, and looked at him with eyes that were almost a mirror image of Cal's own. Cal knew what he was going to ask and wished he'd never knocked on the sacristy door.

"How's the need for a drink lately?"

"It comes and it goes."

"It doesn't help in moments like these, you know that."

Cal chewed on the inside of his cheek. "I know."

"Cal, if you want to talk, that's what I'm here for."

"Thanks, Father," Cal said, and turned toward the door, "but I'm good."

Outside, in the open space of the courtyard, the sharp outline of the church appeared even less distinct now against the darker sky. At the intersection of Tremont and Huntington, people were dark shapes bustling across the trolley tracks. The bell of a trolley sounded farther down the avenue. Cars blew their horns. Tavern doors opened and closed and music spilled out into the frozen night. Cal wanted a drink badly but, hearing Father Nolan's voice sounding in his head, passed the taverns without pause, his mouth set in a grim line.

23

THE CALF PASTURE, DORCHESTER

THE WAMPANOAG CALLED it Mattaponneck, a desolate 350-acre spit of marshy peninsula sticking out into Dorchester Bay. To Cal and Dante it was where they'd sometimes played as kids, a shadowy, mysterious place between the stark concrete worlds of Dorchester and Boston, and later, as adults, a no-man's-land, a dumping ground for the bosses who ran Dorchester and Southie. Beneath its marshes and compressed within its landfill lay the bodies of countless Boston dead, poor and gangster alike.

Cal drove them down the narrow tarmac beltway built for the peninsula's few heavy industries and the trucks bound for the city dump, where ash was dumped by the city incinerator. Dump trucks roared up and down the Mile Road, shuddering past them. Dante stared up at the black clouds bent and coiling in the wind. The dump burned refuse all night, turning the sky red and black, and pouring acrid smoke into the air. As they passed, they saw children playing on dump heaps while their parents scavenged through the debris. Cal gritted his teeth as the car's underside banged and scraped against the deep ruts left by trucks. Whiskey roiled in his empty stomach.

Dante stared out the window. "Remember when we were kids, skating out by the dump when the runoff froze?"

"Yeah, I remember. You'd think there'd be better places for kids to play."

"It wasn't so bad. I don't remember complaining."

Dante looked back out the window, seeing nothing for a mile around but frozen marshes and stacks from the dump and the burning refuse sending black smoke across the bay that would burn one's eyes when the wind shifted, and farther off, the city glittering just over Carson Beach. Out on the water of the bay, a cold, apoplectic light flickered as the sun vented fast-moving low clouds, was covered, and then emerged again. There was a boat out there—a small lobster boat out of the harbor, just rocking on the whitecaps.

Dante smiled, staring through the glass. "Remember the potato chip factory over in Uphams? They used to dump their leftover potatoes around here, all the burnt ones. Me and the Connollys, we'd heat them up over a fire at the edge of the dump, still tasted real good."

"You never had to worry about going hungry when your dad was out on strike or laid off."

"Or in the cooler."

The Calf Pasture pumping station for Boston's sewage rose to the east. They passed the ruins of the coal room and the stone gatehouse with its ancient filth hoist, and beyond, the once stately and now decrepit Romanesque mansion of granite housing the electric sewage pumps and massive engines that moved waste out to the outer harbor on every receding tide.

As they drove the rutted road around the windswept peninsula, squatters' shacks appeared and then disappeared between the mountains of refuse and ash, squalid clapboard and corrugated tin dwellings that looked as if children had put them together.

"This place was never meant to be a place for the living," Cal muttered, as he looked out over the banks of what Dante took to be fog rising from the dumps and floating over the peninsula, but which he realized after a moment was the hot steam of waste, of sewer runoff. He stared at the lights blinking out by Moon Island, and in that light the small darting shapes of rats streaming through the waste by the hundreds as the tide came in and forced them up from the shore and the overflow pipes.

"Shit, this is what it would look like if they dropped the Bomb on us."

Cal steered the car over the dips and swells. "A lot of vets here. It's been that way since the war ended. Poor bastards slipped through the cracks and ended up with this. But maybe it's safer out here than the shelters in town."

"Well, if life ever gets that bad, I'll take the shelters over this."

They passed Boston Consolidated Gas Company, the American Radiator Company, a warehouse for Union Tire. And then the space opened up, and chain-link fence enclosed the three-acre lot of Duffy's wrecking yard. Next to the yard was a row of derelict trailers covered in snow.

Cal perched up in the seat, peering over the dashboard. "Got homeless people living in some of these. Take a look." Cal gestured to a thin, trembling line of black smoke rising over the tops of the trailers at the center of the back lot.

"You really think you'll find this Scarletti guy's trailer here?" Dante asked.

"That dispatcher said this was where they brought their old trailers. I'm not taking anything for granted."

"And you think that's how they got the body to the beach—by truck?"

"Yeah. It seems to make sense, and it's odd that this guy's gone AWOL."

"But it could have been any truck going up and down the highway."

"Any truck," Cal repeated. He rubbed his upper thigh briskly, opened his door so that cold flooded the car, and stepped out. Dante lit a cigarette first and then followed. Bending their heads against the wind, they passed along the row of wrecks. The wind barreled between them, sent the sheet metal trembling so that it bowed and groaned. The snow soaked through their shoes and their feet were soon wet and cold.

A trailer door banged and they looked up, squinted into the windblown strakes. A face, bearded and pale, showed itself around one of the trailer doors, and seeing them, quickly pulled back, the door closing after it. Cal paused, looked about at the other trailers. Some had their doors torn from their hinges, and windswept snow lay inches deep within. Others were hollowed-out frames, exposed wooden slats through which the wind raced in and whistled. From beyond the wrecking yard a horn sounded. Slowly Cal drew his gun from its holster. He glanced back toward their car and the distant hobo shacks, and then moved toward the trailer doors.

He stepped onto the low rail and reached upward and then the door exploded outward as a man barreled out of the opening, and Cal was flying backward off the rail and into the snow. He rose with Dante pulling at his arms. He shook Dante off and at a limping run took after the man retreating across the snow-covered lot toward the wrecker's yard. Dante cursed and, after a moment, followed.

"Fuck, fuck," Cal muttered as he ran. Something warm trickled from his left eyebrow and down his face.

The man was moving at a steady clip, but when he stumbled, Cal pressed his damaged leg to catch up. He hollered at him to stop, raised his gun, and fired in the air—the cracking sound of the shot loud enough to make the man turn, wide-eyed and frantic, and then the sound of the gunshot was gone in the wind and the man seemed to be moving even faster and Cal had to work harder to gain ground. Gradually the length between them narrowed.

The snow was thicker here and the man was slowing. His knees worked up and down as the snow deepened. With his legs failing, Cal made a last lunge forward and tackled him. The man dropped and rolled, swinging his arms as he did, smacking Cal weakly about the head. Cal wrestled with him, batted away his blows so that it seemed they were slapping at each other, and managed to bring a glancing blow from the gunstock down against his jaw before the man threw him off into the snow and was up and trying to run again.

Scrabbling through the snow on all fours, Cal reached for him, and the man kicked, but Cal wrapped his arms about the man's legs, pulled him down. He forced the man onto his back, climbed atop him, and went to strike him again. He grasped his windpipe and squeezed, and the man made a choking sound deep in his throat, tried to pry Cal's hands from his neck, and then shielded his face when Cal raised his fist holding the gun.

Dante pulled up, wheezing, beside them. He leaned forward, hands on his knees, and gasped for air. "Forget it, Cal," he said through staggered breaths. "He ain't gonna do us any harm."

"Please," the man said, and Cal paused with his arm raised, ready to strike. He sat on the man's chest, his breath coming to him in ragged gasps, and stared at the tattered army duffel coat, its olive-green horsehair. The smell off him, sour and rank, the sharp smell of urine.

"Put down your arms," Dante said to the man. "He won't hit you. I promise."

Slowly the man took his hands from his face. His eyes were wide and manic. A scraggly beard covered his face. His lips were cracked and his skin looked burned as if from exposure to extreme cold.

"Why'd you run?" Dante asked.

"I thought you were someone else."

"Who?"

A dog was barking wildly from the wrecker's yard, and as their breathing calmed, Cal could also hear a dump truck rumbling along the Mile Road.

"Tell us who and he won't hurt you."

He shook his head vigorously, his cracked lips peeled back over yellowed teeth.

"We're here looking for something," Cal said. "A friend of ours—a woman—she went missing and ended up dead. We're trying to find what happened to her, okay?" Cal stared into the man's eyes and, slowly, the man nodded.

Cal rose off the man and now realized how bedraggled and small he was. He wore two coats, a soiled sheepskin vest under his olive horsehair jacket and a sweater beneath that. He'd struggled like an animal but without the heavy clothes would probably weigh very little. Cal reached out his hand. "C'mon, get up."

Reluctantly, the man took his hand and Cal pulled him to his feet.

Cal touched a hand to the side of his face where blood had hardened and winced when he pressed against the top of his brow.

"What's your name?" Dante asked.

"J.J. They call me J.J."

"You live in that trailer?"

"Me and about eight others. People come and go, y'know, but mostly there's about eight others."

They trudged back across the snow toward the trailers. The sky had darkened and the temperature began to plummet. The snow cracked sharply beneath their feet. Tired now, they moved slowly, their breath smoking the air before them.

"About our friend," Dante said. "When we mentioned her you gave up the fight. You thought we were someone else."

J.J. lowered his head. "I thought you were here for the trailer."

"What about the trailer?"

"I'm not going in there. I saw it once, I don't need to see it again."

"What did you see?"

"You go over there and find out for yourself."

Cal reached out and gripped J.J's sleeve. "What the fuck did you see?"

"A guy comes with the trailer, he drops it off here. He drives around and picks them up and then brings them back here so he can do what he likes."

"Do what he likes?"

"To women. He likes to hurt women."

"Who?"

"A big tall guy. Real nasty-looking. Kill you as soon as look at you."

"Did he have a fucked-up mouth, a harelip?"

J.J. shook his head. "I don't know. I didn't see that."

"When was he last here?"

"He mostly comes at night. In the morning the trailer's always gone again. This time he left the trailer sitting here."

"For how long?"

J.J. paused, licked at his chapped lips. "Don't know my days anymore. Three days maybe?"

"Which trailer?" Cal asked.

J.J. turned around and pointed to a trailer toward the end of the lot.

"You got a crowbar, something that can snap the chain?"

"I got one inside."

J.J.'s trailer had a makeshift chimney jutting out from the center of the roof. It was made from rusted sheet metal, and black smoke funneled from it and broke apart in the heavy winds. "We light a fire," he said. "Keep it in a barrel and put a pipe through the roof so's we don't die in our sleep. No one ever bothers us over here and we keep to ourselves."

J.J. opened the trailer doors and faces swam out of the dark at them, misshapen in the orange glow of the red flames flickering from a trash barrel at the center of the floor. J.J. waved his hands in a settling motion, told them everything was all right, and they inched backward into the dark. Here and there men lay curled beneath bits of blanket and cardboard and rags. Dante and Cal could smell them, and the heat of them huddled together. Wind banged against the side of the trailer and rippled the thin sheet metal roof. In the dark all they could make out were slivers of raw face, a gleam of broken teeth, protuberant, bulging eyes, as the residents of the trailer moved farther back into the shadows. J.J. nodded and clambered deeper into his trailer. After a moment he reappeared with a tire iron.

"I'm not giving you this," he said. "We need it for protection. And I'm not seeing a thing. I'm not here."

"You're not here, okay, I got it. Give me the fucking bar, would you?"

J.J. handed him the tire iron.

After the exertion of the chase, Cal's leg was stiffening and it had begun to throb with pain so that he had to walk slower than he would have liked. As they walked the row, Cal considered the dented and

134

hollowed sheet metal sides, the snow that had accumulated in drifts between them, the threadbare tires and rusted wheels—wheels that hadn't moved in months but for one, the one that he knew belonged to a red and green Peterbilt. He'd seen the same frozen, ridged tracks along Tenean Beach.

The doors were padlocked. Dante pulled at the lock but it didn't budge. Dante watched as Cal leveraged the bar between the lock and the frame. Cal grunted and the lock shattered. He opened the trailer doors and they felt the ice cold of its interior and the sense of its frozen cargo like a weight pushing out at them. Coughing, he and Dante clambered up into the trailer. Cal banged his fist hard against his thigh, working the blood, trying to get the muscle moving again.

Inside the truck, carcasses of meat hung darkly from hooks, shuddering slightly as wind buffeted the chassis. Heavy drapes of sheer vinyl the color of dog piss separated the trailer into compartments of different meats, kept its insides even colder. It took a moment for their eyes to adjust to the dim light; their breath steamed slowly in the half dark. Between two pale ribbed halves of cow lay the shreds of a torn dress, a woman's underthings: blue panties, the elastic waistband shredded, a white brassiere. A worn leather purse with tarnished clasps. Spooled in a small heap a gold crucifix and chain that made Dante pause. He reached down, held it in his hand, turned it over. After a moment he said, "It's Sheila's."

"How do you know?"

"Margo gave it to her. She gave me one just like it." Holding the crucifix by its chain, he placed it back on the floor, let the chain loop over the cross. His chest felt tight and he fought to measure his breathing, but when he looked around at the hanging carcasses of meat, he could only see Sheila strung up, her arms raised and bound over one of the steel hooks, causing the ligature marks that Fierro had mentioned.

Cal crouched on his haunches, parted the clothing, and surveyed the ground. Blood spatter had turned the metal black. Dante knelt down beside him, touched the clothing he assumed was Sheila's, clutched the things in his hands, and then, strangely ashamed, dropped them back to the floor. When he stood, the tendons in his knees cracked.

Wind banged against the metal sides of the trailer, and the metal warped and bent and popped as if they were underwater and sinking deeper and deeper. Still on his knees, Cal cupped his hands to his mouth and tried to blow some warmth into them.

The trailer was a crime scene now. Sooner or later, he knew that they'd have to call Owen, something he didn't want to do until he and Dante had a little more to go on. Dante glanced at him and fumbled in his pockets for his lighter and cigarettes. He lit one and kept the lighter ablaze.

Beyond the hanging carcasses, shadows seemed to blur and tremble. Cal paused and held his breath, squinted through the rows of chains and meat, in the way he'd once stared and waited in the suspended light of a foreign dusk, waited for the enemy's approach. What the hell was he seeing?

The sounds of the dump yards were gone. Even the seagulls had gone silent. Only the soft rattling and metal tones of the lanyards and chains against the empty gleaming hooks and the softly swaying carcasses of cow.

They moved forward toward a thicker darkness, parting first one vinyl curtain and then another. Outside the wind thrust frozen snow beneath the trailer and it rattled and pinged beneath their feet. They parted the last curtain. Before them, the bodies of three women hung from meat hooks, their mouths in the final rictus of a terrible and tortured death, blood black on their frozen blue-hued skin. Cal put a hand to his mouth and turned away, but the image of them remained, of their splayed and contorted hips and their distended, naked bodies. Dante dropped his lighter and reached for him but Cal pushed his hand away. He was trying to find his way in the dark, and the sense of bodies pushed in on him so that he couldn't breathe. He stepped through the vinyl sheets and moved toward the trailer's doors, and then he was moving faster, feet banging the metal floor, hands searching and scrabbling for the doors, and then he was stumbling out onto the cold, welcome snow and on all fours, gagging, acid bile bursting from his mouth and spilling over his chin.

24

THE CHEVY FLEETLINE sat in the darkness before the wrecking yard beneath a soft dusting of new snow. Cal let down the car window, and cigarette smoke twined out into the night air. He sipped from a cup of old coffee, grimaced, and poured more whiskey into it, shaking the last drops from the bottle. He knew he needed to slow down, but since seeing the women's bodies he'd been unable to see much else, and only the drink blurred the edges of the nightmare. His hands trembled when he raised the cup to his lips, and he cursed them, wishing the whiskey had more of an effect.

Since discovering the trailer, he and Dante had said very little but seemed to have instinctively arrived at the same decision. They knew they had to call it in to Owen, and they knew that once that call was made, they were on the outside again. Even Fierro would have to put up a wall against them. They'd give it one night and see if anything came of it.

The Bruins game reverberated tinnily from the dark interior of the car. Woody Dumart had just split two defenders and, instead of passing to wide-open Peirson coming on the right wing, decided to take it himself as Bill Barilko straightened him up with a high cross-check. A fight ensued between the two, and now two other Bruins were fighting with Fleming Mackell at the top of the crease.

"That cheap bastard," Cal said. "Send the fuck off!"

Dante lit another cigarette. The smell of butane hung heavy in the cold air. Cal watched him staring at the flickering flame, the cigarette smoldering in his hand. Dante clicked the lighter shut, then popped it open again, stared at the small fire-glow. Cal pursed his lips and tried to ignore him.

"Cut it out, would you?" he said after a moment. He shifted in his seat, sneezed, pulled the blanket up to his chin, and squinted through the glass. "We've lost this fucking game," he said. "Our offense is for shit."

He reached over Dante for the extra pint of whiskey he kept in the glove compartment. He unscrewed the top and poured it into his inch of leftover coffee, held it out for Dante, who shook his head.

The far lights of Moon Island receded as he watched. The windshield was freezing over again. He turned the key in the ignition, and the engine hesitated at first and then, grudgingly, rumbled into life. He waited for the engine to warm and then turned on the heater. After a while the glass cleared, and Cal killed the engine again. The game was over. He owed Charlie a fin. The radio spat with static and Cal switched it off.

He sipped his coffee. The hours passed. Ragged men passed in and out of the trailers they called home. The Boston skyline glittered like distant cold stars. Cal's eyes tracked a black shimmer of water from one of the pumping station sluices as, undulating, it flowed into the bay. He turned the radio back on and tuned the station to a soft piano jazz ballad. When the song ended, the deejay's voice sounded as if coming from a great distance, deep timbred and warm, barely above a spoken whisper.

Dante yawned, stretched his arm forward, pulled back his coat sleeve, and by the dim light of the radio checked his watch, squinting.

"It's two o'clock," he said. "Nothing's happening tonight."

Cal shrugged.

"I'd rather be at the Rialto watching Rocky Lane."

Cal blew smoke at the ceiling, rubbed his upper lip with a knuckle. "What was that last one he did?"

"*Vigilante Hideout.*"

"I liked *Frisco Tornado* myself."

"*Gunmen of Abilene* was his best so far."

"Didn't think much of that one."

Cal studied the trailers and then the pasture. He turned in his seat and watched the far and few lights of cars speeding along the highway toward the city. Across the channel the lights of barges bobbed and dipped. He rolled his shoulders, put the window back down to let some cold air in.

Cal stared at the old neighborhood below the South Street Bridge leading to the city. The hulking black shapes of warehouses and factories, J&B Storage and Old Colony Meats, a nineteenth-century abattoir still in use. During the summer months the mewling and lowing of cattle about to be slaughtered used to reverberate down the channel to his parents' tenement on Cardinal Ryan Way. That was before they'd moved to Fields Corner. When he asked his mother what the sound was, she told him it was an Irish wake farther down the avenue. During that summer when he was ten, he heard it most every night, as if people were always dying, for the Irish were always having wakes.

Dante raised the binoculars again, panned the Mile Road. "Why'd you think someone's going to show? Even that bum said the guy hadn't been back in days."

"For shits and giggles, I don't know. It's how this guy gets his kicks. He can't stay away."

"Yeah, but why tonight?"

"It might be tonight, it might be tomorrow night. It might be next week. But he's kept the bodies in the trailer—"

"All except Sheila's." They hadn't mentioned her name since they'd seen the trailer, and Cal paused with his cup before his lip.

"—all except Sheila's, right, but he's kept the bodies in the trailer for a reason. Until he kills another girl, I think he'll keep using them."

Dante grimaced, shook his head. Frustrated, he mashed his cigarette into the overflowing ashtray.

"Do me a favor and dump that out, would you? My car's starting to smell like a crematorium."

"Hold up. What's *he* doing?"

Cal followed Dante's eyes and looked toward the rows of trailers. A bum had pulled down his pants and, hands between his legs cupping his balls against the cold, squatted on his haunches on the far side of the trailers by the wheel wells. The wind whipped his oversized coat about him.

"He's taking a shit."

Dante stared at the man through the binoculars, his brow creasing in concentration.

"Jesus. Let the man take a shit in peace, would you."

After a moment Dante grunted, laid his head back against the headrest, and closed his eyes. Wind moaned through the rusted towers of crushed cars, whistling high then low. The chain-link fence rattled. Cal finished the pint of whiskey, rolled the window back up, and turned the engine over again, allowing heat to fill the car. His head felt thick and heavy. The dashboard radio glowed warmly in the dark. Cal's head jerked on his neck and he swore, inhaled deeply, and forced his eyes open. It took him a moment to see the car with its lights off making its way slowly across the rutted gravel from the Mile Road and between the darkened shacks. Cal tongued his gums and killed the engine, rolled down his window again so that cold air filled the car. Dante didn't move, but his eyes were open and he was staring at the approaching car. Slowly, he raised the binoculars.

"Our man," he said.

"Maybe."

The car, a long-bodied black Lincoln, circled wide and slow before the shuttered and wrecked trailers. It passed beneath the wrecking yard's single halogen lamp and was illuminated, light slipping across its metal like a fish moving through water. Smoke curled white from twin tailpipes, and then it moved though darkness again and pulled in before the farthest abandoned trailer.

Cal and Dante watched the smoke steaming from its exhaust and then the smoke stopped, the driver's-side door opened, and a man climbed out. His footsteps broke the thin surface of ice that had covered the snow and the sound of it came to them.

"Scarletti?" Cal said.

"I don't think so, not the way the bum described him. This guy looks much smaller. Give me a second. I'm waiting for him to step into the light."

Cal leaned closer and stared into the dark, trying to see what Dante was seeing. The man wore a black watch cap pulled low over his head and a long black leather jacket that seemed to shine wetly in the light, its collar raised to protect his neck. He stepped through the snow, the meager glow of a flashlight bobbing before him, and moved without hurry toward the trailer containing the dead women. He knew where he was going all right. Cal realized he had been holding his breath, and exhaled long and slow. The figure reached up to the padlocked chain, and paused. He realized the seal had been broken, and turned, alarmed—the beam of his flashlight arcing crazily through the dark—and Cal flicked on the car's headlights. For a brief moment they could see his face fully and saw that it was Blackie Foley.

Dante lowered the binoculars and surprise hissed through Cal's teeth. Something held the both of them in their seats even as the figure darted from the trailer, and then Dante shouted, "Gun it!" but Cal was already stomping on the accelerator and releasing the clutch, the rear tires of the Fleetline spinning for traction, snow and frozen gravel banging in the wheel wells and digging craters in the snow beneath them. The Fleetline fishtailed to the left and right as they sped toward the trailer. Cal's heart hammered in his chest and nausea swirled in the pit of his stomach. It was the type of fear he'd felt in the war.

At the last moment he locked the car's high beams on the trailer, cut the wheel to trap the Lincoln, momentarily catching a black figure racing toward the car, and then a gunshot sounded and the windshield fractured before them. Glass sprayed their faces, and Cal ducked to shield his eyes, even as he pressed the car forward.

"The fuck!" he shouted, and jammed the gearshift upward, gearbox grinding. The engine screeched. With head lowered to the console, he tried to see through the spiderweb of cracked glass, and then sensing even as he realized it was too late that the tires were floating, riding above the ice, and that they'd lost traction and were gliding forward out of control. "Goddammit!" he hollered as the Fleetline began to turn in a wide pirouette, so at first they were moving alongside the Lincoln—they could see the blurred dark shape of the driver at the wheel through frost-covered glass, and then the Lincoln was roaring backward, barreling across the frozen gravel toward the gates of the yard, its exhaust mushrooming blue—and then they were turned away from it, the rear of the Fleetline like a missile careening toward the sloping drop into the sewage canal.

The Lincoln's retreating headlights momentarily blinded them as they spun. Cal stomped hard on the brakes, held them, and cut the wheel against the spin, released the brake, and wrestled the wheel back. It altered their direction and spun them hard into a wide snowbank. The car shook and the engine whined and then stalled. Cal hunched over the wheel, kept his foot to the pedal as he turned the key again and again until the engine roared into loud, frantic life, air popping in shotgun bursts from the manifold and tailpipes and the heady smell of oil and gasoline filling the interior of the car. Cal popped the clutch, and they spun out of the yard and up the Mile Road. The Lincoln was a distant blur of red tail-lights growing fainter and fainter, the sound of its engine revving at the top coming to them briefly on the frozen air. "You ain't getting away, you fuck," Cal said through gritted teeth. With his legs pressing down, Dante steeled himself against the seat as the car's acceleration forced his head back, wincing as he picked at the tiny bits of bloodied glass imbedded in his cheeks.

THEY CHASED THE black Lincoln into Boston proper, Cal squinting all the while through the shattered glass, his lips pressed together. It seemed as if he was holding his breath, and but for the flush of blood now seeping to his ears, nose, and cheekbones, Dante wondered if he was breathing at all. The cold wind rushed at their faces and made their eyes tear. The car hit a pothole and shook violently. Bits of glass came away from the window frame and with a slight tinkling fell about the car. The Lincoln was still there ahead of them. Dante could just make out its taillights, its sleek black body as it passed beneath the streetlights. Cal pushed the engine as hard as he could and the Fleetline lowered its heavy body to the street, the chassis trembling.

Cal reached into his jacket, pulled his gun from his holster, and dropped it across the car seat. Dante looked down at it and then up at him. Cal's eyes widened in exasperation. "I can't shoot and drive at the same time. Pick up the fucking gun, it won't bite."

The Common passed on their right, the blurred impression of wrought iron railings, bare and gnarled trees, snow the color of pearl, then the Public Garden, the frozen pond with the Swan Boats beneath their black tarps, and the statue of Colonel Thomas Cass, commander of the Ninth Regiment Massachusetts Volunteer Infantry rising triumphantly upon his horse.

Cal cut left across a lane of late-night traffic, which seemed to have materialized out of nowhere, and amid the blaring of horns and bright sparks of metal upon metal the car careened over the streetcar tracks before the glare of an oncoming trolley. In the Theater District he swerved into an alley that let out on Wilbur and then back onto Tremont. He kept his eyes between the road and the Lincoln ahead but they were losing ground. They came over the hill on Massachusetts Avenue, Roxbury with its staggered rows of decrepit and crumbling brownstones stretching before them, and suddenly there was no sign of the car.

Cal glanced in the rearview, looking to the curbs and openings of side streets, checking to see if the Lincoln might have pulled over and killed its engine, waiting for them to pass, or else might have done a roundabout and come up behind them. After a moment he shook his head. "Fuck, we've lost him."

Finally he pulled over, banged open his door, and clambered out, and Dante exited on his side, gun hanging in his hand. Cursing, Cal slammed the metal roof with his fists and then lowered his head, stretched his arms against the roof of the car. The engine idled and coughed as if it might quit altogether. Smoke from its exhaust moved about them heavy and slow, like everything else in the cold. After a moment Cal looked up. Dante was staring at him expressionless and pale, looking as if he might vomit. "This can't be for real," he said.

JUST AFTER DAWN and they were at Kelly's Rose, sitting at the bar and staring out beyond the window at the ashen gray streets. The gray dissipated like a veil being pulled back and the sun crept between the buildings and over the low rooftops, spearing the Scollay alleyways with an unforgiving light. Christy Black had come down from his room above the bar and shaken Peter Kopachek awake from a cot in the storage closet where he'd spent the night, and Peter was now slouched at the counter with a drink in his hand, sputtering as he drank.

Christy had turned on the bare minimum of lights, an ancient low-hanging candelabra in a small booth in the rear of the room, so that the place was thick with shadow. The smell of burning coffee grounds wafted from the small grill behind the bar where Christy was reheating yesterday's brew. A few regulars hunched at the bar eyed Cal and Dante warily, but when Cal looked at them, they went back to their drinks. They were shadows themselves, and if Cal and Dante hadn't already known who they were, they would have had to squint in the grainy light to properly make out their battered features: the cleft lip; the bulbous, vein-cracked nose; the watery, vacant stare. The radio was turned on, sound spitting and whining high as its tubes warmed, until Christy reached up and moved the dial to the morning news, and then Cal stood, holding the stool for support until the blood had worked its way back into his leg, and went to the phone booth at the rear of the room.

He stepped into the booth and swung the door shut behind him. The booth was cramped and stank of old tobacco and beer. A fan thumped into life when he closed the door and whirred loudly above his head. After depositing a nickel, he dialed the precinct and asked for Owen, not expecting him to be at his desk yet, but the desk sergeant patched him through and Owen picked up the phone and he told him what had happened.

"You're fucking nuts," said the voice. "What are you two morons playing at? You know something we don't know, you fucking tell us. You two keep this up and Giordano's going to make your life hell. Fuck! I should send a car around right now and arrest the two of you and just be fucking done with it."

Cal chewed on his tongue as he waited for Owen to finish at the other end of the line.

"Look, what the fuck do you care as long as you have the trailer, and now you have three more bodies to go along with Sheila's and the others, and you know that Blackie Foley's the killer. Tell them some fucking hobo found them and called it in." He made sure Owen knew how to find the trailer, and then even as Owen continued to talk, Cal hung up on him. He picked up the receiver and slammed it down again and then twice more. He leaned his head against the pay phone for a moment, wishing he'd handled things better with Owen, sighed, and pulled back the door, and the light and fan went off. Screw him, he thought. Let him work it out, the bastard.

At the bar Dante had already ordered him another drink and he tossed it back gratefully as he stood. "How'd it go?" Dante asked.

Cal shrugged, lowered himself wearily onto the stool. "Could've gone better. What he does next is up to him."

He ordered them another round. The radio played; men spoke in fragments of words; pedestrians and cars sounded beyond the glass, yet for Cal and Dante the world had gone silent. The regulars of Kelly's Rose shuffled and trudged through the amorphous shadows and glinting fragments of meager light in the barroom, as lost as Dante and Cal with their heads lowered over the bar, helpless before all of the things that haunted their separate imaginations.

25

SAVIN HILL, DORCHESTER

MOST AFTERNOONS IN the warmer months Cal sat on the porch of the triple-decker and watched the neighborhood move through its day. He'd sit there until it became dark while he wondered what he'd do next, if he'd do anything at all. Often, when Lynne came home, she'd come to the screen door and stare at him, the amber light of the kitchen a trembling corona about her black shape, and after a moment—or it might have been hours—she'd call out, "Cal, honey, why don't you come in now?" but when he turned and looked toward her, all he could see was darkness. The doctors up at the VA couldn't find an answer for it, told him it's what happens to all soldiers who have experienced combat and that hopefully things would change with time. Back at the war hospital in Verdun before they'd shipped him stateside, he used to hear the doctors talking among themselves in French, calling the shell-shocked American soldiers cowards.

This rare winter evening with the temperature holding steady at just above freezing, he finished his dinner and then brought a cup of coffee outside as Lynne washed the dishes. Every so often her shadow came across the porch as she passed before the slant of amber light cast from the kitchen and it reminded him that she was there. He sat in his heavy wool pants, wrapped in a winter overcoat and a quilt, stared blankly over Savin Hill's Malibu Beach to the distant traffic moving along the highway and Morrissey Boulevard, and farther, out across the halogen-lit arch bridge toward Tenean Beach, entrenched like a foul, long-gutted clamshell beyond the gray Boston Gas tanks, where they'd found Sheila's frozen, mutilated body.

He waited to hear some word from Dante and dusk emptied into night and with it came a deep cold. The bells of Saint Kevin's sounded the evening novenas and the traffic on the Avenue seemed to still. The moon came soon enough, trembling yellow through a haze of ice. He watched as the wind swept across the frozen water and rattled the bare branches of trees along the street and made him pull his coat tighter about him, and he wondered if it wasn't for Lynne, how he might just allow himself to freeze to death.

LYNNE CAME OUT onto the front porch wearing her hooded wool sweater, the one he'd bought her three Christmases before. She looked at him for a moment and then followed his eyes to the city beyond, blinking through the hazy clouds that formed around its lights at night. "What are you looking at?" she asked. "The view doesn't change, y'know."

He hadn't told her about the bodies they'd discovered in the trailer or of their chasing Blackie through Boston, hadn't mentioned Blackie telling Dante that he'd watched her on the Avenue, and he knew he wouldn't. When he didn't respond, she adjusted the quilt about him, pulled it up his torso. "It's freezing, Cal. You'll catch your death out here."

"Don't worry, I'm fine."

"Okay."

He gestured to the lights of other houses. "I used to sit on my parents' porch and look out at the windows across the way and try to imagine the people there, and the lives they lived. When I was young—"

"When you were an altar boy?" She laughed, and he couldn't help but grin.

"And you were lifting your skirt on the Avenue and pulling down your underwear for the Mulligans and Shays, a nickel a look."

"Cal!" Lynne slapped his shoulder hard. "I never charged a nickel. Never less than a dime for a look-see."

They both laughed with that and he reached for her, pulled her onto his lap, and she curled up her legs and leaned against his shoulder. He stroked her hair, and they kissed. The weight and warmth of her felt good, reassuring. For a moment he enjoyed the silence and the sense of her close to him. A boat was passing out into the bay, shimmering and white in the dark; at the drawbridge the staggered headlights of waiting cars. He said, "Blackie Foley paid Dante and Claudia a visit the other day."

"The gangster? Why?"

"Wanted to scare him, shake him up a bit."

"Are they okay?"

"Yeah, they're fine."

"What'd he owe this time?"

"Not much. He's not deep in to them, not like before."

"But you still bailed him out again, right?"

He remained silent, and she said, "How are they holding up? This whole Sheila thing—I know it must be hard on them. I know it's hard on you."

"They're doing okay. At least they have each other."

"I should go around and see Claudia. It's been so long."

"That'd be nice. I think she'd like that."

He looked at her, and then to her surprise reached out and placed his fingers on her cheek and traced the curve of her jaw. He watched her eyes looking at him. For a brief moment he felt an incredible, heartbreaking love and tenderness as if he were touching her after a great absence. A rush of grief came upon him, but he forced it back and smiled even though it felt unnatural. He clasped his hand over hers and held it there.

"You make sure to be careful when you're coming home," he said.

"Okay? Maybe ask Katie Ryan to ride the bus with you. She works the same shift, doesn't she?"

"Don't tell me you're worried about Blackie?"

"That's all in the past."

"Yeah, but I can tell it's bothering you."

"No, not at all." Cal shook his head. "Just want you to be safe. Crazy things happening these days."

"Like the Butcher?"

"Yeah, the Butcher."

"Don't worry about me, I can take care of myself."

"I know you can. I'm not worried."

She shook her head. "You silly bugger." She looked out over Neponset, Dorchester Bay, the peninsula, the islands, all sweeping back to the city. He watched her for a moment, trying to figure out what she was thinking.

"You never did like it here, did you, Lynne?"

She shrugged. "Like, dislike, I don't know. It's where I was born and raised. It's home, for what it's worth."

"It's home, but you could leave it if you had to."

"Yes, I could leave this. I'd leave it for just about anywhere as long as you were with me." She reached down and squeezed his hand, held on, looked into his eyes with conviction and just a little longing. Did she want him to agree, to say the same thing? After a moment she looked away.

"Sheila wouldn't have died just anywhere, you know. It had to be here."

"What are you talking about?"

"If she was from any other place, she wouldn't be dead now."

"Lynne—"

"That's what I believe. You don't have to agree. It's just . . . what I believe. This city will kill you, too, and you'll let it, Cal. You'll never leave, not for me, not for anything."

That's not true, he wanted to say. *I'd do anything for you, I'd leave this place for you,* but he remained silent, a numbness growing inside him as he watched the glittering windows of other homes. He envisioned himself as a young boy staring out at the dark, across to the windows of his neighbors, knowing that there was warmth there within those lighted rooms, and with a tremulous sense of longing, knowing that it was something he could never be a part of.

LATER IN BED, after she had fallen asleep, he stared blankly toward the ceiling. He sensed her beside him, her breathing sounding the depths of the darkness they lay within. Wind rattled the windowpanes, moaned in the eaves. Something skittered on the roof, and the doorway in the kitchen sighed as the furnace kicked in and the house warmed.

He remembered his second year on the police force, after the war, and one of his worst cases. They'd traced the murdered body of a four-year-old boy to a house in Mattapan where the parents had kept their four children, one boy and three girls, in cages in the basement; for years they'd raped and physically abused them, kept them alive on dog food and water. The place stank of excrement and piss. There was also the smell of the oldest girl's menses. She'd been raised that way since she was eight. When they found her she was eighteen, her body deformed by malnutrition and confinement, by beatings, and by the straps that bound her on a daily basis until they were done with her. The neighbors had nothing but nice things to say about the people—they attended the local Unitarian church, gave to all the best causes, including the Patrolmen's Association.

The children had no teeth left; they'd rotted away, and when they found the children curled up in the cages, their pale, naked buttocks showed the marks of a whip and a razor blade and were caked with shit. As he and a beat cop were letting them out of their cages and another detective called for a wagon and an ambulance, the father came banging down the stairs brandishing a butcher's blade. He was naked and his pale, mealy-colored cock erect. Cal shot him twice in the gut before he'd taken one foot off the bottom step and he dropped like a ton weight. Cal let him howl in pain, curled up in a fetal position, his entrails bleeding out, while they attended to the children. He was still breathing as they bundled the children beneath blankets and guided them up the stairs, and Cal had stared at the father's bowed back, falling and rising slowly, at his hairy, lumpy backside, and suddenly, enraged, had kicked him repeatedly, driven his boot up into his testicles, imagining the man screaming although he was well beyond that. He wouldn't have regretted it had the man died, but he had lived and been electrocuted a year later at Charlestown State Prison.

He thought of the evil in the world, places he'd seen where God had been absent, and sometimes he wondered why he still had faith at all, why he still believed. He turned and looked at Lynne sleeping, caught briefly in the radiance of a passing car's headlights—and suddenly seeming hard and beautiful and incredibly vulnerable all at the same time.

26

THEY OPENED THE front door and a shaft of pale midday light speared the dark foyer of the club, and with it came the cold. Three black men at the bar turned almost painfully toward it. The door finally closed, and Cal and Dante stepped into the dim blue light. The men at the bar let their stares linger before turning back to their drinks and starting into conversation again, louder this time and brash.

"So, this was where you saw Sheila last?" Cal asked.

Dante took his hat from his head. "Yeah, you could say it was one of her regular spots."

"Well?"

"Well what?"

"How long ago was it, the last time you saw her?"

Dante shrugged. "A while, okay? Right around Margo's death. Maybe a few months after."

Cal scanned the length of the place. There were three booths beside the stage, four round tables, and red and green and blue lights blazing everywhere, as if they were aboard a submarine, or at a whorehouse during the holidays. Nautical artifacts hung from the walls. Anchors and compasses, a painting of a sinking ship entrapped within the tentacles of a giant fire-engine-red squid. And photos—lots of photos of well-dressed black musicians holding their instruments. Within the weaving strands of smoke were a miserable sort of shadow people: two bare-kneed bums half asleep at a booth, a round-faced man and a bedraggled white woman starting a binge on cheap wine, a young hophead standing by the men's room seeking some score, and a dusty whore sipping on a ginger ale all alone at one of the tables. As his eyes adjusted to the light, he could see an old man on the small stage holding a tarnished saxophone. The man began to toy with the scales, the brass emitting a sorrowful sound that quickly filled up the close space.

Imagining how the small club would look twelve hours from now at midnight, Cal was surprised to think of Sheila here and comfortable among the regulars, black men and women crammed into this small place as the night turned into morning, the room filled with cigarette smoke and loud, raucous laughter, blaring music, and sweating bodies. But now, just a bit after noon, he saw it only as a desperate way station where people shunned the light of day and carried on in the routine of a slow death.

They took the two stools at the end of the bar farthest from the stage. Dante unbuttoned his worn overcoat, laid it over a stool, carefully smoothed down its creases with his hand, and sat.

The old man blew a few chords of "Don't Blame Me" and steadied out with the gentle refrain of "Body and Soul." Dante found his own left hand tapping the bar top along imaginary keys, fingers arched and striking the notes that sounded in his head. Catching himself, he pulled his hand off the bar, flexed and closed it to break apart the stiffness left over from the cold.

Above the bar, he stared at the ticking neon of a Schlitz sign whose bulb was ready to give out. The conversation at the other end shifted and lost some of its bluster, and Dante knew that they were sizing him and

Cal up, waiting to see what they'd do next. He recognized the face of the guy in the Braves hat, but the other two he had never seen before. They must have been strictly midday drinkers here, their nights resigned to their wives, their families, and now just getting a cheery buzz on before they had to go back out into the world.

The bartender, Bowie, came down the bar to them. Bowie was cross-eyed, a gangly light-skinned man with lots of freckles and a glaring gap between his two front teeth. And to add to his clownish appearance, he always wore brightly colored shirts—lime green, canary yellow, pink, rose red.

"Is Moody in?" Dante asked.

"Yeah. He's just out back." Bowie switched the rag on his left shoulder to the right one.

"No rush. I can wait."

"Something to drink while you're waiting?"

"Two Jamesons," Cal said, "and two beers."

Cal glanced over at the other men at the bar as he rummaged in his pants pocket for his wallet.

"You can at least unbutton your coat, Cal. They won't steal it off your back."

"I was getting to it."

Bowie brought their drinks to them, two old-fashioned glass mugs with white frothy heads. He placed two empty shot glasses on the countertop and filled them to the very top, so that both Dante and Cal had to tenderly raise them to their lips. Cal settled onto the stool, lit a cigarette, and looked along the bar at the photos crammed on the back wall. He raised himself from the stool to get a better look. He wondered if Sheila was in any of them, but not one white face looked back at him.

At the farthest end of the bar, a heavy velvet curtain parted and out came a large man, at least six foot five, holding a case of beer under one arm. He wore an immaculate white apron and a shimmering red collared shirt stretched across his hulking frame. Watching, Cal waited for him to smack his head on the overhang of the bar, or bump one of his wide shoulders against the rows of bottles by the wall, but he moved with a singular grace unusual for a man his size. He turned, looked first at Cal and then at Dante, and came down the bar to them.

"Shit, Dante," he said. "Your face has seen better days."

A younger man wearing jeans and a T-shirt joined the old man on the small stage, raised a trumpet to his lips, and began to add a little cheer to the sad ballad the old man was struggling with. Unlike the old man's saxophone, the trumpet was buffed and polished, and it reflected the red lights above the stage with a gemlike shimmer. Cal listened to the sound of the two instruments careen off the walls and the low ceiling of the bar as if two animals were chasing each other in play.

"This is my friend Cal," Dante said.

Moody reached over the bar and took Cal's calloused hand in his large one and they shook. His arm was laced with tight muscle and corded with tendon and his shoulders were like rounded blocks of stone. Light brown eyes and a nose broken once or twice, set and healed crooked. When he smiled it seemed earnest and kind, even if he might have half his mind set on breaking your arm.

"Are you two here to get drunk like the other bums, or is there something you want?" Moody looked down the bar at Bowie, who was staring at them. When they made eye contact, Moody nodded and Bowie went back to pouring a beer for one of the other patrons.

"We have a couple of questions to ask."

Moody laughed low, almost like a growl, and shook his head. "I knew it. That's what every white bastard says when they walk in here. Next thing you know they're arresting us because we don't have enough soap in the bathroom."

The shot glasses were empty and Moody went to the shelves and came back with a new bottle of whiskey and another empty shot glass. He refilled Cal's and Dante's and then filled up one for himself. "In that case, you're buying me this drink."

Dante pulled two dollars from his pocket and placed them on the bar. "You know Sheila, my sister-in-law?"

156

Moody put down his whiskey, the glass small, thimble-like in his large hand. He shook his head, sucked in through clenched teeth. "I haven't seen her in a while."

"Do you remember the last time you saw her?"

"Like four, maybe six months back, I think it was."

"Was she with anybody?"

"Are you asking with one of us, or one of you?"

"I guess it doesn't matter."

"Yeah, she was. Some guy she'd been here with plenty of times before."

"What did he look like?" Cal asked.

"You'd know him if you saw him, big shot from one of the wards on the other side of town, one of your guys. Can't keep track of all those Irish names. Could be he's a politician or something. Good-lookin' cat, well dressed like a man does behind a big desk."

"An older man?"

"He had white hair, sure, but I'd guess not much older than you two."

"How was Sheila? She look okay?"

"Probably the same as always. She strutted in and gave me some sweetness, then sat at one of the tables and drank and smoked the night away, just like she always did."

Moody gestured toward a table by the stage where dust motes tumbled through slants of daylight, and Dante stared at it as if he might see Sheila there, sipping from a cocktail, and the man, a shadowy and amorphous figure with his back to them, leaning across the table to her, whispering something in her ear, she smiling, pushing him playfully away. The vague recollection of the last time he had seen her came back to him. The man with her that night, Bobby, didn't have white hair and looked too sharp to be a politician, more like some hustler type.

Moody shrugged. "The guy, he kept looking over his shoulder. Didn't look comfortable, I remember. Like he was about to get caught somewhere he shouldn't be."

"Anything else seem off?"

"Well, the night ended in a fight or something. They kept drinking and drinking hard. He was talking in her ear, shouting at one point, and she just kept a straight face and watched the band. Like she was trying to block him out so she could hear every note the band was playing. Like he wasn't even there to her. And when she got up to leave, he followed like an old dog who had done wrong and shit in the house."

"Before this guy, had she come in with other men?"

Moody looked at Dante for a long moment, as if he might be playing a trick on him. "Well, that's a silly fucking question. A woman looking as fine as her, shit, she likes the attention...C'mon. Why all this, really? You're still in touch with her, right?"

Dante took a mouthful of whiskey, let the burn clear before answering. "Since Margo died, we haven't talked much."

Cal looked at him, frowning. Perhaps Moody knew about Sheila's death and was pretending he knew nothing—it wouldn't help to know too much about a murdered white woman, especially if you were the owner of a colored club she frequented—but something was getting under his skin. And why the hell was Dante pulling his chain about Sheila?

"One other thing. There was a guy that came in here looking for her a couple of weeks back. I didn't want to give him nothing on Sheila so I asked for his name, told him I'd leave her a message if I happened to see her. He just smiled as though I wasn't in on the joke. Short little fucker up to no good, but not the type you'd mess with. Still, I wouldn't have served him if he'd asked."

"Another politician type?"

"Hell no. He wore a black cap and a black leather jacket. Real thug type. Craziest blue eyes I've ever seen. Like ice, man—that if you looked at him sideways, he'd be likely to cut you up."

Dante and Cal looked at each other, and Cal shook his head.

"Might have just done some time, definitely had that look about him."

Dante finished his whiskey but left his beer untouched. "And that was it?"

"Yeah, never saw him come back asking for her again."

"Blackie Foley," Cal said. "Fucker gets around."

"You know that guy well?" Moody asked.

"Too well. We all grew up in Fields Corner together. He runs most of Dorchester and Southie now."

"No shit. You don't like him much, huh?"

Cal's face had become rigid, his jaw clenched and his face flushed.

"Let me guess," Moody said. "He stole your girlfriend and broke her cherry before you got a chance. Damn pussy always getting between men." And he laughed deep from his belly, but without any reaction from Cal he let it fade and filled his own shot glass with more whiskey.

Cal stood, pulled four singles from his wallet, and laid them on the bar. He put his hand out. "Thanks for your help, Mr. Moody."

"No problem."

When Moody and Dante shook hands, Moody pulled him close, lowered his voice. "Are you okay? You don't look so hot."

Dante gave him a broken smile. "It's not as bad as it looks."

"You got to stay off the shit, Dante. They don't call it junk for no good reason. I could string up a line of a thousand men I know whose lives were ruined by that stuff."

Cal was buttoning up his jacket and watching.

"I appreciate it, Moody. I always listen to what you have to say."

"Sometimes I fuckin' wonder," Moody said.

Outside, Cal felt disheveled and dizzied by the bright cold daylight. He pulled his collar up tight around his neck as they walked. "You trust him?" he asked. "Him not knowing Sheila is dead and giving us the bead on all her boyfriends?"

"We wouldn't have come here if I didn't trust him. Moody's solid. You don't have to worry about him."

"No, but I wonder if Sheila did. He had eyes for her, you could tell."

"Lots of guys had eyes for Sheila."

"And that's the problem, isn't it? Anyone might have had a reason to do what they did to her."

Dante shook his head. They'd reached the car, and he looked at the cars passing sluggishly up and down Columbus Ave. A city truck with its plow pressing snow close to the curb raked the side of a parked car, shattering its mirror, and kept going. Leaden clouds passed low before the sun over the tenements on the far side of the street. "Not just anyone," he said.

27

THE CITY MORGUE resided in a decrepit four-story brick building just off of Massachusetts Avenue between Albany and Harrison. This time Cal and Dante entered through the main entrance instead of through the underground Boston City Hospital annex and its rat-infested tunnel. The lobby was done up in the Egyptian Revival theme popularized by the discovery of King Tut's tomb at the time of its construction. In the ornate marble lobby two sphinxes greeted those who had come to identify the dead—sometimes family members and lovers, husbands and wives, and at other times estranged children now fully grown, called to give voice and a face to a man or woman who'd abandoned them decades before—and guarded the stairs that led down to the medical examiners and the refrigerated storage drawers in which the dead lay interned. At first it had been a place to honor the dead and comfort those coming to identify them, but in the decades since, the building had fallen into disrepair. Now it was a dark, rambling labyrinth filled with the smells of decay and damp, and the constant sound of dripping pipes.

As Cal and Dante descended the ramp down two floors beneath the city streets, the stinging odor of formaldehyde bit at their nostrils. Underground it was as cold as the day they'd come to view Sheila's body. An elevator clanged open and they stepped back to allow a technician in green scrubs from the city hospital to pass, pushing a gurney on which a body lay beneath a bloodied sheet. They followed the sound of its clacking wheels and his slow, plodding feet down the tunnel.

The doors to the morgue opened, and in the white-tiled room they could see Fierro and two technicians discussing a body they'd just pulled from the storage drawers. On two other tables beneath the glare of white fluorescents lay covered remains. Fierro glanced up, pushing his glasses onto the top of his head, and frowned. He spoke quickly to a technician at his side, pulled the sheet up over the body, and slid the drawer back into storage. At the door, he raised up his hands to block the view and ushered Cal and Dante back into the hallway.

"What the hell are you two doing here?" He raked his fingers through what was left of his limp hair, accidentally knocking his glasses to the floor.

"Need to see if you've gotten anything on the women found in the trailer out at the city dump. Same as Sheila, right?"

"Cal, Dante," Fierro said as he bent over to retrieve his glasses. "Owen's been looking for you for two days. He's already told me not to talk to you two, and he's pissed off as hell."

Cal shrugged, uncaring. "C'mon, Fierro, have they identified the bodies?"

Fierro reached into his pockets for a pack of cigarettes. He motioned them down the hallway between a row of empty gurneys pressed against the damp wall. "You two are going to be the death of me, you know that." He handed them each a cigarette and lit his own. "This office performs most of the state's examinations, almost three thousand autopsies a year. I'm so busy I don't even have time to use the john. I've got a freaking bladder infection, a headache that never quits, and when I come home my wife doesn't want to touch me because she says I stink of formaldehyde."

From down the dim hallway came the distant sound of the elevator doors opening, and after a moment, as the three of them turned out of the hall, single footsteps, sharp and measured and officious, echoed on the floor, followed by a thick, phlegm-filled cough. Before he came into view, Cal knew it was Owen.

Owen's eyes widened slightly when he saw them. He took his hand from his mouth, reached into his pocket for a handkerchief, and wiped his nose. "Sooner or later I knew I'd run into you two."

"You're not sounding too good."

"You're an asshole, Cal." He sounded congested, and he winced when he coughed into his handkerchief.

Owen looked at Dante and then back to Cal. "If you two aren't here to ID a family member, then you're trespassing."

A speckled redness touched his cheeks but left the rest of his face sickly pale. He nodded, resigned. "What has the doctor here told you?"

"Nothing. We were about to beat it out of him."

"I think he's got more important things to be doing than wasting his time with you clowns." He nodded at Fierro. "You almost done with the Hyde Park shooting?"

"Almost."

"Good. I'll be back after I talk to these two."

Inside Mama's Diner it was warm and filled with the chatter of people, the odors of coffee and of meat cooking on the grill. They took a booth by the front windows, and when a waitress came with coffee, they ordered breakfast: eggs, steak, and hash for Owen and Dante, eggs and blood sausage for Cal. Owen was staring beyond the window, and Cal was surprised by how much older he looked; the light reflecting off the snow had turned his face white, transparent-looking, and yet it couldn't erase the lines about his eyes.

"Owen, you have something on the bodies?"

Owen stirred sugar into his coffee and sighed, looked from Cal to Dante as he laid the spoon on the Formica table.

"First off, tell me why you two were looking for a meat truck over at the city dump, and in the early hours of the morning?"

"Got a tip from a dispatcher about a missing truck, that's all."

"Why a missing truck?"

"Trucks are the only traffic down at Tenean this time of year. You see them coming and going like clockwork.

"And then there was the state of her body postmortem, as if she'd been killed on the beach when we know she wasn't. When I saw the tracks at the beach all I could think was that perhaps it had been a reefer. It was a hunch, but I didn't think it would end up anywhere. You had to have thought of that too."

Owen nodded. "Yeah. We'd thought of it."

"So, who are the women?"

Dante turned away and looked out the window. Hiding their faces from the driving snow, pedestrians labored against the wind and passed by slowly.

"Okay, this is what we've got, and I'm telling you only because you found the trailer."

He lit a cigarette, drew on it deeply, and leaned back in his seat as the waitress arrived with their food. She refilled their cups with coffee and then passed down the row of booths.

"We know one of the Jane Does as Margaret Hill, a hooker from Roxbury, pimps for a creep named Shea Mack—"

Dante swore as he slopped coffee onto the table and his hand. Cal pushed his napkin across to him and Dante worked to pool up the liquid before it dripped onto the floor.

"You know this Shea Mack?" Owen asked.

Cal shook his head, but Dante nodded. "I've heard of him." Shaking, he balled up the sopping napkin and put it aside.

Owen began to carve up his meat, placed a small piece in his mouth. "That figures."

He chewed for a moment and then swallowed with obvious discomfort. "Okay, well then maybe you know a little of how he works. Real piece of shit. We've got beat cops looking for him, but no word yet.

"The other victim we identified as Anne Montague. She's from Weymouth. Her parents have had a Missing Persons out for her since the end of December."

From between bites of food he said, "We've been in touch with the State Police and agencies from three other states, Maine, Rhode Island, and New Hampshire. So far they've gotten back to us with nine missing young women from Providence to Portland, all in the last twelve months."

He pushed the plate away from him although he was only half-done.

"This all seems to be the work of the Butcher—maybe this Scarletti character you told me about. Hell, he's got the credentials for it. His record of arrest shows two burglaries and three aggravated assaults: assault with the attempt to cause bodily injury to another person by use of a deadly weapon, assault with the attempt to cause bodily injury to a police officer, assault with the attempt to cause serious bodily injury and have sexual activity with a person under the age of consent."

"What do you mean 'maybe'? We know who did this—it was Blackie Foley! Why haven't you already taken him in?"

"Those are *his* salvage yards, okay? He leases part of the property out to trucking companies so that they can load and unload, switch trailers, or dump them. For years we've known that he's used it as a front for black market smuggling. We've never been able to make anything stick on him, but we've known all about it."

"So you're going to let him slide?"

"Christ, Cal, why would he jeopardize his business by leaving a truckful of bodies in a place he knows we watch? The yards are his property and he has every right to check on them whenever the fuck he wants."

"This is all bullshit, Owen."

"Let me finish. A bum tipped him off about the rig, and as soon as he discovered the trailer, he called it in. He also said somebody chased him halfway across Boston."

"So what did you say to him?"

"That's none of your business."

"Fuck him."

"No. Fuck you, Cal—fuck you both."

"So that's it?"

"That's it."

Owen sipped from his coffee, placed the cup on the table, and squared his hands around it. They were a boxer's hands, much like Cal's. Dante noticed the glimmer of Owen's wedding band shimmering dully beneath the lights of the diner.

Owen pursed his lips, looked at Dante. "So you knew this Margaret Hill?"

"It was a long time ago, Owen. The faces, the names, they all blend together."

Owen stared, unconvinced, pushed his coffee cup to the center of the table. "That's okay. I've got to get back to the station."

"What about Blackie?" Cal asked again.

"Like I said: Blackie had nothing to do with this."

Owen hesitated. He stared at Dante, wiped at his nose with the back of his hand. "I've been dreading this all day. I should have just done it back at the morgue."

"Dreading what?" Cal asked.

Owen ignored him, kept his eyes locked on Dante. "Giordano has been on me these past couple of days. He's pissing blood about how nobody questioned you before."

Cal stiffened in his chair. "What the fuck is this shit, Owen?"

"Dante was the only real relative Sheila had. We got to ask him questions." He stood, pulling his coat about him, and pushed a dollar bill across the table.

A sickly grin pulled at Dante's lips. "You're not going to cuff me?"

"No, and if it makes you feel any better, you can ride up front with me."

"This is bullshit, Owen, and you know it," Cal said.

"It's all part of the process, you know that. I promise to make it as harmless as I can."

Outside, they had to lower their heads against windblown snow as traffic rumbled past. Cal and Dante huddled together for a moment against the side of the building, attempting to light a cigarette.

"Just go with it," Cal said in a low voice. "Giordano is a real greaseball prick, and he'll try to heavy-hand you."

Dante shook the match and inhaled off the cigarette. "I'll be fine."

Cal watched Dante's fingers tremor as he reached toward his lips, took the cigarette, and passed it over.

"I'll be fine," Dante repeated, as if he was saying it more to himself than to Cal.

Owen reached casually for Dante's shoulder, turned him in the opposite direction toward the city morgue. He gestured to Cal with his handkerchief.

"You can follow us in your car if you like. It's up to you."

"Does he need an attorney?"

"I don't know." Owen looked at Dante. "Do you?"

Dante shook his head and Owen nodded. "Good," he said. "That'll make it easier."

Owen blew his nose violently, looked down at the handkerchief, and frowned in disgust. "Jesus Christ," he said, and glared at them. "I wish this fucking cold on you two idiots."

28

BOSTON POLICE DISTRICT D-4, SOUTH END

A SOFT, WET snow came down and the wipers clacked back and forth across the new windshield. Cal had the heater on and sipped coffee; every so often he lit a cigarette and let down the window to blow the smoke out. He'd swung by Scollay Square before following Owen and Dante to the precinct, had shuttered and locked the Pilgrim Security offices, and although he expected the phones to remain dead, he'd had their calls put through to the answering service. He stared through the bleary glass, wiped at it with his sleeve, watched the gray of the street: police cars moving in and out of their spots and cops and pedestrians trudging sluggishly up and down the stairs to the precinct. To the north the lights of the John Hancock Building flashed red, shimmering through the sleet. He checked his watch, and when he looked up, Dante was descending the stairs: so slow and disheveled he looked like a man who'd spent the weekend in the drunk tank, a man with nothing in his pockets and nothing to lose. Dante stood at the bottom of the steps and glanced up and down the street until Cal tapped the horn twice and got his attention. He climbed in wearily, and Cal stared at him, handed him the cigarette he'd been smoking.

"How'd it go?" Cal asked.

Dante sucked on the cigarette, blew smoke out from his nostrils. He looked through the glass and shrugged.

"I would have come in but it would have just made it worse for you. That fucker Giordano hates my guts."

"He was okay. Someone had to ask the questions."

"Was Owen in the room with you?"

"Yeah. He even told Giordano to lay off a couple of times."

"Good for Owen, the prick."

Cal put the car in gear and eased out into the street, past the old redbrick and brownstone row houses of the South End, and then onto Columbus. Dante hadn't looked at him since he'd gotten in the car.

"What did they want to know about you and Sheila?"

"I don't want to talk about it, okay?"

Cal focused on the traffic; they crossed one intersection and then another, idled as they waited for a light to turn green. He coughed into his hand, wishing there was a bottle in the glove compartment. He turned to Dante and noticed his eyes were red and glassy, as if he'd been crying.

"Was there something that happened between you and Sheila that you're not telling me?"

"I told you, I don't want to talk about it." He was staring through the windshield, eyes glistening.

Cal kept his mouth shut, considering. After a moment: "Fine, then. We won't talk about it."

On the road before them a green Ford swerved into their lane. Cal slammed down on the horn, cursed under his breath. The Ford straightened out and moved ahead.

"No matter what Owen says, I know Blackie had a hand in this. And if we get to Scarletti first, maybe we'll find out just what that is."

At the intersection Cal gunned the car as the traffic light went from green to red. "So, this Shea Mack, how well do you know him?"

Dante turned and rolled down the window. Wind rushed through the car, and he sucked in the cold air.

"Shea Mack works Fort Point and the West End," he said matter-of-factly, and turned an odd and strangely disquieting smile at Cal, as if he were opening doors to his past that he would rather have left closed. "And I know where we can find him."

29

A VOICE CALLED from the room beyond the heavy curtains. Local and yet with a fake drawl, sickly sweet as it might come from a man mimicking a child while impersonating someone from the South. "Is that Dante, Honeydew?"

"It's Dante, Shea."

"Well, show him on in. We's just taking care of some business here, ain't nothing old Dante can't see."

The big man called Honeydew nodded, and Cal followed Dante's lead through the curtains.

The back room was dimly lit and full of shadows. At the center a young man with large, pleading eyes sat bound to a wooden chair. His pants and underwear were down around his ankles and his legs were held apart by rope. Half kneeling before him with a straight razor was a grinning Shea Mack. He eyed Cal and Dante as they stepped into the room and pressed the razor against the young man's bruised-looking testicles

171

and then with the flat end of the blade playfully tapped the penis, which lay like a limp, withered worm against the testicles.

Cal glanced at Dante. "What the fuck is this shit?"

Behind the boy stood two young black men, one of them wearing leather gloves that glistened as if wet. Almost lost in the darkness, a large white man slouched on a sofa, his extraordinary belly pushing out of his gray T-shirt. He wore green khakis of the type truck drivers and city workers wore.

Shea pressed the blade between the boy's testicles and drew it back. The boy whimpered and strained against his ropes, the muscles in his thighs tautened, and a stream of urine spat from his penis, splattering the floor.

"Jesus," Shea cried, grinning, "I haven't even started yet." He shook his arm, the shirtsleeve now darkened and wet. "Now I'm gonna smell like piss."

In the corner two other young men lay trussed and naked, kneeling, gags in their mouths, and eyes wide with horror. Another was sitting naked with his back to the wall. By the looks of him, he appeared to have been the first one tied to the chair and tortured. Both eyes were misshapen mounds of black bruise, a barely recognizable slit of an eyeball glistened from his right eye socket. His cheeks and lips were so horribly contorted it looked as if the swelling would soon split the skin. The kid couldn't move the bloodied pulp of his mouth, yet they could hear his moaning.

"You know what these here boys did, Dante?"

This was a mannerism with Shea Mack, a playful and manipulative banter in which the other person was always to assume the inferior role, responding to Shea's rhetorical questions, and so that he always held center court. Cal caught on right away—in the war he'd seen enough megalomaniacs with bars on their shoulders act in much the same way—and he resisted the game, but Dante knew better, and he knew it was dangerous not to play.

"What he'd do, Shea?"

"This boy, and his buddies—fucking frat boys from Tufts—decide they want to get some action in so they come over the bridge and take my Kitty here for a little joyride."

On a stool sat Kitty, legs pressed tightly together, wringing her hands and squirming almost as much as the boy. She wore a floor-length ratty fake fur coat and a bright pink wool hat streaked with grime.

"Well, Kitty tells them how much it's going to be for each one of them and they agree, but when they get her to the room they change their minds and decide they're not going to pay. Not only that but what they want is no longer consensual—you see, these boys want to make her hurt—so they take what they want by force. Y'know, treat her like a dog. A bitch, a piece-of-shit whore they've found on the street. So they rape my Kitty, all four of them.

"They rape my Kitty, sodomize her, and beat her black and blue in the process...and that's not all they do...you'd think they'd never had mothers and sisters, what they did to her...animals...fucking animals." Shea screwed his face up as if something foul-tasting had just come into his mouth, and spat in the direction of the bound-and-gagged students.

He stared over at them now. "Think they got more love for each other, don't you? More love for the little things between their legs. You know, I always figured men who hate women this much must have a love for cock. Bet deep, deep down, they missing their daddy's cock."

Shea shrugged, still smiling. "So, what do you think we're doing about it, Dante?"

He moved the flat of the straight blade back and forth across the boy's scrotum. The ropes strained and the boy began gagging.

"You're making it right, Shea. Teaching them a lesson. They have to know they can't fuck with Shea Mack."

"Yes. They have to know they can't fuck with Shea Mack. They have to understand the consequences." He turned the blade slightly and the boy howled again; a trickle of blood slid down the metal.

"Enough," Cal said, and Shea's eyes moved slowly toward him. Shea smiled coldly. The blade paused against the boy's scrotum. "Tell him why we're here, Dante."

Dante took off his hat and raked a hand through his hair. "We're here about Blackie Foley."

"Blackie Foley," Shea murmured, and his eyes glazed. He seemed to have momentarily forgotten the boy in the chair. Shea ran the flat of the blade over his cheek. "That's one pretty man. Always has been. Ever since I first met him, I thought he was too pretty to be doing the things he did, hanging out with the people he did. Beautiful eyes has Blackie—you ever look into his eyes?"

Cal hacked, spat on the floor. Shea continued to eye him lazily and as if with a strange curiosity. "We think he killed one of your girls."

"Who?"

"Margaret Hill."

"Dear sweet Maggie," and he sighed. "If it's Blackie, poor troubled boy—what are you going to do, Dante? No one in this town's going to step out against Blackie."

Shea tapped the blade against the palm of his hand, stared as its edge caught the light and gleamed. "How'd he do it? How'd he kill her?"

"Strung her up on a meat hook, tortured her, and then sliced her open."

Shea shook his head. "Shame. Even though she'd gotten old far too quick, she was a good girl. She really was. Always listened to what I told her. Always did right by me.

"Strange, though, it doesn't sound like Blackie, the way you describe it, not like Blackie at all. Why'd he do it? What reason would he have to kill Maggie like that?"

It was Cal's turn to smile. "Don't know. Figure he was just getting his kicks, a sick fuck, like you."

Shea cocked his head to one side, and the light reflected off his black hair parted and slicked with grease, his clean-shaven face which had the pallor of a wax figure suddenly come to life. "Oh boy. If you think Blackie and me are alike, you need help, my man. Dante, your friend here needs to open his eyes. He's walking blind."

"Don't worry about him," Dante responded, but Shea disregarded him and kept his eyes locked on Cal.

"I would have expected more from you, war hero. Yeah, that's right. I know you."

"Can't say the same, Shea. But you're almost exactly what I expected."

"You're a funny guy, real funny, but if you're headed to collide with Blackie Foley, you're more of a fool. He'll tear you up into little pieces and send you to the grinders. You're not going to be so pretty when he's done. Shame, really."

Shea tapped the razor absently against his lips, considered Cal with something almost like desire. Blood ran down the blade and onto his knuckles. He looked at it for a moment and then shook his head, glanced back at the boy strapped to the chair, watched the feeble movements of his chest, his legs as the muscles spasmed, the rapid convulsions of his Adam's apple.

"Honeydew! Show these fine gentlemen out. I don't want to offend their delicate sensibilities. We got business to take care of."

30

IN THE WAITING room of the windowless State House office, Dante sat in a chair beneath a bank of flickering, humming fluorescent lights. He squinted against them, felt a headache pressing behind his eyes. Over the last few days he'd measured out the remaining junk from Karl's, made his doses smaller and smaller, and staggered his fixes so that he might come off it without suffering serious withdrawals. He'd taken his last dose six hours before and knew he couldn't last much longer.

In his gabardine pants and stained shirt under an overcoat with only one of its four buttons remaining, he was suddenly self-conscious. He was aware of the stale sweat on his clothes, and how, as they started to warm in the heat of the waiting room, they were beginning to stink. He gripped his damp gloves in his hand, hoping they might lessen the shaking that grew with each minute he waited.

He'd called ahead and spoken to Mrs. Cushing, Administrator of Personnel, and made an appointment for ten o'clock, but the clock on the wall now showed nearly ten forty-five. Beyond the front desk he could

176

hear the insistent tapping of multiple typewriters, as if in some competition to overtake and outduel the other, the noise pulling through his skull like a rusted steel thread. The door to the office opened again, and two clean-shaven men with rolled-up sleeves squared precisely just below the elbows emerged and walked briskly past—each carrying a leather-bound folder that gave them both an air of urgency.

A phone rang, followed by another. A woman's voice answered the first. "State House Employment. Can you hold a moment?" And then another, quickly lifted off its cradle, and as if an automated echo, the same words were repeated. "State House Employment. Can you hold a moment?"

The pit of his stomach expanded sourly as if he might be sick. There was too much noise and too much purpose. The way everybody seemed to have so much direction and intent made the edges blur even more. He wished he'd avoided the impulse to come here, and silently cursed himself because of it. The hallway door opened again, and a man in a tweed suit and an auburn mustache entered from the main lobby, glanced blindly at Dante as he were not even there. The phones dueled for attention once more. He tried to squeeze out the noise of the office, shut his eyes and lowered his head.

A woman's voice, harsh, with a thick townie accent, was calling to him, pulling him back through the black hole and into the office with its loudly thrumming lights and the insistent noise of typewriters and phones and disembodied voices. "Sir, are you okay?" she asked again.

He opened his eyes and saw a woman in a brown business suit standing before him. The suit was too big for her, hanging off her shoulders and falling wide over her hips. Its color matched the chestnut eyes that looked down at him.

"I'm sorry," he managed. "Yes, I'm okay."

"Well, you were nodding off there. Would you like a glass of water or something?"

"No, I'm fine, thank you."

He was surprised to find her smiling at him. He noticed that her makeup seemed far too bright. In the harsh light, the pinkish rouge made him think of a young girl sneaking into her mother's bedroom and using her makeup in hopes of looking more like an adult.

"Unfortunately, Mrs. Cushing can't speak with you. She's been called in to an impromptu, very important meeting."

"I won't take too much of her time. Just a few questions, that's all." He stood slowly, pulling himself up from the chair, and only then realizing that he was trembling even worse. He took his hat in his hands, trying to calm himself, ran his fingers and thumb nervously over the worn brim. He felt like a vagrant asking for spare change after a Sunday service.

"I'm sorry but I'm afraid she has no free time. Today or for the remainder of the week."

Dante raised his voice, louder than he wished. "That other woman said she'd be with me in a minute. I've been waiting nearly an hour."

She sighed and gave him that same childish smile. Her lips curved and exposed large front teeth stained with lipstick. "Again, I'm sorry."

"I just wanted to ask about Sheila Anderson."

"I'm afraid I have to get back to my desk." Her voice wavered. "Perhaps you can try to phone the office next week? You have a good day."

He watched her walk away, her legs moving stiffly, large calves flexing and releasing as her sharp-heeled shoes clacked upon the floor. A run in her stocking stretched down behind her knee toward her ankle.

He went to the office door and paused there, looked over the front desk to the women working behind the partition and arranged in parallel lines. No woman seemed more than twenty-one or twenty-two. They had either platinum or dirty blond hair. And they were beautiful, a mirror image of one another: startlingly vibrant in the same fluorescent glare that made him look gaunt and emaciated. They kept their posture aligned with the backs of the wooden chairs, some of them with unblinking eyes scanning the documents they worked to transcribe with an effortless determination, others with phones cradled against their slender necks, stained lips forming words that were lost in the thrum of the office but that seemed to him precise and well rehearsed through repetition. For a moment he saw Sheila there, auburn head bent slightly, listening to her Dictaphone, then glancing up to look at the women around her. To have worked here she would have been dying inside; the Sheila he knew would have hated this place and these people. Not one of them looked up at him as he opened the door and let it close behind him.

IN THE BATHROOM off the State House lobby, Dante stood at one of the porcelain sinks, polished and glimmering white, and ran his hands under the cold water, bent and splashed handfuls of it into his face. When he could no longer feel his hands, he shut off the faucet. Imprints of flames hung behind his eyes, fanned out and disappeared when he opened them. He dried his face and hands with paper towels and looked at himself in the mirror. In the glare of the light above, his features were pitted and stark, even more emaciated than usual, like something carved from shadow and bone. He hacked and spat into the sink, combed his hair with his fingers.

The main lobby bustled with people bundled in heavy jackets and scarves and hats, and as he attempted to weave through those coming and going, he bumped shoulders with a short, brown-suited man. The man glared at him, and then two women were pushing before him and he was caught in the current sweeping toward the doors. With a sudden surge of panic he pulled himself from the mass of bodies and stood for a moment by the glass windows, waiting for the crowd to dwindle and wondering what to do next. Outside on the street new snow was falling and the winds swept it up off the stairs and the sidewalk in a flurry. He turned back to the lobby and to a vendor who sat on a crate behind a small display of newspapers, candies, cigarettes, and several plastic buckets containing ratty-looking bouquets of flowers.

"*Globe*, please."

The vendor seemed amused by the sight of Dante; a smirk creased his lips, and Dante tried to ignore it. He reached into his pockets for change but had difficulty even with that, and the vendor shook his head. "This weather is for the birds," Dante said, in the hope that he might appear more normal.

Dante shuffled to an empty wooden bench. A security guard with a boozy, heavily veined nose and plum-colored cheeks glared at him as he sat down. Dante did his best to ignore him even though he could feel the man's bloodshot eyes examining him in the same way an ill-tempered drunk sizes up a man before a fight in a bar.

Dante's eyes moved through the front pages of the *Globe*. He saw the headlines but couldn't distinguish any of the words below the bold print. He squinted, but still everything appeared blurred and out of focus. There was a story about the Brink's job, another about the failures of utility companies, the race for the empty Senate seat, and the rise in fatalities due to the worst winter in history. He tried to read the sports page, but all he could think of was getting another fix, how he would make things up with Karl, how he would apologize and then beg and plead with him if necessary.

The sound of a woman's heels came to him across the polished stone floor and echoing up to the vast arched ceiling, and for a moment everything else within the wide lobby disappeared inside a vacuum.

He looked up. The brunette from the office, the one with the bright makeup and the run in her stocking, stood before him. She wore a lilac coat and matching beret that hung over her right ear, slightly askew. She was chewing gum, and her wide jawline pulsed sharply with each movement as she went at the gum. "Why were you asking about Sheila Anderson?"

"It's a bit of a private matter."

"I knew her a little. Not like close friends or anything, but we talked about things sometimes. I don't know if it would help you any."

Dante stumbled for words, folded the newspaper and placed it down on the bench, and stood. "Could I ask you a few questions? If you don't mind."

She grinned, snapping the chewing gum with her back teeth and exposing the glistening pink of her tongue. "I'd be happy to. But I'm as hungry as a wolf. Why don't you be a gentleman and take me to lunch."

She had her hand extended. He reached out and grabbed hold and shook it gently. He turned to the security guard, who was still watching him, and suddenly felt the urge to leave.

"Pamela Grubb," she exclaimed as if he should already know her name, as if she were a person far more important than she really was.

"Dante Cooper."

And as they walked back across the lobby, without his offering, she put her arm through his, turned her face up toward him, and smiled. At the exit, a young doorman opened the door for them and smirked, and once again, a sudden anxiety overcame him. He closed his eyes, focused on the pressure of the woman's arm in his. Outside on the sidewalk the cold air forced him to breathe naturally again. He raised his arm for a cab and was surprised when it turned toward the curb, slowing down and stopping before them.

"Are you a cop?" she asked, looking at him intently. Again, she was smiling.

He shook his head. "Not a cop. Just a relative."

"Well, that's good. My father was a cop, you know..." He stepped toward the cab, held the door open for her. She'd already started in with her life story, where she'd grown up and how her father had treated her and her mother, and Dante put on the vacant grin he gave to people who talked too much, and although she continued to talk throughout the short cab ride, he was thinking of Karl again and of getting another fix and, until they arrived in the Theater District, he didn't hear a word.

31

POOR CLARE SISTERS, FRANCISCAN MONASTERY OF SAINT CLARE, JAMAICA
PLAIN

THE MONASTERY OF Saint Clare faced Centre Street, on which, after the
recent snow, few cars traveled. A city plow growled past him, and Cal had
to veer at the monastery entrance as sand, salt, and gravel thumped and
banged against the sides of the car. He sat for a moment in the circular
driveway and looked at himself in the rearview mirror, saw that his eyes
were red-rimmed and glassy. He got out of the car and closed the door.
He turned up his collar, instinctively blessed himself as he limped through
the entrance.

The gardens were covered in snow—a curving hillside of sweeping,
glistening white. A column of sisters, dark shapes pressed black against
the snow, trudged the far rise into the woods, and their soft chorus—a
working prayer song—came to him across the field.

There were two three-story brick wings flanking the main entrance,
and Cal looked up at their small windows in which lights blazed behind
drawn curtains, and that offered a sense of warmth. A sister, bundled in

a heavy brown overcoat reminiscent of a soldier's field coat and shoveling the walkway, looked up as he approached. Another nun was spreading cinders from a bucket onto the steps.

"Hello, Sisters," he called as he climbed the steps to the door. "Good day for the work."

They smiled approvingly. "Thank God," they chorused. "Bless the work."

Beneath a Romanesque arch the door was wide-planked oak with heavy iron hinges and riveted crossbanding. The doorknocker was a bull's iron nose ring, cold to his hand, and when he let it fall, it reverberated like a hammer in the hallway beyond. He let it fall twice more and, after a moment, heard footsteps upon tile.

The sister who answered the door had quizzical eyes and rotund bright cheeks in a soft, pale face. A tawny patina of reflected light shimmered about her as if the hallway beyond were made of honeycombs.

"I'm here to see Sister Bridget."

She motioned for him to step into the vestibule and said, "Wait here, please." He considered the broadness of her, imagined the heft of her thick calves beneath her habit, not a city girl but a farmer's daughter reared on the prairie or plain, used to rising at dawn and working until the light faded from the sky. He stared after her wide hips for a moment and then glanced about the room.

In the sister's absence the sounds and smells of the place brought warmth and a sense of peace: the muted hum of prayer and chanting, the smell of Styrax, sandalwood, beeswax, and polished wood, the light ashy dust of smoke still in the air from extinguished candles and incense, almost as if the priest had passed through the hall with a censer; on the wall to his right the pictures of the saints and priests of the order, the Blessing of Saint Clare: *May Almighty God bless you. May He look upon you with the eyes of His mercy, and give you His peace. May He pour forth His graces on you abundantly, and in Heaven may He place you among His Saints.*

Cal blessed himself again, stared at his knuckles, red and cracked and swollen, and then Sister Bridget was approaching him from the other end

183

of the hallway, smiling in that way that was at once filled with surprise and sincerity, a happiness in simply greeting the world and all that it had to offer. She was as he remembered her. She greeted him warmly, taking both his hands in her own small, misshapen ones, and then gestured toward a chair in a sitting room directly off the hallway. He waited until she'd settled herself opposite and then sat slowly, extended his bad leg out before him, and placed his hat in his lap.

She laughed slightly. "I remember," she said, and brought a small hand, gnarled by arthritis, to her mouth. "The first moment seeing you just now, how you, Dante Cooper, and the Mulligan twins were the bane of my existence, God help me. I spent many hours praying for patience."

He smiled and shook his head. "I don't know how you managed it, Sister Bridget. We were hell on two feet. I think God must have a special place reserved for you in heaven for how you put up with us."

"We shall see, we shall see." She grinned. "Hopefully at the end I will have done more good than bad. Now, come, on the phone you said this was an urgent family matter and that Father Nolan directed you to us?"

"Yes." He nodded, tapped his fingers on the top of his hat. "It's about Sheila Anderson."

"Sheila Anderson?"

"I understood you taught her at Saint Mark's?"

"If you don't mind my asking, what is your interest, Mr. O'Brien?"

"She was a good friend of mine."

She hesitated; confusion flickered in her eyes. "Why, yes, many of the sisters taught Sheila, but I'm afraid I don't understand. You said 'was'?"

"Sheila is dead, Sister. She was killed about a week ago. I'm sorry, I thought you would have heard."

Sister Bridget's eyes widened, and though she tried to hide it, she seemed visibly shaken. She sank down into the chair, clasped her hands together on her lap.

"How well did you know Sheila?"

She blinked at him. "I remember her as a younger woman, a sweet girl, but troubled.

"A troubled girl," she repeated. It seemed that she couldn't hide her discomfort. Cal eased forward off his chair. "Are you okay, Sister? Do you want me to go get you a glass of water?"

She raised a hand. "No, I'll be fine."

She lifted her eyes to his. "She came to us in labor last month, and was already heavily medicated. It was a difficult situation. Terrible, actually. She was lucky to survive."

"Really? I'm afraid I didn't know that."

"We do what we can here, and the rest is in God's hands. I don't feel comfortable saying any more, Mr. O'Brien. I'm sure you understand."

"Yes, Sister, I do. But the thing is, she was killed, brutally killed. It might have had something to do with this birth."

"Birth? Oh, you're mistaken, Mr. O'Brien. There was no actual birth. The child was stillborn."

"Stillborn? Where did they bury it?"

"Why, out back, in the children's graveyard. I can take you there, if you like, and show you."

"If that's all right, Sister. I'd like to see."

"Of course. I think the fresh air will do me some good."

They walked through the main house and into a scullery, where Sister Bridget took a heavy coat from a coatrack. Cal held it for her and she worked her thin arms shakily into its bulk. A clatter of cutlery and plates came to them from the kitchen. Warm, food-scented steam fogged the glass.

"Take my hand," Sister Bridget said. "My legs aren't as strong as they once were."

"I hear you, Sister." Her birdlike hand grasped at his forearm and exerted such a powerful pressure on his arm that it surprised him. He smiled and placed his own hand over hers.

A loggia in the rear formed a protected walkway, and they followed this between the buildings. Cal looked out over the shoveled pathways and the snow-covered gardens to the ice-topped statues of the Blessed Mother and Child, Saint Anthony, Saint Francis, and Saint Clare.

They stepped into a sheltered cloister with open archways looking out onto a courtyard. Small snowdrifts had accumulated beneath the windows and arches, and though it was cold, Cal was glad for the momentary reprieve from the wind. As they crossed the courtyard, Cal looked back at the building. Lights were blazing in windows here and there and the sky above formed a low vault of dark cloud.

They passed a stone chapel, where amber light glimmered diffuse and warm through the mullioned windows. The haunted chanting of the Divine Office came to them, the wind taking the sound and whipping it back and forth across the courtyard so that it might have come from miles away. A bell tolled from somewhere in the arbor. Although he held her by the hand, it seemed as if she was the one urging him on, insistently, as if he were a recalcitrant child being forcibly led by a parent.

Rock salt crunched beneath their shoes as they walked the stone pathway. Sister Bridget nodded to novitiates and other, older sisters, making their way to the main house or to the chapel.

"I seem to remember an incident," Sister Bridget said after a moment, and a smile touched the edge of her lips, "where you and your friend there, Dante, were responsible for looting the church poor box?"

Cal smiled, thankful for the levity, and shook his head. Sister Bridget squeezed his arm. "No? That's not true?"

"It was the Kinneally brothers who looted the poor box."

"Ahh, and you were their accomplices then?"

"We were witnesses."

"Oh, yes, is that how it was, Mr. O'Brien?"

They passed beneath a stone arch and stepped into the cloistered space of a small graveyard enclosed by a crumbling low wall and by the overhanging boughs of trees, black and bare of leaves. Beyond, the grounds sloped in a sheet of pewter ice toward the dense, wooded lands of the Forest Hills arboretum. Here the wind stilled, and he was keenly aware of their breathing, the long, tired wheeze that came from their lungs, aching from the sharp, cold air. Perhaps two dozen rows of small graves in uneven, staggered lines lay before them. Sister Bridget led him between the rows, stumbling every now and again as she sank into the snow, then righted by Cal's grip on her hand.

"Well, here we are," she said. Her hand squeezed him once again with surprising strength and then let go.

Cal stared at a mound of raised snow and at a small black marble headstone, a white onyx centerpiece in the shape of a cherub with wings. Even with the snow dusting its top, the cuts in the black marble glittered, its surface shone as if lacquered. The child had no name, nor were there the names of loved ones, merely:

Returned to His Loving Care
January 15, 1951

"There's a headstone on the grave already, Sister? It's barely been a month."

Sister Bridget stared at the headstone, bowed her head, and clasped her hands together at her chest. A blackbird cawed in the trees at the wall edge then lifted into the air, causing them both to look up, startled. Heavy snow cascaded down from the branches and thumped the ground. He looked at Sister Bridget's face. She appeared to have aged slightly, as if the walk here had taken its toll on her.

"Why would you rush to put up a headstone?" He glanced about the graveyard, at the empty spaces between the rows of crumbling gravestones and upon bare, snowy mounds where lay a child's doll, an infant's rattle, fresh garlands and wreaths.

"If you don't mind me asking, but who donated the headstone? I think her family would want to know, to thank her benefactor."

"Why, I believe it was Congressman Foley. He has been incredibly charitable to many of the unfortunates from the neighborhood. He's always provided us with funds, has for years. Thank God for him and his kind."

Sister Bridget continued to stare at the grave, her lips pursed. "This child's headstone isn't the first he's contributed to."

Cal looked about the graveyard again. "Unfortunates? Is that what Sheila was?"

"Sheila's life story, her upbringing, as I'm sure you know, was terribly unfortunate. It shaped her life, the paths she took, the choices she made. Sometimes I think that she was determined to fulfill that destiny, that she was hell-bent, if you'll excuse the phrase, on coming to a bad end."

He nodded, rolled his shoulders to bring some life back into them. The cold was getting to him, and there was nothing else to do here. New snow spun down around them, and when he looked up, the sky had darkened to the same gray of the stone walls, the undulating hard-packed ice of the surrounding fields, the older headstones. A snowstorm was swirling in the low, dense clouds, and he wondered how long it would hold off.

"C'mon, Sister," he said. "Give me your hand. I've kept you out in this long enough." She reached for him gratefully; they remained quiet and pensive on the walk back to the convent.

The scullery was warm and welcoming, but Sister Bridget kept her coat on as they passed through the house. Everything seemed as it had been before, but he knew that something had changed for her at the graveyard.

At the door he sighed before giving her an appreciative nod. "Well, thank you, Sister, thank you for your time. I'll pass all this on to her family, and our thanks to Congressman Foley."

"Yes, he has done so many wonderful things for us, for the parish and all its constituents."

"Just like Mayor Curley, back in the old days."

"Yes, I suppose you could say that. They both came from hard backgrounds, hard neighborhoods, good working-class people. Please offer Sheila's family our condolences. We'll pray for her and for them."

Cal turned to her as he stepped out of the convent. "Exactly what happened to the child, Sister? At the end—you said it was stillborn?"

Sister Bridget stared at him from the darkness of the vestibule. She appeared a small, fragile-looking thing now, a dark shape all the smaller, furtive and lost in the shadows. Heavy footsteps padded on the landing above the staircase, and the balustrade shuddered. Sister Bridget moved forward, out of the vestibule. The starkness of her face, the prominent bone of her cheeks, was shocking. The light had gone out of her eyes, and he realized how old and sick she truly was.

"The child, Mr. O'Brien," she said, "is in a better place now, and that is all that matters," and then pushed the door closed.

32

BLEARY-EYED AND disoriented, Dante stared up at the high tin ceilings of Jacob Wirth's and at the numerous steel fans rotating there. The smoke-yellowed tin seemed to be lowering onto him, like one of those funhouse rides, the Shrinking Room, which made you feel that if you didn't run fast enough, you'd be crushed and snapped in two, pulverized bone and gore left behind for some sap to scrape up. Since they'd arrived for lunch, the woman sitting across from him hadn't stopped. When she wasn't chewing, she was talking aimlessly about best-selling books, movies and their stars. How *Point of No Return* and *The Egyptian* were downright bores and took her months to finish. How Bogart's character in *In a Lonely Place* turned her stomach; how *All About Eve* was a hands-down masterpiece, and if she ever wrote a script, it would be penned just like it; how unbelievable and ridiculous and juvenile *Rocketship X-M* was, and how the man who took her to see it, well, she'd never accept another one of his invitations.

"Mr. Cooper, are you sure you're okay?"

He gave her a slight grin. "I'm fine, Miss Grubb. Guess my appetite isn't quite as sharp as yours today."

On her plate was a fat Reuben: thick black bread glistening with a swath of melted butter, folds of maroon marbled meat hanging thickly out of its sides. He'd suggested a quiet bar off of Boylston, but Miss Grubb had coaxed him to this place because it had her favorite sandwich, one in which she indulged once a week. As she began to eat, he had to look away. He took a slow sip of his beer, placed the mug back down, and then licked at the foam across his upper lip.

"I told you already, don't be so formal. Please call me Pam."

Dante kept his eyes off her as she took another bite, stared at the curls and wind gusts nature had designed within the grain of the table.

"You're missing out by not ordering one of these," she continued. "Just the proper amount of dressing, and the rye toasted perfectly."

He turned and scanned the room at eye level, and immediately the same sense of vertigo pulled horizontally and teased his eyes. Off to his left, the long bar was shoulder to shoulder with people, still wearing their coats and jackets, stretching their lunch hour into two. Hazy, threaded smoke twined in the air above them. Most of the men at the bar appeared to be Dante's age or a bit older, and from a distance he could tell that many of them showed signs of too much drink and a weariness in their eyes that made them glisten as if made of glass. But at least they seemed happy, Dante thought, or at least they pretended to be.

"You have the same last name as him, maybe that's why," she said.

He attempted a smile and nodded, even though he had no idea what she was talking about.

"Are you sure you don't mind it here?" She took a napkin to the corners of her mouth, an inquiring look in her brown eyes.

"I'm more than fine, thank you."

"So, back to my question that you're evading: Is there any relation to him?" She looked down at her plate, not eyeing him, perhaps playing some manner of game.

"I'm afraid I lost you there."

"Gary Cooper." She laughed. "I was asking if you're in any way related to him."

Realizing he was slumping, he shifted in his seat, straightened his spine against the hard wooden back. "Excuse me?"

"No kidding, you look like him. No one has ever told you that?"

"Not that I remember."

Her cheeks reddened, and she laughed without offering him the punch line. Is this the way it was with women these days? He had no idea why she would be laughing. Was she merely insecure, or did she find him funny-looking?

"Really, if you put on some healthy weight, washed your hair, and got your proper sleep, I'm sure you'd hear such a compliment much more frequently."

Her lips tightened as if she'd just realized she had offended him, but it didn't seem to stick, for she carried on again, sinking her teeth into the sandwich, chewing for a bit, and then talking around the food in her mouth.

"I adored him in *Ball of Fire,* you know. I'm not that keen on Barbara Stanwyck, a bit too risqué, but Gary Cooper, he's a swoon, I tell you. His eyes are so sad. I think that's what gives him away. Like yours, Dante, such sad, sad eyes."

"Sad eyes, is that right?" He'd heard it before, many times before—from his mother, his aunts, Margo, even Sheila—as if one look at him and they knew that he was suffering, even if he wasn't.

"I don't mean anything by it. Some people have bedroom eyes, fiery eyes, rat eyes...yours are just a bit, you know, weary and pained."

"I'm okay with it," he said.

"You look offended. Are you?"

"Not a bit, not one bit," he lied. "Mind if I smoke?"

"I do mind, actually. I'm filling up so a few more bites. Cigarettes while I'm eating kind of ruins a meal." She feigned a sophisticated air, even went so far as to tilt back her head and show him her upturned nose. He wondered if she knew how much of a fool she was acting.

After he pulled off three mouthfuls from his beer, his eyes steadied and he gave her a closer look-over: thirty-odd years old, a bit full in the face with a fine long nose and thin but nicely shaped lips, brown hair conventionally styled over a lofty domed forehead. From her shapeless office suit came the cloying scent of lavender; whenever she moved, tossed her hair, or returned her food to the plate he could smell it. She wanted to be more than merely a townie, with her antique pin tacked onto her lapel and the affected accent that she slipped in and out of.

She pushed her plate forward an inch, signaling she was done, dabbed at her lips, and laid the crumpled and soiled napkin at the side of her plate. Dante lit his cigarette. When she offered her hand for one, he hesitated, but only for a moment. She placed it in her mouth and leaned over the table toward him. He stared at the cigarette propped like a set piece between her lips, and took his time bringing the lighter to it, watched as she puffed to keep the tip lit and then as she pretended to relish the smoke.

"You weren't all that close with Sheila, were you?" he said.

"No, not really, but we did chat every now and then. I don't think she liked me much. But then that's the way it is with all the other girls. Maybe it's just because I'm a bit older than them." She smiled for no apparent reason, exposing a sharp tooth under a curved pink upper lip.

"She didn't work in the office for very long?"

"Only for two months. Not even that long."

"Last spring?"

"February, March, I think."

"What did she do for the office?"

"What we all do there. Lots of filing, answering phones, meeting and greeting, taking notes. Basic office work. And even though it's not rocket science, she didn't do too well at it."

"Did you know her outside the office, ever go out for lunch or drinks?"

"A group of girls used to go out sometimes after work. Sometimes I'd tag along. Like I said, the young girls often feel threatened by me, so you couldn't say I was part of their circle or anything."

"Was Sheila?"

"I'm sorry?"

"Was she part of their circle? Did she have friends among the other girls?"

"No, she pretty much kept to herself. I always thought she preferred the company of men anyways."

"Why was that?"

She shrugged. "Just by the attention she received."

"Do you know about any men in particular?"

She reached across the table for her glass of wine, put it to her lips delicately but took a big swallow from it as if it were a beer. "I guess a girl like that has many suitors, Mr. Cooper. Gets tough to decide which one is best when there's so many offering up their hearts and wallets to a girl."

He ground his cigarette into the ashtray, then lit another. "She used to go on and on about Bobby Renza. And another guy named Mario. I think she had a thing for the both of them."

The name Bobby Renza caught Dante off guard; he felt his lungs tighten, and a sudden sweat gathered on his forehead. He reached for his beer with a shaking hand, took a generous pull off it.

"Why is that first name familiar?" he asked, feigning nonchalance.

"Don't you listen to the radio?"

"Of course I do. He's a singer, yeah?" Dante flicked the long head of his cigarette into the ashtray.

"He *was* a singer. He had a big hit a couple years ago with 'Let's Fly Away.' Kind of a local hero when his song went high up on the charts. But the way I heard Sheila talking about him, he was working at a photo shop in the North End, doing pictures of weddings, communions, that kind of thing. Can you imagine?"

Dante vaguely remembered the song—a pop tune that radios played in the summer months, and he knew it was something he and Margo would never have paid attention to. Every major city had one Renza, local talent with a bit of gold in their tonsils, attempting to be the next Frank Sinatra, Alan Dale, Mel Tormé, or even Gene Lindell. They all flamed briefly and then faded away. This Renza was the same slick asshole on the Common, the same man at the Pacific Club when he saw her last.

"Yeah, the song," he said, and she pinned on it quickly and began singing. "Let's fly away, and find a land…"

It was a voice meant for the back row of a choir, and he couldn't have been more embarrassed for her. The waitress with pale blue eyes turned from a table to look at them, paused with her weight on one hip, accentuating its sharp angle, and smiled at Dante, almost in a sympathetic manner. When Miss Grubb had sung the refrain, he gave her a grin to appease her, hoping she'd stop, but she continued humming the rest.

"Sorry about that," she said before taking a quick sip of water.

"No problem. We all sound better in the shower sometimes."

She laughed. Color flushed her face.

"So did Sheila and Renza last long? Did she talk much about it?"

"Not much to me. Mostly to the other girls. As far as I know, she was with him the couple of months she worked there."

"So like a boyfriend, not just a tryst."

"That's right."

"What happened to this other guy? What's his deal?"

"Mario? She was always talking about him. I don't know how she had time for it with everything else." She waved her hand dramatically.

"Just Mario, no other name?"

"Just Mario."

"And you never set eyes on either guy?"

"Neither ever came to the office, so, no, I never did." She took another swig of the wine. "Aren't you family…shouldn't you know these things about her?"

"We haven't seen each other in some time, that's all."

A sudden shrieking filled the room, a woman's high-pitched laughter ringing in the air like some wild animal's call, and they both glanced toward the bar. A woman, flushed-cheeked and inebriated, was laughing at something the man sitting next to her had said. When the laughing subsided, she began to snort, pressing a hand to her chest as if to quell the pressure, and the man next to her laughing as well and shaking his head at the noises she was making.

"You mentioned that she seemed to like the company of men. Did she have any suitors within the State House?"

Miss Grubb's lips became rigid and her eyes widened, pulsing with anticipation. He had struck a nerve.

"I've been in this office the longest, and I know to refrain from mixing business and pleasure, but these young pretty faces don't see it that way. They become impressed that somebody from the top compliments them, remembers their names and so on. The big sin is these men are married, and the sadder thing is that these women don't even care. It truly is improper, don't you think?"

Dante nodded.

"She got flowers, and I mean every day of the week, Monday through Friday. Not your everyday bouquet, either."

"So they weren't from the old Greek hawking daisies outside Park Street Station?"

"Ha! They certainly were not. These flowers cost a pretty penny."

"Any other girls get such attention?"

"New women come and go, come and go. This is a farm for bigger and better things. It's a stepping-stone, and because I've been here the longest, I feel like the caretaker. Or one of the stones." She sighed, laughed to herself. "And yes, I can tell there's lots going on there that shouldn't be."

She had her napkin in her hand and was wringing it, but he couldn't be sure it wasn't an act. Her eyes widened, and her demeanor vibrated with the type of excitement that moves through a circle of women gossiping. She bit down on her bottom lip, leaned over the table, and gestured for him to come closer.

When he leaned in, he could smell the wine on her breath, the grease of corned beef and sauerkraut. "Sometimes I'd think of it as a meat market instead of a State House office," she said and began to talk about Senator Gibbons, State Reps. McGhee, Tobin, and Hillsdale, Congressman Graziano, Councilmen Tupper and Millen—matching those names with women's names he knew nothing of. Dante took it all in, finished his beer, and ordered them another round. After she'd listed the names, she gave him the tawdry morsels of rumor that she heard in the lunchroom, the bathroom, and in passing through the State House hallways. By the time Miss Grubb was done talking, they'd finished their second round of drinks. Her eyes shone as if she were in the grip of a fever, perhaps guilty excitement. Maybe she realized how drunk she was getting, and that she was telling too much. But Dante knew she wasn't through yet.

"You've saved the best for last," he said without emotion.

She grinned widely, teeth stained purple by wine. "Yes," she said. "The best."

"So, what is it?"

"Foley," she said, "Congressman Foley. It's the reason she had to leave, and, of course, because everyone knew." She pulled at her napkin, leaving little bits of it on the table.

He had to look away from her, and for a moment stared about the room. Michael Foley and Sheila. Congressman Michael Foley and Sheila. It was hard to imagine. He clenched the cigarette and it broke in his hands. He looked down and saw the tobacco clinging to his moist skin.

"Once Congressman Foley entered the scene, she only had time for him. And not too soon after is when she left the office. And to think, Congressman Foley had a wife at home whom he loved."

"'Loved'... is that right?" he asked, mockingly.

"She," she said, hissing the word so that Dante knew she meant Sheila, and paused, "was merely a plaything. It would never have been love." She shook her head. "Never."

"She wasn't a whore," he said louder than he wanted to.

"But I wouldn't call her an angel," quipped Miss Grubb, unwilling to relent even as she sat farther back in her chair, her smile fading.

"The way you're telling it, she was a girl who'd be foolish enough to fuck a guy for flowers. She wasn't a slut and she wasn't stupid. She knew how life worked, knew how to avoid messes like that." He pushed back as if to leave, knowing that what he'd said didn't ring true to the woman.

Her shoulders stiffened and she shifted in the chair. Her eyes left his and stared over at the crowded bar. "Really, Mr. Cooper, I'm just telling you what I heard. I thought that's what happens in these situations."

"This isn't a goddamn movie."

She looked back and a gleam had returned to her eyes; it was as if she hadn't even heard him. "She's in trouble, isn't she? That's why you're here, that's why you want to know so much about her private life."

"She's dead," he said, and waited until she looked away, pale and unsure of herself. He twisted on the seat and then reached into his pocket and pulled out some crumpled-up bills. He spread one out and ironed it flat with his hand. Just a dollar. The next bill was a five. All he had left. He pushed the five into the middle of the table, crumpled the dollar bill up again, and shoved it in his pocket. "I'm glad you enjoyed the sandwich. Let me hail you a cab back to the office."

As he passed through the smoke and the crowd beneath it, he tried to calm himself, but the bad taste in his mouth intensified.

In the foyer, as he helped her put on her coat, she turned and said, "Dante, thank you for lunch. I'd like to do it again sometime. I'm—I'm sorry, sorry for Sheila, for your loss. If I hear anything, anything at all, I'll let you know."

He saw a fragile, broken expression on her face, and it deepened into self-pity as they stepped outside into the cold of Stuart Street. He hailed a taxi, opened the door for her when it pulled up to the curb. Before he closed it, she leaned across the seat and craned her head toward him, put on a smile that reminded him of his sister Claudia when she tried to show that she was happy when obviously she wasn't. She waited for him to say something, maybe to apologize for getting red moments before, maybe wanting him to ask her out, but he nodded, said, "Good day," closed the door, and turned his back to her.

33

ON THE SIDEWALK, a sudden harsh wind pulled at him, stirring the frustration in him and making him feel like he'd just stepped out of the confessional booth with even more sins clawing at his back. Sheila and Congressman Foley—the politician type that Moody had mentioned. He reminded himself not to take it for truth, for Miss Grubb was just a misfit on a soapbox, that's all she was. A bitter crank.

He tried clearing his mind, but everything faded into the emptiness he understood so well, and all he could do was take those familiar well-worn steps back in time and think of Margo waiting for him to score, her lying on their bed and suddenly alert like a cat ready to be fed when he opened the door, and them exchanging looks, the kind only a junkie would understand, and her clapping her hands like a child. "I can always count on my man, the love of my life."

He tried to pull himself out of the past, watched the wind carry debris through the Theater District. Anger coursed through his veins like broken glass, and he wished that the desperation that followed him wherever he went would subside and break for just a moment.

He needed a reprieve, a way to let it go. He moved in against the shelter of the building, lit a cigarette, and the cold air bit at the exposed skin of his face and his hands so that he felt he could barely breathe. Scarletti was the Butcher, had killed Sheila and the other women, but how did Blackie figure in; or was it, like Owen said, just a coincidence? And Renza, the flash-in-the-pan crooner dating Sheila—where did he figure in to her life before she was killed? Dante imagined the photo shop he had worked at, a front for selling dirty fuck pictures to smut magazines, and he saw Bobby behind the camera, framing Sheila's large breasts, her wide-spread legs, her vacant stare. He thought of the picture he'd found at the Somerville apartment, the one inscribed *"My Only Pin-Up, Mario."* A ripe fucking mess, he thought—and now Sheila linked up with the would-be senator from Massachusetts, Michael Foley, who'd grown up with him and Cal, and who was brother to Blackie Foley. Just a fucking no-good mess.

Sheila's life had been wrapped in all manner of deceits that even he couldn't have guessed at, but did any of it have anything to do with her murder? Her death could truly have been the random act of a psychopath.

He knew he had to do something other than stand out in the cold, thinking about all the men, all the relationships that Sheila had been in. He turned away from the wind, felt an aimless panic pull at him, one that only a visit to Karl could help quiet.

Taxis passed him by, and the urge to wave one down persisted, but he realized he had only a dollar to his name. That wouldn't cover the ride to Cambridge, and if he managed to get there, Karl would only laugh in his face—"I told you you'd be back"—and laugh even harder when Dante asked if he could score and pay him back later.

He walked up to a phone booth, opened the door. Its rusted hinges creaked loudly, and he stepped inside. The wired glass around him was cracked weblike, and the cloying stench of piss and beer overpowered his senses. He felt he should call Cal, let him know how fucked up things were getting. He rifled through his pants pockets, and then the pockets of his coat. There wasn't any change, just the dollar bill he'd crumpled earlier. He picked up the receiver, and the silence of a dead line pressed against his ear. He slammed the receiver against the box and kicked at the bottom panel of glass until it too cracked in a fractured web.

34

DANTE HAD KNOWN Jill years before and had searched her out first, surprised that she was even alive let alone still on the streets. She still used but told him she took it slow, that it wasn't as bad as it had once been, and besides, she'd seen too many friends die. Now she did it to get by, but she knew the difference between that and getting lost. Like a lot of other girls, she'd once worked for Shea Mack, but he'd cut her years before and had no use for her now—he liked his girls young and unmarked.

She told him of dancing at the old clubs in New York City back during Prohibition. How she'd sucked off Frank Sinatra in a restaurant bathroom just before he hit it big. And how all the men from Manhattan to Boston treated her like a queen—jewelry, fancy dinners, silk gowns, the works.

"That's all gone," she said to Dante, who stood there eyeing a pack of four girls across the street. "That's all gone to shit. No respect these days for an old-timer like myself. Men now think of me as a joke—and if they want some, they ask me to do things I'd never think of doing. Stuff that

202

shouldn't be done between a man and a woman, not ever. Like I was some animal, some pot to piss in."

Dante nodded, half listening to her, turned and looked at her, and tried to smile. "Maybe it's time to hang it all up."

"I still got some left, you know," and the strength of her voice wavered and then cracked, as if she knew she was kidding herself. She wore far too much makeup, and it made her appear clownish and crazed-looking. Her age showed in the loose and lined skin of her neck, and even despite her heavy jacket, Dante could see the bulge of her breasts hanging low at her wide waistline. "I try to be a mother to the new girls, give them advice that'll help them survive the right way, but they won't give it much thought, just carry on for themselves as if there's not a danger in the world. If only they seen what I seen, they'd wise the fuck up." She had a voice like gravel being tramped on by horseshoes.

He showed her the picture, the one from his wedding that he'd torn down the middle so that only Sheila showed in her silky gown and part of Margo's arm, but she shook her head. "Pretty," Jill said approvingly. "That's some dress. If I had a dress like that you wouldn't see me out here in the cold. 'Course she's got the body to go with it, too. Not too many girls could get away with a dress like that. I never seen her, though. Was she a hooker?"

"I don't know. I don't think so."

Jill raised an eyebrow. "You don't know much. I thought she was family?"

"She was."

"Yeah, well, that's okay. Family don't always know what's going on with each other. My mother thinks I work at Mass General as an X-ray technician."

"Where'd she get that idea?"

"I took a couple of courses." She shrugged. "I didn't finish the program."

"Maybe you'll go back?"

"Maybe. Yeah, that's what I'll do."

He described Scarletti to her and she nodded. "You've seen him?" he said, surprised.

"Yeah, yeah. Big guy, bigger than you say, but same all the rest. Saw him down by the markets right off Mass Ave. There's a diner there where the girls sometimes go late night. Sometimes they get lucky with the truckers who are about to hit the highway or the guys coming home from the bars and peep shows."

"You mean Mama's?"

"That's the place."

"How'd you know it was this guy?"

Jill took a long pull off her cigarette, her cheeks hollowed, and he waited.

"His mouth—he's got that harelip—and, well, the size of him. The size of him was enough to make you look twice, y'know, he takes off his jacket and sweater because it's hot in the place and he's got these massive arms. He was there for an hour or so chatting up the girls—the owner don't mind any at that time, mostly because she likes the business she gets from the truckers, so she don't stir it up none."

"Did any of the girls end up going with him?"

"Not that night, I don't think, but I got myself a date," and she winked, "so really, I don't know."

Under the light above the doorway, she stepped closer and looked at him. "You okay?"

"I'm fine. Why?"

"You're sweating like it's the Fourth of July. Could be that fever going around. I'd get on home if I were you."

He brought his hand to his face and forehead, felt the wetness there. His hair was drenched. It was as if he'd just put his head beneath a faucet. He closed his eyes and swayed, experiencing a sense of vertigo. When he looked at her again, she seemed somehow out of focus. Behind her the street stretched and narrowed, as if it were unraveling into the distance. Passing cars were blurs of color.

Jill touched his shoulder. "Honey," she said, "you're not right, and you're looking worse by the minute. Go get yourself home," and Dante nodded and turned back up the street, and with the world unraveling feverishly about him tried to focus on the pavement as he walked until, in a little bit, the need for a fix and the fever with all its desperate hunger had subsided.

35

SCOLLAY SQUARE, DOWNTOWN

DANTE SAT AT the kitchen table, allowing the smells of braised meat and onions to find their way into his senses dulled by coffee and cigarettes. He hadn't eaten anything since yesterday, and he sat and watched Claudia at the other end of the kitchen, wearing a starchy white apron over a dress that she had made herself. She chopped some parsley, filled a pot with water and placed it on the stove top, then opened the fridge, peering in, but, as if she had forgotten what she was looking for, closed the door and shuffled back over to the stove and turned on the gas to boil the water.

She was the furthest thing from their mother in the kitchen, fretful and manic, her hands fluttering about the counter and cabinets like crippled birds attempting flight, and at that moment, he thought that she was more like their father despite having the exterior, the dark southern Italian features, of their mother. And to make it all the more tough on herself, she'd chosen to cook them one of their mother's fa-

206

vorite dishes, *paccheri alla genovese,* a classic Neapolitan dish that had many components and took hours to stew. He had to remind himself not to be too hard on her, for in these rare moods when Claudia tried to do things for herself, and for him, he usually cut into her, whether deriding her or just playing with her as many older brothers did to their younger sisters. He didn't see how that would do any good, because with one sarcastic comment, no matter how playful, she'd return to her gloomy old self, and in the end accuse him of never thinking she could do anything right.

He sat at the kitchen table, his legs restless, moving from side to side and pumping in a clockwork piston-like motion, and lit another cigarette, cursed it for his throat was raw and sore. He turned down the radio so the voice of the newscaster became muffled and indistinct, and anxiously leaned back and looked out the window into the cold, empty darkness where the neighboring building appeared closer than it had in daylight.

After he'd left Washington Street and the few hookers lingering there, he had spent the afternoon trying to get some information on Bobby Renza, visiting some of the dancehalls and small clubs in and around Scollay Square and the North End. Some people remembered the name but shook their heads as if he were stirring up a curse, while some enthusiastically referred to Renza as "the Sicilian Swoon" and mentioned the song, "Let's Fly Away," that had given him a taste of fame. Either way, those who did remember him didn't have a bad thing to say about him, but to most, just like his tryst with fame, he was as elusive as he was forgotten.

One old man thought he had moved to Hollywood to make it big, and a middle-aged woman vacuuming the lobby at Storyville said that she'd heard he had died in a car accident after a show down in Orlando, Florida. A talkative old man who worked the ticket booth at a small cabaret club on Hanover Street, the Wild Ace, and who'd known Renza back in those days told him, "He was one of those kids that was good at everything, you know? A real good photographer, too. Got a picture in one of those glossy magazines, you know, *Life, Time,* I forget. He was a cocky bastard, that's for sure, but I felt kind of bad for him, falling off the charts so quickly. Too much drink probably put out his fire, or he knocked up the wrong woman and had to get the hell out of the city."

With nothing else to show for it, Dante spent part of the afternoon in a Copley Square pool hall, seeing if he noticed anybody from the scene who might be carrying, or might know of somebody carrying a score. And when that came up dry, he hung out in a few bars in the South End, down below street level, old speakeasies, basement taverns the size of a railcar with low ceilings and the pervasive tang of urine coming from the lone bathroom, chatting over a beer with some familiar, downtrodden people, and he could see in their faces that they were itching inside just like him. He had ended the afternoon at Collins Pub, a haven for the spent, hunched at a corner stool with his back to the door.

Now sitting at the kitchen table, Dante felt a sharp sense of failure overcome him. He wanted to prove to Cal, more than to himself, that he could get some information on his own. And he'd ended the day, just as he'd expected, with shit, with nothing. And that's because without Cal, he was no good, just no good at all.

Claudia wiped her hands on a dishtowel, walked over to the table, and smiled at him in that overexuberant, childlike way of hers. "Smells good, don't it?"

He forced a grin. "Just like Mom's."

Claudia twisted the knob on the radio until she found some big band number and turned up the volume.

As he watched her twiddle with the knob to get a better signal, the room spun beneath him. His left hand tightened with a strange numbness. Shaking, he put out his cigarette, flexed his hand until sensation came back into it.

"Why don't you do me a favor and open a bottle of wine?"

"Putting me to work now," he said as he moved beside Claudia and ground the corkscrew into the cork, and the same numb sensation gathered in his other hand. He managed to get the bottle open and pulled two glasses from the shelf. He removed the cork with ease and filled each halfway with red wine. And held the corkscrew, turning it against the light above him, imagining jabbing it into the palm of his hand and turning it through skin, flesh, and bone until he could feel again, even pain, just something.

Claudia had shut off the gas and drained the pasta. He returned to his seat and tried to swallow, tried to breathe and just appear normal.

Claudia laid down the plate, a steaming mass of stewed beef chuck, onions, carrots, and a thick, dark gravy spread over paccheri, large tubes of delicate pasta that she'd overcooked, so when he put his fork into it and stirred up the gravy, most of the pasta split apart in a soggy ruin. He leaned over the plate and, in an exaggerated way, sniffed at the steam rising from the food, and gave a pleased sigh, as if he were about to indulge in the best meal any kitchen or cook could offer. Claudia sat on the other side of the table and took a sip from her glass.

"For Mom," he said as he raised his own glass.

She nodded and her eyes appeared to glisten. "For Mom, and for you to get better."

They both bowed their heads, silently blessing their meals, the memory of their mother.

The dish was far too soupy, but after his first bite, he was surprised at how good it tasted. The next few mouthfuls, the stewed meat coming apart in his mouth steaming hot, he nodded toward his sister, who watched him eagerly. "Not bad, Claudia. Not bad at all."

She drank more from her glass. Her face blushed brightly and when she smiled, he saw her teeth were stained with the Chianti.

"I was thinking," she said, eyes widening, "maybe after dinner we can sit by the piano like we did when we were kids. Remember the holidays, all the cousins over and Mom at the table telling us what to play?"

"Maybe some other time."

"Why not tonight?"

He began to raise his hand and remind her what had been done to it years ago, but gripped the tablecloth instead.

"You can still play. It's just like riding a bike, you never forget."

"I said maybe some other time. Let's just eat, okay."

He began to sweat, not just a trickle, but beads moving down his brow with an acidic heat, making his temples glisten. He took a deep breath, dug his fork into the pasta, and ate another mouthful.

An old Gene Lindell song came on the radio. Its carefree refrain sounding much too loud and jubilant in their small, dimly lit kitchen.

"Did you ever hear of Bobby Renza, the singer?" he asked.

Claudia looked up from her meal, smiling at him, exposing her teeth stained with wine—an image that reminded him of Miss Grubb. "Of course I did. He was quite something, a real snake from what I hear. You know Sophie Martino? Lives in the North End."

He shook his head, poured more wine into their glasses.

"She used to date him. He was big then, just had that song become popular. I didn't know her too well or anything, but I worked with her cousin at Schrafft's—you wouldn't believe the things she'd tell us."

Claudia's smile faded. "Remember what Mom used to say about Sicilians?"

"That they had the worst tempers, and never to trust them."

"Well, he was Sicilian through and through, and he used to hit her. I guess real bad, too. Broke her nose and bruised her up. When he wasn't the sweet good-looking man wining and dining her, he was accusing her of all kinds of bad things."

"What made her finally leave him?"

"I guess when he put her in the hospital." Claudia chewed for a bit, swallowed, and added, "but later I remember hearing that she made it all up because he was carrying on with other women. Somebody even said she got so jealous, she threw herself down the stairs and said Bobby pushed her."

Dante took a sip of wine but it tasted bitter. His stomach gurgled and turned over.

"Does he have anything to do with Sheila, Dante?"

Dante looked at her.

"They printed her name in the paper just yesterday. She was the one they found on Tenean Beach last week. They all say the Butcher killed her."

He shook his head. "No, let's not talk about it."

Both of his hands went numb with the suddenness of a slammed door. A sharp pressure rang in his ears. His stomach turned and he caught a mouthful of vomit in his throat. He pressed his numb hand over his mouth, stood, and hurried to the bathroom. Slamming the door behind him, he fell to his knees and filled the toilet with bile, coffee, and what little of Claudia's meal he'd managed to get down. He flushed once, flushed twice, but still his body was heaving and there was no air left in his lungs, so that when his retching ended, he rolled to the floor and lay on his back, gasping.

He stared at the clawed, leonine feet of the white porcelain tub and began to feel his senses return to him—cold tile against his face, water dripping from the faucet into the sink, the muted trumpets of an old Glenn Miller number coming from the kitchen radio—and sensed that Claudia had opened the door and was there now, afraid to speak, watching him to make sure he was alive.

"I'll be okay, just a bug," he said as he got onto his knees, pulled himself up by the tub, and stood with his eyes shut, feeling the ground sway beneath him. Whatever was happening to him was far from over, he realized. His heart throbbed against his ribs, and it felt as if he were breathing his last breaths through a pinhole. He forced himself to the sink, turned on the cold water, splashed it over his face, taking it into his mouth and working it over his dried husk of a tongue. When he spat the water out, it turned the white sink a brackish brown.

"Are you sure you're okay?" Claudia asked at the doorway.

With a towel pressed to his mouth, he looked at her. He couldn't see her face, for it seemed distorted by shadow, and he couldn't tell if she was standing in the bathroom with him or was still in the hallway until he felt her touch his shoulder drenched with sweat.

"You're boiling over. Let me call a doctor."

He tried to speak but couldn't, and he bit down on his tongue, which swelled and choked him, blocking any air from getting in. His eyes rolled up into his skull and he fell back down to the tiled floor. As if from miles away, he heard his sister scream.

SHARP PAINS STABBED at Dante's gut, waking him, and he turned over the side of the bed and puked into the bucket Claudia had placed there. He looked about and it took him a moment to realize he was in his own bedroom. His mattress was soaked with sweat, and the radiator in the room pinged with pressure, hissing out slight drafts of steam. The thick curtains were drawn against the two windows, and he tried to figure out if it was day or night, and he wondered how long he'd been in the room. A half-full glass of water sat on the nightstand. He reached over and took it, raised it to his parched lips, drinking it all at once.

Dante lay back down in his own sweat and remembered glimpses of Claudia coming and going from his room without a word, leaving a baloney or turkey sandwich or a glass of water, and always locking the door behind her when she left, and he thought with a sense of shame of Claudia bringing him here to his room and pulling off his clothes and dousing him with cold water, trying to clean him because he'd shit himself, and getting him into clean clothes. And later, Claudia on her hands and knees cleaning the vomit from the floor.

A fucking mess, he thought. How lucky I am to still be alive.

He heard the doorknob rattling. The door opened and Claudia peeked into the room. Seeing him awake, she smiled halfheartedly and entered, walked to a kitchen chair she'd placed on the other side of the bed.

"The doctor says you'll be okay," she said. "You could have died, but you didn't."

"How long have I been like this?"

"Almost two days. You were real sick, then you slept." Claudia's eyes glistened with tears. "The doctor says you'll be okay," she repeated, bringing a hand to her mouth. "Cal stopped by to see how you were."

Dante felt tears of his own, and he reached out his hand, which Claudia grabbed tightly.

"I'm sorry," he said.

"You just need to get clean, that's all, then you'll be fine."

He tried to form words to console her, but couldn't. He gripped her hand even tighter, shut his eyes, and in the darkness saw the brief glimmers of fire flame before sleep pulled him under once again.

36

LOCKE-OBER, BOSTON

At white-clothed dinner tables before the mayor's podium sat various city officials: the chief of police, the fire marshal, businessmen, civic leaders, a rabbi, ministers, and Catholic clergy from Wards 8 and 9. Cal spotted Sister Bridget among a group of nuns from, he presumed, the Catholic charities in the city to which the congressman had been so kind. When she turned in Cal's direction, her face stiffened, but he couldn't be sure she'd seen him at all. She nodded at whatever the nun on her left was saying but otherwise glanced out at the vast ballroom, the lights from the chandelier glinting in her eyes. Some of the sisters chatted amiably, and now and again laughed. They appeared taken with the congenial, upbeat mood of the moment, and the drink and food and music were fast flowing, creating a contagion of goodwill and exuberance—all of it suggesting how the coming times might be, that things could only be looking up for Boston.

On the dance floor three couples held each other close in a slow dance, pink and blue globes of light swirling over the polished hardwood, and everything seemed to sway to the sounds of the Marv Reynolds Band. A small party of guests dressed in tuxedos sat at the bar and were attempting to sing over the music of the band, swaying, waiting for the bartender to take notice of them. It was the Boston College fight song, and Dante and Cal were forced to listen.

> *For Boston, for Boston,*
> *We sing our proud refrain!*
> *For Boston, for Boston,*
> *'Tis Wisdom's earthly fane.*
> *For here men are men*
> *And their hearts are true,*
> *And the towers on the Heights*
> *Reach to Heav'ns own blue.*
> *For Boston, for Boston,*
> *Till the echoes ring again!*

The men raised their voices as they approached the song's last refrain, and in response Cal banged the bar with his fist.

The lights came up a notch and then dimmed. Marv Reynolds signaled for the band to wind down the last song of the set as former mayor James Michael Curley crossed the stage parquet and stepped up to the podium. He was a short, bluff man who had once been in shape but now hefted a generous beer belly. A cigar smoldered in his right hand. He began talking before the band had completed its final song, so it was difficult to understand what he was saying, but Dante was quite sure he'd taken a poke at the Teamsters, his opponent in the upcoming mayoral race, and the Temperance League of Greater Boston. When he was done, he swept back his short arm and the stage spotlight fell on Congressman Foley. It followed him from his chair to the stage, where he shook hands with both the former and the current mayors and then stepped behind the podium. The crowd applauded and the congressman beamed a wide smile and raised a thankful hand to the audience, who eventually stilled. Dante looked to Cal and Cal raised his eyebrows.

"My friends, my fellow Bostonians," he said, and his voice carried throughout the room, a resonant baritone, his words perfectly paced and emphasized for effect. "Our city is at a grave crossroad, one where we find ourselves losing ground in manufacturing, medicine, and education— once the mainstays of this great commonwealth. We find ourselves beset and besieged by crime and vice. At night our streets are no longer safe to walk. During the day our parks are mostly empty. Our families—parents and their children, the rich future of our city—leave in droves, out to the suburbs or to other cities in other states, because they believe we have for- gotten them, that we have turned our backs, and it is true. Many elected officials of this state and this nation have turned their backs on them, the very class of people that once made this city great.

"But where does such vice come from?" Foley asked, and spread his hands wide. "Where do we begin—how do we begin to create a change and to build for a different type of future, a future where all of our cit- izens have opportunity and the possibility to succeed? Well, right here, right outside our front door. On the streets that hide and shelter vice, that allow vice to spread unchecked like some infestation—because, yes, that is what it is, an infestation that we must eradicate. Did past generations filled with immigrant struggle work so hard so that we, their sons and daughters, might merely bow down in defeat to such forces? Do we not care about our city anymore, about its crimes and the types we let control us and determine our future? No!"

Waiters bearing drinks moved from table to table, replenishing wine and liquor. One of them knocked over a glass, but the echo of its clanging upon the table made few heads turn. The majority of the crowd remained transfixed by the congressman.

"I stand up here with many of the city's finest citizens, dedicated to making this city again the place it once was, to wiping out crime, to clean- ing the streets of vice, to making this city a shining jewel once again, and I ask you for your support. If I am elected senator, I will use my power in Washington to ensure we are not forgotten any longer, that the nation does not turn its back on us. With federal funding and private backing we can rebuild this city, we can rebuild those depressed neighborhoods that have for so long blighted the landscape of Boston, that have caused us to stagnate."

Cal sipped his drink and gritted his teeth. He knew what neighborhoods Foley was talking about, had seen his notion of "redevelopment" firsthand. He doubted any in the room knew people who lived in Scollay or the West End, or cared what would happen to them in the congressman's plans for the future.

"With new developments we can revitalize the economy; we can create new jobs and new opportunities—as a city we will thrive again! And the rest of our nation will turn their eyes to Massachusetts and look at us as we once were, the Cradle of Liberty, the Athens of America, Boston, the City on a Hill!"

Congressman Foley thumped the lectern. Chairs scraped as diners stood and applauded. Foley's cheeks shone bright with passion, and it seemed as if he might be on the verge of tears.

The Boston College boys shouted from the bar and smashed a bottle. Marv Reynolds struck up the band, and they launched into a sweeping number that punctuated Congressman Foley's walk beneath the tracking spotlight from the podium and back down off the stage, among the diners, and amid handshakes, hugs, and cheers, to his own table, where the spotlight finally dissolved.

Dante was at Cal's shoulder. "Do you believe this shit? He couldn't have planned it better," he said. "I've never seen anything like it."

"And I doubt we will again, that is, unless he plans to run for president."

"You think now's the time to talk to him?"

"I think our timing stinks, and it's a lousy idea to do it here, of all places, but I don't think we have a choice."

᪥

CONGRESSMAN FOLEY HAD just put his knife and fork to the pork loin and roasted potatoes, served to him steaming on a gold-rimmed plate, when he caught sight of them at the bar looking his way. He hadn't seen Cal or Dante for years, but it was as if the old neighborhood remained stamped upon their brows. Cal's face appeared to be scraped raw by the cold and by drink. Yet despite this, he had a youthful and cocky demeanor about him, in the way Foley remembered Cal from before the war and his boxing days down at the L Street Bathhouse. At his side, Dante looked awful. He could have passed as an advertisement for a communist soup kitchen, with his thorny five o'clock shadow and his threadbare black-gray wardrobe: Dante the pro-letarian, a silhouette cut from the fabric of a moonless night.

He watched them as they strode between tables, staring at the diners, and them in their hats and coats—a bold statement itself in a place like this. He glanced about the room and a thought spilled and settled into his mind that they were here to see him, and with a slight sense of shame tightening his throat, he realized that he would have to greet them. He took a bite of pork, but he was no longer hungry. He returned his knife and fork to the white table linen, gulped down a generous mouthful from his cocktail. He'd already had three drinks, and that didn't include the two during his lunch meeting with Senator Gibbons. If he was going to continue to drink, he decided, he might as well meet Cal and Dante head-on; no sense in prolonging the inevitable.

The man sitting next to him was a union representative who started talking nonsense in his ear about one of the North Shore pols taking money off the top and paying his mistress with free rent for her and her bastard kid. Foley half listened to the man, didn't really give two shits, and kept his eyes on Cal and Dante as they approached.

"Excuse me for a moment," he said, holding a hand up to the union rep, silencing him mid-sentence as Cal and Dante stopped before the table. The story about the pol's mistress and triple time for city workers plowing the streets on Sundays had mercilessly merged together. "Got to take a walk down memory lane for a bit." He knocked back the rest of the drink, the ice clinking against his front teeth.

"Hello, Michael," Cal said, glancing over at Foley's wife, Celia, and nodding, a gesture that she returned before taking a measured sip from her wineglass. He looked over at the union official, the man in the middle, and the tall thin one whom he recognized from the bulldozed lot in Scollay Square—the man Tim Donovan, his driver, had called McAllister. Two women, a peroxide blonde and a redhead, on either side of them smiling.

"I hear you boys got those plans for clearing Boston's blight already in hand," Cal said, and grinned at the table.

"Who is this?" McAllister asked Foley.

"Just someone from the old neighborhood," the congressman said. "One of our many fine voting citizens, isn't that right, Cal?"

"That's right, Michael. Me and Dante have been voting for you since we were old enough to draw Xs on the ballot."

"Were they invited to this dinner?" McAllister continued. He glanced at Foley and then returned to his plate, carving out the fat from his prime rib.

"Probably not."

"Well, then, they should go, shouldn't they?" he said without looking up.

"We'll let you eat your meal in peace, Francis. I'll be back in just a bit. C'mon, gentlemen, a bottle on me." Foley pulled the napkin off his lap, dropped it down next to his plate, patted the other man in a knowing, commiserating way upon the shoulder, took his fresh drink, a gin gimlet, and then led them past several tables to the bar. Cal glanced back to the table, wanting to make contact with the developer, McAllister, but the man wouldn't give him the satisfaction of a stare-down, and seemed to be taking great pleasure in dissecting his prime rib before allowing himself a bite.

Standing between Cal and Dante, Foley could smell the old neighborhood on them. The tobacco, stale smoke, whiskey and beer, potatoes and cabbage, dime-store licorice candies, gasoline, and cheap musk that came in a tin as if it were oil, all products of the Avenue. It was familiar and comforting, despite the circumstances, and he briefly allowed himself to step into the past and the history he shared with the two men before him.

He set his drink down at the edge of the bar, and the younger bartender went to work on making him another one, but Foley held up a hand, gestured with three fingers, and mouthed the word "Jameson."

"I don't like that fuck," Cal said, gesturing back toward the table and McAllister.

"Oh stop, Cal." Foley waved it away. "It's over. That's what you learn in politics—forgive, but never ever forget. The enemies you make today might be your friends tomorrow."

"Is that right?"

"It most certainly is. You should already know that from our fathers' history."

"Our fathers hated each other's guts."

"And that was politics too. They were friends before any of that."

The young bartender placed three whiskeys before them, left the bottle of Jameson on the marble top, and then moved quickly to the end of the bar. They took their drinks but held them as if waiting for somebody to provide a proper toast.

"To the old neighborhood," Congressman Foley said, raising his glass, and Cal and Dante echoed, "To the old neighborhood." They tapped their whiskeys together before knocking them back, and Foley poured another round.

"Why are you two here?"

"The high life," Cal said. "Just want to see what we've been avoiding for so long."

"You came up to me looking like you meant business."

Cal nodded. "Okay, then. Do you happen to know a Mike Scarletti from Providence?"

Congressman Foley paused with the glass to his mouth, considered the name for a moment, sipped on his drink. "No, I can't place the name. Should I? Or is this a game? And this guy, this Scarletti, he's some gangster my brother's messed up with? Is that it?"

"Not quite." Cal tapped his glass on the bar. "This Scarletti drove a big rig in which they found the bodies of three prostitutes. They'd all been tortured and killed. He also killed Sheila Anderson."

"What the hell are you talking about?" Foley worked his jaw as though he'd just been sucker punched in the face. It was as if the temperature had suddenly doubled in the vast hotel ballroom and wrapped its hands around his throat. He loosened the red-and-black-striped tie he was wearing; a look of revulsion carried through his soft, photogenic face.

"You heard, then?" Dante asked.

"Yes, I heard, but I didn't know about the truck, the other girls."

"Your brother's involved."

"How do you know that?"

"The rig was left out on the Calf Pasture, by the Half-Mile dump. It was left on your brother's property."

"Just because it was on his property doesn't make him guilty of anything."

Cal held his gaze and after a moment Foley nodded. "You disagree, but what do the police think?"

"The police have given him a clean slate."

"But not you."

"No."

He wiped at his mouth with the back of his hand, turned to Dante. "I'm sorry. Sheila seemed like a sweet girl."

"Seemed? You knew her quite well, no?"

"Maybe I'm not on the same page as you."

Cal raised his voice above the music. "Cut the shit, we know about you two."

Foley cleared his throat. "I admit we shared a dance or two. I'm not going to hide that." He ran his hand through his voluminous hair, then poured them another round.

"Then how about it?" Cal's grin was more savage than friendly. "How long was it?"

"Was what, O'Brien?" Foley looked at him, irritated.

"Your affair with Sheila."

Foley turned to Dante, shrugged his shoulders. "It's not my intention to offend you, Dante, but she and I had a brief thing. Call it what you want, a tryst, an affair, it amounted to just a few intimate moments together. I've had my share, names and faces I forgot once they closed the door. So I won't tell you any lies. She was different. I respected her, I was fond of her, and I treated her like a lady."

"Jesus Christ already," Cal said. "How long?"

"Three, four months. Not quite. About a year ago."

Foley shook his drink, the ice clinking against the glass, and drank down what remained of the whiskey.

"Again, I'm sorry. I mean it. And my brother—I still can't believe he'd be involved with anything like this."

Dante nodded. "It's okay, we've no beef with you. We're trying to make sense of it all too."

Down at the other end of the bar, one of the Boston College boys dropped his beer glass and it shattered on the floor. They all laughed and cursed and nobody seemed to pay attention to them, as if wearing tuxedos gave them free rein to act like fools.

"It was a romance," Foley said, and sighed. "We knew it had an ending when we started."

"But it was still serious?"

"Not really...Look, we both had other loves in our lives. She was smitten with somebody else and I am a married man. I couldn't do anything but walk away."

Cal glanced toward the congressman's table. Celia was watching the three of them.

"Would you have left Celia for her?" he asked.

"That's none of your goddamn business."

"It must be at least twenty years, no?"

Foley's eyes gleamed with a sudden anger, as though he had just realized he was in the midst of being set up. "That's a low blow, even for you. I love my wife. But that doesn't mean I have to refuse the occasional woman.

"These women, they're just affairs...I'm not tricking them into something or making them think that I have feelings that I don't. Celia knows deep down...she understands...or she would..."

Dante asked, "And that's all Sheila was?"

"I said it already, she was different from most."

"But the problem was that Sheila wasn't a one-man mistress."

"What are you trying to get at?"

"We heard you were out with her at a jazz club, a colored jazz club on Columbus. Not a class act place like this, where all the blacks are on-stage, or in the kitchen cutting vegetables. They seen plenty of Sheila. Sometimes with you, sometimes with this other guy named Renza, and we heard of a Mario, too."

"Bobby Renza, that half-ass crooner. And Mario, on the side?" Foley held his glass to his mouth and laughed. "You two don't know your ass from your elbow."

"Is that right?"

"Are you two serious? This Mario is Mario Rizzo from the North End, and his stage name, the name that stuck, was Bobby Renza. They're one and the same asshole who introduced me to Sheila."

Somebody at the bar had lit up a cigar, and its smoke lingered in the air around them.

"Boys, please. I don't know what you're driving at, but it's making me uncomfortable. I won't pretend nothing happened. Sheila and I had a good time together, but she had her heart set on Renza."

The band shifted the tempo and started playing a standard swing song that sounded like a Tin Pan Alley version of Jimmy Dorsey. Foley retightened his tie and straightened his jacket. He leaned in between the two of them and raised his voice above the high, shrill sounds coming from the trumpet. "You two saw her?"

Dante nodded, grim-faced. "Yeah, we did."

"How bad was she?"

"She was bad. Lots of hate went into it."

Foley's eyes glistened and he suddenly appeared vulnerable. "I know they'll catch whoever did it, and soon. I have full confidence in our po-lice."

He sighed deeply, his handsome face flushed from alcohol. "Well, gentlemen, my meal has been sitting at the table for a half hour...I apol-ogize..."

He motioned to the bartender with a lift of his hand. "Put these on my tab, and give these two friends of mine a bottle each."

"And glasses, Mr. Foley?"

"No, they won't be staying. I can tell they don't feel much at home here." He gave a laugh as if he were using it simply to clear his throat, and then, as he stood between them, placed a hand on each of their shoulders, a gesture that could be witnessed from afar as either fatherly or downright condescending. "She was a darling girl. For a moment, I admit, she had my heart."

"One other thing, Michael," Cal said as he went to turn away. Foley raised his eyes questioningly. "You paid for the headstone, the headstone for the child."

"The child?"

"Sheila's child. It's buried in a graveyard at the Sisters of Clare convent in JP. Sister Bridget...," and he gestured to the table at the far end of the ballroom where members of the Catholic clergy sat, "sends her regards."

"I don't know anything about any child, Cal. I didn't know Sheila was pregnant." The congressman shook his head in disbelief, and his eyes shone as if on the verge of tears. He cleared his throat. "I donate to the church regularly, and always to the Sisters of Clare. They do what they will with the funds, use it wherever it's needed most. I have no say in that."

He stared at Cal as if waiting for something more, then gestured to the bar. "I see Pat has your bottles waiting, gentlemen, and I have peo-ple doing the same." He smiled in a way that appeared both melancholy and bittersweet. "Good night, gentlemen," he said, nodding, and they watched as he strode toward the banquet tables, a hand raised in greeting to someone on the dance floor, and then bowing in apology to his waiting dinner guests and to Francis McAllister, who turned slightly in his chair, like an aged raptor, to watch them.

"That guy doesn't like us much," Dante said, staring back.

"No, not much." Cal raised the bottle to McAllister in mock salute, and the man finally turned away. "And I'd like to know why."

37

SAVIN HILL, DORCHESTER

IN THE CELLAR beneath the light of a bare bulb Cal worked the heavy bag, worked his taped hands until, exhausted and drenched in sweat, he could barely raise them. He leaned against the bag as if it were his opponent, resting his head against the rough grain and breathing hard, then, driving his forearm and elbow into the bag, gave what he had left in a flurry of combinations and uppercuts.

Too tired to do any speed work, he sat on the weight bench and, with each arm, did sets with the fifty-pound dumbbells. He followed with knee curls. He did seventy-five-pound weights with his left leg and then, more slowly, his right. He didn't look at the leg, didn't want to see the scarring that thickly veined the thigh, but he could feel the hole, the absence of flesh, in the hollow of his hip. He breathed out as he raised the weight, trying to ease through the pain. When he could do no more, he ran water in the slop sink, splashed water over his face, and drank deep from the tap.

He dried his face with a hand towel and pulled on his sweats, sat at the workbench, lit a cigarette, and cleaned his two government-model M1911 Automatics. He dismantled his guns and cleaned their parts. With a toothbrush he took off chunks of carbon buildup, stoked a bore brush through the barrels, then wiped the inside of the magazine well, the ejector, the guide rails, and the area around the chamber. He tuned the radio to the news and caught the sports. His cigarette smoldered on the edge of the wood.

After he was done cleaning, he oiled each gun, the base of the hammer assembly, and then lightly greased the guide rails. Singing "The Wild Colonial Boy," he racked the slides to make sure their recoil springs were set, pulled the triggers and listened to their clicks, then wiped down the guns again and chambered the nine-round magazines. Outside through the squat basement windows he could see that the day had darkened and that it was close to dusk.

He went upstairs and made some coffee, pulled on a dark turtleneck Aran knit sweater over his sweatshirt and a pair of heavy wool military khakis. He slid the guns into twin shoulder holsters, took his old leather jacket out of the back closet beyond the kitchen and his black wool cap. He drank the coffee slowly, wrote a note for Lynne telling her he was going in to the office and would be back late, and left it on the kitchen table. She was working the graveyard shift at the Carney again, and he hoped he'd be home before her.

BLACKIE CAME OUT of the Dublin House with his collar up, the Kinneally brothers in front and on either side of him, standard formation for a lowlife like Blackie who, because he was always stirring things up with rivals, was always waiting for some manner of payback. If there was a hit coming, his boys were going to get it first; Cal wondered if they knew that or if they were too stupid to care. Five minutes before he'd sent a young runner out to check the streets. Cal knew that this was also standard for Blackie, having a local kid—they all idolized Blackie, wanted to be just like him when they grew up—act as a sweeper, checking the way for possible assassins waiting in alleys or in cars. Blackie looked at both sides of the street, took his time lighting a cigarette, and then stepped forward, and two other cronies came out of the bar doors behind him.

They got into Blackie's black Lincoln with Blackie behind the wheel and motored up the Avenue toward Lower Mills, took a right on River Street, and then followed Washington into Mattapan. At McGuire's Package Store on Blue Hill Avenue, Blackie and his boys made their first stop, and Cal knew that they were collecting the dailies from the till. Cal kept a safe distance, and it helped that it was overcast and raining. Visibility was poor, and even close to the streetlights the darkness pressed. When he knew they were about to make a stop, he passed them and parked farther up the street; sometimes he curled back, using side streets, and waited behind the Lincoln until it moved again.

He followed them through Mattapan and then into Roxbury. They went down Columbia Road back into Dorchester, past the darkened Strand Theater in Uphams Corner, and then took Boston Street into Southie. They took a right before the Old Colony housing project and pulled up before a dilapidated triple-decker, spears of ice hanging from twisted and shattered gutters. Cal eased into a spot on the main road, backed up so that he'd have an angle on the house, checked his watch, turned off the engine, and waited.

38

AN HOUR AFTER the murder made print, Cal and Dante stood at the entrance to the alley behind Dempsey's and stared at the dumpster where the latest victim had been found. Dante squatted on his haunches to look at the ground, but Cal stood because his leg was acting up again and it hurt too much to do anything else. A black and white with its revolving blue lamp and squawking radio idled outside the Hub Bar B-Q, but it had nothing to do with the business in the alley. A freezing rain gave the alley a pewter cast, all the cement and stone weeping with damp. It ran off the top of Cal's hat to his collar, and he shivered.

"Not much use looking in the snow. There's been a hundred people through here since they found her."

"Just trying to see him here that night."

"Well," Cal said, and sighed as if it pained him. "It's not Blackie."

"How do you know that?"

"I've been following him the last three nights. He didn't do this."

"Jesus. You want to be careful."

"What, and have him grab Lynne one of these nights? You're the one that said he told you he'd been watching her. Think I'm going to let that happen?"

"No, no, you're right. Just, I could've helped, that's all."

Cal's mood had darkened and he tried to shake himself out of the funk. He nodded toward the dumpster. "Scarletti would have had to drag the body in here. It's not like he used the truck."

"Or maybe she came voluntarily and he did her in the alley?"

"Too much blood; it would have been everywhere. Reporters would have had a field day with that. It'd be a front-page shot for the *Herald*. They said he sliced open her neck, same as the others, but you can see from here clear to the dumpster, and the only thing is snow that's been walked on. He's using another reefer."

"You think so?"

"Kill them, take his time, let the bodies freeze, and then dump them when he likes. Still looks the same."

"So he has another trailer."

"This is a jump from the highway. To get around he'd have to drop the trailer and just run the rig, the Peterbilt."

Cal sighed, stomped his foot to get the feeling back in it. "The papers say it was another prostitute—you haven't heard anything?"

"No one else I've talked to has seen anyone that looks like Scarletti."

The back door to Dempsey's opened and a kitchen hand came out, a bucket of leftover dinner slops held against his soiled apron. No more than twenty, sleeves rolled up, arms scalded pink from hot water. He lifted the top off the dumpster and, grunting, hefted the bucket over the rim, shook it until its contents slopped into the bin. From the sounds of it, the dumpster had been emptied since the discovery of the young woman; foodstuffs splattered and thumped against its metal.

The washer looked up, caught them staring. "What the fuck you looking at?"

Cal was in no mood for a fight, but he didn't like the kid's tone, either.

"We're looking for an asshole. Are you the asshole?"

The kid thought about saying something else and then, sour-faced, went back inside the bar and slammed the door.

"Well, you've ruined his day."

"Yeah. Let's hope."

39

By MID-MORNING THE three limousines were there again, this time farther down the avenue, idling against the curb with white smoke steaming from their exhausts, Donovan standing like a sap by McAllister's car. Cal stared from the office window greasy with condensation, then took his coat and made his way down the back stairway with his car battery. The car had already left him stranded three times in the last week, and since the temperatures had plummeted, he wouldn't leave it to chance.

On the street, Charlie's newsstand was shuttered. After the morning rush he closed up and sat, drinking coffee, at a diner on Brattle until the evening subway commute began. The blue neon cross of the Calvary Rescue Mission shimmered dully through the hard-packed ice that encased it.

As he worked beneath the hood of the Chevy, he lost sensation in his fingers, so that when he cut himself he hardly registered it. He could barely hold on to the wrench. When the battery was mounted and the cables attached, he slammed down the hood and climbed into the car. He sat before the wheel trying to work feeling back into his fingers, pulled out the choke, and then turned the key in the ignition. Wheezing, the engine made half a revolution—he could hear the belts turning—and then it sputtered and stopped. "C'mon, you bitch, fucking start!" he muttered and turned the key again and the engine caught and he gunned it so that it wouldn't stall.

While he waited for the engine to warm and the heat to come on, he wiped at the windows, scraped at the thin film of ice that frosted the interior glass. He stared at the rubble-filled lot surrounded by chain-link fence. Standing by the crane with the wrecking ball that had, days before, leveled another half block of real estate, so that the sun showed through from the West End and the docks where before at this time of day it would have been shadowed and gray, was McAllister, the developer he'd seen at Foley's banquet, and beside him stood Foley, another man Cal didn't recognize, and the union rep. Standing there now, the four looked diminutive, shrunken in their heavy overcoats.

The four men were arguing, but it was the developer, McAllister, who appeared to be shouting the loudest, waving at the surrounding buildings and gesturing toward the West End. At one point Cal thought they might come to blows when the developer, who was no small man, held a finger directly before Foley's face. Foley didn't flinch or budge, but stared at him. The union rep stepped in between them and said something that seemed to calm McAllister, and soon the men parted ways—the rep walking toward his Cadillac and the other three walking across the rubble-strewn lot toward the sidewalk. Donovan held the car door open for McAllister and Foley. After a moment the car pulled out and Cal eased out of his spot and rumbled after them. Riding the brake and the accelerator to keep the car from stalling, he followed them onto Hanover and into the North End.

It still bothered him that Foley had known about Sheila and Bobby Renza, and that Renza had somehow brought the two of them together. There was something wrong there, something that spoke to a deeper connection between the two of them and to her death. For a man who had just been told an ex-lover had been murdered by a notorious killer, and for all his shock and dismay, it now seemed very much business as usual.

The traffic was moving slow and cautious over the slick streets, and he followed behind the car through one traffic light and then another. Donovan glanced in his side mirrors a few times but didn't catch him, and it wouldn't have mattered if he had. There was no reason to be suspicious of him, no reason to think that his driving behind them was anything more than coincidence.

On the narrow streets of the North End other drivers peered through gray, frost-clouded windshields; steam pumped from tailpipes, from sidewalk grates, from the kitchen vents of restaurants and pizzerias. At the intersection of Prince Street and Thacher the car slowed, and Cal held back, watched as it slid long and sleek against the curb before Pizzeria Regina's. Cal pulled into a spot twenty yards back, his bumper knocking over a trash can that a resident of the North End had placed in the shoveled space, and watched as Foley and McAllister entered the restaurant. Donovan stood sentry by the limo. Cal turned off the engine and waited.

The car grew cold and he searched the glove compartment, but he'd finished the last pint bottle yesterday. He turned the car on again to clear the windows and so that the battery wouldn't drain, and listened to the radio for a bit, considered going for a coffee but realized he'd left it too late and might miss them if they came out. Thirty minutes later Foley and McAllister emerged and crossed the street. Cal opened the car door and stepped out into the cold. His muscles had stiffened and his leg throbbed something awful, but he hoped the walk would get the blood circulating through it and that the pain would pass.

He followed the men along Prince Street then down an alley past the Baldwin Place Shul to a four-story faded brick office building, and stood to light a cigarette as they climbed the steps to its doors. He watched a mother dragging her children, bundled and stumbling in their excess of clothing, into the Baldwin Talmud Torah and, after a moment, took the steps and entered the lobby, a small space lit by two rows of exposed tungsten bulbs and smelling of old cigarette and cigar smoke.

The pain in his leg was clouding his vision and making it difficult to think. From his inside coat pocket he took his prescription bottle, emptied three bennies into his palm, popped them in his mouth, and, wincing, swallowed them dry.

Above the narrow elevator door on his right, green lights showed the progress of the elevator from floor to floor. He could hear the thing banging away in the shaft as if it might plummet at any moment. On the left of the elevator a staircase covered with peeling linoleum wound upward.

He scanned the building directory, ran his finger beneath the names, and then paused on the third floor under Rizzo Construction, Roberto L. and Son. Cal pursed his lips. How were they connected? After all, it was Foley who'd told him that Renza and Mario Rizzo were the same person.

A radiator hissed uselessly in the corner, and he stamped his feet to keep the blood flowing in his scarred hip and leg. From above he heard voices and then footsteps. The elevator rattled and thumped as it made its descent, and Cal stepped out into the alley again, hobbled back to his car.

HE DROVE BACK to Scollay disoriented and in a haze of pain that was determined to persist no matter how many bennies he took. What did the Butcher and Sheila's death have to do with Renza, Foley, and McAllister? And if Foley and Renza were connected because of Rizzo Construction, how did McAllister tie in, and if he did, did that mean he knew Sheila as well?

Before he took out the car's battery he picked up a bottle at Court Street Liquors, where the old boy was still complaining that they'd cut off his heat and that they were trying to drive all the poor working people out of the neighborhood. On the street again Cal put the bottle to his lips, but after a mouthful suddenly lost all taste for it and capped it instead. Wind pushed across the lot where Foley and the other men had stood, moaned in the cantilevered braces of the snow-covered crane, sent the chain link jangling, and Cal, freezing and in pain, limped slowly back to Pilgrim Security.

40

BOSTON CITY HALL was located on School Street next to the old King's Chapel graveyard and across from the Parker House, once home to the Saturday Club, the literary elite of Boston, whose members included Henry Wadsworth Longfellow, Ralph Waldo Emerson, and Oliver Wendell Holmes, even a visiting Charles Dickens; it now served as the place where politicians from the State House drank after hours, made underhanded deals, and met their mistresses. Cal supposed that at one time or another Foley had met Sheila there.

City Hall had been built in the mid-1800s in the French Second Empire style, with its high mansard roof topped by a dome, tall windows and doors flanked by ornamented columns, all now pristinely coated in snow. In the courtyard Cal and Dante passed the statues of Benjamin Franklin and Josiah Quincy, a marble plaque that recognized the spot as the original location of Boston Latin, the first public school in America, and then pushed though the massive front doors into the heated foyer decorated with historical murals. Clumps of dirty snow melted on the tile and marble, and an old

237

black woman cleaned the floors with a mop as city workers spilled up and down the wide staircase on either side of the entrance.

Cal paused on the stairs as Dante lit a cigarette.

"Any luck last night?" Cal asked.

Dante inhaled on the cigarette, its tip flaring red, and blew out smoke long and slow. "No, nothing. I'll give it a couple more nights."

He shook the match out. "You think we're going to find anything here?"

"Foley and McAllister aren't tearing down the neighborhood just for the fun of it. The public records will show us what they're up to."

The Office of the City Clerk was a large room on the second floor. Its faded wood-paneled walls had seen better days. As had the two large reading tables in the center of the room, their scarred surfaces illuminated by small lamps. Upon the wall a large clock loudly ticked the seconds. A clerk sat behind an opaque ribbed-glass window that he pushed up when Cal rang the bell. He had a narrow face, dull, watery-gray eyes under thick-rimmed eyeglasses smeared with fingerprints, which reflected the lights of the office when he raised his head to look up at them. His eyebrows and hair were slicked down with oil, and the sharp odor of mothballs came from his tweed jacket. Part of the sandwich he'd been chewing bulged in his cheek.

"We're looking for building proposals or plans for Scollay Square," Cal said. "Anything you might have that's come on the books in the last six months or so."

"A bit more specific would help."

"The name of the firm is McIntyre, McAllister, and Broome, but I'm not sure how you file such things. How about by...zoning region? There can't be that much going on in the city, is there?"

"New building proposals and planning would be under the Superintendent of Buildings and the City Planning Commission. Plats that are awaiting review and approval will be there also."

The clerk took his time chewing and swallowing; he didn't seem to be enjoying it much.

"I can find those records for you, if you'd like to take a seat over at one of the tables."

They waited and listened to the sounds from other offices: typewriters clacking, footsteps on the tiled floors beyond the door, a woman's shrill laughter. Dante finished his cigarette, stamped it out in a tin ashtray still filled with the ash of old cigarettes, and immediately lit another. Cal pulled a damp newspaper from his pocket and began reading the front page, but the words wouldn't stick, so he moved on to the sports section and then the funnies.

The door opened and the clerk came in carrying an armful of cardboard tubes containing rolled drafting plans. When he dropped them onto the table, they counted ten in all.

"Jesus," Cal said. "How many developments does McAllister have in the works?"

The clerk sighed as he took the tops off the tubes. "You asked for McIntyre, McAllister, and Broome, and you asked for Scollay Square, so I got you everything from Tremont to Church Street, and from Hanover to Causeway Street in the North End."

Cal shook out a roll of blue drafting paper and stretched it across the table. Dante held down one side and together they looked at an overhead view of Scollay Square, along Cambridge Street. To the east, past the intersection of State, all the present buildings were gone. In their place were larger divisions and subdivisions: a vast sprawl of concrete plazas and office building skyscrapers. "Shit," Dante muttered at his side. "This can't be right."

Cal's stomach roiled, a sense of panic swelling in him that he couldn't explain. He knew that he was merely looking at a plan, that such things couldn't just happen overnight, that the place he knew couldn't be gone so neatly and so quickly.

Dante pointed toward the corner of the draft and the names that were printed there: McIntyre, McAllister, and Broome, and below that, Rizzo Construction, and Cal's unease grew. This was the thing—the connection—between all of them.

"What about the West End?" he asked the clerk.

The clerk stared at him, and when Cal gave him his best smile, he spoke as if he were speaking to a child.

"McIntyre, McAllister, and Broome have proposals for all the city space I just mentioned. That includes the West End. What you see is awaiting review and approval."

Dante leaned over the draft, the long ash hanging from his cigarette only inches from the paper. "But how can that be? You're talking about one square mile of city real estate. There are homes and businesses there. None of it's been sold—it can't be."

"That's what it says," the clerk said offhandedly, staring at Dante's cigarette.

The clerk pointed to the largest of the documents. "That's a plat of consolidation, which consolidates many parcels of urban land into a single parcel. It comes with the required surveys of the previous parcels attached for approval. As it states there, McIntyre, McAllister, and Broome are the registered landowners."

"They're going to displace thousands of people." Cal sensed he was speaking aloud to the almost empty room. "And nobody fucking knows about it."

The clerk shrugged. "Hey, did you want to look at these or not? I go on my lunch break in five minutes."

Cal wanted to remind him that he'd just been eating. He glanced at Dante. There was no point in looking at the other plans; they already knew what they contained: more empty spaces filled with grid lines, measurements, numbers, dimensions, and architectural line drawings of buildings that would soon be constructed. Cal shook his head and began to roll up the blueprint stock. His hands were shaking. Dante said, "Thank you. We're done."

"You're welcome," the clerk said dryly, and took the plan from Cal, rolled it, and then slipped it into its tube. He gathered up the remaining tubes with a burdened sigh.

"The offices are closed from twelve to one fifteen. If you need anything else, you can come back then." His shoes clattered on the old tile.

Dante whistled and shook his head. "Jesus, Cal, we're talking millions of dollars at stake here—the whole redevelopment of Scollay and the West End, all dependent on Foley getting it pushed through."

"Makes the Brink's job look like peanuts."

"Yeah. And look how much McAllister has to lose in all this. He doesn't seem like the kind of man who would take losing anything too well, does he?"

The glass window squealed as it was pried up, and they turned. There was the clerk's pallid face and his bleary, spectacled eyes staring at them. "The office is closed, gentlemen," he said, pointing to the large clock ticking on the wall, and brought the window down with a bang.

41

KNEELAND STREET, CHINATOWN

FOR THE THIRD night in a row Dante braved the cold and stood on a street corner talking to a group of streetwalkers. Mostly it was the same girls, but every so often a new one showed, and Jill introduced her to him. As the old whore, Jill was the one who ran the show, the one the others looked to for guidance. Tonight her eyes were so bright that for a moment Dante thought she might be high. It turned out she was as angry as he was.

"Cops don't do nothing, they just don't care. I tell the girls to be safe. Like you said, Dante, to watch out for a rig, I give them the description of this guy, but you think they listen? Everyone's out for themselves, especially in this weather. Sometimes it's worth it to give them a discount just to get in out of the cold."

"I've known people who'd do just about anything to get in out of the cold, Jill."

242

"Then why you still here?"

"He's got to show up sooner or later."

"Does he? I've been saying that my whole life."

Traffic pressed tight together moved slowly up and down Atlantic Avenue, faces blurred behind steamed glass. On the far corner of the street, hustling the traffic moving southbound, four girls stood, hands on hips, on display for the passing gaze.

"You already talk to those girls over there?" she asked.

"Yeah, last night. They said they hadn't seen anything, but the tall one knew the latest girl."

"Didn't shake Shirley up any. I've never seen anyone that excited to be standing outside in ten-degree weather freezing her tits off."

"I told them to be careful."

"*Careful.* Not much use for that word around here."

Dante lit up a cigarette and passed it to her. When he realized she wasn't going to be giving it back, he lit another. In an hour he'd have to move on, and he knew the girls would as well. It was too cold to stay in one spot for too long.

"Where you headed after this?"

"Maybe back to Scollay or over to Fort Point."

"Think you'll be back out tomorrow night?"

Dante laughed, despite himself. "Not if it gets any colder, I won't." Jill sucked on her cigarette, shifted from foot to foot, stared down the street. "Maybe," he said. "It can't hurt, right?"

A car slowed and a girl went over to it. The driver put down his window and they spoke for a moment and then the girl climbed in. A few trucks passed, dirty snow plastered to their sides, but none stopped; an old '38 Plymouth with an even older guy peering over the wheel, his wipers beating at the glass, a milk truck, a gleaming sports car low to the ground, shining red as it passed beneath the glow of streetlamps.

Wind came in off the water and turned the moisture in the air hard and sharp. The lights shimmered and crystallized. Dante and Jill watched half a dozen girls get picked up, and then when they'd been the only ones standing there for some time, Jill pulled the collar of her coat tight and sighed. "Got to call it quits for the night, Dante, before I freeze to death or catch my death of cold. You be here tomorrow night?"

It was less a question and more a request, and Dante nodded. "I'll bring us some coffee."

"You're all right."

He watched Jill wave to the girls on the other side of the street and then head away from the water, toward a diner on Causeway. He waited until most of the girls were done for the night and then considered heading back to Scollay. Fort Point could wait. At the far corner the southbound girls had been luckiest. Most had gotten their johns, and the tall one remaining, the one they called Shirley, was hobbling quickly off the curb in her heels, waving toward some customer who had stopped for her. Sometimes, as Jill said, it was worth it just to get in out of the cold.

Dante watched her cross the street toward what he thought was a green flatbed or a white Ford, and then he saw the red and green Peterbilt idling before the light and Shirley passing the other vehicles and moving toward it. He watched her and then looked at the window of the rig and the vague impression of a face staring back. He saw the door of the cab open and the hulking shadow of a man beckon her inside.

"Hey!" Dante called. "Hey!" He hurtled from the curb, hands held up before a stream of cars blowing their horns, and raced toward the truck. He slipped badly, his leg giving out on him before he managed to right himself and keep running. Shirley had climbed into the truck cab and the driver was gunning the engine, grinding the gears, lurching toward the light that still shone red.

The Peterbilt's engine roared and the truck pushed at the cars before it. There was a loud grinding and squealing of metal as its front bumper crushed the rear of the car ahead; thick, acrid-smelling smoke came off the car's tires as the Peterbilt shoved it out of the way, sent it sideways into a row of parked cars, and then began doing the same to the next car in line. The truck hammered its way through the stalled traffic, cars blowing their horns and pinwheeling to the left and right before it.

Shirley screamed from within the cab, and Dante grasped for the door handle, tried to pull himself up onto the running board but slipped again and almost fell beneath the rig's moving wheels. He righted himself and banged on the metal, hollered, "Open the fucking door!" The driver cut the wheel sharply and Dante lost his footing, fell hard to the street. From inside the cab, Shirley was still screaming.

The truck pushed aside the last car and was now picking up speed, the cab jolting as the driver went through the gears, and Dante raced after it. For a moment he and the truck were parallel, Dante running down the center lane beside it, eyes locked with the driver's, whose face appeared and then disappeared in the stuttering light from the streetlamps above. He saw the orange-red hair, the disfiguring harelip, and then the driver smiled and the rig pulled ahead, and though Dante tried to keep up, eventually his legs faltered. Breath steaming from his mouth, he stood in the middle of the street as cars continued to move about him, and stared down Atlantic to see the Peterbilt's taillights blink red once, twice, and then disappear.

42

DUBLIN HOUSE, UPHAMS CORNER

Late the next morning Cal insisted that he and Dante drive over to the Dublin House in Uphams Corner and get a drink. The bar was done up in a fake Tudor-Irish style: white-painted walls now turned a greasy shade of vanilla crisscrossed by interlaid wood beams painted to look as if they'd been covered with pitch. The ceiling was low, and beams in the same style split the nicotine-stained ceiling above their heads. Smoke spiraled from cigarettes slouching in ashtrays on the bar as men, engrossed in their orations, spoke softly to one another, boots and heels banging the wood, scraping at the metal rungs of the stools as they straddled their seats and the day wound down through the slow hours before dusk.

It was their fifth or sixth pint, and Dante tilted his glass from side to side, stared blearily into its almost empty bottom. "I could have stopped him," he said. "And now we have no idea where he's got to. He won't be coming back to the same spots again."

"You couldn't have done anything more than you did," Cal said, and scanned the room from their corner booth. "And you got his plates. He'll

246

have to dump the truck now and find another, and that might take him some time. We'll see what Owen does with them, but I was hoping we'd get to him first."

A waitress came in for the late-afternoon shift, when working stiffs stopped in for food, and she did a good job of keeping the drinks coming. Dante was speaking when Cal next looked up and twilight had fallen on the Avenue and another bartender stood behind the bar. Cal knew him, too; he was one of Blackie's boys, a wiry guy named O'Leary from some backwater bog in Cork. Originally a former world-class welterweight who had turned to knife blades one night after a fight didn't go his way. His opponent had damaged O'Leary's right retina, and since he could never box professionally again, he took the Old Testament adage "an eye for an eye" seriously: he stepped out of a crowd at Dorchester's Sons of Erin Hall after his opponent's next match six months later, came up behind him and knocked him to the ground, kicked in his face until the man wasn't moving anymore, and then went down on his knees and sliced the man's right eye cleanly out of its socket. Everyone knew it was O'Leary, and there had been at least a dozen witnesses to the stabbing, but no one ever tagged him for the crime. Since then, and that was ten years ago, he'd become even better with knives. The stories ran rampant through the old neighborhood of what O'Leary had done with a knife and to whom, and of his alliances and betrayals with half a dozen Irish families still wreaking vengeance upon one another, retribution and revenge for a hundred wrongs done in the old country when Boston was still rising out of a swampy spit of land in the harbor populated by sheep and cows.

A familiar loud voice sounded at the bar and Cal's shifting gaze slowed. A slim youth in a leather jacket and black watch cap was talking to another man and, between sips of his drink, looking about the bar. His shock of black hair made Cal pause with his drink to his mouth. The door to the bar opened and the man turned to see who had entered, and in that moment Cal could see his face clearly and knew he must have come in from the alley entrance at the back of the bar. The youthfulness was still there but in a face hardened by violence and cruelty. Blue eyes flickered

247

lazily across the room, taking in the newcomer, and then went back to his drink.

From where he sat, Dante had the better view of him and was looking at him now. Perhaps he'd noticed him all this time and hadn't said anything about it. The laughter at the bar grew louder as more men congregated around Blackie. Cal recognized the Kinneally brothers—the fat bastards—and four from the O'Shea and Walsh clans from the D Street and L Street projects. They stood on either side of Foley, listening intently as he spoke between sips of beer and laughter, and nodding as if taking orders.

Dante noticed the joyless smile on Cal's face. "You knew he'd be here," he said.

"Sure."

"You're an idiot. We should drink up and move on."

Cal put his glass down. "I'm not forgetting."

"Forgetting what?"

"Him following Lynne."

"Oh, for Christ's sake."

Cal bit down on his bottom lip and grimaced. "Just seeing that short bastard makes my teeth ache."

The whiskey was giving Cal a bad drunk, and he thought about Blackie watching Lynne, following her along the Avenue. There was a part of him that wanted to grab a glass, walk up to Foley, and smash it across his face, to tear into him as if he had been the one who'd murdered Sheila and the other girls, but even drunk he realized how foolish that would be.

"Time to go," Dante said. "I don't like the look of this."

"Yeah," Cal said, but remained sitting, and when the waitress came he ordered them more drinks. An odd languorousness settled upon them, as if the scene had slowed to match the cigarette smoke swirling in the tea-colored light.

Blackie glanced back at their booth and paused. "Dante Cooper! Cal O'Brien!" he called out, and the men around him turned their eyes in their direction, and Cal knew that Blackie had no idea who had chased him through Boston the week before. "Will you look at this! The war hero and his Polack sidekick." Foley grinned humorlessly and moved down the bar toward them while the rest of his men watched.

"Cheers, Finn," Cal said, knowing that nobody called him by that name anymore, and raised his glass. "The other day we bump into your big brother, and now you. You must be proud. Michael's come a long way from his old stomping grounds, a long way from Adams Street."

Foley thumped the bar with his glass. "The next fucking senator for Massachusetts." The men behind him raised their glasses and cheered.

Cal laughed, nodding. "As long as he doesn't stick that little prick of his in the wrong hole. Or mess around with any more girls who end up dead like Sheila Anderson. You know Sheila Anderson, Blackie? Know anything about a truckful of dead women out on the Calf Pasture?"

Foley's grin faltered.

Cal glanced at Dante, who kept his eyes on his drink, and forced a smile. "Growing up, we always knew you were fucked up, but this fucked up? Doesn't sound like the type to be the next boss of the town. Shit, I heard you couldn't even get a straight cut from the Brink's job. You ever find the guys who did it?"

He raised his glass toward Blackie in mock celebration. "Let's just hope Sully has somebody else in mind when he hands over his crown."

Blackie's goons crossed the barroom and had Cal and Dante up by their collars faster than Cal could have thought. He realized the drink had got to him when he tried to shake them off and helplessly flailed under their grip. One moment he was laughing and the next his legs were dragging against the wooden floor and chairs were being overturned. Two goons kept a manacle-like pressure on his shoulders until the sockets burned and he could no longer feel his arms. The sounds of the bar seemed very far away, a steel door opened before them, and then they were out in the alley and he was thrust up against the brick wall. The first punch to his gut doubled him over, had him gasping for air, and the second and third, a right roundhouse followed by a left, rocked his head upon his neck and sent his mind reeling. If the hands let him go, he'd be on the ground. He spat and tasted blood.

Dante hollered and struggled against the men who held him. "I don't think that's so wise, do you, Blackie?"

"What the fuck are you talking about?"

"Me and Cal are investigating a murder, helping the police, talking with your brother, the would-be senator, two nights ago, and now this. We end up in trouble and who you think they're going to link it back to?"

"Fuck you." Blackie reared back and struck Cal successive blows to his mouth and nose. Cal could feel the blood filling up over his tongue. His head was becoming unmoored; his vision wavered with spots of light, fading and simmering and then flashing again. He managed to raise his head. Blackie undid his jacket and handed it to one of the Walsh brothers. The Kinneallys held Dante immobile against the far alley wall. When he struggled, the bigger one bent him double with a punch to his gut.

"You two," Dante said breathlessly, trying to raise his voice. "You two make him see sense. Anything happens to us and everything leads back to Michael. You let this happen and if he's lucky he'll be a fucking councilman for Southie the rest of his life."

A punch shut his mouth, snapped his head back, and sent a razor-like charge down his spine. Then they held him and he watched Blackie unleash a flurry of punches to Cal's face and head. Cal fell forward and then strong hands were pulling him upright again. Blackie went into working his body and Cal knew he would soon lose consciousness. He couldn't breathe, his nose felt shattered, and blood was dripping from his mouth and dampening the front of his shirt.

There was a sudden squeal of car tires. Headlight beams cut through the darkness, swept across the brick walls, and moved toward them. The car bounced up over the curb, entered the alley, and its front end smashed into a garbage can, sent it crashing against the wall. The driver hit the brakes, a door opened and slammed shut, footsteps crunched on snow, and a voice hollered, "We found him! Blackie! We fucking found him!"

The Kinneally brothers had come forward and were trying to pull

Blackie off Cal. "He's done, Blackie, he's done. You heard the prick. We go too far and it could come down on Mikey. We've got to go."

The driver in the car honked the horn. In the narrow alleyway the sound of it was deafening.

The other Kinneally pulled at Blackie's arm and shouted, "You heard Sean. They fucking found him."

But Foley relented only slowly. Breathing hard into Cal's ear, he whispered, "You're a fucking dead man, O'Brien." The hands that were holding Cal let go and he slipped forward to the ground, hard, face-first into the snow. His eyelids fluttered and he turned on his back, coughing and gasping for air. His nose sprayed the snow around him with blood.

Up between the buildings, above the alley where the sky showed itself, he could see the stars. White smoke rose from rooftop chimney stacks. From somewhere came the clanging of a church bell. He imagined he heard Mel Tormé's "Christmas Song."

"Cal? Cal? You all right?" Dante was on one knee, leaning over him, and Cal reached up to touch his face. He could feel his ribs contracting sharp and jagged against his diaphragm and he feared they were broken.

"I'm okay," he managed.

"You're a fucking idiot." Dante grabbed under his shoulder to help him up, but Cal shook him off.

"Give me a moment, would you?"

He lifted himself up on his elbows and lay there for a moment, his ragged breaths steaming white in the darkness of the alleyway. He turned and hacked out a mouthful of blood that in the moonlight looked like oil, and then he rolled onto his side.

"Christ, Dante. I think I need a doctor."

43

DANTE SAT ON a bench in the hallway outside Cal's room and vacantly watched nurses and doctors passing on their rounds. He went to light a cigarette and then realized that there was one already hanging unlit between his lips. He shook his head and slipped the other cigarette between his fingers back into the pack. He lit a match and watched the flame and felt that same sense of guilt all over again. He held the flame, and the tobacco blazed a pulsating ember as he inhaled with small, staggered breaths.

A hand came down upon his shoulder, squeezed gently. He looked up at Lynne, wearing her nurse's uniform. It was the first time he'd seen her in it, and she looked authoritative in the crisp, well-ironed white, her blue eyes radiant despite the flesh around them appearing swollen, as if she'd gone without sleep.

"You doing better than him, I hope?" She smiled, but it was clear she was tired and the smile disappeared.

"I'm trying my best, Lynne."

"Well, you should try harder. Haven't seen you since summer, and you look like you'd barely push one hundred and forty on the scale."

Dante smiled, sucked on his cigarette. "It's all part of the jazz diet. Strictly cigarettes and gin."

"Yeah, and that other stuff."

Dante turned his eyes away from her and glanced down the corridor.

"I'm a nurse, Dante, and I've seen it all. I can tell when somebody is strung out as opposed to hungover."

I'm not strung out, he wanted to say, but his voice broke, and she sat down beside him on the black bench. An intercom cackled with static, clicked and clicked, but no voice came through. The squealing roll of a wheelchair carried down the connecting corridor.

"Will he be all right?" he asked.

"He'll be all right," she said without emotion.

Dante let the cigarette smolder between his fingers, scratched at the stubble on his cheek. The lighted end of the cigarette came dangerously close to his eye. There was silence, and the hospital hallway was suddenly still. The hairs on his neck stood. It was a similar sensation to somebody whispering in his ear, like Margo did so many times when she had woken up before him, beckoning him from sleep with a soft kiss to his cheek, his temple.

Lynne shifted on the bench and sighed. "It's time I got back to my shift," she said. "You check in on him one more time for me, and then go get yourself some rest."

He nodded but couldn't look her in the eye. If he did, he'd be able to see contempt, or worse. She blamed him for Cal's beating.

He watched as she walked down the hallway, and when she turned the corner, he noticed the sunlight coming through the high windows and dissolving over the linoleum tiles that had just been waxed this morning, illuminating them to an almost liquid appearance.

His cigarette done, he stood up from the wooden bench and walked into the room where the blinds were drawn and a lone lamp by the bed was turned on, giving that part of the room a comforting glow. He sat in a chair by the bed and watched Cal as he slept, glanced over his still body covered in a wool blanket, and to the bandages that seemed to hold his face together.

He lit another cigarette and spoke through the gray smoke that carried in a stream from his nostrils. "We're going to get those fuckers. This ain't the end of it."

The threat felt empty to him, so he repeated it word for word, but still without true conviction, and the words fell flat and blew away with the smoke billowing in the room. Beyond the drawn blinds there was the sound of ice pelting the glass, and he felt a chill in his bones and a tightening in his throat. When he spoke, his voice cracked. "I promise."

44

ADAMS STREET, LOWER MILLS

SEVENTY-FOUR-YEAR-OLD PATRICK Burgess, out for his early morning walk, and attempting to slow his heart, which banged painfully against his chest as he labored for breath in the chill air, stopped on the Adams Street Bridge in the Lower Mills section of Dorchester. He leaned over the latticed iron railings of the Baker Dam, stared out at the narrow, twisting Neponset River which wound its way through the divide between factories and homes, cascaded in a steaming froth over the low weir supplying power to the Walter Baker Chocolate Factory mill. As he worked at slowing his heart, there came a white cloud of smoke billowing from the massive orange brick chimneys of the factory, and on that smoke, a startling yeasty smell and the acrid odor of burnt cacao beans. He blinked at the chalk-colored chimneys of Diamond Chemicals & Plastics on the shallow, farther shore, and saw something caught down on the ice about twenty feet beyond the falls. Something half in and half out of the water and misshapen through the peripatetic light cast by the mist and steaming spray of the river.

After a moment of staring, Patrick realized that he was looking at what might be a person, and when he descended the stairway to the dam and crossed the wooden footbridge to get a closer look, he saw it fully: a pale, perhaps once heavily muscled torso, crude sailor's ink on both biceps. The body was bloated and swollen, a strange disjointedness to the limbs, and beneath the crushed skull a head of orange-red hair. Without these male features the thing before him might have been a man or a woman, for it had no face.

He lurched back across the footbridge, clambered up the narrow, frozen staircase to the bridge, and frantically looked about him. At this time of the morning the streets were mostly empty; a car crossed the intersection of Washington Street and was gone. Then the dreamlike sight of the number 34 bus shuddering down the hill toward Ashmont, its vacant interior illuminated by amber light, and the lone driver at the wheel staring ahead into an overcast dawn emerging above the rooftops, a cigarette dangling from the side of his mouth, and Patrick clutched at his chest and rushed into the street to wave him down.

45

EVEN IN THE blackness there seemed to be swirling movement. Cal's eyes rolled beneath his closed eyelids, and his body twitched as if in some intense struggle. He was in the Hürtgen Forest again, and he could feel the cold, deep in his bones and so numbing he wished only to sleep. He tried to move but his limbs were too heavy.

The soldier—he looked no more than seventeen—was caught on the barbed wire and pleading with him to shoot. Heavy German voices came through the sharp-smelling cordite fog to them, then their gray shapes moving ghostlike through the mist, and the boy's eyes widened in fear. Cal raised the gun, raised it to the boy's temple, stared into his eyes.

"Kill me," the boy said. "Please, fucking kill me, fucking kill—" and Cal pulled the trigger and shot the boy in the head. His head rocked backward as the bullet, in a spatter of gore and bone shards, exited the rear of his skull, and then his body fell forward onto the barbed wire, swayed, and then, after a moment, was still.

This was what he dreamed at times—only he hadn't shot the boy.

257

Instead he'd thrown himself to the ground and buried himself among the bodies of his dead comrades when the first advance cleared the fog. He watched as two Germans came and the boy hollered out, writhing and struggling, twisting frantically as the soldiers leveled their bayonets, and then screaming as they began taking turns spearing him, gutting him. Cal dug himself into the trenches of dead bodies that lay in parts across the frozen forest floor, tried to still his breath, tried not to scream, and pulling one of the corpses over himself, he waited.

He could feel the fading warmth of those bodies all around him, and with that warmth came the knowledge of how recently they had died, but time was lost here and minutes felt like hours. It seemed the boy's screams lasted forever, and Cal was never sure when they had ended, if perhaps he was only playing the boy's single scream over and over again in his mind, for long after he knew the boy must be dead, the screams continued like an echo reverberating in his ears. He couldn't breathe under all these dead bodies—they would suffocate him if he were to remain—but he also knew that to climb from beneath them would mean those same bayonets would find him. He tried to calm his breathing and listen to the sounds of the soldiers who were now talking to one another. He could feel the bodies shifting and tremoring with each bayonet thrust into them and then withdrawn. They were coming closer.

The bodies stirred around him, shifting as bayonets struck bone, hooked intestines and organs, and lifted them. He could hear the German soldiers using their feet to pry the bayonets free. They were directly above him. He opened his eyes briefly and looked into the face of a corpse: pale eyes staring from their sockets, lips pulled back from yellowed gums and frozen so that the man appeared to be leering at him.

Cal closed his eyes and tried to calm himself. He raised his sleeve to his mouth and bit down on the heavy wool. He could take a bayonet; as long as it missed his vital organs, he might live. The German voices were louder, garbled words that in some strange way he felt he understood.

The corpse above him shook and was still, shook and was still. A soldier at some distance called out and a voice sounded loudly above him, and then the corpse to his right jerked. His mouth had eased its clamp upon his coat when suddenly the bayonet speared soft flesh on the inside of his hip. He bit down as the knife twisted in his muscle, felt tendon and sinew exiting the wound as the knife was withdrawn. Warm blood came up over his groin and flowed down his pant leg. His breathing came in ragged gasps and he knew that if they speared him again, he would die.

A bayonet ripped into his thigh again and he howled madly in his head. Blood filled his mouth from where he bit into his sleeve. Pain and darkness were pressing down on him, and he knew that he must fight to stay awake. In this glimmering half consciousness his eyelids fluttered, and he opened and closed his eyes, and into this flickering space came the leering face of the dead soldier lying prostrate beside him.

He heard the voices move farther away, and in that moment thought of what would come next: Panzers bulldozing the clearing, rolling across the fight zone, giant tracks crushing the frozen dead beneath them. When he tried to move, kicking and pushing himself up through the bodies around him, burning pain shot through his hip and leg, but he rose steadily nonetheless, pushing and pulling himself to the top.

He eased his head between two bodies and tried to catch his breath. A thick gray-white fog rolled over the corpses, hid the tree line from view. Through the mist he could see the back of the soldier who had speared him. The others were spread a few yards apart from one another and had already advanced much farther, barely visible through the haze. He began to pull himself toward what he thought would be the tree line, and stopped. Another company of soldiers were coming, treading their way around blast craters and bodies and toward the line of barbed wire on which the dead soldier hung.

Cal remained still and through slitted eyes watched their advance. They moved deliberately, scanning the trees, giving only an occasional glance at the bodies strewn across the ground. The mist was separating them, elongating their shapes as they moved past. He had to stem the bleeding and make some type of tourniquet if he was going to live. He had to get to the tree line. He reached down to his waist and, with difficulty, withdrew his bayonet from its scabbard. He began to move again, crawling over corpses and parts of corpses, pausing every now and again and remaining still, hoping that in the mist he would not be detected.

But now someone else was coming. He heard a loud voice, a sudden exclamation of surprise, and a soldier was making his way back to the wire, treading slowly with his gun raised. Cal lay on his side, pressed into the body of a man who no longer had a face. The soldier swept his gun through the mist before him. There was a moment when Cal heard nothing, as if the solider had turned and moved away, but then there was the sound of splintering ice and a black boot came down a foot from Cal's ear. Cal breathed slow and deep, tightened his grip upon the bayonet. The soldier took a step forward and Cal lunged up from between the corpses, grabbed for the back of the soldier's head. His right hand found the man's mouth as he drove the bayonet up into the man's lower spine, and as his leg and hip gave out on him, his weight pulled the soldier back to the ground. The man lost his hold on his gun and flailed with his arms, scrabbled at his back frantically. Cal held him there in that strange, intimate embrace, hand clasped to his mouth, pushing the bayonet with all his force deeper into the man until his strength began to ebb and finally the soldier's struggles ended. Cal felt the man's last hot breath exhale upon his hand, and then his arms fell to the side. Cal lay beneath the body, breathing deeply, and soon got up enough strength to rotate and push to the side, where it rolled off him.

It began to snow again, soft thick flakes spilling out of the dark sky above. When he looked up into the sky, the sight of the snow mesmerized him. It was like looking though the windshield of his father's car when he was young, the many nights he'd sat in the front seat of his father's beat-up Chrysler, bent for warmth against the heating vent as a snowstorm came down, and accompanied his father to the union hall and to union rallies during the winter. He thought of that heat now, and felt sleepy and strangely content. He could smell his father's tobacco which filled the small space of the car, the pleasant odor of pomade in his freshly combed black hair, and his cologne, which he'd put on after he showered and shaved. His father was talking to him in that deep-timbred accent, a voice that was soothing and yet somehow violent at the same time. He couldn't make out what he was saying but it seemed to have something to do with his mother. The snow was rushing down from the sky into the headlights, and his father squinted at the glass, sucking on his cigarette intensely. The wipers made their squeaking sound as they moved back and forth, staggering across the glass, and it was as if he and his father were alone in the world, lost in the streets of Boston and the snow and the dark.

He didn't know how much time had passed. Snow had dusted the German soldier's body; it covered the corpses that lay about them. He had to move again, do something. He felt blood dripping around his waist and down into his crotch. He stared up into the sky and blinked. Everything was becoming blurry and indistinct. He reached into his jacket's front pocket, hands stiff and barely working, and struggled with the small packet to pop out two morphine capsules into his bloodied palm. Once he got them down his dry throat, he lay there staring up at the sky, at the snowflakes falling into his eyes.

The sound of gunfire and explosions echoed deep in the forest. Flares ignited the corners of the sky. The war was starting up again. The pain began to ebb, like little candle flames extinguished one by one in the dark cave of his skull. What warmth he'd felt had left his body, and time passed and the morphine took him away and the snow covered him and he knew that he would soon be dead.

The early light of dawn came through the window sharp and bright, reflecting off the snow that had fallen again in the night. Wind pounded against the windowpanes. A receptionist was barking though the intercom for a doctor, and for a long while as Cal felt the sheets about him, hearing the hospital bed creak and whine as he moved, he couldn't distinguish if it was English or French the nurse spoke, and in a perplexed moment he thought that he had awoken in the French hospital again, and that he could feel the bayonet in his upper thigh, the frostbite upon his fingers and toes where they'd turned almost completely black.

Dante was sitting in a chair by the door looking haggard, his eyes sunken and sleepless, the black of his unshaven face stark against his pale skin. He was staring at him, a cigarette smoldering from between his fingers. His voice moved toward him through the smoke.

"They found the Butcher," he said.

"What?"

"Scarletti. They found him."

Cal shook his head in a confused manner, his eyes still adjusting to the dueling contrast of the bright light from outside and the dark shadows that gathered by the corners of the room. "Where?"

"He's here, on the third floor. They brought him in this morning. I guess he's in bad shape. I met Owen in the lobby and he told me."

Cal pushed the blanket and sheet off his body, grasped for the bed rail so that the iron bed frame shook with a sudden, loud tremor.

Dante put out his hand, palm up, and moved forward off the chair. "You're not going anywhere."

"He's that bad?" Cal eased himself into an upright position, inched his way down the length of the mattress. His bare legs dangled over the edge of the bed. He pressed his feet against the floor and grimaced, used the bed rail to hoist himself up, the tendons in his forearms and neck strung rigid with the effort. He pushed his feet into slippers, yanked his arms into a robe, fumbled with the ties at its front. He was already breathing hard.

Dante shook his head, mashed his cigarette out in the ashtray stand by the door, then stepped out into the hall. A moment later the door opened and he rolled a wheelchair into the room.

"What the fuck's that for?"

"For Christ's sake, just get in," Dante muttered. "It'll be easier on the both of us."

⤸

THE BUTCHER'S ROOM was on the far side of the ward, the full length of the building and through a double door to a registration desk and then a dozen rooms beyond. Dante pushed the wheelchair slowly, giving the appearance of a fatigued family member suffering from both a certain kind of grief and helplessness, but when Cal tried to take control of the wheels and propel himself forward so that they might move more quickly, Dante swore under his breath, leaned over, and pushed his hand away.

Nurses and attendants bustled past, oblivious to them. Here and there a nun walked by, white face pulled taut by a white wimple. From one room a priest stepped out slowly, pulling a stole wearily from his neck. The door to the room remained partly open, and as they passed, they could see a family huddled at the end of a bed, heads bowed down in either mourning or prayer. From another room came a startling phlegm-choked wail, and a young rusty-haired attendant rushed from the nurses' station. The head nurse sat rigid, unmoving at the registration desk, and as they passed her, in machinelike fashion, she picked up the telephone ringing shrilly on the desk before her.

"Owen said it was room three thirty-seven, second to last, at the very end."

They turned into the corridor, and at the end of the hallway Owen stood at the door to room 337 talking with Giordano and a young, pale-faced uniform to their right, trying to look purposeful and austere.

Inwardly Cal groaned; he'd been waiting for this but wasn't ready for it now. He straightened in the wheelchair and lifted his head, though it hurt to do so. The sound of his wheelchair turned their heads. Frowning, Giordano looked from Dante to Cal and his eyes paused; it took him a while to recognize him, thanks to Blackie's fists, but he must have heard what had happened. A smile came to his face.

Giordano had never been a lean man, but he had put on weight since Cal had seen him last. He wore an expensive pin-striped Italian suit beneath an overcoat that reached his ankles, to flaunt, Cal supposed, his new rank and to make him look slimmer.

"O'Brien," he said grinning, and his jowls quivered. "I almost didn't recognize you. Jesus, look at your face. What've you been eating? Bad pussy?" His smile grew wider; his face had the flush of constant exertion particular to the obese.

"You've always been a class act, Giordano."

"You ain't so tough now, though, are you?"

Dante paused with the wheelchair, gave the two of them some distance just to be safe, and Owen stepped between them.

Giordano looked to Owen. "What are they doing here?"

"Lay off," Owen said. "They're family."

"Family my ass."

Cal said, "It looks like someone did your job for you."

"I don't think the press or the public will care about that. All they'll care about is that there's no longer a mass murderer on the streets. And in the end, they'll thank us for it."

"And you don't care that someone almost killed him? You know it was Blackie who did this, and why? Because he doesn't want you to find out something. Why the hell would the Butcher, a truck driver, leave Sheila's body somewhere where everyone would know it had to have been dumped by a truck? It doesn't make any sense."

Giordano looked down at Cal. "Want to know why you were kicked off the force?"

"Sure, go ahead, tell me."

"Because you have no self-control. That's always the problem with you micks."

He reached into his overcoat, pulled out a cigar, took his time unwrapping it. Cal noted that his fingernails were manicured. He chewed on the end of the cigar, spat into the trash bin by the door.

"He was good police," Owen said, and held Giordano's gaze when he turned his way.

"Yeah, well," Giordano muttered, staring at Owen and chewing on something stuck in his teeth. "He ain't no police now. Him and his buddy can look at the stiff if they want to, it doesn't mean shit to me. Then the room is off-limits to everyone." He nodded to the uniform standing just outside the door. "You, what's your name, you got that?"

"Kokkinogenis, sir. Yes, sir."

"Good. And you," he said, gesturing to Owen, "come with me."

He went to step past Cal's wheelchair and then paused. Cal turned his head painfully to look up at him. Giordano was smiling again, trying to antagonize him, and taking as much pleasure out of seeing him in a wheelchair as he could. Giordano's jowls trembled as if he were laughing silently to himself. He put the cigar in his mouth and turned away and Owen followed him.

THE MAN'S NOSE was gone, the lips torn away, and his mouth an open leering cavity absent of teeth. From within a purple, pulpy mess a single eyeball gazed lifelessly up at them. An oxygen tube was taped to his throat, and through this he breathed in a wet, gurgling, clawing way that made Cal want to keep his distance. The man might as well have been dead. He should have been dead.

"Christ, how is he even alive?" he said. He stared at the man's arm and the deeply inked tattoo of an anchor, a dark serpent coiling around it, the only recognizable thing left on his body.

"I guess Blackie and his boys found him, all right," Dante said. He moved from behind the wheelchair and stood beside Cal. "Owen said his tattoos were the only way they could identify him. They found the Peterbilt a little ways away from where they discovered the body. Shirley was in the truck, with her neck cut open."

Cal leaned back in his chair, felt the chill of the room pass through his threadbare hospital robe. "Blackie made sure we could see those tattoos for a reason, but why did he leave him alive?"

"Maybe just to teach him a final lesson, spread the word not to fuck with him, I don't know."

Cal continued to stare at the faceless man breathing through a pipe shoved down his throat, and the slow movement of his chest up and down, the shape of him growing more amorphous as sun reflected off snow and came into the room. The man's body seemed to dissolve into that stark and almost violent glow, and they squinted, focused on what was left of his face, the single blazing eye. The sound of his breathing intensified, a labored and thick, wet wheezing, like a broken sump pump attempting to suck water from a flooded basement. Both Cal and Dante thought that they were watching his final breath, but the machine returned to its even up-and-down grind, pushing air into a body that wouldn't last much longer. In the hallway beyond, a gurney passed along the tile on squeaking rubber wheels, momentarily startling both of them.

Dante rubbed at his jaw, exhaled. "So, it's all over now."

Cal tongued his swollen mouth, rolled his shoulders. He was staring at the man again, and the whole room seemed to blur, leaving only the gruesome face in a sharp clarity, and for a moment he thought how the two of them shouldn't be here in a room with the near dead, that only family and loved ones should have this moment to say their final prayers. He clenched his jaw, and his mouth filled with fluid that might have been blood, and he wanted to spit on the floor.

He swallowed, coughed into his hand, his throat bitter and hoarse. He felt cold and weak and wanted to be back in his own bed. For the first time in a long while he had no desire for a drink, and that, despite everything else, seemed like a good thing, even if the danger of sobriety was being able to feel and see everything for exactly what it was—the whole shitty world and everything in between: the neighborhood within the neighborhood that was Boston.

46

BLACK JACK'S, SOUTH BOSTON

BLACKIE FOLEY SAT at the end of the bar, slowly sipping a beer, and, squinting through the cigarette smoke, watched the door. It opened only occasionally, admitting a flash of brief, bright winter light through which the black shapes of men passed, their feet thumping loudly on the old wide-board floor toward a stool or table. The lights in the place flickered and dimmed each time wind gusted down the avenue, and the barman had begun to light candles—waxen stumps and butt ends—at the back of the bar as if anticipating a power outage. With the electric fluctuations, the lights of a jukebox in the room also flickered, a quivering glow cast through yellow marbleized Catalin, its once vibrant and translucent colors dulled by smoke and grime. The music droned, winding down and then starting up again, causing Lee Wiley's "Can't Get Out of This Mood" to vibrate back and forth between a strange baritone and a sweeping falsetto that filled the room with a strange, ghostly dissonance.

There was loud laughter in the corner, and a man with a green scally cap pulled low over his forehead joined Blackie at the bar. He had a stocky build, broad shouldered and narrow hipped, a thin crosshatching of scars just under his temple by the cheekbone. His blue and green flannel shirt was open to the waist. Still laughing, he gestured to the barman in a way that insinuated Blackie had his next round paid for.

"Do I know you?" Blackie said, his voice resounding in the long, narrow space. The man turned his head to look directly at Blackie, and noticing something, he started slightly. "I'm Jerry Hayes…" He looked confused. "I live over on D Street."

"Do I know you?"

"I'm—"

"Do I fucking know you, Jerry Hayes?"

"We once were out—"

Blackie repeated himself, this time much louder so all the chatter in the bar stopped, allowing an uneasy silence to fill the smoke-laden air. "Do I fucking know you, Jerry Hayes?"

"No…no." He took a step back, half raised his hands in apology. "You don't know me, Blackie."

"Then what the fuck are you doing in my fucking space? Get the fuck out of my space."

Casting his eyes downward, the man backed away, and when Blackie was sure he'd gone, he drank from his beer. A look overcame him, as if he were thinking back, trying his hardest to put two and two together and remember something.

"Petey," he said, "get that fuck and his friends a round of drinks on me and a round of chasers. Tell them I don't mean anything by it."

"You got it, Blackie."

Blackie tipped back his glass and wiped at his upper lip. A copy of the *Herald* was spread out on the bar, its pages dampened by the wet rings of beer glasses. He grabbed it and turned to the front page, looked again at the photo of his brother, the chief of police, lead detective Giordano, and the mayor posing before the police headquarters entrance—POLICE ARREST KILLER. THE BUTCHER'S REIGN ENDS. A fucking joke, he thought.

The lights flickered and the song on the jukebox wavered in its strange tremolo of alternating speeds, fast then slow. When the congressman entered, the clock above the bar read a quarter past four, although Blackie knew it was fifteen minutes slow.

The congressman shook snowflakes from the collar of his leather coat, nodded at the bartender for a drink. He waited with his leg cocked on the tarnished bar rail as the bartender pulled on the tap and filled the glass, then grabbed a bottle of whiskey and poured a double. A semi rumbled past toward Old Colony and the building trembled.

Blackie continued to stare at him, until the congressman turned slowly toward him and grinned.

"C'mon," Blackie said, and motioned with his head toward a back booth, and the congressman followed him from the bar. Blackie sat down in the booth, slapped the paper on the table, and sipped at his beer as if it were bitter. His jaw flexed; he watched as his brother drank casually from his whiskey. He gestured toward the newspaper. "Nice picture."

"Think it'll serve me in my run?"

"That's all you've got to say?"

"Give it a rest."

"No. You fucking owe me."

"I worked hard to get here, Finn. I didn't come this far to get fucked by my little brother, the fucking gangster."

"Don't talk to me like that, Mikey. You're not that big that you can talk to me like that, and not here. I'm always trying to do the right thing by you."

A silence overcame the space between them. Blackie took a tug of beer and the congressman took a generous one off his double whiskey.

"I brought you up after Ma left because I promised her that I'd always look after you. I was there for you when you were in and out of juvie. I was there for you after you got out of Concord and Danbury. I've gotten you out of more scrapes than I can fucking count."

"The Butcher is the least of what I did for you," Blackie said.

The congressman raised a finger, pointed it across the table, silencing his younger brother. Blackie waited a moment, watched the congressman sipping his double. Color had risen up his neck to his cheeks.

"You helped me out of a jam, Finn, and I appreciate it. For Christ's sake, I had nowhere else to turn."

The congressman put his glass on the table. When he spoke he was slow and deliberate.

"Look, if I didn't show appreciation for what you did, if I didn't thank you enough, then I'm sorry."

"You and that silly little twat. You sent me on a wild goose chase, Mikey. You said she was connected to Renza, and now they're both gone, and I'm still out my share."

"I don't care about the Brink's job and I don't care about your fucking share. You know I don't give a damn about any of that. I told you where she lived, I told you what she had going with Renza. What more do you want from me?"

"I want a cut of what that McAllister and that fat guinea Rizzo have. I want Scollay Square, between Cambridge and Broad."

"You don't think Sully or half the other racketeers in the city want a part of it too? You're nuts. What would Sully say if he knew?"

"Fuck Sully. You give me a part of what you and McAllister have going on and it puts me in a position to take over."

The congressman raised a hand in exasperation and surrender. "Okay, okay, but there's still too many loose ends. McAllister is getting worried. No one gets anything for nothing here."

"I've already taken care of the Butcher, already made everything nice and easy for you."

"Jesus, you want me to ask Sully to take care of this because my own brother can't?"

"No. I'll take care of it."

"There's a reason why Sully is boss. He finishes things off."

"I said I'll take care of it."

The congressman nodded. "We're brothers. We stick together." Spit glistened on his lower lip. "But this needs to get done, so just do it." He pushed out of the booth and rose, adjusted his shirt and coat with an odd grace. He looked down at the picture on the front page of the paper. "Not bad, is it? I think they got my good side."

At the bar he pulled a five-dollar bill from his pocket, placed it on the scarred countertop, nodded at the bartender, and strode toward the door, coat fanning out behind him. Blackie watched him exit the bar, his hulking figure momentarily transfixed in the doorway surrounded by a corona of light, and he saw the two of them as small boys of some summer long ago, when they still had their mother and before their father had remarried. They were in a small cove where waves crashed and the sand was hot beneath his feet, and once he'd made it into the water, his brother's grip strong and reassuring, pulling him through the water, drawing him farther and farther out where the water swirled gray and cold and mysterious, his brother telling him to look into his face, at his eyes staring intently back into his own, forcing him to trust him, convincing him that no matter what, he would not let him go—he would never let him go.

47

CARNEY HOSPITAL, BOSTON

CAL SAT UPRIGHT in bed, looking out at the snow-topped evergreens swaying against the glass and the sounds of the hospital in the hallway beyond: the shuffling of soft-heeled shoes, the whirring of gurneys and trolleys, of nurses and doctors and the double *bing* of the intercom and a page for a doctor or family member. A young nurse's aide named Maggie had managed to get him some bennies to calm his nerves and he'd asked her not to mention it to Lynne, but when Scarletti's face came to him—or what was left of his face—he could die for a drink. Scarletti was barely alive, sucking air through a tube; in a matter of days he'd probably be dead, but it wasn't death that scared Cal, it was the way one died.

He'd first seen death as a boy on the streets of Dorchester, a man stumbling from a bar, bloodied from being cut with a smashed beer bottle. It had been in the summertime and near dusk, although true night seemed very far off, for the streets were still busy with the noise of workmen on their stoops talking and smoking, sharing a beer after work, women calling children in, and radios blaring from open windows.

He was walking the sidewalk when the door to the Adams Street Tap slammed open and the man stumbled out before him. The man reeled, his legs crumpling beneath him before he'd even made the curb. Blood flowed brightly down his face and from his neck. The chest of his blue work shirt turned black. He clutched at his throat, oblivious to the blood flowing from the gash at his hairline, and then fell onto his back. He turned in Cal's direction and stared at him and gasped something, and it was then that Cal realized the man before him was Mr. Welch—Julie Welch's father, who worked at Necco confectioners over the bridge in Cambridge. On Dorchester Day he'd bring bags of candy and pass it out to the kids. He even rode a float in the annual parade. Cal had never seen him inside a bar, and he'd been inside most of them on the Avenue, at one time or another, searching for his father. Mr. Welch gasped some more, blood frothing from the wide, ragged slit in his neck. His eyes searched Cal's and held them for a moment as if he had something very important to tell him, and then he closed his eyes and lay very still and Cal knew that he was dead.

But that type of death, as shocking as it had been, had never touched Cal physically. He had no fear of his neighborhood or its streets; he knew he could never be hurt here, not like that. And then, a year before the war, sitting at the Blarney Stone in Fields Corner having a beer, and Blackie and some of his buddies from Charlestown started a fight with him. There had been a mick, a small weasel of a man but tough, with a boxer's nose and fast hands, whom Blackie had goaded into fighting by telling him he couldn't take Cal, and the mick had come up to the bar and slapped the beer out of his hands and followed with a cheap right, grazing the side of his head. When it looked like he was going to handle the mick one-on-one, Blackie set the others on him. Outnumbered, he'd smashed a beer bottle and stuck it first into the mick's eye and then one of his buddies' throats. He'd acted out of desperation and fear, but with this came an anger that provided its own momentum and energy, a conviction that he wouldn't stop until he had hurt as many of them as he could.

In thinking about it now, Cal clenched his fists. His shoulders and neck became rigid and his breathing deepened. It felt as if his lungs were being pierced by his ribs, his heart a heavy, swollen thing working hard in his chest. Air whistled through his broken nose and it began to throb painfully, forcing him to breathe through his mouth.

In the end, when Blackie's boys had driven him to the floor with their fists and boots, Jackie Doyle, the bartender and an old friend of his father's, had saved him. He took a bat to the back of one of Blackie's punks, held three of them off, and as Cal rose to go at them again, slipping in a pool of blood on the wooden floor, they fled, bleeding and cursing their way out the door and fucked off up the Avenue. For months Cal had waited for retribution from Blackie in the typical manner of the neighborhood—a tire iron to his skull one night as he stepped drunkenly out of a bar, a shiv to the eye—but none ever came. Jackie Doyle wasn't so lucky. Blackie came through a crowd on the street during the Saint Patrick's Day parade and gutted him, left him to bleed out on the street while parents with their children milled about.

He had survived because of that desperation, because he didn't cede an inch, but if he'd stayed and never left Boston for Europe, that desperation would probably have also gotten him killed. And he realized this in the same way that he realized he was lucky to be alive now. He had pushed Blackie too far, and he was lucky to be seeing and thinking and breathing, and not like the sad bastard down the hall who'd had his face torn inside out.

When he'd first come back from the war—a six-month-late transport home thanks to stops at French hospitals in Bar Le Duc, Clichy, and Verdun—Lynne had tried to comfort him, soothe him, and be sympathetic. But even after the injuries to his body had healed, all he'd felt was a numbness, a black nothing that gradually gave way to fear and then to incredible waves of anger and resentment—anger at nothing he could name, and yet the source was everywhere around him: it was Lynne with her calm tenderness and sad, pitying eyes; it was the neighborhood with its people and reminders of the life he'd left behind and could never return to; it was those people with their talk and memories of his parents, of his mother, silenced into submission by his father's fists, hiding in their small kitchenette in her housecoat and apron, staring blankly out at the Ave, waiting for the phone to ring, for a neighbor to call and visit, smoking one cigarette after the other, the gray haze of it always swirling in threads against the stamped tin of the ceiling in the small room; the shift horns from the docks, the shipyards, and the Edison plant, the clock chiming five thirty; and the downstairs door opening and his father's footsteps sounding on the narrow, crooked back stairwell as he made his way up to their second-floor apartment, with no bathtub or hot water and only a coal stove in the middle of the kitchen to heat water and an icebox to keep the food cold. It was this neighborhood, with its boundaries and petty grievances and vendettas and its long, never-ever forgetting.

There was still something wrong about the whole Butcher thing. Cal knew this. It all seemed too easy to have a suspect in custody who would soon die without ever giving voice to all the terrible things he'd done. But perhaps Lynne was right, perhaps it was time to get out, now while he was in this state of mind, now while the rage for retribution and payback did not burn within him or the deep-rooted fear that the not-acting, the not-doing-anything-at-all might mark him as a coward, as someone who'd hidden beneath dead bodies in order to stay alive and then slunk away like a rat to safety beneath the cover of night. He knew that sooner or later he'd die—everyone died—and the only thing that frightened him was that he didn't want to die like Mr. Welch, Jackie Doyle, or even Scarletti, the Butcher.

48

THEY CHANGED HIS bandaging before they checked him out, and Maggie handed him sixty Benzedrine wrapped in a towel, which he placed in the canvas duffel bag Lynne had brought from home on the night he'd been admitted. With his bag he limped to the elevator, waving away a nurse who was insisting that Maggie bring him down in a wheelchair, and rode to Lynne's ward on the second floor. She wasn't at the nurses' station but he knew where she was.

The hospital pool was fogged by moisture and heat, and he had trouble breathing. Empty wheelchairs crouched in the shadowy corners gleaming. Lights were set into niches under the lip of the pool, casting strange undulating reflections onto the tiled walls and ceiling. Cal stood at the edge of the pool, feeling sweat gathering between his shoulder blades and on his eyelids and his upper lip. He removed his hat to wipe the sweat at his temple.

Lynne, in a black bathing suit and a white goose-pimpled bathing cap, was floating on her back with her eyes closed, her knees flexed slightly and parted, arms outspread. Water lapped over her breasts and stomach. The pool lights shimmering beneath her created a corona of luminescence around her body, darkening and blurring her features so that at first he felt that he did not know her, that it wasn't really his Lynne at all but someone other, and he felt ashamed and guilty for his intrusion. Lynne rolled onto her front and did a lap of freestyle. He watched her long, lean legs pumping and the muscles of her bottom tensing with each kick. On the return, she turned onto her back and began to swim with strong backstrokes toward him. She turned and completed another lap and then another.

She reached the wall and paused there, treading water for a moment, and then, grasping the sides of the metal ladder, pulled herself up out of the water. When she stepped from the ladder, he found himself standing closer than he had expected. She stared up at him for a moment, wide-eyed and startled, and then stepped back. "Jesus, Cal, how long have you been there?"

Even in the thick, moist heat of the room he could feel the watery chill emanating from her flesh. He shrugged, pawed at his hat. "Not long."

She pulled off her bathing cap and shook her hair, stepped past him, and bent to pick up her towel. She toweled her front, the insides of her thighs, turned her back to him to adjust the crotch of the swimsuit and cover herself more fully, as if he were a stranger and not her husband.

She pulled on a white terry cloth robe that lay stretched across the chair and sat, lifting her legs up beneath her onto the chair. In the distance came the sound of an ambulance siren. She sighed. "What are you doing here?"

"That guy in room three thirty-seven," Cal sighed, gesturing toward the door suggesting the third-floor room, as he lowered himself onto the chair next to her. "They say he's the Butcher—the one who killed Sheila and all those women."

Lynne paused in wringing her hair with the towel. "But you don't believe it?"

"I don't know."

"Why can't you let it go? Just look at what happened to him."

278

"You didn't see what was done to Sheila."

"No, I didn't, and I wouldn't want to. Most normal people wouldn't."

"But I do, that's what you're saying?"

"Sometimes you seem to thrive on it."

Cal lay back on the chair and grunted, touched his ribs tenderly.

"I'm asking you to do something for me for a change. Will you please let this whole Sheila thing go?"

Cal stared at the water, the slightly undulating surface and the shimmering lights it cast upon the walls. He felt like he was in a dream and falling, and that if only he could have a drink, he'd wake up and everything would be still around him again.

"Would you? Would you do that for me?" she repeated.

"I can't," he said.

"You can't?"

"No, I don't think I can."

"We once talked of getting out of Boston, and of having children. You used to talk about us getting a small cottage in Truro. You said that the Cape, facing the Atlantic, was the best place, the only place in the world to raise a child."

"Yeah, except in the winter."

"You didn't care about the winter then."

"You're right. I didn't."

Lynne shook her head. "I don't know what you care about, but it's not the important things anymore."

Their voices traveled out over the water and struck faint echoes from the walls. She was studying him. She began to speak and then paused, tried to follow what his eyes were looking at. "We're still young," she said. "If we tried... if you wanted to try."

"You're young, Lynne." He shrugged. "Maybe. Maybe we try, maybe we give it a go."

She gazed into his face and he could see her not believing him. She sniffed, and laughed, and buried her face in the towel, and held it there for a long moment, and he wondered if she might be crying.

The reflections off the pool, calmer now that the water had stilled, moved in dreamy helixes on the glass wall and ceiling, reminding him of mortar shells exploding above the tree line, raining showers of burning metal as colorful as fireworks seen through the blurry gaze of concussion.

Distantly, in some other part of the hospital, an intercom sounded and a doctor's name was called, a clock struck a single, silver note, and an instant later from farther off came another chime, and yet another, farther off still, and then the silence settled again. The glass was bright and opaque although the room had grown dark around them. The pool shimmered green in the center of the darkness. Lynne stood and, taking her robe off, walked through the lights toward the locker rooms without turning back, without any further acknowledgment that he was there.

AT FITZGERALD'S RINK over at Neponset, Cal stood against the boards and watched the skaters gliding across the ice. He stared at the couples there embracing, arms around each other, pulling each other close, clutching at each other as they stumbled and slipped, laughing. A few couples looked at him, startled by the sight of him: heavy stained gauze plastered across his nose, eyes still red from the blood that had pooled in them, and when he tried to smile at them his face felt lopsided, as if the nerve endings had been somehow severed. He wondered if they would heal at all.

When the cold got too much he took a bus down to Carson Beach. Inside the L Street Bathhouse it was warm and smelled of sweat and urine. A young welterweight was jumping rope; a couple of older boxers worked the heavy bags. Joe Castiglione, the manager of the bathhouse, pushed a mop and bucket across the stone floor, paused and frowned when he saw Cal.

"Jesus, what the fuck happened to you?"

Cal waved him away. "Never mind me, what have you got on the cards?"

"Nothing that would cure what you got, not enough to cure a hangover."

Cal laughed, felt his ribs pressing like splinters into his lungs.

They spoke for a bit about the upcoming fight in March between Jersey Joe Walcott and Ezzard Charles, Joe, leaning on his mop handle, telling him of the next great in the back room who'd whup both of them soon enough.

Passing through the gym Cal nodded and said hello to those he knew, and a few veterans of the war who'd found a place to lose themselves—a phantasmagoria of worn-out, mangled faces: busted cheeks and scarred necks, bloated, pockmarked noses, stooped shoulders, split brows, flop ears, and weary, stupefied eyes, as much a result of the war as of boxing, and of the city and the larger yet no less forgiving world beyond. Stepping into the back room Cal was glad to suddenly enter the realm of the young. Even the effect of light and the smell of sweat seemed different here, somehow less desperate. Cal watched the young boxers as they stepped in and out of the ring and at the ring's center as they stumbled and tripped and sometimes danced and strutted beneath the caged lights.

Recognizing Cal, one of the young men in the ring took his mouthpiece out and called to him, asked about the other fella's face and if he'd gone a couple with Rocky Marciano and his entire corner, hollered for him to get in the ring and spar, to show them what he had, wondering if the old man still had anything left in him, and his trainer and others in the room called out also, echoing the young man. Cal grinned and waved them away.

Back outside he stared at the sea, sharp-looking whitecaps shearing the tops of the gray Atlantic, feeling the pleasant stinging warmth of the sun against his face and hands. He could feel pain beginning to build like a wave, and popping some more bennies, he tried to ignore it, turned his head toward the sea wind. He grabbed a grilled cheese at the Farragut House on P Street, walked up to Old Colony Ave, and caught a bus to Uphams Corner, saw a movie he didn't care for at the Strand, rode the streetcar to the end of the line and then back, and finally walked to Mickey Doolin's at the corner of Savin and Franklin Street, where he sat and waited the two hours for Lynne's night shift to end. He reclined his head between the seatback and the cold window and closed his eyes and waited for the clock to chime the hour so that he could be moving again, and then restless as if something were gnawing at him, he went to the pay phone at the back of the bar and waited for the switchboard operator. The clock ticked over the bar and the operator finally came on the line and he asked for the address of McIntyre, McAllister, and Broome.

49

LOUISBURG SQUARE, BEACON HILL

THE OFFICES OF McIntyre, McAllister, and Broome were in a three-story redbrick Greek Revival in the city's charmed Louisburg Square on Beacon Hill. Cal paused before the weathered steps on which fresh salt was drying and regarded the black-shuttered windows, the silent cobblestone streets, narrow as alleys, and the small private park with its frozen statues and fountain, placed exclusively in isolation, away from the rest of the city and just the way the people living here wanted it. Cal's bandaged hands rested upon the elaborate black iron railing. The roof's copper flashing was weathered to a rich green hue, and above that on the slate rooftop, snow so perfectly white it looked as if it were part of some Hollywood set.

In the vestibule he stamped snow from his feet and paused, breathing in the warmth and the rich smells of wax and pine and mahogany, of brass and metal polish. A thick red carpet ran the length of the hall and his footsteps moved softly over it. Interior double parlors to the right were shrouded in darkness, broken by a brief flickering amid the shadows—the sound of wood crackling in a fire.

To his left an ornate staircase wound its way upward to other offices from which came the sound of opening and closing doors and voices in conversation, rising and falling and muted like the hiss of waves upon a shore yet distant. The hallway opened into a large reception area, where a receptionist sat at a shiny polished wood desk before the wide double doors to McAllister's offices.

She was turned away from him and he could see the angle of her face, sharp and rodent-like, although he could tell she fancied herself a beauty. Her hair was dyed a cobalt black, so black it shimmered blue in the light; she'd applied red lipstick beyond the thin line of her lips to make her mouth appear pouty and full. As he approached, she was looking at herself in a compact. He could hear the hiss of nylon against nylon as she crossed her legs and rubbed them against each other.

He raised a hand as he passed. "Committeeman O'Brien from the Eleventh Ward for Mr. McAllister," he called out. "We've got a ten thirty time arranged at Franklin Park." Her hands dropped, but the compact remained opened. Her blowsy mouth opened in surprise. "You can't," she managed, and Cal pointed to his teeth, made a scrubbing motion that had her picking up her compact again, and then the doorknobs to McAllister's offices were turning in his hands. He locked the door behind him and a moment later he heard her heels clattering on the tile, and then she was tugging at the doors, calling for him to leave the office at once.

The room was empty and done up in much the same manner as the entranceway: burnished mahogany wood paneling and plush red carpets, a large desk behind which hung an ornate gilt-framed painting of a group of stags crossing a great plain, a single door to his right, which perhaps led to other offices or back out into the hall. He eyed the desk quickly: framed pictures of children splashing in the surf at some small beach—he could see a rocky coastline jutting out into the water and as it curved to the sea a house sitting at its end, the North Shore perhaps or, farther, Maine—another of a woman who he assumed was the wife in an elegant wide-brimmed bonnet, holding its top as if it might be swept away by the wind; a large daily planner, two blue half-unrolled architectural plans, various forms dealing with city planning and building codes, a stack of letters with the firm's name stamped in formal print that caught Cal's attention.

The intercom on the desk suddenly buzzed, its light flashing. After a moment it stopped. Cal leaned farther over the desk, risked lifting the letters, fanned them out. There was one addressed to Michael Foley, with a Gloucester address. He held it to the light so that it became almost translucent. There was a check inside, on yellow stock, and nothing else; as he turned it, he could almost make out a name and the amount.

The sound of a man clearing his throat came from a door to his right, followed by a hacking of phlegm and then the flushing of a toilet. A belt buckle jangled. Footsteps sounded on tile. Cal placed the letters back on the desktop and sat in a chair before the desk.

The door opened and McAllister stood there looking at him, hand on the doorknob.

"Who are you and what are you doing in my office?"

"I told your secretary we had an appointment."

"Then you lied, and I shall have to ask you to leave." He stepped into the room and the door shut behind him. He was a tall man, well over six feet, and lean, thinning white hair combed to the side. Cal half expected him to move as an old man might, but there seemed to be nothing old about him. Looking at Cal and drying his hands on a paper towel, McAllister strode to his desk, dropped the crumpled paper into a wastebasket. His lips tightened in consideration, but he remained silent, waiting for Cal to speak.

Cal imagined that this was what he looked like in board meetings and how he intimidated everyone else in the room. He felt an urge to speak and to offer an explanation for his intrusion; the man's silence seemed to demand it.

The intercom buzzed on his desk again and McAllister finally broke eye contact. He sat and then clicked the speaker button. "Yes?" he said.

"Mr. McAllister, I'm so sorry but a gentleman who said he was from the Eleventh Ward and had a time scheduled with you..."

"Yes, yes, I know. Thank you, Susan." He clicked the speaker off and turned his attention toward Cal. "You're the one from the banquet," he said. "What do you want?"

"You've got plans in at City Hall to tear down all of Scollay and all of the West End."

"You were at Congressman Foley's Senate dinner. He sees great things for Boston, and it begins with its revitalization, with tearing down the old, but what I have to ask is what concern is it of yours? I thought you were looking for the killer of Foley's old fling."

Cal stared at him. He knew more than Cal had suspected.

McAllister smiled. "Congressman Foley told me of their relationship very early on."

"Did you know her?"

"Did I know her? There were times when the congressman brought her to a dinner or an event and we shared the same table, but that was the extent of it."

"So, you know she had a name as well."

"I think it hardly matters now, does it?" McAllister turned his attention to the appointment calendar on his desk, took up a pen, and wrote something there. Without looking up he said, "Are you done, or should I call the police?"

Cal could feel the anger rising in him; McAllister was doing a good job of pushing all of his buttons, and he tried to turn the conversation. As long as McAllister was letting him speak, he wanted to see if he could push back.

"The properties on which your plans are built haven't been bought and you're already tearing down buildings. Nobody has sold a damn thing to you—"

McAllister finally looked up at him. "The buildings we've torn down were already condemned by the city. No personal property has been touched—yet. Congressman Foley made all this very clear at the dinner."

"Like shit he did. Not one person in that ballroom knows what you've got planned for those neighborhoods."

"I can assure you they do. It shows how little you know."

"You're not from around here," Cal said matter-of-factly.

McAllister eyed him and then dismissed him.

"The moment I first laid eyes on you and your friend I knew you were trouble. The world is full of people like you, Mr. O'Brien, trying to get a free buck wherever you can and reap the rewards from what others have worked hard to accomplish. Men like you were born to tear things down, because that's all you are capable of doing. I don't know what your relationship is with Congressman Foley and neither do I care. As you say, there are millions of dollars riding on this project, on the revitalization and development of this fine city, and trust me, nothing, especially not you or your threats, will stop that from happening."

"No?"

McAllister smiled and shook his head. "This is tiresome. You really don't have any idea what you're doing and who you're fucking with."

"Is that what you said to Foley's 'fling,' Sheila Anderson?"

"Go back to your sacred neighborhood, Mr. O'Brien. Call your councilman, call City Hall, call the mayor for all it matters. I think you've wasted enough of my time."

"You must have been shook up to hear about Foley and this woman, to hear about how she was threatening to blow their affair out of the water, to splash it all across the newspapers. What would have happened to all those investors then, all those political promises, all those federal dollars, all those tax breaks? A scandal like that and Foley's chances for Senate are gone. What would your investors think then, after everything you've promised them?"

Snow was knocking against the tall sash windows, small drifts accumulating beyond each chevroned frame. The world outside was white and without sound. The haloed globes of light from the old gaslights on Beacon Hill seemed to float upon the cloudy glass. Cal measured his breathing and worked to calm his pulse.

"Before you leave, Mr. O'Brien, I want us to understand each other perfectly. McIntyre, McAllister, and Broome is one of the biggest developers in the United States. I built this company from the ground up and made it what it is. So that you know, I've never had a problem getting my hands dirty, if that is what it takes. I know all about you and your connections, how you're related to every piece of shit that has ever crawled out of a Boston sewer. If you wish to pursue this, no one will help you. By the time I am done, no one will admit to knowing you, do you understand?"

McAllister smiled, thin-lipped.

"Good-bye, Mr. O'Brien. We won't be seeing each other again."

Cal stared at McAllister unmoved, and then he smiled back, baring his teeth. He tongued some tobacco there, spat it to the carpet. McAllister went to take a cigarette from the case and Cal lunged, grabbed the hand, and yanked McAllister so that he was bowed over the desk. He grasped his head and drove it facedown into the wood. McAllister's head bounced as if it were on a spring, and Cal drove it down again and held it. McAllister, his face turned sideways toward the wall, sputtered and spewed rheum and blood.

"You think you know me. That's your first mistake."

Cal held his hand there, atop his head, and pressed so that McAllister gasped. He whispered in his face, "How do you know Bobby Renza?"

Through broken teeth McAllister sputtered, "His uncle—" and blood filled his mouth and Cal waited for him to spit. "He's the contractor for our redevelopment."

"Why him?"

When McAllister remained quiet, Cal pushed steadily down on his head and repeated the question. When he spoke, Cal knew he'd broken his nose and lost a few teeth, and the swelling was making it difficult to understand him.

"Foley, it was Foley, so he could be with the girl."

"With Sheila?"

McAllister's eyes opened and closed. When Cal let up on his head, he moved it slightly as if in a nod.

"Even though she was with Renza?"

"Yes."

"How did it happen?"

"At one of Rizzo's restaurants in the North End. Everybody was there. Renza was with Sheila. Foley got all hot for her and asked Rizzo who she was. Rizzo told his nephew that she needed to go with Foley, smooth out the deal..." McAllister began to cough more blood. Cal twisted the man's neck harder. "He needed Sheila to make Foley happy."

"You're telling me Renza pimped out his own girl so his uncle could land your bullshit contract?"

"Yes."

"What's your relation to Foley? How are you two connected?"

Cal had to push on McAllister's head again. His anger had faded and now he took relish in it. Across the tabletop a thick film of blood pooled.

"I knew his family," McAllister said finally.

"Bullshit. You didn't know the Foleys."

"Foley's mother worked for my parents. When the Foleys were children, they spent the summers in a house owned by my parents."

"You're lying."

The secretary was banging on the door now. He let go of McAllister's head but then for good measure grabbed it and slammed his face down against the tabletop once more.

"Call the police if you want," he said, and walked to the door.

50

_____

OUR LADY OF PERPETUAL HELP, MISSION HILL, ROXBURY

THE RADIO HAD forecast heavy snow, but only a few plows were on the
deserted roads as the trolley made its way up Huntington Avenue. Two
inches of snow lay on the ground and it continued to fall thick and heavy,
but there was no wind, and to Cal the snowfall seemed to make the city
even quieter and stranger. From the window of the trolley he saw no traffic or pedestrians and only now and again a glimpse of a plow working,
its swirling amber lights sparking in the gloom. There was only one other
passenger on the trolley, sleeping fitfully, and the driver didn't even bother
to turn on the interior light, so they passed through the city in darkness,
the trolley's bell clanging vacantly at empty intersections, and he stared
from the window and watched the snow coming down. Because of ice on
the tracks, the trolley trundled along the line like an aged arthritic, and it
took him forty minutes to get to Mission Hill.

He sat near the front of the church, his head lowered, hands clasped
and resting atop the pew back before him. He had his eyes closed, and
his senses filled with the muted voices of prayer murmuring throughout

the church—so purposeful and insistent in seeking solace, peace, the intercession of the saints and of the Virgin Mary on behalf of a loved one. And though he tried to pray, he couldn't focus; for the third time he forgot what prayer he was reciting and began it again and then, frustrated, whispered the words so that he might hear them. Still, the words and their meanings passed through his head as if it were a sieve and he remained empty-feeling and agitated. He exhaled and looked up.

Above the altar the hands of Christ were held to the cross by the spikes driven through his palms; he stared at the hands, the rigid tendons of his alabaster wrists, flexing as if from the pain as the weight of his body and the force of gravity drew him down and the nails tore through his hands, and for a brief moment Cal was inside the cold of the trailer again and staring at the hands of the dead women bound by chains to dangling meat hooks.

AT MICKI'S ON Tremont, Cal ordered a double whiskey and went to the pay phone by the betting board at the back of the room and called Dante. The operator patched him through and he listened to the flat whine of a dead line and remembered their phone had been cut. He picked up the receiver again, stared blankly at the day's races marked in white chalk, the horses, and their odds, as he waited for the switchboard operator. At the morgue the phone rang and the operator cut in twice to ask if he wanted her to keep trying. Finally a breathless technician picked up and Cal had to wait while he went to look for Fierro. Through the static on the line he could hear the squeal and slam of doors being opened and closed, and what he took to be the whirring buzz of a dissecting saw. Two drunk men by the jukebox with their arms about each other's shoulders began to sing "You're Breaking my Heart," a painful baying that brought the hairs up on the back of his neck and forced him to lean in over the phone. The operator cut in again asking for another nickel and, cursing, he rummaged in his pocket for change, deposited a nickel and two dimes.

The familiar moribund voice came on the line, wheezing as if he'd picked up Owen's cold: "Fierro."

"It's Cal, Tony. I need your help."

"Cal, I really don't have the time. I've got four bodies from a car that went into the Charles at dawn, I've got—"

"I need you to look at the bodies again, just the photos. I need to know something."

"What's this about, Cal?"

"Just look at the photos and tell me if the markings on the wrists are different. If Sheila's markings are different from the other girls'."

"Cal, I can't—"

"Tony, this is the last thing I'm asking you in the world."

Fierro paused on the other end of the line and he heard the strike of a match and a soft exhale and knew Fierro was smoking. After a moment: "All right, give me a couple of minutes to pull the file."

While he waited he placed the phone down and went to the bar to get another double, then returned, put the phone back to his ear, listened to the odd hiss of static from the line, the distant, muted sounds of the morgue. A gurney rattled by once, amplified and close, like the sound of the elevated subway passing, thumping in his ears, then the line became quiet again. He sipped his whiskey slowly, rolling it in his mouth but not really tasting it anymore. Three men stood to his right before the betting board discussing the horses running later on the West Coast, and he turned his back to them, knew that once they made their picks they'd want to use the phone to call their bookies. The door of the bar opened as someone stepped inside and a blast of cold air traveled the length of the room.

Fierro came on the line clicking his tongue, as if with annoyance. "The ligature marks aren't the same," he said, and Cal could picture him frowning. "The others were clearly bound by some kind of metal cuff. It didn't fully bind the wrists, so there are only marks at contact points on the wrist. Sheila's looks to be a thin rope of some kind—you can make out the braid of the different fibers. I should have noticed that, but I don't see how that changes anything. The killer probably used what was at hand."

"Yeah, you're probably right. I just needed to know."

"You sure that's all?"

"That's all. Thanks, Tony. I owe you one."

Cal put the phone down, stared at the wall, and slowly finished his drink. He sensed one of the three men to his right waiting for the phone, and he turned away from him. He picked up the receiver again and tried calling Kelly's Rose to see if Dante was there, but there was no answer and he hung up, walked back up the bar, mulling the discovery in his head. Sheila wasn't killed in the trailer with the other girls; it was only made to look that way. He saw Blackie climbing into the rig down at the Calf Pasture, checking and knowing the seal on the doors had been tampered with because, of course, he'd already been there a few nights earlier depositing Sheila's torn underthings, the purse, and the crucifix, placing them where he knew they'd be found.

51

CAL EASED THE beat-up Fleetline into a parking space along Wollaston Beach and waited. An empty public works truck hulked at the far end of the lot, nose pointed toward the islands, but otherwise the lot was deserted. Before him the water stirred, and farther off the rotted remains of what had once been a pier stretched through the frothy white straits toward Squantum and Moon Island. A yellow snowplow rolled slowly along Quincy Shore Drive, its plow lowered and raising sparks as it struck clear tarmac.

The stacks from the pumping station out on Moon Island stood in black relief against the horizon. Smoke, seeming to glow white, churned into the sky and across the bay—a still picture through which the lights of a plane bound for Logan intermittently broke.

In his rearview he watched the lights of a shiny blue Plymouth sedan as it slowed and, tires losing traction upon a stretch of ice, angled itself awkwardly through the lot's entrance. When the car parked, Cal looked over, opened his door, and climbed out. Shaw met him on the cement walkway before the breakwater. He wore a long dark tweed overcoat, and pushed down over his big mick red head was an olive wool cap with ridiculous-looking earflaps. From where they stood along the vacant beach they could see the low Boston skyline across the black water, lights glittering through a smoky haze of ice.

"I heard about that," Shaw said and gestured at Cal's ruined face. "You look like shit."

Cal shrugged, lowered his head against the wind.

"We all know that Blackie's a reckless fuck. Out his goddamn mind these days." Against the wind, Shaw sucked his teeth, reached up his leather-gloved hands to tighten the collar of his overcoat.

"What do you want?"

"Sully's got to protect his interests."

"Yeah. What's that got to do with me?"

"Don't be a fucking idiot. There's only one guy that needs to get fingered in all this."

Cal dug his hands deeper into his coat pockets, hunched his shoulders. "You're asking me for a favor, aren't you? A goddamn yellow-belly favor."

"No one's going to be looking for payback, that's all I'm telling you."

"A fucking bookie's coming to tell me this? You must be real important these days."

"I'm just speaking for Sully, Cal. Take it while you can."

"For all I know this sounds like a way to get me to do your dirty work, a setup with me as the fall guy, piss off half this city's scum on your behalf. No thanks."

Shaw raised his hands in frustration. "Jesus, Cal, you know I'm telling you because of what he did."

"That's a load of shit, Shaw, and you know it."

"We're all family men, right? We always respect the old neighborhood and the people in it. Sully's word on this. The O'Sheas and Kinneallys and everybody else will fall in line. Through thick and thin, we look out for our own. All we want is that he's gone."

Cal laughed, but without humor. "Except none of you have the balls to do anything about it."

Shaw pressed his hands deeper into his coat pockets, squinted out toward the city lights.

"What makes you think *I'm* going to do anything about it—risk my neck for this?"

Shaw lit a cigarette, the flame of his lighter bending back and forth in the wind. He handed one to Cal.

"Because since you came back from the war you're a fucking mess. You're a fucking bozo, a rummy." He smirked in an all-knowing manner, blew his smoke out at the water, but it returned into his face and into his eyes. "Because you got nothing to lose, Cal. You're a fucking joke. Everyone knows that. They've been taking bets on the street on who's in a coffin sooner, you or Dante."

"Yeah? What are the odds?"

"Odds on you, three to one."

They stood in silence and watched the skyline in the distance shimmering like a cheap crown. The refraction of light through ice gave the city a strange illusory quality, made it seem to have moved closer as they spoke. "We'll give you enough money to start over, Cal. You and Lynne can get out of town. Go. You'll never have to look back."

Cal looked out over the water, at the way it disappeared in blackness a hundred feet from shore.

"Well, that's it," Shaw said. "I'm not standing like a jackass out in this fucking cold any longer. You got what you need to know. You can do what you want with it."

"Why should I trust you? You're the ones who stand to gain in all this."

"Sure, everyone does. And especially you, O'Brien. You get to kill him before he kills you."

"Is that right? It still feels like a setup to me."

Shaw shrugged. "I ain't got no beef with you, Cal. Yeah, we could set you up, but there ain't nothing in it for us."

"For fuck's sake, just kill him yourselves. Not the first time you took out one of your own."

"You know how tightly wrapped this city is. That would start a war, and an Irish gang war would tear this town apart."

"Why isn't Sully telling me this himself?"

"If it all goes down, Sully can't be associated with you. What, do I have to write a fucking book for you?"

"You're afraid of him, and Sully's afraid of him, and that's why you're freezing your ass off talking to me here."

"Sure, that's it, Cal."

"Fuck off, and tell your buddies if they want Blackie taken out to take him out their fucking selves. I won't do your dirty work for you."

"Whatever you say, Cal."

"And another thing."

"Yeah?"

"You touch Dante again, I'll kill you."

"It's business, Cal, purely business. You know that."

"And my business is what I'm telling you now. Your boys touch him and I come after you. As you said, I've got nothing to lose." He spat tobacco from his lip and threw Shaw's cigarette into the snow.

"Fair enough."

"Good, then. Now go fuck off."

Cal watched Shaw climb into his car and start the engine. The windows had iced over so he had to climb out and scrape the glass, and though it took several minutes, the two didn't speak again. When the car had left the lot, fishtailing onto the Shore Drive, Cal climbed into his own car and turned the engine over. He was tired and cold, but his conversation with Shaw had made the world about him seem sharper and more distinct.

He lit a cigarette and exhaled. The water chopped against the cement and stone, washed over the large ancient iron mooring hooks and the mushroom-headed bollards, but otherwise the sea was still. Peddocks Island was a black fortress to the southeast and the lights of an oil tanker, passing out of Boston Harbor, blinked beyond it.

52

IN THE MORNING when Cal woke it took him a moment to remember where he was. Lynne was hanging sheets on the clothesline strung on a looping pulley wheel between the triple-deckers, pulling over yesterday's clothes made flat by ice and wind and smelling of bleach as they warmed on the rack in the kitchen. Even though he knew she was in the other room, he reached over to feel where her body had lain next to him in the night. He caressed the sheet, inhaling the smell of her. He had slept through the night without any dreams, without any nightmares. He could smell the air of the room, the sharp winter scent coming in off the bay like a whiteness brightening his senses. Coffee was brewing in the kitchen. He pulled himself up, pressed his feet onto the cold floor, and sat, smiling, on the edge of the mattress as he stared at Lynne's sheer nightgown stretched across the bottom of the bed.

In the kitchen she was at the stove in a white terry cloth robe, and he stood for a moment in the doorway looking at her. She turned and smiled at him, gestured for him to sit at the table, then went back to cooking.

"Eggs okay?" she asked over her shoulder, and he nodded to himself as he grasped the chair.

"Good, eggs are good."

He rolled his neck and listened to it crack. He smiled, and when the words came, they surprised him. "I want to get out," he said. "I'm ready to leave."

Lynne turned from the counter to look at him, wide-eyed and with concern. She probably thought he was sick and running a fever. He laughed at the look of her, at the strange relief and comfort he felt. It was as if he'd been holding his breath. "I want us to move somewhere, any-where you want to go. We'll start over."

She came to him and he pulled her onto his lap, wrapped his arms about her.

"You mean it? But how are we—"

"It won't be easy, it might even be hard at first, but we can do it, Lynne."

Her face was against his. Her chin trembled and he could see her fight-ing back tears. He pulled her tighter, felt the subtle tremors that shook her body. "I love you," he whispered against her ear. "I love you, and I don't want to lose you." He put his face into her hair and breathed her in. He kissed her ear, her neck, her soft cheek.

Now it was her turn to laugh. "I almost believe you," she said.

He pressed into her, felt the fleshy heat of her, and she grasped at his face as they kissed, her tongue working against his. They groped at each other's clothes, hips grinding and thrusting, half dragged each other to the floor. Clothes wrapped about their ankles, entwined about their legs, they moved into each other. A breeze came up from the bay and whipped and snapped and smacked the clothes on the clothesline and the door to the porch closed itself and they listened as soft clumps of wet snow, like rain, began to tap upon the kitchen windows and stream down the glass in steady rivulets that sent thin, sinuous shadows on the wall above them bending in sudden, violent tremors.

When they were done, they lay on the floor together, his hand between the cleft of her bottom. Lynne's skin was pebbled with goose bumps, and they were both sweating although it was cold. When he stroked her with his free hand Lynne shuddered, and though she smiled, her eyes were big and dark and distant. He could feel her heart beating beneath the center of her breasts. He wanted to say something that would show how grateful he was that she was with him and had stood by him and show how very much he loved her, but something inside him was opening, breaking, and he could put no words to it. Perhaps it was the look in her eyes, but for no reason that he could explain he felt panicked, as if he were falling from a great height.

"Are we leaving, really leaving?" she asked, and he saw the doubt there, as if in the time since he'd said it he might have changed his mind.

"Yes," he said, and he did mean it. "We're leaving. I promise."

With sudden urgency, before the sensation of darkness engulfed him completely, he needed for them to make love again, and he pulled her to him, rolling her on top, his hands spreading her bottom wide. He felt her thighs, the strong, taut flesh trembling as she pushed against him as eagerly, he wanted desperately to believe, as he did against her, and that in some strange, inexplicable way, this was what, in the end, might save them both.

53

CAL WORKED TO keep himself busy, but there was little to do at Pilgrim Security, and he found himself staring blankly out the window, from which he had to wipe condensation every few minutes, looking down on the Square. Shortly before the noon spill of bodies from the subway and the heave of pedestrians along Cambridge Street, an old rummy of an ex-cop named Casey came in, looking to see if Cal had any work going. Cal made a point of looking at his watch and then at Casey. Finally he shook his head. "Jesus, you come looking for a job at lunchtime? You booze through the night and snore it off while the rest of us working stiffs are up at dawn? How'd you think you're gonna get a job like that?"

Casey licked at his lips savagely and blinked dumbly at him. He looked pretty rough. Cal could smell the booze coming off of him from where he sat. It seemed to float in slow waves of heat and stale sweat, and his skin looked patchy and purple-hued as if he'd spent the better part of the night in a frozen alley being blasted by the cold. Casey's parboiled eyes gazed blankly back at him. The last time they'd talked, Casey had still had a wife and a teenage daughter; he didn't even want to ask how that was going, and he stopped himself from asking.

There was no work for him, and after the two guards Cal had sent out earlier that morning to Necco, there was nothing about to come in on the books, although he had hopes for some of the parking lot details down on Causeway once the winter broke. In the end, he gave Casey a quarter to get a burger and a cup of coffee at Joe and Nemo's, and told him to go see Charlie. He knew that Charlie needed someone to jump for the *Herald* trucks, counting papers and running them into stores. Charlie had been complaining all winter about his paperboys quitting the morning shift because of the cold—and the morning setup, when the local newspaper delivery trucks dumped their stacks, was his busiest time of the day. As long as Casey stayed on the straight and narrow, he could probably do him for at least an hour every morning, perhaps more, and perhaps some in the evening, too. It wasn't much, but it might see him through until the winter was over.

When he was gone, Cal looked at the schedule for the week. It had barely changed in months; he called the men on detail for the week to confirm their assignments, then called the operator and asked for an answering service for the following week. He didn't know when he'd be picking up a phone again.

THERE WAS A rumor that people were disappearing from the low-rent streets of the West End on Scollay's skid row border, and when Cal walked Warren Street, he saw it was true. In the lower end the buildings became even more decrepit and abandoned, as if someone had spread the word that the Bomb was going to drop. The alleys were filled with garbage, and many of the stores were vacant. Along one half of the street the destruction of two buildings was near completion. Their front façades were gone and only the brick and wood shell remained, the bedrooms and living rooms where people had once lived snow-covered and visible to the street; on one fourth floor, tattered wallpaper and window draperies flapped in the wind. He'd had friends who'd grown up here in the tenements and played ball in the bustling, narrow streets and alleyways filled with the chatter of Jews, Irish, Italians, Chinese, Polish, Greeks, Albanians, Syrians, and Ukrainians.

Cal walked between the tightly packed four-story tenements, desolate and empty of families. It was like walking through a ghost town, even as he heard the distant sounds of traffic and the rest of the city moving through its day. He stared at the curtainless windows and looked in at empty rooms through the smeared glass. He knocked on a door and it swung open when he tried it. Inside, vandals and vagrants had already been here. Fires had been lit in the living room, the ceilings scorched and blackened with soot, and in one house what looked to be animal sacrifices and black magic rituals: a pentagram sketched on the floor in blood red, a wall covered with unintelligible words.

The West End wasn't a slum, although McAllister and Foley made it out that way and wanted the public to believe it. It was low rent because the landlords didn't care about their immigrant tenants, but now it looked so far gone, no one would be convinced it was worth saving. It looked like McAllister would have his way. There was no one left to battle the redevelopment, and if the houses were in such disrepair they couldn't be sold, they'd be condemned by the city, and that fit McAllister's plan as well.

Cal stood on a stoop smoking a cigarette. At the end of the street an old woman pushed a cart of groceries along the pavement, the wheels of the cart buckling and squealing. He watched her work the lock of a door, pull the cart in behind her, and then the door closed and the street was empty again.

McAllister and Foley were doing it, all right, either through intimidation or payoff. They were displacing thousands of people, just as the plats at City Hall suggested.

IN THE EVENING he attended vespers at Mission Church but, too distracted to pray, he rode the trolley downtown and walked four blocks to the Littlest Bar, where he passed the next two hours sitting by the window drinking whiskey and staring out through the ice-covered windowpanes at the business district stiffs passing. The bar was warm and smelled slightly of tobacco, burnt coffee grounds, and greasy sirloin; familiar, comforting smells that did not seem all that different to him than the incense in the church he'd just come from. He wanted to think about Sheila's murder and the dead girls, about Renza, Foley, and McAllister, knew he needed to be thinking about them, but his mind was empty, a sieve through which only blackness fell. He and Lynne were getting out after all, and none of it was his concern anymore. He simply had to kill a man, which he'd done in the war, but now someone was going to pay him to do it, and that made it different, made him into something other.

At a news kiosk at the corner of Fulton, he bought a pint of whiskey and then caught a trolley home. He trudged down the Avenue past the brightly lit storefronts wreathed with faded Christmas decorations, past bars and corner markets. Crowley's Funeral Home still blazed its Christmas lights, and small candles sputtered and sparked blearily through the ice-covered windows.

Cal lowered his head. The temperature had dropped, and with it came a windchill that felt like ten below. Everything sparkled and shone beneath a sheen of ice: the gutters and trash cans, the dented fenders and worn, weather-beaten shingles of the three-story houses, twinkling in much the same way as, when he leaned his head back, the first stars coming out where the day ended, high in the winter sky. Shouting children, smears of snot frozen on their upper lips, ran and ducked between parked cars along the curb, hurled packed snow hard as rocks at one another.

A trolley sparked electric on the Avenue. A mother called from a porch for her child. And then came the blaring of sirens. As he climbed the hill past Nash's Pub, two fire engines and a cop car roared past him, sirens wailing. Flames, a shifting reddish glow through the tops of the black frozen elms that lined the Avenue, settled like a hazy sun over the tops of the triple-deckers. Black smoke churned upward in wide-spiraling funnels into the sky. The smell of ash and gunite and of roof tar heated as if it were summer.

He walked faster now, forcing the taut tendons in his hip and thigh to bend and flex, his eyes fixed on the end of his street, where two fire engines, lights swirling, had formed a V before his triple-decker. On the third floor, smoke mushroomed from the windows of their apartment, consuming the rooftop and obliterating it from view. He ran lurchingly then and the pint bottle fell from the folds of his coat and shattered upon the street. Ignoring the pain in his hip, he raced toward the fire engines and the flames that seemed to grow larger and more violent as he neared. At the house he stumbled to the side of the engines and charged the front door, but two firemen grabbed him and pushed him onto the street.

The hose water rushed in great twining ropes that turned black as they fell back from the burning building. Icicles hung from the fire hydrants and from the moisture that beaded upon the firemen's faces. Their eyes seemed white and large and driven with panic in the fiery glow and the flashing red lights of the engines. Thick, blazing embers floated down from the sky. More sirens sounded, and another two engines from other parts of the city whined past Cal and joined the two engines already fighting the blaze.

An explosion blew out the windows of the third-floor living room and sent Cal and half a dozen firemen to the blacktop. As he began to rise, crouching low against the heat of the flames, a series of smaller explosions from within the apartment above sounded, and the windows of the kitchen blew outward, frames shattering. He saw a flaming shape—Lynne on fire—racing past the blackened windows, struggling against the flames that engulfed her. With hands clutched to her head and long hair blazing, she burst through the doors to the balcony and, without slowing, launched herself over the railing.

"Lynne!" he screamed. "Lynne!" He rushed forward, but two firemen reached for him. "That's my wife!" he cried out, as he tried to shake them off. "That's my wife." Burning debris fell about them, small timbers, slates, and shingles skittering alight across the sidewalk and down onto the engines.

"Keep him back, for Christ's sake!" one of the fireman shouted as Cal glared at his ash-streaked face, someone he knew he recognized but could not place, and then more arms were grabbing at him and pushing him back. The hoses writhed and whipped, and men glistening with water turning to ice struggled against them. For a moment Cal fought but finally relented when he saw Lynne's mangled, smoking body on the sidewalk. Steam rose off the blackened, twisted shape of her. The contraction of tendons and ligaments, before they'd been burned away to the bone, had pulled her body into an inhuman contortion—the spine bowed into a severe fetal cocoon, and the neck twisted sideways so that her blackened face held its mouth open in a silent scream. The firemen didn't even bother to cover her. There was no point.

Water flowed through the valves, and men continued to work the pumps to prevent the lines from freezing. Water gushed from the hydrant and valves onto the road, rushed down to the bay, and slowly began to freeze, merging with the black, icy glassiness of the beach. Cars— gleaming pinpricks of headlights—continued on the highway as if a world away, as if nothing had changed.

Cal stumbled backward and stared glassy-eyed at the body before looking away, but the neighborhood around him was unfamiliar and alien. He was cold, his clothes soaked from the hoses, sodden and sticking, freezing to his skin. Ladder 29 and Ladder 26 from Dorchester station houses, and from farther, Engine 49 out of the Hyde Park fire station rumbled by him. A long-bodied black Lincoln idled at the farthest corner of the street, lost in the shadows before the far triple-deckers and beneath the bare branches of the elms. White smoke curled from its dual tailpipes. Condensation fogged its glass. The light of the flames slid in sinuous flickering snakes across its dark metal. Movement stirred within; someone wound down the window and threw a cigarette butt through the gap.

Cal stepped away from the blaze and, gazing more intently at the car, began moving toward it. The alcohol was leaving Cal in a rush, as if someone had just given him a kick of epinephrine. He could see a Kinneally, the big white face leering, staring at the fire from the driver's seat. Cal reached for his gun, extending it before him as he strode, more quickly now, toward the car. The taillights came on as they spotted him. A large goon whom he recognized as one of the Flanagan clan clambered from the back, a gun in his hand. He was laughing. They were all laughing.

"What the fuck you gonna do, O'Brien," Flanagan called, and then Cal began firing, running as he went. The first bullet struck Flanagan high on his chest and his mouth froze in shock. He reached for the door and managed to fall back into the car. The door remained open and Cal could still see Kinneally staring back at him. Cal fired again and the passenger-side window exploded, and then the car was peeling away from the curb, tires squealing and grasping for traction on the ice, its rear door swinging wide, Flanagan's legs dangling over the seat, his feet dragging on the ground, one black shoe bouncing off into the gutter.

He chased the car down the street, shells snapping from the chamber of his semiautomatic, as onlookers watching the fire fled from their front porches back into their houses. The car reached the intersection and Cal continued firing. The rear window shattered, and he could see Blackie and another man in the front ducking for cover. They careened onto the cross-street without braking as Cal emptied his clip, and as they slid across the road, it gave Cal time to draw his second gun. He pumped five more bullets into the passenger door before the car accelerated up the street toward the Avenue. At the intersection his legs gave out and he finally stopped running. Breath steamed from his mouth, fogged the space before his eyes. His arm remained extended, the gun barrel smoking, the car still in his sights but now too far gone. He reached toward a lamppost for balance and slowly slid down to the ground, sat splay-legged on the curb, staring down the street.

Black ash drifted down, mixed in with the snow coming down upon the houses and bringing forth a vast, muffled silence. It buzzed in his ears along with the other buzz that was the effect of alcohol, and he closed his eyes, but the darkness made him feel queasy. Things were spinning in the dark, and out of this vertigo images were emerging, ash-blackened faces and flashing red lights, orange flames racing up the side of a building, windows exploding, glass bursting in the heat and raining down upon the black sidewalk and flames licking at the same space where just moments before there had been windows. He had to open his eyes again, but when he did, he continued to see Lynne burning and blackened and mutilated and made unrecognizable by fire. He realized he was shaking and sobbing so loudly it racked his body. A bubble of rheum burst from his nose. Gasping, he fought to breathe over the tears, but still he could not stop crying. Finally he stood and walked down the street toward the Avenue, away from the flames and the fire and their home and with still more engines wailing down the street toward the blaze.

54

THE DAY PASSED beyond the shuttered blinds but Cal was unable to move. He stared into the mirror above the bureau in Owen's guest room. At times he held his head in his hands and sobbed, and at other moments he raised his head and stared blearily before him. Then, in a matter of seconds, an indescribable desperation overtook him, a spiraling helplessness that threatened to choke him, and he felt that if he didn't act he might be buried alive. Panicked, he lashed out at the furniture. He swept the glasses and ashtrays off the bureau top, punched the walls, and finally shattered the mirror with his fist. He fell back on the bed screaming, clutching his hand, thin shards of glass embedded in his knuckles and blood streaming down his fingers and wrist.

Later he found himself on the floor, not knowing how he had got there. He had drunk too much whiskey, and was feeling dazed and unsteady. He was partially dressed but had stripped to his undershirt. His shoes were sodden and the bottoms of his pant legs were wet. Three new pint bottles glared at him from the bureau.

He fell asleep and then woke again and he was on the bed, the room darker now; thin bands of sunlight retreated to the floor beneath the window, shimmered at the edge of the shutters. The bedsheets were caked hard with blood. He flexed his fingers and pain shot up his arm and so he lay still again. He stared for a while at the ceiling, at the cracked plaster, and saw his and Lynne's bedroom ceiling with the water damage from when a nor'easter blew the shingles off the roof the year before, and he turned, imagining her there, smelling her skin, sensing the heat of her naked thigh stretched across his lower abdomen, the heady musk of her moist sex filling his senses, before he realized he was alone.

When he woke he was sprawled in the chair with his head bent at an awkward angle, the sides of his mouth wet with spit and drool. He reached for his drink, but after taking the first swig he began to cough, and soon he was doubled over on himself, falling out of the chair, gasping and shuddering and dribbling mucus on the carpet.

Lynne was standing a little way from him, twisting something in her fingers and looking out through the glass toward the distant, dark line of the sea. "Lynne," he said tentatively. "Lynne?" And she turned and smiled at him with such openness and love—of the kind he imagined was always there at the beginning of their marriage—that his heart pressed achingly in his chest, and he held on to that smile in his mind, even as the figure before him swirled gray and faded before his eyes and he called out once more to the empty room. "Lynne?"

Sweating now from the alcohol in his blood, and clutching a pint of whiskey, he tottered out to the porch and collapsed into a chair covered in ice. But he was no longer drunk.

An overwhelming fear pushed him deeper into his chair and held him as he stared, wide-eyed and trembling, out onto the boulevard. Everything familiar was now hostile to him. The landscape of the neighborhood with all of its memories was a sort of ruse, taunting him with the power it held over him. Knowing he could never leave; knowing that, as Lynne had said so many times, he could never step fully out into the world and be free of it. She'd known the truth.

❧

DANTE STOOD BY the window in Owen's living room watching the morning traffic on Day Boulevard, a few scraggly soot-colored gulls screeching as they fluttered above the rooftops, and the wind whipping the flagpole by the bathhouse. He was antsy but didn't know what to do. Cal was sleeping off a hangover in the other room, and he hadn't been in great shape when they'd talked earlier. He'd recited the events of the firebombing in a flat monotone, as if it were merely a recording, as if he were transcribing an event that had happened to someone else. It had been like talking to a stranger, and Dante didn't know if Cal had fully registered his being there. What he did know was that he was helpless in the face of such grief and of little help to Cal.

Owen's house was so silent he could hear the timbers creaking in the three-story frame. Not even a sound from the other tenants. He wished Owen would turn on the radio or the record player, anything other than the silence. But then, that's probably what Owen wanted. He was hoping the tension that inhabited the silence would get Dante going, start the need for a fix. When he turned, Owen, dressed in his police blues, was sitting on the sofa watching him. Dante knew he was waiting for him to speak.

"Well," Dante said, "I guess I'll be going."

Owen nodded, but kept staring.

"You got something to say, you should spit it out."

"I'm just wondering how much more of you I can take."

For Cal's sake, Dante ignored him. He wasn't going to fight with this asshole, not now. "When he wakes, tell him I'll stop by tomorrow."

"What have you ever done for him but drag him down to your shit?"

"This isn't my shit."

" 'Course it is. You think Lynne would be dead if Cal hadn't gotten messed up with you and Blackie Foley?"

"Cal and Blackie have their own history that has nothing to do with me." Dante picked up his hat off the side table, moved toward the door, but Owen wasn't done yet.

"When will he stop having to look out for you? When are you gonna start taking care of your own problems? I'm fucking sick of hearing that he's bailed you out again from the bookies or that he's spent the night searching the town's flophouses for you, worried that you might be dead. You've never given a shit what looking after you has cost him."

Dante paused at the entrance to the hallway; he fingered the rim of his hat. "You're wrong. I know what it's cost him."

"Well you don't act like it. Did you ever give a thought to what he lost over there? Huh? You think he was the same when he came back? While you were shooting up with all the town's lowlifes and faking a 4-F so you didn't have to fight, he was over there doing what you should have been doing."

"I wanted to be over there fighting. They wouldn't take me."

"It's always fucking someone else, isn't it? Always the dealer or your wife or the junk. You and your damn scapegoats. In all the years I've known Cal, I've never seen him blaming his problems on anyone else."

Dante tugged the hat down on his head, raised his coat collar. "That's because he's a better man than I am, and a better friend. Tell him I'll see him tomorrow."

55

FOREST HILLS CEMETERY, JAMAICA PLAIN

NEAR DUSK DANTE rode the El from one end of the city to the other and then back again, watching vacantly as the day began to darken and the cityscape seemed to change and alter itself beyond the windows as the first snowflakes came down like moths through the dark. They pattered against the glass before his face. He thought about the way Blackie's boys had killed Lynne and he imagined her burning alive, the pain she must have felt and the terrible slowness of it, and how Cal had seen her die like that. He thought of Owen's words, that he was a coward who had never taken responsibility for anything in his life, and the price that Cal had paid for his cowardice over the years.

The train car rattled and pressed through the dusk light, and Dante looked down from the elevated tracks above Washington Street at the cars waiting below at the various intersections. Amber slivers of light showed from second- and third-floor apartments as they passed, so close it seemed he could reach out and touch them, their brick and stone and wood façades turned black by soot. Below, the homes and shop fronts drab and gray and crumbling, and to which only meager slants of sunshine showed themselves during the day. It was a part of the city the rest of the city had forgotten and would never remember again. The train's screeching brakes sounded out in the darkness, and electrical sparks showered down upon the world below.

At Forest Hills he finally roused himself. The train had reached the end of the line, and he stood and exited through the doors before the train headed back into town once more. He descended the ancient wooden escalator that clicked and clacked like a set of large revolving teeth, and through the empty station where his hard soles echoed on the brick floors, out onto the street, where the snow came down in big flakes that evaporated once they hit the ground. He crossed between the cars on Washington to a florist, bought a dozen white roses. It was all they had, and the petals had already curled, their ends bruised-looking and black.

On the corner by Kilgarriff's restaurant and the old apothecary a coal truck idled, swirling gray-black smoke churning from its exhaust. The driver, emptying coal into a cellar chute, cursed the cold as he rattled the stubborn metal swing arm encased in ice. Dante walked the length of Tower Street and entered the pedestrian gate and the cemetery's woods. His feet were already frozen, and he wished he'd worn another pair of socks. The path through the trees, slippery with the recent cover of snow, curved downward to the left, and he took each step cautiously.

The cemetery office, crematory, and columbarium with their backs to him were already closed for the day, the granite and puddingstone buildings dark shapes hulking at the main entrance beyond the Gothic gateway, the mullioned windows glowing slightly with a dim light from within. Briefly the peaked roof and stained glass windows of the Forsyth Chapel showed through the trees, and then he was angling eastward and through the woods again. The smell of brewing hops from the Haffenreffer Brewery half a mile away on Amory Street came to him on the frigid air.

The lamps had come on along the graveyard road, even though it wasn't fully dark yet, and as he walked the winding pathway through the grounds, their amber glow shimmered here and there upon the shoveled paths cutting between gravestones.

It was a large old graveyard, and it took a long time to reach Margo's grave. Along the VFW Parkway cars motored slowly and their headlights were small flickering embers through the ice-covered hedgerows and black tree branches.

Every time he visited he traveled a familiar path, past the crypts and graves of Revolutionary soldiers, politicians, statesmen, and he remembered when he and Margo used to visit the arboretum and Victorian gardens here in the summer months, along these same winding paths, surrounded by flowers then and rose bushes, and the pond with its two swans always coasting across the placid surface. He never imagined that he would end up burying her here, and he wondered if Sheila would also be here once the ground thawed so they could dig her grave—not in the same plot, for there was only one spot next to Margo, and he reminded himself that it was for him.

The path turned in to a grove, briefly illuminated by the glow of lamps, hazy amber orbs trembling through a brittle-looking latticework of leafless tree limbs, and then he was at her grave.

He glanced down at the flowers. The rose petals looked ghostly against the white snow at his feet. They appeared to have browned and wilted even more on his walk here. He wiped at his chapped lips with the back of his hand, knelt on one knee, and lowered the roses before the gravestone. MARGO COOPER. OCTOBER 1, 1921— JUNE 24, 1950.

"I guess I'll never be able to pick you good flowers," he said aloud, his voice cracking. "Always a little worse for wear. It's the thought that counts, you'd tell me, even if you were embarrassed to put them out in the vase."

Raising himself back up, he brushed the snow clinging to his knee, flicked the smoldering cigarette back toward the path. He reached into his coat pocket and pulled out the revolver he had retrieved from his closet this morning after leaving Cal at Owen's. It was a gun he'd won in a card game years ago, the kind of game where everybody playing was broke and scavenged their meager belongings to put something, anything, on the table.

The only time he had ever pointed it with a target in mind was at himself. After a month at Mattapan State, he had returned to their bedroom for the first time since she'd died, and he had sat on the bed for hours, hunched over, elbows on his knees, head in his hands. He had tried his hardest not to think about it, to try and remember what the doctors had told him about coping with tragedy and moving on, but all he could focus on was where he was, sitting on their bed where the police had discovered him with his arms wrapped around Margo. It still felt as though it was all just a dream, a horrible dream. And that was when the idea had come to him.

He'd found the gun at the bottom of the dresser drawer, wrapped in a towel, and he'd gently slid the barrel over his bottom lip, pressed at his tongue, and eased his thumb over the trigger. He didn't know if there were any bullets in the gun, had no memory of ever loading the gun before. When he pulled the trigger and heard the dry click, it took him a while to realize the gun was empty, but still he pulled the trigger again and again. He'd eventually rewrapped the gun in the towel and put it back in the dresser drawer. It had been a rehearsal, but now he knew that he could do it if he had to.

A delicate wind came through the headstones, stirring up the fresh, unpacked snow, raising it up in the air and sending it drifting about his eyes, cooling his forehead, which was hot as if it were the focal point of the fever that gripped him. "I guess this is it," he said aloud.

Bare branches swayed above him, scratching their crowded limbs against one another before the wind quieted and the branches suddenly stopped moving. A pressing silence followed, pushing at him and making him feel breathless.

He bowed his head and tried to finish a prayer to Margo, but nothing came to his mind except warbled melodies and lyrics of old songs that Margo used to sing to herself. He shut his eyes tightly; there was light coming through the darkness.

It was spring 1945, a month before the Allied victory in Europe. Margo sat at one of the tables spaced around the small dance floor of the Tap Room, wearing the blue dress he'd bought her on her twenty-third birthday. Her hair was done up in a victory roll, eyes shadowed with mascara, lips painted a cardinal red. At the other tables and along the bar, patrons were silhouettes and shadows. Their conversation carried on softly and out of range. Every so often he looked up from the piano keys, glanced at her, and smiled.

Most Tuesday nights she'd walk into the club halfway between his first two sets and sit at the same table. He would play all her favorites, one after the other. "An American in Paris," "I Remember April," and ending with "These Foolish Things."

Midnight arrived, and the bar lights came on fully. People got up to leave, chairs scraping against the wooden floor. A teenage colored boy with a cigarette angled behind his ear came out with a broom and began to sweep the floor. At the table, Margo finished her whiskey sour, stood and fanned out the wrinkles in her dress, and then walked to the bar, asked the bartender for a last drink. Dante lit a cigarette, reached into the large brandy snifter he used for tips, and pulled out the dollar bills. He unfolded them, stacked them together, and began counting.

"Look at Rockefeller counting his money," she said, and gently nudged his shoulder with her hip. He moved so she could sit beside him. She placed his drink, a whiskey with one ice cube, on the piano top.

"Have a drink and stop worrying about paying people back. It'll all work out."

She kissed him on the cheek. And with her perfume lingering in his nostrils, a sweetly fragrant whisper in his ear: "Play for me, just one more song. One more song."

Dante listened to snowdrift whisper along the frozen ground. Rheum dribbled from his nose and crept down to his upper lip. He reached up and rubbed at it with the cuff of his jacket. Off in the far distance a crow cried out, and farther off, a car horn blared impatiently.

He opened his eyes and wiped at them. "Sorry, Margo," he said. "You don't know how sorry I am."

Dante turned from the gravestone, walked back along the path into the woods. He slid the gun into his coat pocket, turned up his collar, and, holding his hat down against the wind, quickly walked an adjoining path toward the lights of Forest Hills, and as he moved farther away, only wishing he could turn around and say good-bye to his Margo one final time.

56

AT THE FRONT door, Dante pressed the doorbell twice. There was no sound from within. He waited, cupped his bare hands and blew into them, even though they were already slick with sweat, and then went around to the side walkway that led to the back of the house. Sometimes Karl left the back door open for his customers. The small backyard was littered with scraps of steel and aluminum, a child's bicycle upended, its front tire angled off the rusted frame. Racks of empty pint bottles were stacked unevenly upon one another and several torn bags of trash. Putrefying garbage was strewn about the snow. Even in the cold, Dante could smell it.

Snowdrifts were piled against the dilapidated fence, where gaping holes were covered with chicken wire, and from the other side Dante heard the movement of a big dog, its panting heavy with phlegm. It sensed Dante moving, and barked. Other dogs farther off in the neighborhood barked in return, a chorus of dogs calling out to one another as if in some secret warning.

Maneuvering over more scrap that cluttered the yard, he made it to the back door, turned the knob, and pushed at the frame until it budged. Before he stepped inside, he noticed a foot-long length of rusted pipe on the ground. He reached down for it, cold against his palm, and entered the house. On his right was the door leading to the first-floor apartment. He heard a radio playing in a kitchen, disembodied voices of a soap opera aimlessly chattering away, and the sounds of dishes clattering in the sink.

The hall stank of piss, cigar smoke, and something foul that he couldn't quite place. He moved up the stairs, reached in his coat pocket, and touched the revolver to make sure he still had it. At the door, he knocked once, twice, and, after the third, he heard movement on the other side.

"Gimme a minute." A woman's voice, abrasive and raw. A chain lock rattled and scratched at the wood. She opened the door slowly. Light suddenly cut into the darkness, dizzying him. His eyes refocused and the woman appeared before him. He watched her rounded face look at him and then a coy smile exposing a missing front tooth.

"I need to see Karl," he said.

She laughed, raspy and carefree. "Well, he's sleeping off a hangover." She opened the door wider, turned, and stepped back into the kitchen. She was wearing pale blue panties, and her buttocks hung below the hemline, doughy and marked. Dante looked away. Light came in from the dusty, grease-speckled windows.

"The front bell, it's broken."

As though she hadn't heard him, she said, "I've never seen you here before. What's your name?"

The woman was nearly his height, a wide, round face on a thin neck and broad shoulders with barely any breasts pushing at the fabric of her tight man's T-shirt. Her lipstick was dry and caked and her eye shadow smeared, giving the appearance of a bruise.

"It doesn't matter."

"You're right, you'd probably give me a fake name anyway. They all do, you know," she said.

He passed her in the kitchen, and suddenly his senses sharpened. There were eggs frying loudly in a pan. The faucet dripping into the sink full of dishes and glasses, each drop tapping hollowly against a tin tray. A cigarette burning in an ashtray, smoke churning upward in dusty blue tendrils. A newspaper spread out on the floor, darkly stained and stinking of cat piss.

"So, you here to get high or get fucked?" the woman said as she reached over and pulled his arm closer to her. He smelled reefer on her breath, and the stale bitterness of alcohol. "I'm not like one of Karl's little girls who don't even know how to please a man yet. We could have a good time, you and me."

He looked down at her hand holding his: the index and middle fingers were gone, scarred stumps up to the knuckles. She saw that he was looking.

"That was from the Fore River yard in Quincy, working the night shift building ships for the boys overseas. I hated that job like you wouldn't believe."

He pulled his hand away from hers and, to avoid her eyes, looked at the kitchen table. It was covered in dirty plates, balled-up tissues and napkins, foil, cigarette boxes, newspapers, and smut magazines yellowed with age.

He asked for a cigarette. Her watery chestnut eyes moved to the side, head gesturing with a sideways nod to the kitchen table. He eyed a pack, grabbed it, and shook it. It was empty. Then he found another pack, pulled one out, lit it with his lighter, and took a deep drag. On the table were several of the plaster Jesus Christ figurines he had seen the last time he'd visited Karl, each one split into powdery pieces as if dismembered; a head on its side, a split torso, raised arms broken off from the shoulders, little hands with nails the size of thorns pinned in their center.

He touched the plaster torso that no longer seemed part of Christ, no longer seemed part of something sorrowful and holy, but something obscene. He pressed his thumb into it, crushing it apart until there was nothing left but dust.

"Get your clothes on and get out of here now."

"What'd you say?" The woman smiled at him, as if he were setting up a joke.

"I said get your clothes on and get the fuck out of here."

Looking down at the pipe in his hand, her eyes widened, suddenly aware. She stepped backward into the bathroom, flicked on the light, and closed the door.

Dante took a deep drag off the cigarette, let it burn inside his throat and chest, and then pressed the cigarette into an ashtray overflowing with ash and crumpled ends. He passed through the narrow, cluttered hallway. His stomach turned and he paused before entering the living room. There was a quavering groan, followed by laughter, throaty and deep. Something about it was oddly childlike. Feet were banging the floor as if someone was throwing a tantrum.

In the living room a boy sat upright on the couch. Or it looked to be a boy at first, but the head was so large and misshapen, with patches of hair missing where the hairless lumps made the skull seem inhuman, like a sculpture of a head whose clay had not yet hardened, and the eyes sunken into the skull left nothing but shadows, as if the boy had no eyes at all. The boy reared his head up toward him, and Dante saw that he was blind.

From one of the bedrooms he heard a man growling, grunting like some beast in heat as he fucked one of Karl's girls. As the sounds became louder, the boy on the couch began to mimic the noises, grunting gutturally, his lips slick with saliva. He pounded both feet against the hardwood floor so violently that the end table and lamp shook. He grinned, showing a mouthful of crooked, oversized teeth.

There was a heavy wool coat next to the boy, and Dante knew that it was the kid's father or caretaker who was in the next room having his way. He shook off the disgust building in him and moved toward the bedroom door. The boy quieted, cocked his head to one side, and the blind, sunken eyes turned and followed Dante across the room.

The sounds from inside hit a violent peak. A headboard banged and

324

thudded against the wall. The man grunted pig-like over the muffled moans of a girl in pain. Suddenly the ruckus faltered, stuttered, and then silenced before the man released a sickly groan. Dante turned the doorknob. It was locked. He stepped back, gained his foothold, and launched forward, kicking the door. Wood splintered and the door bowed in, but the lock still held. He reared back again, raised his leg, and slammed his boot into the doorknob. The door broke open and banged against the inside wall.

On the bed, a man's white, pockmarked ass bounced up and down, the large body pressing down on the girl beneath him. The man lifted himself off her and, as much as his fat neck would allow, turned around. "What the fuck!" he shouted. "What the fuck, asshole!" His face was flabby and unshaven, the skin flushed and glistening with sweat. He slid off the girl and stood with his fat cock dripping.

He raised his arms and rushed toward Dante. Dante stepped to the side and brought the pipe down on the man's right arm. A dull crack of bone just under the elbow, and the man cried out and bent double, cradling his arm against his bare stomach. The girl screamed, and Dante could see that she was much younger than she was made up to look. He guessed she was no more than fourteen.

"You." Dante nodded at the girl while keeping the pipe raised for another blow. "Get your clothes on and get moving."

Tears in her eyes, mascara dripping dark streaks down her cheeks dusted pink with rouge, she moved up off the bed, and with the sheet covering her naked body, she rushed out of the bedroom.

The man shook his head. "You're gonna pay for this, cocksucker," he said.

Dante rushed in, swung the pipe at the man's face. The impact of cracking his skull shook through Dante's hand. The man fell sideways, bounced off the bed frame, and fell to the floor. Dante watched as he got to his knees, fingers pressing at his wound, smearing blood across his face. Dante tossed the pipe aside and reached into his coat for his gun. He jammed the barrel into the man's mouth, the metal chipping his yellowed front teeth. His finger quivered on the trigger, but then he heard the boy in the living room crying out again, and dragged the man to his feet, pushed him across the room. Whimpering, the man stumbled to a chair and found his clothes.

Karl was standing in the doorway, an ashen pallor to his face, his black hair raked back. His protuberant eyes glistened, locked on Dante. He held a baseball bat in his hand. Dante had seen firsthand what Karl could do to people with a bat, and there was no way now that Karl was going to let him leave without exacting his pound of flesh.

"Maloney," he said. "Get your retard son and get out of here. I'll take care of this."

Pulling up his pants, the man nearly tripped out of the bedroom. He rushed to put on his white T-shirt even as the blood pouring from his head turned the shirt red. He grabbed his son by the arm, pulled him off the couch. The boy cried out and tried to wrench free from his grasp, but the man pulled harder and with a bloodstained hand cuffed him on the back of the head. The boy mewled like an animal, his lips and teeth glistening with spittle. Both scrambled out the door, their heavy footsteps pounding in the hallway and down the stairs. Dante felt the house rattle as the front door slammed shut.

Karl stared at the gun pointed at him. He reached down to his stained robe and scratched at his crotch. He sucked on the cigarette between his lips, and smoke poured from his nostrils.

"What the fuck you think you're doing, Dante?"

"I'm making things right."

Karl gave him a sickly grin. "For what, Dante?"

Dante felt sick, felt his fever double up. He tried to swallow before talking but couldn't.

"C'mon, just give me the gun and we talk about this. Just give me the fuckin' gun and I'll make everything better."

Dante raised the gun and moved toward Karl, who backpedaled into the living room. "C'mon, man." He dropped the baseball bat and it clattered onto the bare floor.

"Don't tell me this is about Margo. That's old news, man. Just let that shit stay buried."

They passed through the living room into the kitchen. Looking into Dante's eyes, Karl realized that Dante wasn't high but completely sober and in control, and suddenly he began to feel fear. "Just because your wife's last dose was from me doesn't mean anything," he whined. "She was already sick and you know that. All this, it's fucking ridiculous, man."

The bathroom door was shut, and Dante heard movement from within: the whimpering of the girl being quieted by the woman who'd let him in.

"Let's forgive and forget, man. We get our heads back on straight and I give you the dose of a lifetime. No problem, I'll forgive you for all this. Trust me, my new shit will get you higher than the heavens. C'mon, your wife would have done anything for a taste of it."

A shadow of a smile crept over Karl's face. "And I mean 'anything'—anything I wanted—you know that."

The bathroom door banged open and the woman, screaming, rushed at Dante, pulling at his shoulder. The gun almost fell from his hand, and he turned and stiff-armed her. She fell backward and collided with the refrigerator, sending empty bottles on top to the floor, and glass shattered about them.

Karl grabbed a steak knife off the kitchen table and lunged at him. The blade cut the air an inch from Dante's throat and Karl howled with pleasure. They banged into the stove and sent the pan of eggs clattering to the floor, hot grease splashing the linoleum. Grinning, Karl stabbed again and slashed Dante's cheek. Dante staggered and pulled the trigger. A flash of pale light, and Karl's head snapped back. The bullet blew through his forehead, just under his hairline. Blood bubbled out from the hole and streamed down his face.

On the floor, Karl twitched as the life rushed out of him. His eyes rolled white and, as Dante watched, a black puddle pooled around the back of his head.

He glared at the woman, who stood watching from the sink, moaning. "Shut up," he said, but her moaning increased. "Shut the fuck up!"

He pointed the gun at her. "You take that girl, and you go someplace safe," he roared. Her eyes glistened wide in shock. With a hand clenched to her mouth, she nodded. Dante put the gun back into his pocket and walked to the stairs. At his back, he heard the cries of the woman become louder as air came back into her lungs, but all of his sympathy, all of his remorse was gone. He no longer cared about anyone.

57

BLACK JACK'S, SOUTH BOSTON

THE ILLUMINATED SIGN for Brubaker Beer hung crookedly above the entrance like a guillotine that might soon lose its hold and slice through whichever drunk stumbled out at the wrong time. Dante watched the red and white lights tick and hum in their glass tubes, began to see spots in front of his eyes, and looked back down at the windows of Black Jack's, covered with mustard-colored curtains. His reflection shimmered in the pockmarked glass, and he imagined it would remain there long after he stepped inside the bar.

Hand in his pocket, fingers touching the gun, Dante pressed back into the shadows near an empty stoop still covered in snow and watched the bar and the men who entered and exited: rail workers, longshoremen, and laborers, an old barfly stumbling slightly in a tattered fur-collared coat. He smoked a cigarette, and then another, felt the smoke singe his raw throat. On the other side of the street a beat-up sandblasted Chevy rumbled up to the curb. Three men got out. The driver stood for a moment in the street, jangling his keys in his hand and laughing at something one

329

of the other men had said. Dante recognized two of them as the Kinneally brothers, and the other as one of the goons who had helped pin him against the alley wall outside the Dublin House. He watched them enter the bar, and began to get the shakes again, feel the fever creep back under his skin.

He stepped out of the dark and stood by a bus stop, pretending he was waiting for the next bus to arrive. A few men walked by him, eyed him with that questioning, invasive glance peculiar to those living in Southie. He nodded toward one of them, thinking that he recognized him, but the man glared back at him with the same cold stare, as if seeking a fight but too damned tired to start one.

He moved toward the door of Black Jack's, grabbed the handle, and, holding it for a moment, looked at his hand. It was a junkie's hand, but he was no longer shaking, and it was steady now. He opened the door and stepped inside. The harsh, treble-heavy sounds from the jukebox echoed sharply in the room, fiddle strings wildly playing alongside a woman's high-pitched voice. His eyes adjusted through the smoke and he saw the long oak bar on his left, the hunched shadows of men lined up against it, and on the other side, tight low booths. A man with rolls of fat hanging over his belt sat on the bar stool closest to him; he had a cigar clenched in his mouth, and its yellowish smoke moved over his wrinkled face slowly like ink traveling through water. The bartender, thin and acne-scarred, placed a drink on the bar before him, glared at Dante, and asked, "Who the fuck are you?"

Beside the fat man, a woman wearing a lopsided wig turned on her stool and looked at him. She had a man's chin, a man's Adam's apple, and she winked at him as a man might to a child after telling an off-color joke. Dante pulled out the gun, kept it at his side, visible enough to anybody who cared to look. The bartender shook his head in an exasperated way, as if pondering the mess he'd have to clean up afterward. "Don't be a cunt, fella, just move it the fuck outta here."

"Blackie Foley."

"Who?"

"You heard me."

The bartender paused as if pained, and then moved down the bar illuminated in reds and blues by neon signs hawking Miller and Brubaker. Dante stiffened and walked deeper inside. At the farthest end of the bar, the bartender was talking to someone. Blackie. He leaned back, slowly moved off a stool, and stood there for a moment. When he recognized Dante, his eyes widened and he started laughing. He pulled up his belt, making sure his shirt was tucked in, and walked toward him. The Kinneally brothers and the other goon rose off their stools and followed him. Another one watching on the opposite side of the room left the darkness of a booth and rushed Dante. From the corner of his eye, Dante saw him. He turned and sidestepped, striking the man with the grip end of the gun. The steel tore into the man's jaw and sent him to his knees. Stunned, the goon reached up to his bloodied mouth with fat fingers. When he tried to get to his feet, Dante aimed the gun at his face. "Don't fucking move," he said. He looked back up at Blackie, who stood a few yards away, grinning.

"What's up with the gun, Cooper. You need a fix that bad?"

Blackie's boys laughed with a sadistic playfulness.

"Does the fucking thing even work?" called out one of his men, but there seemed to be so many of them Dante couldn't pick out which one had said it. Sweat stung the corners of his eyes. He took a step back, raised the gun off the injured goon, and aimed it directly at Blackie, who had stepped toward him. When two of his boys moved alongside him, Blackie raised a hand, telling them to stay put.

"I guess you're playing revenge here, is that it? You're here to show us that you're more than a coward. Seriously, I got no beef with you, Cooper. Never had much of a beef with you. Messing with junkies ain't no fun."

Another voice called out, "Somebody just shoot the fuck and get it over with."

Blackie moved closer. "If you're here to get some payback for putting that prick O'Brien in the hospital, then be a man and drop the popgun and try to take me."

"Like a real man!" some drunk echoed. Someone clapped, egging him on; a few muttered harrumphs and taunts from observers at the bar. Laughter followed and it seemed to fill the room, then it faltered when Blackie raised a hand again to stop it. The last note from the jukebox faded. Nobody got up to put in another nickel. Somebody in a booth flicked a match to light a cigarette, and it was the only sound left in the world.

Dante cleared his throat. "You were looking for Sheila. You found out where she used to live in Somerville. You were looking for something. And you killed an old man. Bashed his fucking head in."

"You're fucking loony, Cooper. Out of your fucking mind."

"And then Lynne. You torched Cal's place. You knew she was inside."

"You're talking out of your ass, Dante." Blackie raised his right hand, palm-side up. "Just put that gun away, say you're sorry. C'mon, old neighborhood, we stick together."

There was a blur of movement from behind Dante and he turned and fired, and the acne-scarred bartender's eye exploded in a blood-pink plume and he dropped to the wood. The crack of the revolver silenced the barroom. Time slowed, and Dante felt as if he couldn't move, but as Blackie reached for his own gun, Dante shot him. Blackie recoiled and twisted sideways, knocked to the floor. Dante got off another round and the bullet tore into the neck of the Kinneally beside him, hands clawing at his throat as he fell to his knees. Flashes of pale fire lit up the room. Most of the patrons made a break for the back door, a panicked flurry of footfalls, chairs tossed aside, and people pushing one another to get to the exits.

Dante fired again even as a volley of bullets ripped chunks out of the wood around him. A sudden pain tore into his shoulder and he lost his footing, slammed sideways into the jukebox. He glanced down to where a black circle smoked in his right shoulder. A surge of blood bubbled through it, dripped from between his fingers and onto the floor. He regained his feet and fired off another round, stumbled away as bullets shattered the domed glass of the jukebox, the lights within flickering strobe-like before sizzling out. He emptied the gun into the crowd as he pushed against the door and stumbled out onto the avenue.

He slid on a layer of ice into a gutter piled high with debris, regained his foothold, and began to run. He fumbled with more bullets from his pocket, which he fingered but couldn't quite grasp. The gun barrel singed the skin on his hand and he fought against the pain, popped the cylinder open, and jammed in as many bullets as he could.

He glanced back as he ran, fired four more rounds at the goons rushing out of Black Jack's so that they had to dive into the snow and behind cars parked along the curb. Gunshots popped like firecrackers. To his right, a parked car's windshield shattered, a snowbank erupted into plumes of ice. Pedestrians huddled in storefronts, rushed for cover in alleyways and behind trash cans. When the pain in his right shoulder became too intense, he switched the gun to his left hand and fired haphazardly. Above the door, the sign for Brubaker Beer exploded in white sparks and showered down on the cowering bodies below. He kept firing until the gun clicked empty a second time.

He made it to an intersection, stumbled off the curb and into the street. Car headlights blinded him. Drivers laid on their horns. A blackness pulsed at the edges of his vision; he felt the ground sway and bend beneath him. A hundred yards ahead he saw a taxicab coming down the avenue. He crossed into the middle of the street, raised the gun toward the headlights that grew larger and enveloped him in their light. The driver hit his brakes, and the car spun across the icy road before coming to a sideways stop, smoke steaming from its tires.

He winced against the blinding glare of the headlights, aimed the gun at the driver's side of the windshield, and stumbled to the passenger's side. Inside the cab, he held the gun at the driver. The man was old, with a frightened, impoverished face and a white beard that thinned out at his chin. He shook his head, said something in a language that Dante knew was Polish.

"Turn the car around," Dante said, his hand trembling and spittle flying from his lips. "Turn the fucking car around!"

The staccato flares of gunfire came from the other side of the street, the sharp echoes popping off into the night. Bullets tore through the taxi's back door, and the side window exploded, broken glass skittering across the hard leather seats. The driver put the car into gear and pressed the gas. The tires spun, caught traction, and the engine roared as the car straightened out and sped ahead. Dante held his free hand against his shoulder to stanch the flow of blood, but there was so much of it he could taste it. He fought against a wave of burning pain carrying through his arm. Bile filled his throat. The darkness was coming and he had to hold on; he blinked and tried to will the adrenaline through his veins, while in his head he replayed how he'd seen Blackie go down and he prayed with all the strength he had left that it was a head shot.

58

THE PAIN FORCED Dante into a fetal position on the small cot at the back of Pilgrim Security. His shoulder felt as if it were on fire; beneath the bandages it throbbed and pulsed like some manner of animal, something no longer part of him. With clenched teeth, he grabbed Cal's army-issue blanket off the chair next to the cot, shakily wrapped it about him, feeling the coarse wool scratch at his skin like a scouring pad.

The room didn't have much in it. One lamp that occasionally flick-ered, sometimes going off and leaving him in darkness, or beaming so brightly he'd see spots if he looked at it too long; a radiator constantly pinging with pressure and hissing out steam; and one window to remind him that a world still existed outside. From the other room came voices softly talking, and then the door opened. Cal gave a weak attempt at a smile and stepped inside the room. Behind him came Fierro, wearing a heavy wool coat with the collar turned up and eyeglasses slightly fogged over. In his right hand he gripped a leather satchel, making him appear like a small-town doctor on a house call instead of the city's medical examiner. He labored to catch his breath.

"Claudia," Dante managed. "I've got to get Claudia." He tried to rise, but Cal motioned him to be still.

"She's okay. She's at Owen's."

Dante nodded and lay back. "Thanks."

"You're an idiot. You should be dead after what you did.'"

"Did I get him?"

"No. Word on the street is that he got you."

Fierro placed his satchel on the wooden footstool, took off his glasses, and rubbed the lenses with his thumb, wiping away the moisture. He put them back over his wide inquisitive eyes and attempted to appear professional before turning back to the satchel and rifling through it.

"First, Dante, I want you to take some of these pills; they'll help you sleep. Wash them down. And then I've got to check that wound and get the bullet out, that is, if you want to keep living."

Dante reached out for the pills, his good hand shaking so horribly that Fierro had to hold it steady as he placed them in his palm, and then as he lay back on the cot, he felt Fierro undoing the dirty wrappings about his shoulder.

FIERRO CAME BACK into the office, sat down heavily in the chair opposite Cal's desk.

Cal looked at him. "So he'll be fine?"

Fierro, his neck stiff and tight, eyes appearing owl-like behind his glasses. "He'll live, but he's not fine. That wound is bad. I got the bullet out, cleaned it up best I could, and rewrapped it with clean gauze and bandages. Another day or two, gangrene would have set in. I gave him something that should help him sleep a bit, but he isn't right. Not right at all."

"Just tell me he's fine. That's all I want to hear."

"Cal. He's not fine."

Cal moved behind the desk, sat down in the chair, and reached for the half-empty bottle of whiskey on the glass top.

From his desk drawer he took two shot glasses. He filled them to the rim and slid one across. Fierro tossed it back in one go. He winced briefly, suddenly warmed over.

"Really, Cal, I have no idea what you two are up to, but whatever it is I don't like it. The next time I see you two, I don't want it to be because I'm performing an autopsy on you. Christ's sake, you look almost as bad as him."

"Don't lecture me. I'm not in the mood." Cal downed his whiskey, grabbed the bottle, and refilled his glass but not Fierro's.

Fierro glanced down at his empty glass and back up at Cal. "You should stop with all this cops-and-robbers shit. I mean it. Go back to chasing cheating husbands, missing persons, and cats stuck in trees, whatever the fuck you do."

"You have no idea what's going on."

"To tell you the truth, I don't want to know."

Fierro pushed up his glasses, eased forward toward the desk. "That's supposed to be your best friend in there. Do what's right and bring him to a hospital. And you, you should lay off the whiskey for a while."

Cal shrugged indifferently; it was as if a great weariness were pulling him down. "Fuck you, Fierro," he said, but without much feeling.

Fierro stood, took his leather satchel and hat off the desk. "I don't know if you've listened to the radio the last couple of days, but there's a real bad storm coming up the coast. Might be the worst one this winter. You'll want to stay put. Keep an eye on Dante, and if his fever gets worse, you'll know what to do, right?"

Fierro waited for Cal to speak, but he didn't.

"I guess that's it. Take care of yourself."

Cal fought to find words to thank him, to offer him an apology, an excuse, anything, but nothing came to him, and all he could do was pour a third whiskey and keep his eyes downcast, staring at the shot glass filled with its amber liquid and not looking up as Fierro opened the door and left the office. He listened as Fierro's footsteps padded down the hallway and then faded in the stairwell. The curtains were drawn but he could tell it was snowing again, could hear the slow, dull thump of thick, heavy snow against the glass and windowsill. From the back room came the sudden sound of Dante heaving painfully, as if he were vomiting his guts and everything else within him onto the floor.

59

CEDAR GROVE CEMETERY, DORCHESTER

THEY HELD A Mass and funeral service in the Cedar Grove chapel with Lynne's coffin positioned before the altar with flowers and wreaths set upon it. The ground was too frozen to dig, and so the body would rest in the graveyard's charnel house until the ground thawed and she could be buried. Father Nolan, who divided his time between Mission Hill and Saint Brendan's on Gallivan Boulevard, said the Mass and spoke a brief but tender eulogy. He'd asked Cal the night before if he wanted to speak, but Cal declined. Words wouldn't have come to him if he'd tried; all he felt was a dull numbness, as when the nerve endings of one's body have gone into shock and no longer scream with the pain of some terrible wound. He was thankful that the funeral home, Father Nolan, and Owen had done most of the funeral plans. It if it had been up to him, he wouldn't be sitting here now, but Owen had arranged the car service—one black Lincoln for Cal, Owen, and his wife, and another for Lynne's parents—that had picked them up in Southie that morning, and so he'd had no choice. He tried to think about how important it would have been for Lynne, how she would have wanted this, but even that wasn't enough, for nothing seemed to matter anymore, and when he stared at the coffin he saw only the burned and charred remains, a skeleton that could not be his Lynne and yet he knew it was.

In the pews sat mostly Lynne's friends, co-workers from the Carney, others from the old neighborhood whom she hadn't seen in some time or from Savin Hill and to whom she had always been kind. There were also cousins and aunts and uncles of his, the ones who attended every wake and funeral in the city as if it were a special dispensation that their Irish souls demanded of them. Her mother and father were sitting at the front across the aisle from Cal, Owen and his wife, Anne, Claudia, and Dante, pale and disheveled in a tie and black suit, one shoulder raised and crumpled from the thick gauze that wrapped his wound; but they refused to look his way, and when he'd tried to approach them before the Mass, Lynne's mother had shook her head fiercely and begun to sob, and Matty, her husband, jaw-clenched and pale, put up a hand warning him to keep his distance. When he glanced toward the back of the church, he caught sight of Fierro along with half a dozen cops he knew from his days as a detective.

Outside, the air felt cold and hard despite the sun. As if, without the cloud cover that they'd been under the last month, what little heat there had been was now gone. The sky was blue, but the only bird was a seagull shrieking forlornly over the Neponset River and the flats winding out to the bay and the sea. There was the soft peal of a bell, and Cal watched a trolley car bound for Mattapan Square trundle along the tracks that bisected the cemetery. Lynne had often joked that when the time came for them to be buried here, they could still take the trolley into town at midnight and go dancing together at Storyville.

He didn't realize he was crying until he felt Owen's wife hugging him, and then, awkwardly, Claudia did the same thing. Lynne's parents had already climbed into their Lincoln, and he watched as the driver eased the large car between the granite gateposts and out onto Adams Street. And he let them take him to the car, even though it felt as if their combined weight, one on either side of him, were weighing him down.

In the dining room Owen and his wife had laid out a platter of cold cuts, bread, and cheeses; in the kitchen a large pot of stew simmered over a low flame. Mourners stood in various corners of the room talking quietly. Anne went about turning on the standing lamps while Owen refilled whiskey glasses or passed out bottles of beer.

After he'd shaken hands and listened to condolences, to which he vacantly nodded and said thank you, Cal stood to one side of the bay window in the dining room and looked across the boulevard at Carson Beach. He spooned stew from a bowl and chewed slowly; he couldn't taste a thing, but knew he needed to eat.

There were a few stuttering notes on the upright piano, and then Dante began to play "Carrickfergus." The piano was out of tune and many of the keys dead, notes that sounded out wooden and dull, but Dante's gnarled fingers did their best, slowly letting the notes hold their pitch. His head was bent to the keys and cocked sideways, and Cal couldn't tell whether this was from the pain of his shoulder wound or if he was listening for the absences and tremors in the range his damaged hands would allow. And there was something about the sound of the ruined piano and its player that lent a melancholy quality to the song.

Cal glanced over from the window. Lynne would have appreciated the song—even with all of its flaws, it was beautiful. More, he thought, she would have been happy that Dante was playing again.

After a moment, Owen placed his beer on the mantel and joined him, singing. Owen was a natural tenor with a fine falsetto and his version of the song brought most people in the room to tears. Together they played "The Galway Shawl" and then "Blackbird" and "She Moved through the Fair," and the haunting treble of Owen's voice filled the room.

They played together for a while longer, moving from the traditional Irish ballads to World War II standards, and then the sound of them drifted slowly into the swell of talk and lament and the giving of blessings and leave-takings, and it wasn't until Dante stood at his side with a bologna and cheese sandwich and a beer that he knew the whole thing was finally and mercifully over.

"How you holding up?" Dante asked.

Cal nodded. "I'm okay."

He flexed his bandaged hand then looked back to the window. Dante watched him staring blankly beyond the glass. He finished his sandwich and sipped his beer.

"What do you want us to do?"

"Do? Do about what?"

In the living room someone turned on the radio and a surge of static filled the room, followed by the loud, jubilant sounds of a swing number, and they quickly turned it off. Dante followed Cal's eyes; the street looked gray and deserted. Not even a car moved. It was as if the world had been stilled and was waiting to move forward again.

Voices from the living room came to them, louder now thanks to the whiskey and the beer, everyone more comfortable with their grief and letting go the decorum of mourning. Dante touched Cal's arm lightly and Cal looked at him. "What do you want us to do?" he said again.

Cal rolled his shoulders and it hurt; he realized that his body had been rigid for the last half hour, and that he'd been standing in the same spot without moving. He still felt the tightness and pain in his muscles, the ache of nerve and tendon after the surge of adrenaline from three nights before. He exhaled slowly, trying to let the tension go. Felt the holsters beneath his jacket. Since the fire he'd kept them close and hadn't left the house without them. It was time to let them go, too. All of it needed to end, and there was only one way.

"I want to burn the fucker down," he said softly. "All of it. I want to light him up."

"Good," Dante said. "That's good."

60

FROM THE FRONT seat of the battered DeSoto Dante had jacked in Jamaica Plain, they watched the lights beyond the plate glass windows of McGuire's Package Store on Blue Hill Avenue and the clerk bent, slope-shouldered at the cash register, closing out, taking the cash, adding up the receipts, and then walking through the narrow building, extinguishing the lights one by one. They watched as a beer truck made a late-night delivery, the driver carting kegs and crates of booze on a two-wheeler dolly through the side entrance. After the truck was gone, they watched as the clerk wiped the snow from his car and then as he drove out of the lot, turning left onto Blue Hill Avenue toward Franklin Park and the city.

Cal hunched low in his seat, knees against the dashboard, thumbing bullets into the clip of his automatic. Dante sucked his cigarette slowly, let a thin stream of smoke escape from between his lips and drift out the partly open window. A truck bearing the placard RUBENSTEIN'S KOSHER MEATS growled down the deserted avenue, big band music drifting from its cab. With the heel of his hand, Cal pushed the clip into the chamber.

On the darkened street Dante opened the trunk of the car. Six five-gallon metal gas cans stood upright, side by side, a seventh lay turned on its side. With his good arm he reached into a nook beside the upright cans and pulled out a pint bottle. "For your miseries," he said, lifting the bottle in mock toast, and they both took swigs from it.

Cal looked up and down the street to see if anybody was watching. The wooden triple-deckers and brick-and-clapboard houses, the poorly shoveled sidewalks, mounds of plowed snow and parked cars squeezed between them; the whole neighborhood encased in a bone-white moonlight that made it all appear frozen, as silent and still as a photograph in a rarely opened photo album. He ran his fingers through his hair, hacked, and spat phlegm into the snow. He heaved out one of the five-gallon canisters and then slammed the trunk shut. "All right, then," he said, and in the moonlight Dante could see Cal's face, rigid and hard as stone.

In the back lot a line of low pine trees silhouetted the mottled sky, charcoal clouds covering the moon. The back door of the building was encrusted with ice. A drift of frozen snow covered the bottom steps in a sweeping arch. Cal kicked at the door once. Three more times and the door snapped open, the dead bolt tearing through the weathered wood.

First thing that hit them was the smell. Dante moved about the center of the room with the flame from his butane lighter leading the way. After several minutes he found a lone string hanging from the ceiling. He pulled down on it and a bare bulb illuminated a room with concrete floors and walls constructed of cheap plywood. A couple of worktables stood against the wall off to their right, boxes of bootleg liquor stacked beneath them.

A cot covered in bedsheets and blankets rested in the far-left corner of the room. Above it, photos of women with powdered faces exposing their pointed breasts were tacked on the wall, and besides them, a gas station calendar two years old, pinned open to October 1949.

"Jesus Christ," Dante said as he pulled back the sheets, revealing a large blackish-brown stain in the area where a head would have rested.

Cal moved to the boxes under the table. They were full of water-damaged papers and files, now dry to the touch. He poured gasoline on them first, and then, taking small steps sideways, his arms moving in a careful pendulum motion, poured gasoline in splashing arcs on the walls.

When the can was empty, he walked back to the center of the room and lit the cigarette in his mouth, inhaled slowly, seeming to savor it. He flicked the cigarette and it landed under the table, and the vacuum sucking noise of conflagration was followed by a rolling, bellowing hiss as everything caught fire. He walked over to the bulb and pulled down on the string so the only light was from the flames that carried up the walls in a brilliant blue, orange, and white wave.

Outside, it took a third attempt with the solenoid clicking before the engine roared and then settled into a steady grumble. Cal hit a switch, and headlights rose up from the sides of the hood. Two beams of light fluttered, washed trembling light across the snowbank before them. The engine grated and made a straining noise as he put the car in gear and slowly moved out onto the empty street.

He kept the whiskey bottle between his legs as he drove, took a small pull before taking a much larger one, then passed it to Dante. He flexed his hands, rolled his shoulders, pressed back into the car seat, and watched the snow falling slow and thick before the wavering beam of the head-lights.

They finished the bottle of whiskey outside the second building, a small warehouse on the Milton–Hyde Park line. It was as if it was all meant to be. The door to the small warehouse wasn't even locked, and inside a large pile of dried splitting firewood sat in the corner, as though the Fates bore matchstick fingers and had placed it there just for them. But farther in amid boxes of cigarettes, imported canned goods, clothes, kitchen appliances, was a row of male and female department store man-nequins standing there as if guarding the stolen goods. Grinning, Cal began moving about the room like the boxer of old, jabbing the air be-fore the mannequins' faces. He shuffled down the row and then paused at a dummy with a pencil-thin mustache. "Ahh, you fuck!" Cal shouted.

347

"Thought you'd sneak by me, didn't you, you dirty bastard!" and he struck it a left uppercut and then a right and the dummy toppled to the floor. Dante shook his head, helped drag one of the wooden men into the center of the large room, poured gasoline over its bald head just like dousing a wick, and then, branching out trails of gasoline in all directions, made sure the inferno would catch to every corner.

LEARY'S SAT AGAINST the tracks behind a steel-wire fence crested with tight coils of barbed wire: a one-story building that looked as if it had once been a canteen for the local mill workers. It was well past one o'clock, and all the lights were out. Cal and Dante moved around the perimeter of the building until they found a cellar window. "It's Saturday night, they got better places to be," Dante said as he kicked the glass in, tapped at the sharp fragments with the tip of his boot until it was clear enough for them to climb through. They made it up the staircase, listened at the door, and when only silence came to their ears, they moved quickly inside. Dante found a light switch, which illuminated the small barroom.

Dante moved behind the bar, swiped a bottle, broke its seal, and drank from it. Cal poured gasoline along the oak bar and the stools whose cushions were tattered and torn, wide strips of electrical tape keeping them from falling apart. When he lit the cigarette and flicked it over the bar, Dante stood farther away, unzipped, and let loose a streaming arc of piss onto the jukebox by the entrance, watching the fire reflect off and dance on Cal's profile. "Now we can celebrate!" he shouted.

BLACK JACK'S HAD its back to the Fort Point Channel, beside an arch-covered alleyway that veered crookedly out onto Old Colony Way. Plaster crumbling in places revealed the horsehair between the framing joists. Empty beer glasses and overflowing ashtrays lay on the windowsills from the night before. Dante glanced at the shattered glass, the places that showed bullet holes and blood, and the floor near the door where a pool of blood had soaked into the wood, turning it black, and then he and Cal went to work, dousing the tables and booths and bar.

As Cal and Dante set the fire, there was a sudden swell in the channel as a barge passed slowly in the night; waves pushed up against the stone embankment, and the building seemed to shift, a wavering tremor beneath Dante's and Cal's feet as if they were at sea, and as if the place were built on pylons instead of stone, and then they rushed out to the car, which they'd left idling.

They crossed the channel and drove into the city. The windows of the lone tavern on the far side of the South Street Bridge blazed with light like a distant flame, and then something inside ignited, perhaps the gas mains from the stove or the heater, or more secret things stored in the bar's cellars, for an explosion sounded across the water, and they could feel the vibration of it through the chassis of the car, and a pillar of bright flame shot through the bar's roof, sending shingles and splintered joist beams and black tar paper hurtling into a sky lightening with more snow.

They moved through the dark, deserted city, blankets of white snow in drifts between buildings starkly white, and the firelight caught like candle flames in black, empty windows. Dante tugged at a cigarette while Cal wove the car lazily through the darkness, fishtailing back and forth on the deserted streets of downtown. The lights of Jimmy's Lighthouse blazed in blue and amber. Atop the John Hancock building the weather beacon flashed red. And the snow fell thick and soft before their headlights, swirling before the windshield and the wipers, and then swept back along the car's sides and into the blackness.

61

CITY DUMP, THE CALF PASTURE, DORCHESTER

THEY DROVE THE DeSoto to the city dump, where they'd left Cal's car parked beyond the mountains of refuse, hidden among the crushed cars from the wrecker's yard stacked eight high. Thick, churning smoke billowed up from the tire plant; the smell of burning rubber swept across the frozen marshland. Here and there, plainly visible in the darkness, feeble white smoke twined sluggishly upward from the roofs of hobo shacks scattered across the point. Tonight it seemed too cold even for the rats, and nothing moved. The crushed chassis shuddered and groaned about them as wind off the water came rushing over the peninsula, and Cal turned his head slightly against the wind, convinced for a moment that he'd heard a fragment of an old dancehall tune come drifting across the bay.

They splashed the remainder of the gasoline on the stolen car, smashed the windows, and doused the interior. Dante lit a matchbook, stood for a moment watching the matches curl, blackened, into a small blaze, and then he pitched it through the shattered windows and onto the front seat, where it at once ignited the gasoline. Blue-tinged flames raced through the interior and then on rapidly flickering tendrils about the roof of the car, across glass and metal. In a moment the upholstery of the seats had caught and the interior became a revolving fireball. The front and rear windows blackened, torqued, and then shattered. Flames shot upward, illuminating the towers of crushed cars.

They stepped back, twenty feet or so, and watched. Even from such a distance the glow of the burning car shone upon their faces. "I was starting to like that car," Dante said. The adrenaline of the night was all but gone, and a sickly metallic taste remained in his mouth. His limbs ached dully, and he was suddenly extremely tired. Blood had seeped through his bandage, and he felt the wound throb with a sharp, bullying pain. Cal looked pale and washed out, his eyelids opening and closing heavily as they watched the car burn. He lifted the whiskey bottle to his mouth, but it was empty, and he let it drop to the snow.

He trudged to his Fleetline, climbed in, and started the engine—it turned over grudgingly and caught on the third attempt—and fixed Dante in the headlights as he pulled slowly out from between the rows of crushed cars.

Cal rolled down the window, gunned the engine as the idle faltered, and motioned with his head for Dante to get in the car. "I've seen enough fires for one night," he muttered.

They drove back along the Mile Road from the dump, past the tire factory and treatment station, and the lights of the city blinked into view before them, and it was as if they'd suddenly emerged from some strange, hidden country, a place that existed outside the world they were returning to; and with this came a sensory realization, the overpowering smell of gasoline, sulfur, and ash, burnt hair and charred clothing, of sweat and alcohol. Cal's head slumped forward as he drove, his eyes mere slits as he peered through the glass. His shoulders shook and his hands gripped the wheel so tightly the big, scarred knuckles shone white. It took Dante a moment before he realized that Cal was crying. He said nothing, and Cal's eyes tracked the road before them and they drove on blindly through the dark.

62

CAL WASHED AND then slept through the afternoon on the office's foldout couch in his underwear, a blanket wrapped about his lower legs, sweating although the room was freezing. When he woke, he looked in on Dante. He was sleeping fitfully but seemed stronger than he had the day before; some color had come back to his face. He boiled water for coffee, breath steaming the cold air, and couldn't help but smell from their overcoats the acrid scent of ash and gasoline. He lowered his nose to his skin and sniffed; even after bathing, he could still smell the gasoline and fire on his skin.

Too agitated and stir-crazy to bide his time sitting in the office any longer, Cal wandered the streets again, his senses alert to every holler or shout or passing car. A reluctant winter dusk came down upon the city and the lights came on. In the distant bell tower of the Old North Church in the North End, a lamp glowed golden-hued, and seemed to guide him. He walked the old West End, passing small tenement houses, working-class shuls, Italian butcher shops and bakeries, grimy storefronts seeming

352

to lean in on the narrow streets, and alleyways entrenched in snow and through which no cars could now pass, and then along the river back into the North End, along Copp's Hill, where Cotton Mather lay in his grave, and down the backside of Hanover Street. He passed Clough House and the Paul Revere House, the Standard Saloon, infamous political club of the old ward bosses.

"What do we do now?" Cal said aloud, and a group of passing pedestrians stared at him.

He passed the Langone Funeral Home on Hanover, where over ten thousand mourners had paid their respects to Sacco and Vanzetti back in '27. And the tenement where ward boss John F. Fitzgerald had been born, worked his way up from ward heeler to city council to state senator to congressman for the Ninth District, and, finally, mayor of Boston. The Ladies' Auxiliary were standing on the steps of the shul on Salem Street, and despite a strake of snow and wind rushing at his face, Cal looked up and tipped his hat as he passed.

A regiment of streetlights came on above his head with a slight buzzing hum. Along the street thick clouds of steam spiraled slowly upward from manhole covers. On Thacher Street he found himself before the restaurant that just the week before he'd waited outside as Foley, McAllister, and Renza's uncle had their meeting. The red and green neon sign glowed in the frozen air, its windows lit brightly from within, and he stepped inside into the heated air thick with the scent of garlic and fresh dough.

Cooks shouted in Italian at one another, flattened and oiled the dough, dressed it with various toppings, pulled pizzas steaming from the ovens. On the wall behind the counter, under grease-spotted frames, numerous pictures of smiling Italian crooners, pop stars from years past, all autographed to the pizzeria.

He ordered a pizza and took a beer to a stool before the window. On the opposite wall more framed pictures crowded the wallpaper, peeling in the steam of the room: local figures, sports heroes, politicians—a picture of Mayor Hynes, Pope Pius XII; Italian boxers staring at the camera lens and frozen in permanent flat-footed rigor, their fists raised against invisible opponents just beyond the photographer.

From a radio came the standards from a decade before, crackling and hissing over the noise from the kitchen, and between songs the deejay, bright and exuberant, describing the year of the song, the various singers and band members, and national events occurring at the time of the record's release. Cal drank the beer slowly, reluctant to head back to the office, and then his pizza came and he ate.

Sam Shaw's "Wish You Were Mine" followed Dinny Cochrane's "A Splendid Thing" from 1942, the year they completed the Alaskan Highway, *How Green Was My Valley* won Best Picture at the Academy Awards, and a fire at the Cocoanut Grove supper club on Piedmont Street burned it to the ground, the year Cal shipped out for Europe. He and Lynne had taken a final trip to the Cape the month before, and Dante and Margo had joined them. He hadn't known then that it would be the last time he'd visit the Cape. It was near the end of the summer, and even with the new food rationing program, the local stores were out of vegetables and fruit, even bread and milk were in short supply, and they combined their money and their ration coupons to buy what they could: a small amount of coffee, eggs, and chocolate. From a local fisherman they purchased a crate of beer and a bushel of oysters. It seemed like it was all they ate for three days.

At night they lit a bonfire on Long Nook Beach, and each couple huddled against the wind coming in off the sea, surf booming on the sand, he imagined, like the distant guns in Europe waiting for him, and Dante made up stories about the acts of heroism Cal O'Brien would perform during the war, the medals he'd be wearing on his shirtfront when he came back, stories so absurd that they all laughed. It had been a good time, a happy time, but when he returned, the world had changed, gone slightly off-kilter, and so had he. In the time that he'd been away, Dante had lost himself to his addiction, Margo was slowly killing herself, and he wondered if Dante would ever be the same. But at least now, after Dante's withdrawal, if they could get him cleaned up, off the junk, and healthy again, it would be a start.

One of the cooks was singing in broken English along with Sam Shaw, and Cal smiled as he ate, looked absently at the pictures of Celtics and Bruins teams, the horses at full gallop at Suffolk Downs, and then of greyhounds at Wonderland curling about their track, of a grinning man holding a winning betting ticket aloft, of greyhounds curled up, asleep in their cramped kennels, and another of a gaunt-faced man, eyes bright with humor, walking four greyhounds on a leash, his slick black pompadour seeming to defy gravity.

Cal paused with the pizza in his mouth, began chewing again until he could swallow. He took a swig from his beer, almost draining it, and looked back at the photos again, at their stark black clarity, the sharply defined foreground. He looked about the room and to the signed photos of pop stars and crooners over the counter where a group of old men now sat.

"Hey!" he said aloud to himself. "Hey!"

He squinted and stared at the row of three pictures of Wonderland: the greyhounds racing, the greyhounds asleep, and the man with the black pompadour holding the dogs' leash. They were all done in the same style as the ones they'd found in Sheila's box.

The amber glow of the streetlights pushed through the three windows at his back, like the flames of a dimming furnace, lighting the long, narrow room. He looked at the picture on the wall, and then stood to look at the autographed picture of the crooner above the register. "It's fucking him," he whispered. "Bobby Renza, Mario fucking Rizzo."

"Hey," he said to one of the men working the ovens, face shimmering with sweat from the heat. "You know this guy?" He pointed to the photograph of the crooner on the wall.

"Of course," he said. "Everyone know that guy."

"Yeah, yeah," he said, "but what about this guy," and he gestured to the photos on the back wall so that the man had to come out from behind the ovens to look. He shook his head. "I no know this guy, I no know who he is."

Some locals seated at stools at the counter turned his way. "You know this guy?" he asked. "This guy in the picture with the dogs, you know this guy?" But either because they spoke only Italian or because they distrusted him, they refused to answer and only shook their heads.

He turned to a stocky man who sat at a small booth studying a betting slip, the thumb-end of a cigar clenched between his teeth, its thick smoke swirling above his head.

"This guy," he said, "in this picture, it's Mario Rizzo, right?" The man had arms that seemed carved of granite, each tightly layered with cords of muscle and coiling black hair, and each crossed over the other and leaning atop his generous stomach. He gave off the appearance of some golem, a morose statue perched still on the toilet, contemplating nothing but the well-earned stones he was about to purge from his bowels.

Cal ground his teeth in frustration. He might as well have been talking to a man taking a shit, and was about to turn away when the man nodded once slowly, and then looked back down at the betting slip on the table before him.

Relief came over him. He shoved pizza into his mouth, chewed at it voraciously, and washed it down with the cold beer. He looked again at the pictures on the wall before him. He stared at the photo of Mario Rizzo on one knee, stroking the back of a dog. Another of a greyhound at full sprint and leaning into the bend of the track, looking as if it were levitating, lean muscles bulging from thin bone, and he imagined Sheila there, just to the right of the camera lens, leaning on the railing, watching the dogs racing past, and in a moment she would be captured within that frame herself, smiling beautifully forever.

"I know where to find you, Mario Rizzo," he said. "I know where to fucking well find you."

63

WONDERLAND DOG TRACK, REVERE

HE WATCHED THE two men appear on the horizon, two black figures against the snow-packed field and the sky above, colored like wet stone, its clouds breaking and rolling in slow liquid movements. One was tall and lean, bowed slightly, the other a little shorter, compact, and moving with a stiff determination even as he seemed to be limping. A tingling sense of déjà vu came over him, some future memory that seeped in from the spaces between dream and premonition, and he lowered his head wearily and sighed. It was time.

One of the dogs nuzzled against his leg. She sat beside him, and he dropped to one knee and pulled her to his chest. He felt her shivering, the sharpness of her ribs beneath her thinning coat. Her one good eye glistened wetly from the frigid air.

"Maxine, my old lady, I know it's too damn cold. Go join the others and get those muscles worked up before the big storm." He stroked her head and then said, "Go on now."

The old greyhound gave him a worried look, as if she knew that the two figures approaching were carrying some bad news, but she obeyed his command and ambled off as well as her arthritic legs would allow, joining the other two dogs, Norman and Sierra, who moved through the snow quicker than she could, their heads bobbing as they rushed each other in play.

He stood and wiped the snow sticking to his knee. The two men were getting closer. It seemed they knew he wouldn't make a run for it.

Norman and Sierra noticed the men approaching, and they hustled back and paced around him, craning their necks up as they circled, occasionally barking while their panting spurts of breath steamed the cold air. He wondered if they could feel what he was feeling: the fear and yet acceptance that everything would soon be at an end. The sound of the world felt contained, as if nature were holding its breath. He reached out to Sierra, and she nudged his hand before mewling a sad strange song. "It's okay, sweetheart," he soothed.

With their hands stuffed inside their coat pockets, the two men were close enough now so that he could see their faces. They didn't look like killers, nor did they look like police. The taller one seemed somewhat familiar, unshaven and gaunt and looking as if he'd been through the wash one too many times. It seemed as if he were barely on his feet and might fall any minute. The shorter guy was clean-shaven; his square face shone, reddened by the wind. As they came closer, he could see the shorter man's eyes, bright and blue in bloodshot whites.

The shorter guy said, "Bobby Renza."

"I don't go by that name anymore." His voice cracked as he spoke, as if something were catching painfully in his throat. The dogs moved toward the strangers. Steam fell from their open mouths, tongues hanging as they panted, brown mottled with pink.

He shrugged, scratched at his beard, cigarette smoldering between nicotine-stained fingers.

"We need to talk," the shorter man said.

"What about? I don't know nothing and I got nothing to say."

"Maybe. It's about Sheila Anderson."

"Are you here to kill me?"

The shorter one paused at that.

"We just want to talk."

Renza knelt by Norman, rubbed his hackles, as Sierra came and licked at his other hand. He looked at the two men, who eyed him flatly, the stone-faced blue-eyed one and the thin, sick one giving off such a buzz he could feel it. So many things he could do right now and perhaps make a getaway, but he felt so damn tired. He nodded toward a little wooden shack attached to a narrow extension where they kept the kennels. The shack's stovepipe chimney funneled a gray smoke into the even grayer sky.

"All right then," he said.

THE ROOM WAS dimly lit but for the flickering light that came from the woodstove in a corner on which a blackened coffeepot sat, and from a small window above a cot piled with discolored sheets and wool army blankets. It smelled of warm dog hair, tobacco, old animal feed, stale sweat, and of bedsheets that hadn't been changed in some time. The dogs followed them into the room, and Renza closed the door behind them. The older-looking dog pulled herself up onto the bunk but continued to stare at them.

Renza left them while he put the other two dogs in their cages, and from the kennel there came the sound of scratching and a chorus of excited barking. When he returned, he put two splintered logs into the fire, poked at the embers beneath them until flames shot up and licked, crackling, at the wood. "Sierra and Norman get a little wary around new people, but don't worry about Maxine here, she's a harmless old lady." The dog looked toward him, nervously stole glances at the two strangers.

"All the other greyhounds are down in Florida for the winter. These here with me didn't make it. They're way past their prime, not one race left in the tank." He walked to an industrial wooden trestle turned on its side to make a table, picked up a bottle of rum and a dirty glass.

"If you're not here to finish me, you might as well pull up a chair, help me finish off this bottle."

Bobby Renza was not what Dante had expected. His marquee good looks had long since faded. Bloodshot eyes burned from deep-set shadowed sockets. He had an unruly black beard. The pompadour was gone. Now his hair was long and swept over his ears, a black stocking cap tight on his head. He wore a tattered red and black flannel jacket, frayed at the collar and cuffs. The place around him was just as disheveled. Magazines and a stack of old newspapers and empty cans of beans and empty bottles of Coca-Cola strewn about, and above, exposed ceiling beams that seemed to bend, ready to snap and cave in from all the snow packed onto the flat tar roof.

Renza stared at Dante. "Now I know who you are. Sheila kept a picture of you and her sister on the dresser. She used to talk about you sometimes."

Dante stepped closer to the fire, seeking some warmth to thaw the numbness in his bandaged shoulder. "We know all about pictures. We found some nice ones you took of her, the kind of smut they pass around at stag parties. Was she proud enough to put those on the dresser?"

"Those were just for the two of us," he said and closed his eyes for a moment. "Most of them anyway."

Cal pulled out a cigarette and lit it. "And the rest for Foley?"

"A few."

"You're a real piece of shit."

A sad smile crept over Renza's mouth. He coughed weakly and then cleared his throat as he sat down at the table. "I loved that girl like you wouldn't believe." He filled up the small glass with rum, took his lips to it, and drained it.

There was a moment of silence in the room, interrupted by wood popping in the fire. And as if the rum had already made him drunk, Renza continued. "You know, it was that faraway look in her eyes. First time I met her, back when I was singing still, I noticed it and immediately thought she was trouble. Not the kind like in the movies where she sticks a knife in your back when you're not looking. No, it was never that way. Just like something damaged, something that you know you can't fix but you damn well try your hardest anyway."

"That damage attracted you," Dante said.

"Yeah. And not just me."

"She left you for Foley, didn't she?" Cal asked.

"You've got it wrong, all wrong. She was always my girl. Even he knew that."

"Then come clean." Dante sat down in the chair opposite him, took off his hat, and placed it on the table.

They watched him pour three fingers' worth of rum, then drink it down.

"Day in, day out, stuck here hiding like some sick fucking dog. Somebody knows they can use you and they hand you a lot of money, you take it and feel this is it, the big payday. I thought I'd get what I finally deserved, take care of Sheila the right way by giving her everything she ever wanted."

He paused as he filled his glass again. "Well over a million in bills and bonds. They wouldn't notice the difference, right? A few thousand here and there out of a haul like that? Peanuts, right? But we all thought that way, you know, taking from the top and then some more."

"The Brink's job," Cal said.

"Yeah."

"And Sheila knew too much about it. She knew what you were up to, but that's not what got her in trouble. It was your uncle, the contractor, right? He forced you to give her up to Foley. She was there to grease the deal. Foley had his fun, and now your scumbag uncle is in charge of tearing down and rebuilding Scollay, and it's on her fucking grave."

Renza took three tugs off the bottle, pulled it roughly back from his chapped lips. "I loved that Sheila like nobody else ever did. And she did everything to protect me, kept her mouth shut..."

"What about the Emporium, room eight-oh-oh-one?"

"What about it? That's Foley's penthouse suite, where he and her used to meet. After I introduced the two of 'em, she went regularly by herself, whenever he called, the fucking shit."

"Where's the money, Bobby?" Dante asked.

"They killed her...you think it'll make any difference if they get their money now?"

"I don't think she died for the money, Bobby, but it might be the only thing that can save you."

Dante pushed his chair in closer, the sound of wood scraping wood. "Who killed her?"

Bobby shook his head. "Honest to God, I don't know." He wiped at his eyes with the back of his hand.

"You knew she was pregnant?" Cal asked.

"Of course I did."

Dante's head was beginning to throb. "So you know what happened to the baby?"

Renza shook his head and took another hit off the bottle. "Dead and buried in a landfill for all I know. I have no fucking idea." He slammed the bottle against the table, made a fist, and clenched his teeth.

"I don't know shit. She could have been fucking half this city for all I know. A bunch of politicians at the State House, trading favors for favors, or at the jazz clubs she always went to, going down on some niggers just so they'd play her favorite song. And that makes me the sucker, don't it?"

"You're the one that sold her out, Bobby, pimped her like she was a whore."

But Bobby no longer seemed to be listening. His bottle was almost empty. His head swayed and then drooped and stayed that way; his fingers lightly touched the bottle before him.

Dante clenched his jaws. "Hey," he said, and kicked at Bobby's feet. "Hey!" He wanted to hit him, but he knew that Bobby probably wouldn't feel a thing; he was too far gone.

"Fucking wet-brain," Cal said. They both knew he wouldn't last much longer even if he did decide to run. The old greyhound on the cot eyed them sadly and groaned. Dante stood and made for the door, and Cal followed him.

Outside the cold air felt good on Cal's neck and face, sharp in his nostrils, stinging his eyes so they watered. The snow-packed field was covered in shadow, and in the dusk-lit distance they could see the shell of the Wonderland racetrack, with its gleaming frozen track and empty stands, looking like something skeletal, just bones and the vast emptiness that seemed to hold it all together. It appeared as though it was much farther away, and that the walk back to the parking lot would take them nothing short of an eternity.

They began walking, and then paused when they heard the slight stirrings of a song. It was Renza's voice coming to them, bending against and falling into the wind that whirled throughout the grandstands and onto the open field before them. It was a familiar ballad, strange and haunting, from which all the ravages and drunken slurring had lifted, and Renza's voice was as golden in timbre and cadence as it had ever been on the radio all those years before.

> *Come take my hand, my love*
> *Hold it tight and never let go*
> *Under a night without stars, we'll dance one more time*
> *Come take my hand, and never let go*
> *Forever and ever, the night sky we will climb*

Dante shivered and pulled his coat more firmly about him. The dead still sing, he thought as he and Cal trudged back through the field, the sky above darkening with night and neither of them saying a word to the other but instead merely listening to the last ghostly echoes of Renza's song fading throughout the old iron balustrades and tin roofing and then, almost at its end, broken by a dog's howl.

64

OUR LADY OF PERPETUAL HELP, MISSION HILL, ROXBURY

A FLUSHED-CHEEKED ALTAR boy swung the censer back and forth, its incense blurring the air in slants of gray smoke, drifting across the altar. Cal watched from the second pew behind the left transept. At the shrine to Saint Peter on his left, over which hung hundreds of canes and crutches dating back over a hundred years, the wood shining, a polished luster as if encased in amber, a half-dozen disabled parishioners were lighting candles and praying. Cal watched several of them bless themselves and rise, struggling from their kneelers, and totter to the center aisle, genuflect, and make the sign of the cross again before leaving. In the vestibule an old woman, stout-hipped and bow-backed, in a black shawl murmured the Stations of the Cross. A ragged run in her stocking cleaved the back of one thick calf as if it had been sliced by a blunt razor blade.

He watched the altar boy, who had paused in his swinging and then looked upward at the high domed and glittering ceiling as if an image of God might appear among the clouds and angels. The sound of footfalls, sharp and distinct on the tile, came to him only after he had registered the presence of bodies settling into the pew behind him.

He turned slightly, and Blackie's voice stopped him.

"Keep looking straight ahead, O'Brien. Just keep praying."

Cal arched his neck, felt the muzzle of a gun there at the base of it.

"Did you think I wouldn't know it was you two fuckups that torched my places, my fucking bar?"

Despite Blackie's warning, he turned to the right, glanced at Joe Kinneally, and then to the left, Pat Mulrooney, and in the vestibule, the slender, stoop-shouldered figure of Shaw. He saw that Blackie's left arm was held in a sling, and he took some satisfaction in that. "Dante got you after all," he said. "You prick."

Blackie pressed the gun sharply into Cal's neck, prodding him to turn back to the front. Shaw moved up the aisle toward the altar, genuflected and blessed himself, put his hands together in mock prayer.

Blackie eyed him and scowled. "I told you to wait in the fucking car. What are you, a fucking idiot?"

Shaw shrugged, indifferent to Blackie's insults. "You want me to go back to the car?"

"Nah, stay here now that you're fucking here. It's bad enough that Sully says I got to bring you with me wherever I go."

Shaw laughed uneasily, his face burning red.

The gun barrel pushed harder against the back of Cal's neck. He should have been scared, but he wasn't. This is how it's going to end, he thought, and felt a strange calm. In his own church, no less.

"So," he said, "what was it with you? The Brink's money or just the kicks?"

Blackie laughed, but it was harsh sounding, rueful, and filled with resentment. "That was the Butcher, not me, the sick fuck. I get no fun out of doing something like that, and I made an example out of him, didn't I? Found him even when the cops couldn't."

Cal shook his head, felt Blackie jab the barrel into the base of his skull.

"He killed the other girls, all right, but you killed Sheila. You discovered the truck at the yards and found the perfect way to get rid of her, the perfect cover."

"If I want to kill someone, I kill them plain and simple."

"Like the old man out in Somerville. Like my wife."

"Yeah, just like that."

"So why did you kill her then? If you find her, you find the money. Unless she refused to talk? So you found her, but she never gave him up, never led you to the money and Bobby Renza."

Cal could feel Blackie's anger, palpable as heat, surge at the back of his neck. The gun wasn't moving now, and he wondered if Blackie would wait to shoot him.

"I told you, I didn't kill the cunt."

"How did you find out about Sheila and Renza anyway? How'd you know he was connected to the Brink's job?"

"You always talk too much, O'Brien. Shut up for once, why don't you."

"I know you put her clothes in the trailer to make it look like the Butcher, and she wasn't killed on Tenean Beach. You killed her somewhere else—but where? And why dump her at Tenean?"

"I said, shut the fuck up."

They waited as the church emptied. Soon the altar boy was gone and the old women doing the Stations. Shaw strolled toward the transept, feet echoing on the tile, looked around at the few parishioners who remained: a dark-suited man bent over the votive candles praying, a woman wearing a shawl dropping coins, clattering, into the empty poor box, and then glanced back to Cal.

He moved to the left and then to the right, pacing. When the man and woman were gone, he reached inside his wool coat and withdrew a silver-plated automatic. He checked the clip, opened and closed the chamber with a swift metallic click.

Blackie looked up at him. "What the fuck are you doing now?"

"Nothing."

"Well your nothing is bothering me. Stay still, will you?"

"Sure."

Cal turned his neck so that it cracked, and Blackie clubbed his ear. Thoughts were rushing in his head now and he couldn't have stopped them had he wanted to. It was like telling someone a story you once knew but could no longer remember the ending. "You never found Renza, did you, Blackie?" he said quickly. "You never got your piece of the Brink's job, and your brother cut you out of everything else. Imagine the money he and McAllister are going to make on the Scollay deal, and all without you."

"I told you, O'Brien, you're a dead man."

"I bet Sully's getting his take, you can guarantee it. That's what the boss always does."

Sucking on his teeth like a dimwit, Shaw raised the gun until it was level with Cal. Cal and he met each other's eyes.

Joe Kinneally rose from the pew. "What the fuck did Blackie tell—"

There was a gun blast, and Joe's face exploded in a black mist of blood and gore; part of the back and side of his head splattered down onto Cal's cheek. Blackie and Pat struggled to their feet, and the gunshots seemed to come to Cal in a delay. Instinctively, he half turned from the gunfire as Shaw fired another round and Pat fell into the transept. Blackie stepped into the aisle, gun raised and firing, and Shaw scampered toward the altar before Cal lunged and drove Blackie into the votive stand before Saint Peter's shrine. The tall brass candlesticks clattered to the floor. Votive candles sparked in the dark. Blackie tried to raise his gun, but Cal knocked it away, drove his fist into Blackie's cheekbone and then again into his mouth. He felt teeth and bone tearing the skin of his knuckles.

Blackie pushed him off and, crawling on all fours, went for his gun. Blood streaked his gums, stained his teeth. "You fuck, O'Brien," he said, and snatched his gun off the tile. Cal scrabbled for a grip on the brass candlestick and swung it like a sledgehammer down onto Blackie's hand. Blackie howled, and the gun fell from his fingers. Cal struck him again in the head, and he fell onto his back. It took Cal's two hands to fully heft the candlestick, and he brought it down with all his force into Blackie's face. Blackie screamed and thrashed, but Cal had all of his weight upon him. When he lifted the brass, blood and skin were stuck to it. Bone poked out pink and viscous through Blackie's torn cheek. He sputtered, trying to talk; blood flowed down his gums, over his shattered teeth. "My brother," he said, chokingly, "it was my brother," and reached feebly to protect his face.

Cal brought the metal down again, crushing Blackie's nose and eye sockets. The body beneath him no longer struggled, but he raised the candlestick a third and then a fourth time.

"Cal!" Shaw shouted, but sound came only slowly, and then Cal was aware of his chest rising and falling, the thumping, heavy sense of his lungs working like a bellows. He let the candlestick go, and it clanged to the floor.

There wasn't anything left of Blackie's face below the hairline. Nothing to tell that he'd been a person, for even the skull beneath the skin was gone; no sockets or nose or teeth—all the bone within the pulpy mess had been shattered into hundreds of pieces.

"That's for my wife," he said, and climbed shakily to his feet.

Shaw had been shot and was holding his arm. Blood seeped from between his fingers. The other hand held the gun still. He stared, pale-faced, at Blackie's body and sucked at his teeth.

"Jesus Christ, Cal."

Shaw coughed, raised his hand weakly to his mouth. Cal stared at his long, arrogant face, but now Shaw seemed shaken and his voice didn't carry any authority. "Sully was sick of his shit. I guess that makes you one lucky son of a bitch, don't it?"

Cal nodded, and Shaw, clutching his arm, made his way to the vestibule. Cal listened to his heels padding on the tile. He waited, and then the door of the church opened, a thin stream of streetlight glanced down the center aisle of the nave, and then Cal was in gloom once more, illuminated by flickering votives and the meager sconces high on the wall. Blood from Blackie's head pooled darkly across the tile.

Cal looked at Blackie's body and then toward the crucifix beyond the altar, and resisted the urge to genuflect and bless himself. He cocked his head as if listening for something—distant sirens, a screech of tires, the rest of Blackie's goons come to finish him off—and then when only silence came, he exhaled long and hard. He glanced at the body sprawled in the transept, at Joe Kinneally bunched between the pews, and then wiped some more at the blood spotting his neck, the angle of his jaw, his cheek. He stared bleary-eyed at the crucified Christ. The lights of the altar flickered on his blind eyes. Cal ran his hand over the side of his face again, stared at the gore he'd wiped onto his skin, then, hand shaking, reached for his hat and followed Shaw out into the light.

65

FOR MOST OF the ride north Cal and Dante said very little. They watched the strange morning mist blending with the snow clouds that darkened the horizon. Cal eased the car along Route 1A as it curved back and forth along its snakelike trail north of Boston, through the coastal towns of Swampscott and Salem. The heater ticked and hummed, and snow, heavy and thick and driven by the wind, fell out of the sky. The big car began to slip and slide, its engine revving, its tires losing traction. Cursing, Cal finally stopped at a corner store that seemed to come at them from out of the squalls with its dimly lit signs advertising Ipswich Beer, Wonder Bread, and Happy Time soft-serve ice cream, up against an inlet where small dories lay upon their bellies, scattered here and there along the ice, broken wind-bleached backs humped with snow.

Cal asked for directions in the store while Dante eased the car into the attached single-bay gas station and paid two dollars to have chains put on the tires by a boy in a denim burlap jacket with a ribbed collar. He had large parboiled eyes and terrible acne, and smelled of booze.

As they waited, they stood in the shelter of the garage bay.

"You don't look so hot," Cal said, eyeing Dante. "Will you make it?"

"Yeah, I'll make it okay."

Dante's pallor was ashen. He coughed into his hand, and he raised his other hand in an apologetic way as he stepped out from the garage into the snow. He turned his back to Cal and began to heave, his shoulders bowed and shuddering. When he was done, he wiped at his mouth with the back of his hand, breathed deeply, took off his hat, and let the snow come down onto his face.

"Me and Sheila," Dante said, and Cal looked up, wondering if Dante was talking to himself. "We had a thing, Cal. I fucked up. I didn't mean for it to happen, but it did. It started months before Margo died, and she knew about it but never said a word."

"Were you two together after Margo died?"

Dante nodded. "I should have told you."

Cal squinted at him through the snow. "I don't think it matters much now, do you?"

And then the boy was done and staring at them, wisps of cigarette smoke drifting from his vacant mouth. Cal pulled the car out, and Dante opened the door and moved stiffly into the front seat. Cal rolled down the window, his bloodshot eyes glancing in the rearview mirror, and steered them back to the road.

When they came into Beverly, the temperature dropped, and moved into the car's interior through the dashboard, doors, and windows. Strakes of snow appeared suddenly, flung in from the sea miles distant yet, drifting across the road, and as they came to Cape Ann, heavy winds buffeted the car.

They crossed a drawbridge and looked out at houses squatting against the coastline, the cranes and the fish and ice storage warehouses of Gloucester Harbor. Washington Street curled and spiraled inward around Flats Pond and Grays Harbor. They looked about them, at houses pressed in against one another, smaller, uniform clapboard turn-of-the-century cottages of quarrymen and once upon a time the Irish, now the province of the Italians, Portuguese, and Swedish, the homes of lobstermen, cod men, and swordfish men, those who sailed out toward the Grand Banks and were gone for a week at a time. But fishing was over for the season, and the economy had blighted the area. Everything seemed meager and tamped down. Here and there a light burned within a window. Small lobster pot buoys, strung up as decoration along the tops of fences, banged hollowly against wood.

Cal drove farther inland and by abandoned quarries, and the houses parted on their left, revealing a small stone jetty and the sea crashing against the rocks. A tall abandoned church tower leaned capriciously in a snow-covered clearing, and then they were descending another rise and a small bay opened up on their left. At the southern promontory a ledge of granite rocks jutted out into Ipswich Bay, and upon it sat the large colonial house from the photograph on McAllister's desk, and at the same address as the check he mailed to Foley.

Cal slowed the car and, as the engine quieted, they listened to the wind whistling in the wheel wells, the door runners, the sound of waves battering the rocks in white spumes.

"The Foley homestead," he muttered.

McAllister's family had once lived in that home and rented a cottage to the Foleys. Cal could see the young Foley, entranced and awed by the wealth such a house implied, imagining a life in which he was one of them, not merely poor Irish from Boston but one of the Brahmins, the elite. How, even as a young boy, he had envisioned something other, something greater, a way out of the squalor of the Southie and Dorchester tenements. How could one not be impressed and awed by it?

Foley had risen up the political ranks and bought the house from the man his family used to rent from. Was that when he and McAllister began their business relationship, one in which Foley the politician ensured the success of McAllister's developments, of his proposals getting city and state approval, and of local contractors working on the cheap, and all of them pocketing federal monies? Or perhaps the house had been a part of that deal also.

Beyond the debris-strewn sand of the deserted cove lay ragged rows of wrack and straw, pushed up like drifts, and farther still, raw-looking whitecaps on the waves, and Cal could imagine the younger Foley brothers playing on that sand with their father of a summer, he grasping them in turn beneath their arms, scooping them up in his large longshoreman's hands, probably callused and bent in the way of his own father's, and throwing them out into the spray and spume of high tide, and a warm sun beating down upon them, the houses on the coastline of Ipswich glittering in the sun from across the bay.

Out on the rocks of the compound an American flag whipped to and fro and snapped against a tall metal stanchion. Most of the surrounding houses were closed and shuttered for the season. Snow-covered gravel crunched beneath the car's tires as they made their way up the winding driveway toward Congressman Foley's summer retreat. Bare trees loomed on either side of the car. Bushes came into view, evergreens trimmed in all manner of shapes, a topiary of strange, obscene animals, turned fantastical now, overgrown and misshapen.

The doorway was unlocked and the hallways were silent. It seemed the hired help were gone for the weekend. From somewhere upstairs came the strains of an opera playing softly. Wind chimes sounded from the eaves of the house, echoing the louder warning bells from the buoys tossing out upon the whitecaps, marking the treacherous coastline.

They followed the sounds of the music, listened as the stylus lifted off the record and then slid, crackling, back into the groove again. The room, a pastel blue, was warm and seemed impervious to the storm outside. At the center of the room a fire burned low in the grate, its coals glowing. With eyes closed, Congressman Foley reclined in a rattan chair covered with thick quilts to the left of the fireplace. A sleeping infant lay stretched, face turned sideways, upon his chest, its cheeks flushed a bright and healthy pink. It wore a red-striped cotton one-piece. Small sheepskin boots covered its feet. A half-empty nursing bottle stood on a side table with a glass tumbler of scotch or bourbon. The congressman's eyes were closed and his breathing was as soft as the baby's. Watching the congressman and the baby, Dante was aware of the cold, like a block of ice that surrounded him and Cal, as if they had brought the storm in with them. From the phonograph a soprano's voice pleaded to her love or to God or to some other torment of the heart and soul. The congressman's eyelashes flickered and then opened. He took them in slowly, and then his eyes widened.

"Cal," he managed. "Dante." His voice was hoarse and thick with sleep. He hacked to clear his throat and blinked. His hand reached protectively around the sleeping baby.

Cal stepped into the room and Dante followed, settled himself on the arm of a sofa just inside the door, plucked at the top buttons of his coat until the coat dangled open at the front and he seemed to sink down inside it. His eyes looked more sunken than ever, his cheeks hollowed out by a hunger and exhaustion.

"Hello, Michael," Cal said.

"What are you two doing here?"

"We're here to bring you news. Your brother was killed late yesterday." Cal waited for a response. The congressman opened his mouth and then closed it again. It seemed as if he was thinking of the correct thing to say.

"My brother? How?"

"I killed him, though it wasn't supposed to happen that way. But then you already know that. You knew that Sully was going to kill him."

The congressman looked at Cal and then nodded. "Yes."

"You put the call in to Sully, and Sully went along with it."

"I did it because I had to, because of what he'd done, because of all the infighting and mob factions he'd created in the city. He was tearing the city apart. I did it for the good of the city. You know that better than anyone, Cal."

Phlegm rattled in Dante's throat, and Cal glanced over at him. He was leaning forward. He hadn't taken his eyes off Foley and seemed purposefully not to be looking at the child.

"I couldn't care less that your scumbag brother is dead, but you put a hit out on him for more than that," said Cal.

"I had to, because of what he'd done to Sheila."

"Because you loved her," Dante said acidly.

"Yes, that's right. I loved her and she loved me and he fucking murdered her." The congressman's voice rose, and he lowered it almost immediately. Color had risen to his cheeks. The baby moaned, kicked out with a foot, and then was still again.

Dante felt a pressure pulsing in his forehead. Dark spots seemed to be spiraling down before his eyes, blurring everything. He tried to measure his breathing. He felt the cold again, encasing the space in which he stood.

"But she didn't love you, did she?" Cal said. "She never really loved you, and when you found out about her leaving you for Renza, you wanted to teach her a lesson, teach her that no one says no to a Foley. Kind of like what your father did to your mother, isn't it?"

"You don't know what you're talking about. What the hell have my mother and father got to do with anything?"

"Your mother had an affair—I remember it was the talk of the neighborhood—but it got hushed up, and over time the story changed. All that we remembered was how your father had her sent up to Danvers, had her institutionalized, saying that she was unfit, mad, how he had to drag her home from the bars every night, telling everyone about her various infidelities, how she'd fuck anyone in the back of McGann's for the price of a drink. Everyone felt so bad for him, that poor man and those poor boys with the crazy mother. Except she wasn't crazy, was she? And she wasn't no whore. Just a woman who ended up on the wrong side of the Foley men."

"My father was a good man, a proud man who served the city his entire life. She brought him down. She ruined him."

"Like Sheila could have ruined you—ruined you and the deal you and McAllister had going."

"I loved Sheila. I'm telling you the truth."

"But when you found out about her and Renza, how they still had a thing together, you had to teach her a lesson."

"I knew who she was with. I knew where she got her money. I didn't care about any of that."

He looked over at Dante now, pleading. "Dante, I loved her. I truly did. I never wanted this to happen. I only wanted her to realize what she had in me, what we had together, and not to throw it away on some piece of shit like Renza.

"Blackie was like a caged animal about the Brink's job. He kept going on about how they'd taken the food right out of his mouth, how they'd come onto his turf and he needed his cut. I told him about Sheila's connection, how she was close with someone on the inside. She used to brag to me about it to get me jealous. I never thought that he would hurt her. I never thought he'd kill her. I just thought that he'd scare her, make her see things right, and that she'd come back to me."

"Look at me, Foley," Cal said. "Dammit, look at me."

The congressman turned back to Cal.

"You're lying. Blackie didn't kill her, not like that—it wasn't his style. He was covering for someone else. And there's only one person I know who Blackie would cover for."

Cal sighed, wanting Foley to explain, wanting him to say something that might make all of this right. The baby stirred in its sleep, mouthing as if it were at its mother's nipple; the small arms and legs flailed and then became restful again.

"You were the one that killed Sheila. You killed her at the Emporium, killed her because you were angry over her relationship with Renza, angry because she was going to spill the beans about your affair, about your crooked dealings with McAllister, and splatter it all over the front page. Blackie had alreday discovered the Butcher's trailer out at the salvage yards and knew he had the perfect out for you."

The congressman shook his head, raised a hand in protest.

"I—I didn't mean to, Cal. We argued—she said she was going to tell Celia, that she was going to tell everyone about our affair, about her child—she was going to ruin everything—and I hit her, it wasn't even that hard—dear God, I've never hit a woman in my life—"

The congressman nodded. "I'd been drinking, God, I'd been drinking all day. I didn't think I'd ever see her again, and then suddenly she shows up at my suite..." He stopped for a moment and then added, "She fell and hit her head. I thought she was fooling around, but she didn't get up again. I didn't know what to do, so I called Blackie. He said he'd take care of it."

"And he did. He made her death look like the work of the Butcher. He took her body from the Emporium, slit her throat from ear to ear, and left her naked body at Tenean, and you carried on with your run for Senate. That was why he had to get to the Butcher before the cops, so that they could never prove otherwise. And that was why you had to call in the hit on your own brother, because, in the end, you didn't feel you could trust him, did you? You were worried that eventually he'd talk and your career would be over."

Foley's jaws clenched. He closed his eyes for a moment, and his Adam's apple bobbed up and down. "Cal," he said, "you know I would never do what you're saying, that I never meant to hurt Sheila. It was an accident, you have to believe that—you don't understand how I loved her. If it wasn't for her and Rizzo—"

"Cal," Dante said. "Cal."

Cal looked at him.

"Bundle up the baby and take her out to the car."

Cal stared at Dante for a moment, questioning, then nodded and stood. His eyes flickered momentarily over the congressman's face and then back to the baby.

"You can't take my child," the congressman said.

Dante spoke again to Cal. "Wrap her up good in blankets. Turn the car on so it's warm."

Cal took a large blanket from the couch and stood before the congressman.

"Move your arm," he said.

"You can't do this."

"Move your arm now."

Dante took the .38 revolver from his pocket, aimed it at Foley. "Do as he says."

The congressman pulled his arm back from the infant, and Cal gently lifted the baby from his chest, bundled her into the blankets in one swift movement, and lay her snoring against his shoulder.

"Cal, you know this isn't right," the congressman called as Cal left the room. "Cal!"

The congressman gripped the arms of the chair. "Dante, you don't need to do this. Think of what this means for the child. Look at what I have to offer her—a good home, a good school. She'll never want for anything. What can you give her? She'll be living on the streets, no better than Sheila was when I first met her."

"You're right. I should let the man that killed her mother watch over her."

"I won't let you get away with this."

Dante cocked his head toward the hallway, waited several minutes until he heard the front door open and then close, imagined Cal's careful footsteps above the snow-flecked gravel, bending his body to protect the child from the wind and the snow. The last few remaining embers crackled in the hearth.

"Dante," the congressman began, "I was wrong, there doesn't need to be trouble between us. I only want what's best for Sheila's daughter, for *my* daughter—"

The stylus lifted off the record, and Dante waited for the needle to settle into the groove again. A long *hisssss* preceded the soprano's voice. He stared at the congressman as the soprano's voice rose up the scales. It resounded in the quiet of the room, pressed loudly in Dante's skull till he could hear nothing else, so that when he spoke, his voice seemed strange and faraway, as if coming from across some great distance.

"Who ever said she was your daughter?" he said and his gun boomed in the small blue room, obliterating everything else.

66

IT TOOK A long time to drive back to Boston. There were more snow flurries, and Cal kept up a low moaning as he negotiated the winding roads out of Gloucester and along the coast. To Dante it sounded as if he were at prayer, chanting to the saints, his head lowered and squinting against the snow and the ever-disappearing boundaries of the road before them. Dante held the baby against him, using his heavily bandaged shoulder as a cushion for her head, and leaned back in the seat. So far she'd slept the entire way. His anxiety about holding her had gradually lessened as he watched and listened to her in sleep, and he studied the small moon of a face.

Cal glanced in the rearview at the two of them in the backseat. "What do you think Claudia will make of it?"

"I think," Dante began, and then paused. "I think it will make her happy."

"You think we were right to do what we did?"

Dante remained silent. He stared at the baby asleep in his arms. The wind rocked the car lightly.

"I'm not sure about what's right."

"The law wouldn't see it that way."

"The law didn't do much for Sheila, did it?"

"Are you going to lose sleep about it?"

"No."

"Well, good, then."

BOSTON WAS DESERTED. Swirls of snow swept over the sidewalks, and in the roadway the tracks of cars were lined with brownish slush. The car's chains tapped and clanked in the places where the roads had been cleared, sparking briefly on the desolate streets. The frame houses and triple-deckers crouched against the cold and the snow, and they seemed to shudder with each gale. A trolley car trundled up the avenue, showering blue sparks as it dragged the power lines. The streets seemed empty and dark; Cal peered at the houses as they passed.

"All the lines are down. The electricity's out."

"We'll be fine," Dante said.

"I'm just thinking of the baby."

They drove through Scollay Square and pulled up before the building with its crenulated black fire escape dripping with dark icicles before each shuttered window. A halite sheen on the recently shoveled steps glowed like silver. For a moment they sat in the warmth of the car, waiting, and watching the streets. A few bums sheltered in the alleyway before Moran's. A couple exited the butcher shop and quickly crossed the street to Kendall's pharmacy. Other than that, the street was deserted.

A deep bone-tired weariness came upon the both of them as they sat in the last of the heat escaping quickly from the car. In the silence the baby's soft, insistent, yet fragile breathing filled the interior of the car. Cal glanced at Dante in the rearview, and Dante nodded, climbed out of the car with the baby bundled against his tattered coat. Cal watched as Dante took the steps slowly, the baby held tight against his bowed chest, the wind whipping the coat about him, and then he opened the front doors to the building and stepped inside.

67

KELLY'S ROSE, SCOLLAY SQUARE

DANTE STARED INTO the mirror above the sink, the mercury plating showing through the cracked surface corroded by mildew and age, and saw only himself transfixed in the stark light cast by the bare light-bulb dangling from the ceiling. He left the toilets and walked down the hallway, stepped to the door of the bar, and opened it. For a moment everything seemed to slow: Cal at the bar, sunlight slanting down the scarred mahogany glinting off glass so that at first he was merely a black silhouette, and then from the brightness emerged his face, and Dante stepped forward, into the light, and the door to the hallway banged shut behind him.

"You all right?" Cal asked, hand momentarily paused around his glass, brow pinched in concern.

"Yeah." Dante nodded, sipped from his drink, and then smiled. "I'm good."

Cal looked at him for a moment longer. Dante fumbled with his pack of cigarettes, put one between his lips but didn't light it.

"There'll be a lot waiting for us when this storm ends."

Cal swallowed his whiskey, grimaced. "Don't worry about it."

"Don't you think they'll link it back to us?"

Cal squinted at the window rattling as the wind moved the snow sideways, swirling before the glass. "They won't find him for days, and with all this snow, they'll have to dig him out. Everybody knows Blackie was searching for the Brink's money. Maybe they'll figure that's the connection."

"What do you think became of the money?"

Cal shrugged. "I don't think we'll ever know. Whoever got the money is probably sunning it up poolside in Acapulco, a cocktail to his lips and a couple of girls on either side of him."

A man entered the bar, his mouth covered by a thick scarf. Eyes squinted in a face made ruddy by the cold and swollen by booze. He shuffled to one corner of the bar and sat down heavily. Outside the sun had disappeared again behind low, thick snow clouds, and the street was still. The bartender placed a glass before the man and then turned on the radio at the back of the bar. It took a moment for the radio to warm up, its transistors humming loudly, and then through the crackling speakers came the Rosenberg trial and the bartender fiddled with the knob until he found the hockey game. The Bruins were beating the Canadiens, 3–1, but had already been eliminated from the playoffs.

Wind pressed against the bar's window so that the glass seemed to bend. When it eased, a strange silence followed. Cal sipped from his drink, pursed his lips. The bartender glanced at them while he worked the dial on the radio above the bar as the signal faded and they lost the game. "Worst storm in history, the papers say," he said.

Cal nodded, and Dante stared toward the snow-streaked windows. Outside, jagged-looking icicles quivered and the flattened shapes of passersby marked the slow decline toward a dusk indeterminate and indistinguishable from day. The radio whistled, high and piercing.

"We'll have another round over here," Cal called, but the bartender could no longer hear him over the squeal of the radio and the wind against the transom and Cal and Dante emptied their glasses and waited.

EPILOGUE

༄

SCOLLAY SQUARE

ON THE TOP floor of the derelict Anvil Building, whose gilded molding and frescoed façade had once so elegantly greeted tourists and sailors and out-of-towners to the Square, a handful of homeless men pressed around a large rusted barrel in which a fire blazed. Through holes punched in the metal sides, orange flames pushed back the darkness and the cold.

The vagrants stood around the blazing barrel and fed it with paper, wood, and the cheap ashy coal that one of them had stolen from the coal tipple at the rail yard. The flickering orange flames cast shadows writhing across the floor and walls, where here and there the plaster was torn away exposing the horsehair and lath beneath. Through the splintered lath the exposed copper wiring hung from the walls like the guts of some eviscerated animal. The wind howled in the corners, hammering against the bare clapboard and through the frame, and they squeezed together for warmth, pressed up to the barrel against the holes they'd punctured in its side and from which the orange glow leaped. One of the men placed a thin, flat iron grate across the top of the barrel, and someone laid four potatoes on it.

The biggest man stood by the barrel idly whistling "The Wild Colonial Boy." Another took a swig from the bottle they were passing around, and handed it to the blind man. He looked up with pale, whitewashed eyes, but his hand, swift and assured, closed around the bottle and brought it to his mouth.

Searching for more wood to burn, one of the men shuffled to the corner of the room where odd remnants of furniture had been left behind, two-by-fours that they'd pried from the floor joists and sections of paneling they'd torn from the walls. From the floor-to-ceiling windows, one of the men looked out upon the Square, at the Old Vic, the Howard Athenaeum, the Scollay Theatre, at its smoke shops, taprooms, hash houses, and liquor stores, the marquee billboards filled with faded pictures of the women who had once performed there: nude legs parted and scissored in the air, large bared and glistening breasts with tasseled nipples, a row of plump, oiled bottoms raised toward some unseen audience of men, and the performers looking back over their shoulders at the ghosts of another time.

The man looked toward the Old Vic with its awning bowed and warped by the weight of snow and ice. Its marquee bulbs continued to blaze even though it was shut down for the night. Its upper windows were mostly dark. Here and there a shadow moved behind an amber-hued shade, stood in that warm rectangle of golden light, something so small and brief and insignificant in all that darkness that it seemed to intensify the sense of isolation and emptiness so that the feeling of desolation grew larger still. From so high up, the whole street seemed like some vast ocean liner abandoned at sea, its once elegant salons and stairwells and ballrooms dark and empty now, absent of laughter or joy or life, as if everyone had left her to the terrible sea and she merely awaited her end.

The flames cast their orange light amid the debris, the soiled mattresses and threadbare, hollowed-out chairs and sofas, the piles of horsehair blankets, and the cardboard and timber lean-to at the far end of the room where they squatted to relieve themselves. Even with the cold, the room smelled of human waste. In the coming months the wrecking ball and the bulldozers will reduce the building to rubble, but the man and the others will already have moved on to another section of the Square, seeking shelter in one abandoned building after another until there are no more left, and the Square and its illustrious and shadowed past is gone.

The skin of the potatoes began to brown, and the smell of it made their bellies roil with hunger. The men crowded for space around the barrel. Their bottle was empty, but tonight they felt lucky, for someone appeared with another. At times the men looked upward through the latticework of joists and roof beams to the stars, and as they became inebriated, that view held their gaze, the momentary flicker of another lifetime pulled achingly at their thoughts. Their shadows lengthened, stretched sinuously across the wide-planked floor of the loft and into the dark corners where the rats scuttled, and the moaning of the wind echoed through the old building.

In the crawl space between the plaster lath and the exterior wall, tightly pressed together, lay half a dozen large square packages wrapped in black plastic bags. Orange flame light and black shadow spilled between the cracks and gaps and coalesced like oil upon their surfaces. Over the last couple of weeks, the rats had been at the bags, shredding the paper they held, using it for bedding. When the wind sheared down through the torn flashing at the edges of the roof and inside the clapboard walls of the Anvil, it sent the wrapping of the parcels shuddering, their loose corners flapping. Two rats scurried across one of them, nibbled absently at its corner, and then, pausing to listen to the muted sound of men from the other room, moved on, pale tails flashing in the orange light. From the torn hole gaped the shredded edge of a stack of thousand-dollar bills. A banknote fluttered in the wind, and then the wind took it and then another and, slowly, one by one, ripped the contents of the bag clean away.

ABOUT THE AUTHORS

THOMAS O'MALLEY was raised in Ireland and England. He is a graduate of the University of Massachusetts, Boston, and the Iowa Writers' Workshop, and currently teaches on the faculty of creative writing at Dartmouth College. He is the author of the novels *In the Province of Saints* and *This Magnificent Desolation.* He lives in the Boston area.

DOUGLAS GRAHAM PURDY grew up in the Boston area. He is a graduate of the University of Massachusetts, Boston, and currently works in Film and Media Studies at the Massachusetts Institute of Technology. This is his first novel.

MULHOLLAND BOOKS

You won't be able to put down these Mulholland Books.